Valvina Ariana Goodfellow

The Goblin Chronicles, Volume 3

S. M. Sutton

Published by S. M. Sutton, 2026.

This is a work of fiction. Similarities to real people, places, or events are entirely coincidental.

VALVINA ARIANA GOODFELLOW

First edition. May 13, 2026.

ISBN: 979-8992352962

Written by S. M. Sutton.

Table of Contents

To my mother,

who encouraged me to believe

every little girl was

a princess.

"Dancing round the Faerie Ring;

Magic makes our hearts sing.

Wildflowers in our hair;

Colored dresses for us to wear.

When you have a silver ring;

Perhaps a prince will become your king.

Until that day, we have each other;

And all the magic from your mother.

The secret is part me; part you.

If you join your hand with mine,

The power we wield

Will be combined."

Chapter 1: Her Whispered Words

Caz and Faith began the dance pattern at the head of the aisle made by the other dancers. Clapping hands matched the music's beat. Faith danced out a sequence of steps, and Caz followed, mirroring the pattern. Each time it was her turn, she added more steps to her choreography. As they moved down the row, the more complicated she made the steps. Her skill delighted Caz. She was as good a dancer as Saffron was.

Near the end, Faith grabbed Caz's hand. He put his other hand on her waist, and they paralleled their moves to the very end, where he dramatically laid her back into a deep dip, making laughter bubble out of her. The pair went to the end of the line and took up clapping along with the crowd, as Aliah and Garrett went next, stumbling through the gauntlet, not a matching step between them.

Val rushed up to Faith, her cheeks flushed. "You were amazing! When did you learn the steps? Did Saffron teach you? Come on, you've got to show me."

Before Faith answered even one of the barrage of questions Val had posed, she was being pulled along by her friend to the front of the dance queue to wait their turn.

Two additional groups arrived for the moot. Robin went over to welcome them. The Aurora Borealis was in full swing, filling the horizon behind them with flashes of shimmering light and color. The newcomers were a mix of goblins, Fae, and humans. Spread out along the road, they were talking in clusters, introducing themselves to one another near the end of the dance corridor.

The crowd let out a cheer. Robin turned to see Val and Faith facing off in the back and forth of dance patterns, moving down the peopled corridor. He explained to the new arrivals that everyone was just letting off a little steam and having some fun. The Northern Lights were acting as a stage background for the dancers.

A large man stepped out of the group to get a closer look. He focused on the lovely Fae girls twirling down the dance-way, colors of green, silver, and red casting shadows across their faces.

"It's her!" the stranger exclaimed to himself. He pointed at Faith and Val, who'd almost reached the end of the dance line. "She's the long-lost daughter of Lancer Goodfellow! Rumored dead all these years." The stranger shook his head in disbelief as he talked to himself.

The noise level rose amidst the audience, clapping and congratulating the girls on their dance.

"What did you say?" Robin shouted, grabbing the man by the collar with both hands.

"It's her! I'm sure of it. She was only a babe when I last saw her," he told Robin. "But I was shown a vision of what she would look like as a grown woman long before we were told the babe had died. I'd know the Goblin Princess anywhere. She's Lancer's daughter alright." His excited voice was loud, and a few people in the crowd caught his last words and whispered among themselves.

Finished with the dance, Val and Faith looked around to see who the stranger was pointing at. The audience fell silent.

Shaking his finger at the two of them, the man's hood fell back, revealing his dirt-streaked face. Faith sucked in a sharp gasp of breath. The Northern Lights kicked up in a wild dance behind the girls' silhouettes, and he made his declaration, still pointing, "She's Valvina Ariana Goodfellow. She's alive, and I've found her!" The two sister-friends stood stock-still, stunned. Holding one another's hands, they stood staring into each other's eyes. Both their mouths were opening and closing like fish, uncharacteristically speechless.

VALERIE VICTORIA PUREHEART squeezed Faith's hand, conveying her panic as they noticed the crowd staring at the two of them. Of one mind, the girls turned and ran in the opposite direction of the stranger. Black and opalescence wings snapped open. In seconds, they were airborne, headed for the shoreline, away from the crowd.

Cazzidy shouldered through the press, rose on the balls of his feet, about to follow. Before he could release his wings, Robin grabbed him by the shoulders, hissing in his ear, "Wait! Give them some time to sort it out among themselves. Besides, we promised not to reveal *our* wings until Faith gives her speech in two days, yeah?"

Caz's whole body gathered as tight as a bowstring, but he lowered his heels back down to the ground and turned to look Robin in the eye, urgent words pushed out in a whispered rush, "How can you be so calm, mate? Someone just declared one of those two girls to be your sister! What's what?" snarling at his friend.

"The keyword you said was 'someone'. I had two of the lads take the stranger to my tent. I'd like your help in questioning the old man. Could be he's touched in the head?" Robin spun his finger in a circle to show Caz that he meant the man might be crazy. "Let's find out who he is, how he would have come by such knowledge, and just what makes him so sure he was actually seeing Valvina? Especially since we know she was just a newborn babe when she disappeared, yeah? The rest of the world was told she had died at birth. Are you with me, Cazzidy?" Caz gripped Robin's upper arm and nodded.

Robin surveyed the crowd, pulled up his friendliest face, and put on his best routine. "Alright. Alright now. The show's over. We've gotten the old man somewhere to rest a bit, take a meal, and see if we can figure out what's going on in that addled brain of his, yeah?" People mumbled, shifted about. A few chuckled. Still, some kept their whispers among themselves in small groups.

Robin's face lit up with a smile when he saw Zeeka wave at him. "Well now," his voice loud to get the throng's attention, "it seems we could use a little music to go with dinner. Mistress Zeeka has just signaled me she's got her special venison stew ready to serve. Please everyone, let's go on with our celebration. I'll let you know what's what, soon as I have more information."

As if on cue, the lads started to fiddle and flute. That seemed to break the spell. A steady stream of people headed toward the cook's pavilion. A few even danced again to the lively music.

Green shimmers filled the horizon, adding their own surrealistic feel to the situation on the walk toward Robin's tent. When Caz and Robin were about a hundred yards away, Aliah and Garrett stepped into the lads' pathway, bringing them to a halt.

"Aliah, Garrett," Robin addressed them. "What's what?" Caz rolled his shoulders and jutted his chin out.

"What's what?" Aliah scoffed, "We're going to be there when you ask that stranger questions, Robin. That was my sister..."

Garrett interrupted, his voice full of emotion, "And Faith!"

Aliah rolled her eyes at Garrett, continuing, "Val and Faith, yes, that old man pointed at the two of them, claiming one or the other is the missing daughter of Lancer Goodfellow. We will not be left out of your interrogation," Aliah jutted her chin out at Caz and squared her shoulders.

Garrett pressed the bridge of his nose between his thumb and forefinger. He could feel a headache coming on. Seemed to be a recurring issue whenever the Aurora Borealis became active. Garrett gently wrapped an arm around Aliah, grounding himself, and coaxed, "Come on, Lia," he whispered. "Robin and Caz aren't trying to keep us in the dark. We can help listen to the details of the stranger's story and see if anyone of us pick up something odd, yeah? He's old, but he reminds me of someone. I just can't put my finger on it."

Robin pulled one shoulder forward, cocked his head toward the tent, showing they should follow. His long strides covered the ground quickly.

"Um, er," Garrett stuttered. Aliah pinched him and he jumped, blurted out the question, "Just exactly who is Valvina Ariana Goodfellow, anyway?"

Robin had reached his tent, hand on the entry flap. He turned his hooded dark eyes to the Foxfire and replied, "My dead stepsister." Pushing open the canvas, Robin ducked inside, Caz right on his heels.

A small table and two chairs sat in the center of the large tent. A lamp was lit, smoke visible, curling up and out of a small vent directly above; its flame casting shadows across the canvas walls. They had given the stranger water with which to wash. Though his clothes were dirty and tattered, the man's clean face had a regal look to it. His escorts had brought a bowl of Zeeka's stew, crusty bread, and a mug of Bedwer's beer. Zeeka had hauled four barrels of that beer with her when she'd left the clan to travel to the moot.

"Greetings, good sir," Robin started. Pointing, he said, "This is my friend Cazzidy Beaumont Touchstone. The lass here is Aliah Bethany Pureheart." Aliah smiled shyly. "Our other friend is Garrett Emmon Gladheart. We've got some questions we'd like to ask while you finish your meal, yeah?" Robin turned to the two lads who had guided the stranger to the tent and said, "Thanks for making our guest feel at home, lads. You two should be off to be sure you don't miss out on Zeeka's stew," the Goodfellow smiled. They wasted no time exiting the tent.

Aliah noticed the stranger wore fingerless gloves as he ran his hand through his thick, white hair. He kept his eyes on Robin and took a generous swig of beer, wiping the foam off his upper lip with the back of his hand. "A pleasure to meet all your friends, lad, but I don't believe you introduced yourself." Those gray eyes held Robin. Caz stepped forward, but Robin blocked him, holding out his arm. "My name is Robin Wilum Goodfellow. Your name, sir?"

The flame in the lamp flickered, and Garrett sat down, put his head to his knees, casting a shadow of a fox on the canvas, but remained a man before their eyes. Aliah kneeled next to him, rubbed the back of his neck and shoulders. "The northern lights bother him," she murmured to no one in particular.

"Well now," the stranger settled back in his chair. "Robin Goodfellow, is it? You've got the look of Lancer. I knew your father, son. Long time since we've seen one another, but we knew each other well." Opening a leather pouch he pulled from his waist, the old man took out a pipe and packed the bowl with tobacco, struck a match. He drew on the tip three or four times, the smoke curling upwards, his gray eyes never leaving Robin's.

"Your name, sir?" Robin repeated. "You've made a bold statement calling out a lass who is a friend of ours as Valvina Ariana Goodfellow. It's well known that she died at birth. I'd like to know who's making such a wild claim and why?" His question ended with a soft growl.

"The lass is more than your friend, Robin. She's your half-sister. Though there's not much of it left, I'd bet my life on it." The stranger winked at Robin.

No longer able to hold himself back, Caz stepped forward. "I'd say you've already made that wager, manno." Caz ground out his words. "Enough of this! Tell us who you are!"

A miserable Garrett lifted his head, the ache across his forehead visible, eyes seeing double. "I remember now. He's Faith's long-lost father, Lennox Jakson Stargazer. He looks much older now, but I saw a portrait Faith drew of him, an exact likeness except that he's aged. The impression stuck with me because it enthralled me when I found out the man was the King of the Northern Fae. Faith was able to create the sketch based on a verbal description given by...um...one of her cousins. You know how an imprint like that sticks with you. It's him all right."

The stranger stood, gave a curt bow from the waist, and said, "Lennox Stargazer at your service." When Lennox came up from his bend, he brandished a knife, blade pointed directly under Robin's chin. Everyone tensed. "Back off," Lennox roared at Cazzidy. Caz put his hands up and backed up two spaces. He didn't want to make a move that would get Robin hurt or killed.

Behind the stranger, Garrett suddenly shifted. Caz couldn't believe it as he watched the bloody coward slink away in his fox form. Instead of working with him to take down the man threatening Robin, he crawled under the canvas to escape.

"Let's talk, son," Lennox said to Robin. The old man cocked his head, indicating Robin should move over to the chair. He pushed the Goodfellow into the seat and swiftly took position behind him, moving the knife, putting light pressure on Robin's jugular.

"First off, I've no quarrel with you, sir," Robin offered. "Why the attack? All we've done so far was offer you food and drink, along with requests that you answer our questions?"

"So, you have," Lennox agreed. "But my entire mission in getting here is based on information. Word is, your brother Rupert and your stepmother, Queen Morveena, are planning on capturing my daughter Faith and selling her to the Gugwe Emperor. I can only assume you're in on their plan."

The canvas entry flew open, and Faith came in like a storm cloud. Val and Garrett were right behind. "Your assumption couldn't be further from the truth!" she hissed at her father. "Put that knife down! Please, Papa. I'm in no danger here. These are my friends," she insisted. "Please. Papa?" she whispered to him and opened her arms, inviting his embrace. "Where have you been all these years? You're alive and I've not had a single word from you!

I couldn't have meant very much to you, sent away to be raised as an orphan, identity buried, no knowledge that I had family or was a Fae, much less a worthless princess daughter."

Lennox Jakson Stargazer watched as his daughter's eyes welled with tears, but none fell. He felt his throat close up, and he swallowed hard at the sight of the distraught girl, a grown woman now. He sheathed the knife and crossed to her, gathering her tightly in his arms. "Thank the stars you're safe. Safe." Tears leaked from the corners of his own eyes.

Caz went to Robin and asked. "Alright, mate?"

"Yeah. No harm done," he answered.

The two lads stared at Val. She felt a flush run up her neck to color her cheeks as she realized the man was Faith's real father. She felt physically ill when it occurred to her he must have been pointing at her when he made his declaration. A wave of dizziness swept through her. Then Aliah was there, wrapping her arm around her sister's waist, supporting her.

Caz looked at Garrett and said, "I owe you an apology, mate."

"Yeah? What for?"

"I thought you were acting a coward slinking off earlier, but it turns out you knew just what we needed to diffuse the situation. Sorry, mate," Caz said earnestly.

"I probably would've jumped to the same conclusion, Cazzidy."

"I doubt it, Gladheart. But I won't make that mistake again, yeah?"

Garrett clapped Caz on the shoulder in response.

Faith took charge, surprising her father. She clapped her hands to get everyone's attention. "Papa, much as I want and need to hear the story about where you've been all these years, I'm afraid we're really short on time. I can hardly wait to hear the explanation of why you couldn't have gotten word to me. Ever. Why was I never told my real identity, even by those you sent to watch over me? In fact, I understand you had people give their oaths not to tell me my heritage." She squinted her eyes in anger at him. "So much has happened since you and my mother abandoned me; suddenly, it seems most of it occurred in the last several months." Faith glanced around the faces of her friends and heaved a heavy sigh. "You've picked a fine time to show up out of the blue. We're about to hold a big moot with goblins, Fae, humans, gargoyles, and anyone else that wants to help us. There's a dangerous race of monsters called the Gugwe. They intend to make all of us their slaves."

Faith's father grunted, "I know the Gugwe well and their bad intentions."

"The People's Alliance needs a plan. We need to gather and train an army if we're to have any chance at all to win a war for our lives, our freedom. Robin is with us on this, Papa. He's already saved my life once. Some of his clan helped us escape when Morveena, Queen of the Goblins, held *both of us* prisoners recently." Her eyes narrowed as she eyed him carefully to be sure he understood, then went on, "Morveena is pure evil, but Robin is as good as can be. Don't you see, Papa?" she looked up to catch Robin's eyes, but he'd moved across the tent, over by where Val stood, holding her hands, their foreheads touching. Faith felt her heart contract and freeze. Caz reached out and brushed her cheek with his knuckles, and she turned away, offering him a smile, a silent thanks for his support.

"So," Faith swallowed, finding her voice again, "please explain all that wild talk you were spewing when you arrived, pointing at Val and me? You were talking like a madman, saying you'd found Lancer's daughter, Valvina Ariana Goodfellow. Please help us understand. Val," she pointed at her friend, "has been part of my whole life. She and her sisters live at Uncle Robert's hold. Val couldn't possibly be Robin's stepsister. We grew up together. She's my best friend and...and she's like a sister to me. Do you see how you've made a mistake?"

Faith's troubled face broke Lennox's heart. He'd been away for so many years. Now that he was finally back, it seemed all he offered his daughter was heartache. Lennox pulled a chair over and sat down heavily with a sigh. "I'm sorry I didn't handle this differently." His gaze drifted over to Robin, who acknowledged the statement with a nod. "Lancer Goodfellow and I were the best of friends over many years. When Lancer's first wife, Robin's mother, Alora, died, Lancer grieved hard. Lost himself for a time. Had no interest in anything or anyone in his life, including his two sons."

Robin kept his eyes on the ground, unable to meet the looks of sympathy from those present.

Lennox continued. "Morveena had accused the Fae court, Aleta and myself, of murdering her father, Munro Marcellus Montestrell, who served as the Goblin emissary to the Fae. She took her wild tale to Lancer and

Alora. Lancer, always a clear thinker, came personally to the Fae court in order to investigate Morveena's accusation. He found Montestrell's body exactly where the girl said it would be. It was a frame-up; she had planted the evidence. Lancer reassured us he had counted us as friends for as long as he could remember. He believed we had nothing to do with the envoy's death. The Goblin King decided he would return home to look into the ambassador's daughter's story and that we would talk again. We later learned that he arrived back at his castle only to find his wife, Alora, had died giving birth to Robin."

Val leaned into Robin's side and laid her head against his shoulder.

"In no time at all, gossip raced through the grapevine that Lancer had become ill. The Goblin King fell into a deep depression. There were rumors that Montestrell's daughter had moved into the Goblin palace and was caring for young Rupert and the babe Robin. No one explained how that arrangement came about. Months went by, and the next news we had was that Lancer had wed Morveena. It was only two years later that they were expecting a child. Aleta and I tried to visit, but they refused us any courtesy. On our last try, Morveena herself came to the gates and told us Lancer did not wish to see us, that murderers were not welcome at the Goblin palace. Aleta was more troubled by this than I. That's when your mother told me she was pregnant and expecting our own child. Winter passed, and when the snows melted, spring was upon us. Lancer surprised me with an unannounced visit to my castle. He and Alora had long known of a secret entrance we had. Lancer had used it as he used to, to gain secret access to the Fae court. This time, Lancer had secreted away his newborn daughter, Morveena's babe. Valvina Ariana Goodfellow."

Lennox's regard moved to Val. "Lancer begged me to hide the child away, to be fostered by a loving, stable family. He couldn't bear the idea of the lass growing up to be tainted by her mother. You must understand, Valvina, your father explained he noticed abusive behavior toward his boys. Goodfellow confessed he would tell Morveena that the child was stillborn. His plan was to lie to her and spin the story that he'd buried the baby's body while the Queen was recovering from the difficult birth. When Lancer arrived at our castle, he'd conveyed his visions using a complicated mind-link. It was he who showed me what the babe Valvina would look like as a full-grown woman." Lennox took a sip of the beer on the table, his throat dry. "A few months later, Aleta gave birth to Faith." He nodded at his own daughter.

"Well, that's convenient," Aliah said. "Lancer's been missing for years, and you just happen to be the only one shown a vision of what Valvina would look like today." She tsked, feeling his story incredible, king or not.

"You can kind of see her point, Papa," Faith said in Aliah's defense.

"Of course," Lennox agreed. "But there's one thing I haven't told you yet," he suggested.

"Tell us then," Aliah scoffed.

"The babe, Valvina, was marked at birth."

Both Robin and Caz stiffened. Val watched the group warily. Aliah had turned two shades paler and looked green around the gills.

"Marked how?" Val ventured.

"A tiny star-shaped mark under her left breast," Lennox revealed.

Aliah put herself between Val and King Lennox. "Val's my sister. I've taken care of her since she was a baby."

Garrett spoke up. "Um...er...I," he stumbled over his words.

"For heaven's sake, Garrett! Say what you're trying to get out," Aliah stamped her foot in frustration.

Garrett looked around the room, unsure of himself, but pushed the words out because Aliah had insisted. "Well, I thought your parents adopted you and your Pureheart sisters right around the same time I was adopted."

Aliah's mouth fell open, as that was the last thing she expected him to say.

Faith's mouth fell open. Garrett knew he was adopted!

Val looked at Faith. The two of them moved shoulder to shoulder and linked arms. "We both have the same birthmark," Val announced.

"Impossible!" Lennox gasped.

Aliah pulled both girls to the back of the tent. She grabbed Robin's bedroll to use as a curtain to give the girls some privacy and demanded both girls show her Val's declaration. Aliah held her hands high and dropped the makeshift screen, her face a pasty shade of pale, her hands shaking.

"Well?" Robin demanded.

"They're both marked, just as Val said," Aliah admitted. "I knew Val had the mark. I practically raised her."

"So, that means...?" Robin considered out loud.

"It means they fostered Valerie Pureheart with a good family, but she is really your step-sister, Valvina, son. I know my daughter. Faith is not your sister. I was there when she was born to my wife, Aleta. My wife took care of both babies for a few weeks. She was the one who came up with the plan to send both babies into foster homes. Aleta was convinced that if Morveena found out Lancer had secreted her babe away, our child would be in terrible danger. I didn't know Faith had a similar mark, but I was directly involved in placing Valvina with the Pureheart family at the same time Faith came to live as an orphan with Reatha and Robert." He offered the words softly, with no cruelty intended.

Val and Faith hugged, at a loss for words. Val turned, dashing to Robin, and stood, her hands clasped in front of her, eyes full of questions. "Wait!" Faith called out. Val turned to her sister-friend, cocked her head to one side. "I just remembered something. When I talked to my mother through a scrying pool, she told me to tell Robin that he would find his sister when he saw the Aurora Borealis. The Northern Lights are putting on a show tonight. She also told me Robin's sister would know the words he seeks. Her whispered words, I think she said." Faith held her breath.

Aliah bowed her head, defeated.

Val looked at Aliah with surprise, then back at Robin. "It's just a song I know. Aliah used to sing it to me when I was little." She hummed a bit, then sang softly.

You struggle with the memory,
trying to recall;
the dream from your childhood,
it didn't seem real at all.
The room filled with light and shadow;
Your memory is full of holes.
Her golden hair hung in waves;
Her sapphire eyes held your gaze;
Her essence sweet, like a spring in May.
Her whispered words;
a spell, hidden deep down in your soul;
You'll not recover what you lost, the part of you she stole.

Her slender fingers held at bay; a Trillium.
She gave the flower's name to you
and in the name, she told it true;
the one who picks the flower anew,
will wake the magic left in you.
Wake Robin. Wake Robin. Wake Robin.
The years will pass;
the time will come
and when the hour does strike;
You'll protect a maiden fair,
she too has golden waves of hair.
When your task is done,
You'll find you've lost your chance,
only to regret you didn't dance the dance,
to match your steps in life with her;
to hold her in your arms,
as she became impervious to your many charms.
Her whispered words;
echo loud,
the Trillium's leaves begin to wither,
you've missed your chance to be with her.
I tell you now, good fellow;
the flower will fade from white to yellow.
If you fail to act in time;
the death of love would be a crime.
Fate, as fickle as the wind that blows,
the enchantress, the only one who knows;
how you alone can break this curse.
A simple rhyme; an easy verse.
Wake Robin. Wake Robin. Wake Robin.

WHEN VAL FINISHED SINGING, Aliah stood, tear tracks dried on her cheeks. "Nursie used to sing that same song to me, too." Faith told her. "I guess that settles it." She turned and looked straight at Robin. "My mother said your sister would know 'her whispered words.'" She reached out and took both Val's hands in her own. "Val, you must be Robin's sister."

"I always just thought the song was a sad tale of a prince under a spell, but didn't think it had anything to do with me," Val confessed.

Robin took Val's hand. It felt as if a weight had lifted off his shoulders. "That's the spell I remember being put on me as a child. Word for word. I always called it the Trillium curse." He shook his head, couldn't believe his sister was here in front of him. "Val," he said with emotion, pushed a tendril of hair from her eyes, and hooked it behind her ear. "Valvina," he breathed out in a hoarse, rough voice, "My father... our father," he corrected, "tasked me to find you, but never told me how or where to look. And now, here you are standing next to me."

"Everybody out!" Val ordered, keeping her eyes locked on Robin's. "My brother and I have a lot to talk about."

Chapter 2: Nothing is ever as it Seems

Faith wasted no time moving toward the door. She gripped Lennox's right hand in her left as she pulled him along. Caz stood nearby. Faith stopped, her eyes locked with his, her expression pleading, and he gave her the barest nod. She reached out with her free hand, welcoming Caz's warm grasp. The Beaumont led Faith and her father out the doorway, heading toward the beach where he'd found her earlier that evening. Not a word passed between any of them as they made their way around the perimeter of the camp to avoid running into anyone.

ALIAH STOOD, SHOULDERS drooping, hands and arms hanging limply at her sides. Her face had a defeated look, but she held her tears at bay. Garrett stood behind her, not sure what to do for either the girl next to him or one of his best friends a few feet away.

Val was staring at Robin, searching his face. She didn't move, but her voice carried her command: "I said get out, Aliah. I need some privacy with Robin. Please help her, Garrett, if she isn't able to leave on her own. Aliah, I promise I'll find you later. Just leave us. Don't make me beg this of you." Her voice broke, and Aliah turned on her heel, hurrying from the tent, Garrett right behind her.

Finally.

Alone.

Val made a slow, deliberate circuit around Robin. "So," she breathed.

"So," he quipped back to her. "You must be boiling over with questions. I know I am." He craned his neck around to track her movement.

"Ask," she directed him.

"The Purehearts adopted you and your sisters?"

"Yes, fifteen years ago. Aliah said I was just a babe."

Robin blinked several times.

"I guess that makes me about the right age, yeah?" Val put her hands behind her to hide their shaking and leaned against the central tent beam. "Tell me what you know," her words coming out in a whisper.

Robin ran his fingers through his dreadlocks. "Lennox had the right of the backstory. Of course, Morveena twisted some things over the years. In fact, I've had a recurring dream since I was a wee lad. In the dream, I was with my father when he supposedly buried Morveena's stillborn child. A story he invented in order to spirit you away, and one that would stop your mother from moving heaven and earth to find you. A couple of years later, my father confessed his secret to me: that he'd hidden you away as a babe. He insisted I promise to find you and, when I did, to protect you. What Lancer failed to tell me was *where* I could find you. Oh, he said he planned to give me more details later, but later never came, and then he disappeared. I think he was trying to find out where you had been fostered out. Lennox Stargazer's story puts some of the puzzle pieces together on why he didn't disclose where you were raised. The only information of any value Lancer provided was about the birthmark. He insisted my sister hadn't died at birth. That a spell of forgetting was put on the two of us for our safety. According to Lennox, Faith's mother, Queen of the Northern Fae, blocked our memories. Lancer acknowledged sneaking you away from Morveena shortly after the delivery and sought help in fostering you out to another family to keep you safe. I would have been all of two years old when we went to the Fae castle and turned you over to Queen Aleta and King Lennox. Desperation drove our father to keep you from Morveena's cruel hands."

"Want to see it? Confirm I really have the birthmark?" She quirked her mouth at him as a flush ran up his neck and brushed both cheeks.

"What?" he squealed. "Don't you dare!" He pointed at her as she put her hands on the buttons of her vest in jest, as though she was going to pull her shirt over her head. Laughter bubbled out of her. Robin took two steps back.

Val shoved him playfully on the shoulder. "Don't be ridiculous! I will not introduce you to the girls, silly."

His forehead crinkled. "The girls?"

Amusement lit up her face. "You know."

He shook his head and squinted his eyes in question.

Valvina cupped her hands under her breasts, raised her eyebrows at him and repeated, "The girls."

Robin rolled his eyes at her.

"I think you were tempted to kiss me last night," she asserted.

"I was not, and you know it. You know how I feel..." he shook his head. "Thank the Aurora that didn't happen!" He smiled back at her, realizing she was baiting him.

"We look alike, you know."

"You think?"

"Yeah." She dug around in the leather pouch at her waist, held up a round shape, "Come here and see."

Robin walked over and sat in the chair, and Val moved behind him. She blew on the round and buffed it against her shirt sleeve, then held it out in front of both of them, her head over his shoulder, their cheeks touching. With her free hand, she gathered her hair and pulled it behind her neck, just like Robin's was bound. Their two faces reflected back at them.

There was no denying it.

After that, neither could unsee the resemblance. It was uncanny, really, Val thought. Their skin and hair coloring were nearly the same. The only exception was where the bridge of his nose was pressed flatter. Other than that, their eyes matched, chins and cheekbones as well.

"I'm not sure how to get used to the idea that I'm not really me," she sighed. "At least you can still call me Val. It's just that it's short for Valvina instead of Valerie. I feel all mixed up inside. Weird. Also, I've never had a brother."

"I've never had a sister."

"Somehow, I always knew I didn't match my sisters. I didn't have any features in common with any of them. The three of them all share similar characteristics." Her voice drifted off as she wondered how this would change things with the only family she had ever known. Wondered how she could cope with being two different people.

Robin cut in on her thoughts. "Actually, you have two brothers."

"Ugh, Rupert," she whispered, goosebumps breaking out on her arms. "Faith had nothing good to say about him while the two of you were prisoners of Morveena." She bit down on the ham of her thumb. "Oh, gods!

That horrible woman is my mother!" Anguish twisted that last word, and Val/Valvina wrapped her arms around herself.

Robin moved behind her and enfolded her in his arms protectively. "But *you* are not your mother," he whispered in her ear. "You also had a good man for your real father. Actually, you remind me of him, now that I think about it." He turned her by the shoulders to face him and released her, put a finger under her chin and raised her eyes to meet his. "You were lucky to be raised by loving adoptive parents. You shared a wonderful childhood with three older sisters watching over you. If Morveena raised you, well, let's just say you wouldn't have so many happy childhood memories, yeah?" She nodded, and he felt her taut muscles relax a bit.

"We'll have to make a plan. Morveena was told you died at birth. Rupert won't take well to finding out he has a sister, let alone a child that is Morveena's daughter.

She cocked her head. "Why would Rupert care?"

"Because it makes you an heir to the throne. A throne she currently controls as Queen Regent. You're a princess, Valvina. *The* Goblin princess. Rupert has craved the throne for himself for as long as I can remember. Our brother is not well-liked among the clans. He'll see you as a threat to that dream. Plus, he won't trust Morveena to give him the carrot she's been dangling in front of him all this time. Not if she finds out *her* only child is alive. She'll want her own blood to inherit the throne, yeah?" Robin raised his left eyebrow, questioning if she understood what he was trying to convey to her. "Then again, you never know. Morveena herself might just see you as a threat to her own power. After all, you're also the daughter of Lancer Ian Goodfellow. Our father claimed you would somehow save our people." His face was grim with worry.

"What about you, Robin? Don't *you* see me as competition, being an heir to the Goblin throne?"

"I've never, ever wanted to sit on the throne. I'd be happy to put it in your hands, yeah? Rupert will make as bad a ruler as Morveena, just in different ways."

"Well, brother," Val steepled her fingers at her chin, "I think you may be right. Best to act with caution before we know what dangerous reactions this news could stir up, yeah? We should keep my birthright a secret until we have a plan on how to handle this situation. Besides," she shrugged, "rumor has it the lads and the clan have been discussing following you as their leader, Robin. I want you to know I support you if you decide that's the best thing for the people. Who knows how things will be turned upside down? We have to deal with the Gugwe problem first. Since we found out about the link between the Goblin people and the Fae lineage, maybe all the old traditions won't matter. They certainly are meaningless if we're all forced to become slaves of the Gugwe. I think we need to see how everything plays out before we worry about who succeeds Lancer on the throne. You have had no confirmation that Lancer is even dead! We've promised to back Faith up, and nothing has changed that vow for me at this point. The princess of them all, remember?"

Robin's face split into a wide grin, proud of how she had set her priorities. "I think we should get to the others who were witnesses to Lennox's untimely announcement. Let's instruct them that for now, you," he tapped the tip of her nose with his forefinger, "are to be their best-kept secret. I can work out a cover story with Faith's father. Be prepared, because Caz will pledge himself to you as our Goblin princess. Do you think you'll have any trouble convincing your sister, um...Aliah, or your good friends Faith and Garrett to keep this revelation under the table?"

"They'd do anything to protect me," she told him with confidence in a soft voice. Suddenly, she realized how much she'd lost. All her sisters, her mam, and da. Her whole life as she'd known it. She was sure it would be some time before she realized what she'd gained. "I'll meet you back here in an hour, after I've talked to everyone and asked them to keep our secret," Valvina squeezed his hand. "I still have lots of questions, mind."

With a time-sensitive mission at hand, she rushed out of the tent and ran for a clearing where she could open her wings safely. No one could learn about this yet. Everyone knew her as a fairy. People expected the Fae to have wings and use them. No one except her closest circle of friends now knew the actual truth: she was actually a goblin. So, by flying right now, she wasn't stealing Faith's thunder about the huge misconception that goblins weren't supposed to have wings. Right now, she was still considered a fairy. Two days, she thought. In just two days, Faith would tell the truth and send everything sliding sideways. It was for the best. People needed to know the truth. She heaved a heavy sigh. Nothing is ever as it seems.

Just as she reached the clearing, a ray of sun shone down on a trillium. The bloom was long gone, but the leaves were still on the plant. Val cautiously looked around, stooped, quick as a red squirrel, and pinched the stem off and whispered Robin's name.

Nothing happened.

So, she surmised, the song 'Her Whispered Words', were the key to breaking the spell that had been on Robin. Even as she regretted the loss of being able to summon him at the pluck of a trillium, she looked forward to telling him the good news.

Val bounced three times on the balls of her feet. She took a few running steps as her wings snapped out, straining against her shoulder blades, working hard to lift her. A wind current came up and gave her just enough boost to gain the height she wanted, eyes scanning the ground below as she searched for her best friend.

SURPRISE WROTE ITSELF across Val's face when she spotted Faith, only to discover Robin had beaten her there. He was walking down the beach with Faith's father, their heads together in serious conversation. She dropped slowly to the ground and retracted her wings, making a mental note to ask Robin about his ability to move with preternatural speed without the use of wings. An irrational fear twisted her stomach into a knot. Would her sister-friend reject her now that she knew she was a goblin? No, she told herself firmly. Faith said, 'One for all and all for one,' and she meant it. It couldn't matter, could it? Technically, goblins and the Fae are related. That was *the* big secret. Val swallowed hard, hoping Faith believed what she said was true.

Caz tapped Faith's shoulder and whispered. Faith's eyes snapped back to find Val standing ten feet away. The two girls met in the middle of the distance between them. Val gripped her thighs to keep her hands from shaking. Now that they were face to face, she didn't know what to say.

Faith opened her arms, and Val tumbled into the embrace, returning one of her own. "Are you okay?" Faith whispered. "I mean, *really,* okay?"

Tears sprang to Val's eyes, and she wiped them away in irritation. "Yes. I am. A little confused. Maybe unsure of myself. I'm not confident about dealing with being two different people. At least you can still call me Val, despite the formal name change and all; my short name still works. I think I'm reacting fairly normally, don't you?"

"Val," Faith cupped her cheek, "I'd be a basket case. But you...you're so strong. Are you disappointed Robin has turned out to be your brother, rather than...um...I mean..." her words trailed off. She could think of no way to finish the questions and no way to retract the words.

"Rather than a boyfriend, you mean?" Val asked with a smirk on her lips. Faith nodded. "That was never going to go anywhere."

"But you spent so much time together...oh, hell's bells," Faith admonished herself. "I don't mean to sound jealous. It's just that I missed you, and I admit I was envious of all the time you spent with him...instead of me." Her own eyes were brimming with tears, but she didn't dash them away.

Val let out a relieved laugh. "I've missed you, too. I was green-eyed over all the time you were spending with your cousins. It seemed like your old family wasn't important anymore. I was lonely. Don't get me wrong, I'm happy that you found you had other family, but you know... Besides, pretty much most of the time I spent with Robin, I was answering his questions about you. You were his favorite topic of discussion."

Faith's eyes opened wide. "Really?"

Val nodded. "I'm sorry."

"Sorry for what?

"I'm sorry I didn't tell you all this before. Obviously, I knew he was attracted to you. Thought maybe you were interested in him too. I said nothing because all I could imagine was even more of what little free time you have would have been spent with Robin, besides the time spent with your newly discovered family and well... Selfishly, I was already missing you, so, I kept up the ruse. I didn't want to lose any more time with you." Val's eyes swept down to the ground, ashamed. "I hope you can forgive me."

"Let's make a promise to each other that we won't let anyone—brothers, sisters, friends, family, or anything—come between us again. Promise we'll talk about it if either of us feels lost or left out. You'll always be my best friend and sister."

"Does that include talking about big things, like our secret?"

"Especially that! And things like being the Princess of the Goblins and the Princess of the Northern Fae. I need you, your strength, your support. Most of all, your love. All those things from you help keep me grounded." They squeezed each other's hands.

Val took a step closer, pressed her lips to Faith's ear and said conspiratorially, "Robin is asking your father to keep my secret. He thinks if Morveena and Rupert find out; I would be in danger."

Faith shivered at the mention of those names and the memories that came with them. "I agree with his thought process. The few of us who know will protect your secret with our lives until you are ready to reveal it." Faith promised Val fiercely.

"Thank you. I knew I could count on you. I've got to find Aliah and Garrett and impress the importance of secrecy." Her eyes caught on Cazzidy. "You'll tell Caz as well?" Faith nodded. "Seems I see the two of you together everywhere these days," Val said casually.

"Yeah," Faith confessed, "Caz is the kind of friend who is steady, solid, and dependable. He's really been looking out for me."

"That's good. You need all the friends at your back you can get, right?" Val's eyes moved back and forth between the two. When Caz caught her staring, she looked away. Time would tell, but she kept that thought to herself.

"It looks like Robin and your father have finished talking. Have you actually had a heart to heart with Lennox yet?"

"Not yet. I think that's next. I can't help feeling angry about how long he's been gone. How he couldn't be bothered all those years with sending some kind of word to me or to Reatha and Robert, so they could tell me about my heritage?"

"Caz can come back with Robin and me. That will give you some privacy with your father," Val offered.

"Actually, I asked Caz to come with."

Val raised her eyebrows in surprise.

"I'd ask you to stay with me to talk to my father, but you need to have several serious conversations yourself. Caz's support will give me some backbone."

"Yeah, I get it. Promise you'll find me later?" Val prompted.

"I promise. I'm sure I'll need a good 'Val lecture' and your advice after this discussion."

The two friends exchanged smiles. Val turned, bounced on the balls of her feet three times, and took off with the snap of her wings.

ALIAH WAS PACING BACK and forth in front of the campfire outside the tent she shared with Faith and Val. Garrett fed two more logs into the flames.

"Stop worrying," he told her. "Val will come to find you as soon as she's talked with Robin and gets her head around things." He stood and gently took hold of Aliah's shoulders. "There's nothing to worry about. She'll always think of you, Carlisse, and Delainey, as her sisters. I'm sure of it. She loves you. Nothing can erase that."

"I only hope she'll forgive me," Aliah groaned in anguish.

"Forgive you for what?" Val said as she slowly glided down by the campfire.

Panic raced across Aliah's features, and Garrett stepped in front of her to give her a moment to compose herself. He took three long strides and wrapped Val in his arms. "Nothing's changed between us. I hope you know that," he assured her and rested his chin on the top of her head. "Are you okay?" Garrett held her away just enough so he could look into her eyes.

"I'm fine. Really. I..." she swallowed. "I'm trying to get a grip on what this all means. But thank you. Knowing I have your continued support and friendship helps."

He could see in her eyes that her words were heartfelt. The tension left his body. Val sidestepped him. Garrett knew it was best not to get between any of the Pureheart sisters if they were going to argue, but he wanted to stay for both of them. Still, he asked, "Do you want me to go? Give you two some space?"

"No!" Val and Aliah responded in concert. The two sisters circled the campfire, eyeing one another.

"Um, er...I'll just be over by that oak tree while you talk." Neither girl objected, so he moved off twelve feet and sat down, leaning against the solid trunk. He took out his pocketknife and retrieved a small piece of wood he'd been working on and bent his mind to shaping it, ignoring the strain between the two sisters. Now and then, he would steal sidelong glances at the two of them, keeping his hands busy with whittling.

"What would I need to forgive you for, Aliah?" Valvina asked again. "Did you borrow any of my clothes without asking? Did you break something of mine or lose one of my earrings?" Val asked with a touch of anger lacing her question. "Well?"

Val moved faster around the circle they'd been dancing in and found herself face to face with her oldest sister. "Funny, Aliah," she said sadly. "For a seer, you sure didn't foresee this coming, yeah?"

Aliah was backing away from Val now, shaking her head, tears making tracks down her cheeks. "I love you, Val, always have and always will."

"I love you too, Aliah, but you haven't *always* loved me, have you? You didn't have any insight into this big secret because you already knew! Admit it! You've always known. Isn't that right?" Val shouted.

Garrett looked up, confused by Val's accusation. He could see Aliah wringing her hands together, tears streaking her face. He didn't know what to think. "Val," he hissed.

"Stay out of this, Garrett," she warned, shaking her finger at him while keeping her eyes focused on Aliah.

"Time to fess up, sis," Val came to a stop in front of Aliah, crossing her arms in challenge. "Admit it, Aliah. No vision came to you about my real heritage, my true parentage, because you've always known the secret. All the pieces of the puzzle started coming together for me when Faith and I stripped to show you the birthmark. You showed no surprise at all to see the mark on me, but it shocked you to see an identical one on Faith." Her voice was passionate with emotion. "You've known ever since I came to live with the Purehearts. Oh, part of the story was the truth. Johnson found you three of you abandoned in the woods. But I didn't arrive at the same time as you, Carlisse and Delainey, did I? I didn't come until *after* they'd already adopted you three. Isn't that so, Aliah?" Val's voice broke then. "If you ever had any genuine love for me, please, I beg you, tell me the true story. Tell me what you know," Val dropped to her knees in front of Aliah. "Please tell me true," Val whispered.

Aliah wiped her tears with the back of her hand and used the edge of her tunic to wipe her nose. She tentatively reached out her hand to Val, but dropped it when Val pulled back from her. Grabbing a lock of her own hair, Aliah began twisting it round and round, would let it fall, then repeated the action again and again as the words flowed.

"I never meant for you to find out this way, Val." Aliah swallowed hard. Garrett's face was a mask of horror. He wanted Val to be wrong, never believing Aliah would keep such information from someone she loved. His heart ached for Val.

"You were just a baby, not even a year old. MaeElla took you from my arms when I presented you. It was as if you were the most precious gift she'd ever received. You were the best child, hardly ever crying, interested in everything and everyone around you."

"I don't need you to rehash my happy childhood, sister. I want to know *how* I came to be there? *Who* brought me? How did you know about the birthmark? Quit stalling and give me the full truth!" Val demanded.

Aliah continued twisting her hair. "I just want you to understand how much you mean to all of us. How much we love you."

Val narrowed her eyes, glared at Aliah, her lips pressed flat.

"Okay, okay. I'm getting to it," Aliah bit her lower lip. "You arrived about a year after the three of us were taken in by the Purehearts. It was the same time Faith and the old nurse came to Robert and Reatha's fortress. It was a quiet arrival. Secret. No fanfare or welcome feast. Robert made it clear he didn't want any notoriety about the visit. Reatha had never had a baby. She was barren. Everyone said it thrilled Reatha to have a child of her own to care for. It didn't turn out to be a *visit* at all. Faith and her nurse stayed. MaeElla sent me to the garden behind our house the afternoon after the nurse had arrived with her charge, to pull weeds. It was a cloudy day, but warm. I remember there being bees all over the goldenrod flowers. It smelled as if it were going to rain, but it didn't. A long shadow fell across the patch of ground I was working on. When I looked up, I found that the old woman was standing there. I'd only seen her for a few moments the day before when she got out of the carriage, cradling baby Faith in her arms. Not wanting to be rude, I stood, brushing the dirt from my knees and hands. The old lady stayed on the other side of the garden fence."

Aliah was twisting her hair in a manic, repetitive action. Val sat cross-legged on the ground, her face solemn, hands cupped together in her lap. Aliah stole a glance to see if Garrett was still there. He was, but didn't meet her eyes.

She let out a soft sigh and continued. "I asked the nurse if she wanted me to fetch my mother, MaeElla, thinking it was likely that was who she'd come to visit. But she shook her head, put a finger to her lips to quiet me, crooked her finger, beckoned me to the fence. Bending down slightly, she said she had something for me. Something that would be an enormous responsibility. My responsibility. I didn't dare refuse. She had an authoritative air about her. Remember, I would have only been six or seven years old. When I got to the fence, I could see a wooden apple crate down by her feet. She'd lined it with soft sheep's fleece. Evy leaned over and pulled back a blanket, just enough so I could see a baby's face. But it wasn't the same baby I saw her get out of the carriage with the day before. It was your face, Val."

Val blinked twice, but said nothing.

"Anyway, the old biddy told me you were a gift for MaeElla. She said it was important that I keep the secret about where the baby came from. I was never to tell anyone, she said. She picked you up out of the crate and kneeled down by the fence so I could see you better. I was to be your guardian angel, she declared. Nurse made it clear to me you were secretly my responsibility. Evy threatened to hold me accountable should anything happen to you. She confessed that she'd had a vision. Told me that sometime far in the future, a time would come when it was right to reveal the truth: that the Purehearts had fostered you, but you weren't a child of their blood or of the same blood as your sisters. But until that time, how and when you came to live with the Purehearts was to remain a secret. Then, the old nurse looked around to be sure no one was listening to our stealthy conversation. It was then she foretold to me that a stranger would claim you were another person. Not only that, but the stranger would know of the perfect little star under your left breast, a mark you had from birth. She lifted your gown to show me the birthmark and made me touch it with my forefinger. When I touched your mark, I felt a strange tingle that ran up my arm and jolted my heart. I didn't realize it then, but as I grew older, I knew it was a binding between us. Magic had tied me to you. From that moment on, charged with watching over you. It's how I always knew when you were hurt or in trouble, or causing mischief. You were like a magnet, drawing me to your side. Anyway, Evy said that I was a witness, and when the stranger came, the mark would confirm who you were...are...um...I..."

"Go on, Aliah, finish," Val prompted.

"I didn't know *who* you were, Aliah. Please believe me. I did not know. She didn't give me any clues. My suspicion that the story she spun for me all those years ago might actually come to fruition didn't really start until two years ago. I had recurring dreams and trouble sleeping. That's when Carlisse and Delainey went with me to seek the Dream Weaver. Even her fortune only hinted at things. We had to deal with that horrible creature to have my fortune told, and I didn't really gain any new information. Still, nothing was confirmed until today. I swear, Val, I didn't know you were Robin's sister or a...a princess."

Val heaved a sigh of relief that Aliah didn't mention her sister was a goblin, just a princess.

"Evy disappeared into the woods, heading back to Reatha's. I picked you up out of the crate and rushed to the house, babbling about the story she'd prepared for me, about how I found you abandoned behind the barn. I gave you into MaeElla's arms. Not once did she ask for any further explanation. After that, I hardly ever saw the old nurse again. Oh, sure, once in a great while we would cross paths at a fortress celebration, but she was Faith's nanny, and she never spoke to me about it again. After a while, it all seemed like a dream. It was just as if you had always been with us. The years passed. Nothing happened. You and Faith grew up and became fast friends. If the nurse had wanted to tell you anything, she had had many opportunities. So, it all faded into the background, forgotten. Life went on as usual."

"Until today." Val deadpanned.

"Yes, until today. The only instruction I could remember was that I had to acknowledge the stranger's claim and confirm you had the birthmark. But

Val, you know I take my binding to you, my loyalty to you, seriously! I will always do whatever I can to protect you. Please believe me!"

Val opened her palm, puckered her lips, and blew Aliah a kiss. "I release you from your binding."

Aliah's body jerked, and her skin pebbled with goosebumps. She could physically feel the binding pull up roots and drift away from her. "Val! What are you doing?" Aliah cried out.

Val held her palm up to silence her sister. "I release your binding." Aliah's face sagged, stricken with horror. "But...never fear. I will always need your love, Aliah."

Aliah dropped to her knees, and the two girls threw their arms around one another, rocking back and forth, each comforting the other.

A person loudly cleared their throat behind them, interrupting their embrace. They turned, ready to admonish Garrett for interfering, but Garrett wasn't there. Instead, Lennox Stargazer stood before them.

"I think it's time you and I had a private talk, Valvina Ariana Goodfellow. Shall we take a little walk?" Lennox raised his eyebrows and held out his arm, inviting her to take it.

Chapter 3: A Private Talk

Valvina held Faith's father's forearm for about a dozen steps, then let go, putting a few inches between them. Lennox felt the cool air replace the girl's closeness.

"Did you kidnap me when you had the old nurse bring Faith and me as orphans to Sir Robert's?" Val stared at him out of the corner of her eye.

"Where did you get such a notion?" he said sharply. Lennox shook his head and huffed, "The answer is unequivocally no. I did not kidnap you. Lancer gave you to me to keep you safe. A request from your own father. A favor he *begged* of me. He asked me to hide you away, to make sure you fostered in a good, loving home. The only way I could honor his request was to put you with a family unknown to the Goblin Court or the Fae Court. I couldn't raise you myself. That would have put you in real danger. The same danger that threatened my daughter. But one thing I could do was keep a distant watch over you if I placed you in a suitable home near Faith. It was best if both of you appeared to be orphans. Over time, Reatha, and Robert had adopted Faith as their own. If your mother ever found out, well, let's just say it wouldn't have been good for you or for us. Your mother was bent on revenge against us for reasons Aleta and I could never really figure out. So, just as Lancer requested, I hid you away, along with our own daughter, to keep you both safe from Morveena Morgan Montestrell Goodfellow. Lancer made me swear I would never even tell him your whereabouts. Said he didn't want to know as a precaution. That way, the information couldn't be tortured out of him. The last time I saw him, years and years ago now, he begged me to tell him, but I kept my word and held my tongue. It wasn't easy. Your father was my friend, and I could see the desire, the longing, the desperation in him for the knowledge. Lancer was angry when we parted. He did everything in his power to convince me that enough time had passed, that it was finally safe to reveal to him where I had secreted you. He claimed that the danger had passed. But from everything I knew, Morveena had only grown more dangerous and crueler over the years. You would have been only five or six years old. Word was, he disappeared shortly after that." Lennox paused and sat upon a great stone when they reached the top of the ridge. He surveyed the valley, allowing himself to be distracted by all the bodies in constant motion in the camp below, making preparations for the moot.

Val's mouth was like dust, her eyes dry. She couldn't produce enough spit to give herself any relief. Lennox surprised her when he pulled a pocket flask out and passed it to her. She pulled the stopper and took a deep swig, coughing, feeling the burn to the bottom of her gut. Her stomach warmed and churned.

"Better have another," Lennox advised. Val tipped the flask again, wiped her mouth with the back of her hand, and offered the vessel back to him reluctantly. She felt the ground spin beneath her feet. She'd only ever been allowed watered wine, and then only on feast days. The sharp liquor hit her with a mild wave of dizziness, sending her to sit on the rock next to him.

"How much do you know about your mother?"

"Not much," Val provided, a small burp coming out with the words. "I hear she's some kind of monschter," the last word slurred. Lennox handed the flask to her again. She reached for it, but he pulled it back a bit and told her, "Just a small taste for your nerves, mind." She hiccoughed and snatched it from him, managed a quick gulp before he stoppered it, spirited it back into a hidden pocket inside his great wool coat.

"Your father's actions were born out of love for you, Valvina. He wanted to protect you. Lancer agonized over the fact that he thought it was too late to save Rupert, knew that he hadn't protected either of his sons as he should have. Still, he felt it necessary to leave Robin in place, to keep someone on the inside of the Goblin Court working against his stepmother. A big job for a young lad. Not long after putting you in my care, we didn't see Lancer again for a long time, until he sought me out years later for information about you. By that time, Morveena's reputation for being a blood magic user, as well as her evil and cruel ways, had become well known throughout Sharas. The goblin clans feared her. I would have taken your secret to the grave to fulfill my original promise to your father. He was furious with me for refusing to disclose where I had fostered you. I never saw him again."

Lennox looked at Val's eyes and raised his brows, inviting questions, but she shook her head. She was thinking hard about all he'd told her, endlessly twisting the silver ring the old nurse had gifted her a few weeks ago, round and round her forefinger. The silver glinted as a ray of sun broke through the canopy. Lennox noticed the bauble. "Ah, so you have one of Aleta's pretties. She always put a bit of magic into the things she made. I'm afraid I don't have the faintest idea of what that one does. Faith has one too. You might ask her about it," he suggested.

"So, what happens now?" Val asked cautiously. "Robin was going to ask you to keep my identity a secret. He thinks if Rupert or Morveena find out I'm alive, I could be in danger. Do you think that's true?"

He bent to pick a patch of black-eyed Susans and wove them together. "Robin would know. He's lived with the two of them his whole life. It would be wise to heed a warning if he gave you one. The lad knows what his brother and stepmother are capable of. The few of us who know the truth of who you really are respect the fact that it is your secret to keep or divulge. You can trust me to keep the information safe. I apologize again for the way I blurted that out in public, but I promise you I will put it right. I'll make sure people just think I'm a confused old man spewing stories. It's just that when I saw you, I was shocked to find you at all, much less discover you attending a moot between Fae, goblins, goyles, and humans, no less."

She nodded her understanding. He placed the flower crown he'd made on her head.

"I'm glad you and Faith have each other. Your friendship is strong," he told her. "I've been gone so long. We wanted her to believe she was an adopted orphan. It was part of the plan to keep her safe. She needs someone who's a constant in her life and a person she trusts completely. I'm afraid there's going to be some rough times ahead for both of you."

"The only plan I have right now," Val told her best friend's father, "is that Robin and I committed to supporting Faith while this prophecy plays out and she figures out what it means to be 'the Princess of them all'. At least I don't have *that kind* of pressure on me. Did she tell you about it? The Dream Weaver's foretelling? No? Well, ask her about it. That prediction is the driving force behind this moot. So, do you have any other advice for me?" She looked up at him shyly from under her eyelashes. She blinked her eyes a few times to dispel his double.

Lennox pulled the flask again and took a drink, setting it down beside him. "I'll not lie to you, Valvina. It will be hard to figure out who you are. Each day will push you to meld together, part of who you've grown up to be, emerging with the person you think you should be, now that you know your lineage and true name." Lennox stared off into space as Val snuck another swig from his flask. The whiskey's warmth spread across her body, down to her toes, giving her cheeks a rosy-red glow.

"You already know 'who' you are as a person. Who you are is defined by what you think is right and wrong; what you consider fair or cheating; who you love and who loves you. You've become *you* through your actions and reactions. A name can't change what you are inside. You're *not* your mother. Rest easy about that. You far outmatch her in power, because your power comes from goodness. Hers is deeply seated in hate and bitterness. Just be true to yourself, Valvina, and all will be well."

Lennox's face softened. He turned to look back at his secret charge. The flask was lying on its side, empty. Val's chin slumped against her chest, and he could hear soft snores emanating from her. "Hmmm, too much pressure all at one time, so you've chosen to numb it for a while. Fine, until you wake up with the aftereffects. You'll see," he mumbled, chastising himself for not keeping a better watch on the silver flagon.

Pocketing the flask, he scooped up the thin girl in his arms. "Come on, then. I'll take you back to your tent so you can sleep it off. When you wake, lass, your fears will be buried and you'll face the world with bravery, real or feigned, as you always have," he whispered in her ear.

Once inside her tent, he laid her on a bedroll, gently untangling her arms from around his neck. Her eyes flickered, and she gave him a kiss, as light as the brush of a feather that tickled his whiskered cheek, and breathed out, "All for one and one for all." Then Valvina Ariana Goodfellow turned on her side. Lennox covered her with a blanket and stepped out of the shelter. He set off, dusk covering the landscape. It was time to have a long-overdue conversation with his own daughter.

CAZZIDY BEAUMONT TOUCHSTONE tapped Faith on the shoulder when he saw her father, Lennox, approaching. She fed the two logs she had in hand to the beach bonfire, stood and brushed the sand off her knees. A mild wind blew her long hair away from her face, and Lennox's heart ached at how like her mother she looked. He didn't miss the determination written across her features. A look that brought back memories.

"Your mother used to wear the same face you are projecting when she'd decided about something and was willing to fight for it." He offered her a sad smile.

"First, before we walk down memory lane," she said firmly, "I think you owe me an explanation. I know your face only from a verbal description provided by Dedo. I made a portrait from that description, and he confirmed it was an excellent likeness of you. You sent me as an orphan to be adopted by Reatha and Robert. Never once has anyone told me what happened to my mother. I had to find out from others that she had been kidnapped shortly after you sent me to Aunt Reatha. After that, you apparently disappeared yourself. Of course, I didn't know until recently that Reatha was truly my aunt. You abandoned not only me, but the Fae people as well."

Lennox heaved a great sigh and lowered himself to the ground. For several moments, he stared into the flames, taking himself backward in time, remembering. Caz quietly patrolled a two-hundred-foot perimeter. He was making sure no one was going to interrupt their private conversation. Faith held a long, heavy stick she used to poke at the fire as she waited patiently for him to speak.

His voice cracked when he finally told her his story. "I never meant to leave you for so long. I deliberately sent you to Reatha, knowing you would be safe and loved, but that's no excuse. Your mother and I thought it would only be a short period. When we determined it was safe again to bring you home, we would expose the ruse. I admit I've been a poor father to you, Faith. I accompanied Evy, your nanny, about half-way to Robert's fortress. When I returned to the Fae castle, I found your mother missing. Naturally, I immediately left on a mission to find her, and then...well, then I found I couldn't stop looking for Aleta. All these years, it blinded me—my obsession to rescue her. Now and then, I would remember my responsibility to you, but somehow, another rumor would surface of Aleta's whereabouts, and off I would go. The hope of finding her kept me alive year after year. Over time, I noticed changes had occurred everywhere in Sharas. The Goblin people had scattered, broken into smaller clans that stretched from north to south all across the Shara's upper and lower peninsulas. The Fae fractured into several factions after our court was attacked, and Aleta disappeared. You're right. I abandoned our people. Left them to fend for themselves and focused only on my efforts to find your mother. You must know I love you, Faith. After all, you're my child. But can you understand Aleta was my world? I felt like I had lost everything when she was abducted." His eyes flicked up to hers, but she kept her gaze on the hot coals as she stirred them about with her fire poker.

"I still don't know if Lancer betrayed me to Morveena or if it was the Gugwe. No one knows if Aleta's even still alive. It was a big surprise, living in squalor outside a Gugwe community, that fate put me in a position where I recently overheard Morveena and Rupert's plan to capture you. Their scheme included selling you to the Gugwe emperor. That was what finally broke the chains that had tied me to my dogged failure in my never-ending search for your mother. After Lancer begged for our help to hide Valvina, it was your mother who hatched the plan for me to see Evy on the road south to Robert's hold. She suggested we leave you safely with Robert and Reatha. I didn't want to make the entire trip, as I was eager to get back to Aleta. Also, I thought the ruse of an orphan arriving at the fortress would be less suspicious if I didn't accompany Evy all the way there. Originally, Aleta's plan was only to leave you with Reatha until she felt sure Morveena didn't know about you or, worse, that the wicked witch had somehow found out that the babe she had borne didn't die at birth. Aleta worried that the evil woman would take revenge on our own daughter for helping Lancer hide their baby away, so Aleta sent you south into Reatha's loving hands with a story to cover your identity. Nursie, you, and Valvina traveled the rest of the distance alone. Evy was to arrange a good, loving home for Valvina. She took complete charge of the two babies, and everything fell into place for Val with the Purehearts. I learned later that Reatha was besotted with you, not having any children of her own. I used that news to justify my not immediately coming for you when I found your mother was missing."

A single tear made a track down his sunken cheek. "Fate changed the course of our grand plan. I arrived back at the Fae castle to find the court in chaos. Our home was attacked and overrun by Gugwe. Your mother missing. They took hundreds of our people as slaves. Hundreds were dead. Hundreds had fled. Your mother had occasional dealings with a gargoyle named Dedo, and he was there when I returned and provided a sketchy accounting. He confirmed Aleta had been taken, but he couldn't say if the Gugwe were responsible or Morveena, who had been sighted in the area. I certainly couldn't make any inquiries of Dedo or anyone else about whether Montestrell's daughter had discovered Lancer's ruse and my help in spiriting her baby away. It was a secret I had to take to my deathbed, because if she truly *didn't* know that Valvina was alive, my asking questions would give the secret away. I commanded Dedo to go south to watch over you. I required a blood oath, and he swore on his life to protect you. A few years later, word reached a few Fae still loyal to us. It was they who reported the news that Lancer, the Goblin King, was missing, possibly dead. For the first few years, I returned to the Fae castle regularly for short stints to gather news. I had convinced myself I would have known if Aleta were truly dead. I stuck to my mantra that she was alive. Believing I had only to find and rescue her to achieve success and take our life back. Unfortunately for you, that focus became all I lived for. All my efforts went into finding my wife, your mother. As you can see, I failed. I failed you both." Lennox covered his face with his hands and rocked back and forth, caught up in his misery.

He felt Faith's hand on his shoulder, then her words washed over his tortured soul. "It seems fate has let you come to a place that has another clue for you to pursue." He turned to look at his daughter, and she let her words touch him softly. "Let your heart be at ease. Let your guilt and grief go. They loved me and cared for me." She used her fingers to sweep his graying hair out of his eyes, bent and whispered in her father's ear. "I don't know *where* my mother is, but I *can* arrange for you to talk with her."

"What? How can that be possible?" he whispered, his gaunt face filled with hope. Lennox covered her small hand with his rough one, his body wracked with great, heaving sobs. They stood that way for a few moments until he cried himself out. Caz respectfully kept his gaze on the Milky Way, counting falling stars each time he saw one shoot across the sky.

THE NEXT MORNING, FAITH, and her cousins huddled in deep discussion. When Val came around, she saw the group and spun on the ball of her foot to get away. "Wait! Val, wait up!" Faith called out as she jogged toward her friend.

"I didn't want to interrupt," Val said lamely.

"Don't be ridiculous. I thought we had covered all of that yesterday. You are my family, too!" Faith chided. "My cousins just came from their own conversation with my father. He had some news about each of their fathers. My uncles have been keeping a secret watch on certain Gugwe tribes just over the border in Adana before they came here to help us set up the moot. Lennox has agreed to stay on to help train all the volunteers we can recruit, so we can defend ourselves from the Gugwe. Travis and Shaun are going to Adana as directed by their father. Their task is to do reconnaissance and report back on the Gugwe's actions. Lennox is confident that between him and your uncles, they will teach our recruits the battle skills we need. We just have to raise an army."

"That would be one prayer answered." Val agreed. "With men who are skilled in warfare, training and leading us, we might actually have a chance. Are you ready for your big speech tomorrow to open the moot? Everything hinges on your words being able to convince all the people to unite and fight our enemy together. You are the key to raising an army. A united army. It's imperative that you persuade them to put their differences and old grudges aside. Otherwise, nothing we do will matter. We'll all become slaves of those Gugwe monsters. I want you to know that I believe in you. I know you can do it!" Val said with conviction.

"I'm glad you have such confidence in my words! But I worry words won't be enough," Faith said, nerves firing on high. "Listen, I was wondering if you would do me a favor?"

"Anything," Val responded.

Faith pulled a wad of folded pages from her pocket and handed them to Val. "This is my speech. Can you look it over and make any additions or edits you think are important? I've got to take my father on a brief trip. I'll be back by nightfall, then I can practice the speech with whatever changes you make. You've always known just the right things to say, the right words to use. Please?"

"Of course, I'll help you. It will keep my mind off my own worries. I need to kick this fear of Morveena finding me out."

"Oh, I almost forgot. I asked my cousins to keep a special watch over you. Marianna, Chris, and Brittany said they would keep an eye out for anything suspicious," Faith assured her.

"Umm...oh," Val stammered, amazed that Faith's cousins would actually look out for her.

"Don't worry," Faith picked up on Val's discomfort. "I didn't tell your secret. I just said Robin heard a mysterious rumor that someone had threatened to hurt you, and they were all in on volunteering to protect you. Extra eyes can't hurt, yeah?"

Val nodded and smiled, opening the folded papers to run through the speech Faith had written. Messy handwriting filled the pages. There were smudges, cross-outs, and tiny words written sideways in the margins. She wasn't surprised, having seen Faith's schoolwork for years. When she looked up, Faith's gossamer wings were backlit by the sun as her friend flew across the sandy beach to meet up with Lennox.

Chapter 4: Zeeka's Cast Iron Oven

Val had read Faith's speech repeatedly, jotting notes, making corrections. But her stomach was growling, distracting her from making any further progress. If she were going to get any meaningful editing done, she would have to take a break and get something to eat. The dinner hour was long past. It was likely no one would be in the kitchen, but she thought she'd at least be able to find something to quell her gnawing hunger. Folding up the pages carefully, she stowed them in a deep pocket of her tunic, treating them like valuable jewels. She hummed a little tune as she made her way across the camp to find the cook's house. Her back itched as though someone was watching her. She looked over her shoulder several times, but no one was there. When she reached the food pavilion, it was dark. She worried she might have missed her chance of any kind of meal at this late hour. To her delight, there was a small woman stirring a pot on the biggest cast-iron stove Val had ever seen.

"Have a seat, dearie. I've just the thing for your rumbling stomach," the woman said without ever turning round to look at Val.

"How did you know I was here and looking for something to eat?" Val asked, sitting down at the table behind the cook.

"Why, I could hear your stomach growling when you were halfway across camp!" She laughed good-naturedly.

"But shouldn't you be finished cooking for the night? Dinner was hours ago," Val told the woman as if she hadn't noticed that night had fallen. "I was just hoping to snag an apple, maybe some cheese and stale bread. You're probably tired. I don't want you to go to any trouble for me." Val noticed a pile of fresh vegetables on the table, a board, and a knife laid out next to them.

"Here's the truth, lass." Cook turned and pointed her long wooden spoon at the vegetables. "Where there's a large group, the cooking starts again for the next meal as soon as they've finished the last one and the washing up is done. The crowd will be round again with empty bellies, ready for the next repast in no time. The morning people and the night people have some crossover, but mark my words, before the sun is up, there'll be plenty with rumbling stomachs like your own. I've got good news for you. I can do you better than an apple and cheese, lass."

The cook produced a wooden bowl and a clean spoon. The next thing Val knew, she'd placed a hot bowl of stew in front of her. She drew a deep breath, the spicy aroma making her salivate. The friendly cook set a thick slice of bread with a generous pat of butter down next to the bowl. "This bread has just cooled enough for you to have the first slice, lass." The woman smiled at her charge. "Now then," the wooden spoon pointed directly at Val, "what's got you up so late and kept you from your dinner this night, hmmm?"

"I have a lot to think about. I guess I just got caught up trying to solve some problems." Val confessed as she shoveled down the food to slake her hunger. "This is delicious," she mumbled around another mouthful. "Thank you so much." Val expressed her gratitude as she scraped the last of the stew out of the bowl, using her slice of bread to capture all the gravy.

Looking on, the woman commented, "Well, I'll hardly need to wash that bowl."

Pleased with the girl's manners, the woman turned back to her oven and wrapped her bony fingers with a thick cloth. She set down her spoon, folded her apron over her other hand. Pulling hard to open the oven door, she deftly pulled out six freshly baked loaves, then set in another half dozen she had ready to bake from the sideboard. Val looked on with fascination as the woman pried the top off the side compartment on the stove and chucked in two more logs to the wood burner. Taking up her spoon again, she gave the food on the stovetop a quick stir, cocked her head, listening. She turned to find the young girl she'd just fed peeling and chopping the pile of vegetables.

"Here now," the cook told her, waving the spoon in her direction. "You don't have to do that!"

"Oh, I don't mind," Val offered. "I'm grateful for the hot meal. Besides, I have a lot of sisters, and chopping vegetables was always my job at home. Actually, it's work that helps me think."

"Truly?" the woman asked. "You remind me of another lass who did her best thinking while chopping. While you're stewing over your troubles, look for the common threads in the pattern, lass. That's what I counseled her to do. You'll always find your answers there." She winked at Val and waved her spoon. "Now, only half the pile, lass. You've got to leave some work for Hazzel. Otherwise, it won't take long for that one to fall back into her lazy ways."

"Hey," Val said as a memory clicked in her mind. "I bet your name is Zeeka, right?"

"That's the truth!" Zeeka replied, surprised at the comment.

"My friend Saffron told me about you and what a skilled cook you are. She mentioned looking for the common threads and how they fit into a pattern when we were on kitchen duty together at Stone House Camp. I'd forgotten that bit of advice. Thanks for reminding me." Val smiled at Zeeka and continued chopping vegetables. Zeeka left her to her thoughts. Smiling at the memory of Saffron, she went out the back door to bring in another box of herbs and spices from her wagon. Her goblin-enhanced hearing caught a sharp gasp and words half-whispered from inside as her late dinner guest declared, "That's it!" The girl cleaned the knife and her hands, calling over her shoulder as she headed out of the pavilion, "The pattern! I've got it, Zeeka. I'll see you tomorrow. Thanks again!"

The lass was out the front of the building before Zeeka came back in. She took up her wooden spoon, crushed some dried sage into the pot, gave it a thorough stir, humming a tune she'd last heard Saffron sing. Zeeka jumped two feet into the air when someone tapped her shoulder.

"Sorry, Zeeka. I didn't mean to startle you!"

Zeeka held her hand, spoon intact, to her chest, heart beating like a drum. "Thought you'd left, lass."

"Yes," Val confirmed, "but I didn't get far when a thought struck me. I had to come back and ask."

"Ask me what, child?"

"Well, I know you were the cook for the clan that Robin, Caz, Saffron, and Rolland were from. There's another friend from there named Raven. Last I saw him, Raven was headed to your clan to check on everyone with some lads. There was a female Fae with them, and I just wondered..."

"Wondered what, dearie?"

"Did you see them when they came back, or had you left to travel here before they got there?"

"Course I saw them. Was Raven who told us about the moot and the reason I came here."

"How was the girl with Raven? Did she seem well?"

"Ha!" Zeeka yelled. It was Val's turn to jump, surprised. "Now I know who you remind me of! Leastways your manners, if not your looks so much. Raven's Ambassador, the Fae lass named Carlisse..." Val nodded her head, eager to hear about her sister. "Oh, you'll be proud. Miss Carlisse is a prize; she is. Charmed the pants off every goblin in the clan. The first time a Fae Ambassador has ever reached out to our kind that I can remember." Zeeka had a dreamy look on her face. "Anyway, you must be one of Carlisse's sisters. She told the clan about her family. Why can you believe Miss Carlisse took the time to meet every single one of us? And asked to be introduced to all of our own kin?" Zeeka laughed a great guffaw. "The last I saw her was when I was pulling out with my wagon loaded to make my way here. Why, she had a line out the door and down the cavern hallway waiting to get what they were calling a 'Carlisse Tattoo'. The people loved her."

Zeeka waved her spoon at Val. "Off with you now. You had the threads of a pattern coming together that will help you align your solutions. I can tell you agreeable solutions to put your heart at ease. We can talk of Miss Carlisse more tomorrow, after the moot, dearie." She waved her spoon over and over at Val, shooing her out, watching from under the arch of the pavilion as Val pushed open her black gossamer wings and took flight. She was in a hurry now to get back to work on Faith's speech, ideas fresh in her mind. Zeeka's forehead crinkled as she squeezed her eyes down to slits, focused on the lass's movement, and thought she saw someone follow in Val's wake. But she couldn't make out anything clearly in the dark. It nagged at her as she went back to her cooking, catching the contents of her pot just before it boiled over the lip of the pan.

Chapter 5: Surprise Visits

"There she is," Robin pointed at Faith, sitting cross-legged by the small campfire in front of his tent. She looked up to see the Goodfellow and her father approaching. She balanced her sketchbook on her lap.

"Have you seen her drawings, sir?" Robin asked Lennox. "She's very talented."

Faith blushed, having heard the compliment. The two men walked behind her to look over her shoulder at the sketches open before her. She turned the pages slowly, enjoying the attention, then abruptly closed the book, declaring, "We have better things to do than look at my old drawings, yeah?"

"Wait!" Robin exclaimed as he squatted down, putting a hand out to flip the book open again where she'd left off. "This drawing," his eyes roamed across the details on the page. "I haven't seen this one before. Who is the woman in this portrait?" he wondered aloud.

It was Lennox who answered Robin's question. "That's Aleta. My wife and Faith's mother," the old man's eyes teared up, "How did you get this?" he whispered.

"I drew it, Papa," she said gently, moved by his emotion. "I asked Dedo to describe her to me. As he gave me the details, I created this portrait. Does it resemble what she really looked like?" Faith held the book up so they could better see the picture she'd rendered of her mother.

"It's her," Robin declared, drawing in a sharp breath.

"What are you talking about, Robin? I don't know who you think this is, but I can assure you it's a likeness of my mother."

"That's a face I could never forget, Faith. Though you've drawn her likeness using coal, her hair was golden, her eyes sapphire blue, and I...I remember her essence was like springtime in May." His mouth hung open, his eyes seeing something far away, long ago. He nodded to himself in sharp affirmation. "She's definitely the woman I remember from my childhood who cast the Trillium spell on me. I'm sure of it."

Faith shook her head. “It couldn’t have been her.” Faith argued and clutched the sketchbook to her chest.

“It’s possible,” Lennox said, scratching his beard, “your mother followed the threads far into the future. She was a powerful seer. Maybe she planted the seeds so Robin could save you when the time came. Robin had been to our castle as a wee lad with his father, Lancer.”

“Well, that settles it,” Faith declared. “Robin is coming with us, Papa. She can confirm or deny his recollection.”

The color drained from Lennox’s face. “What are you talking about?”

“Oh, that’s why I’ve been waiting for you. I know the gargoyle’s secret. A way to travel to a scrying pool that my mother had spelled ages ago. Dedo has communicated with her. He’s been doing it for years. Claims she swore him to secrecy.” Faith held out her hand. Robin pulled her to a stand. She studied his face, but he betrayed no emotion. “Will you come with us, Robin? It’s not dangerous. I’ve been to see her once before. She may have other answers for you, or maybe nothing, but worth the chance, yeah?”

He was at a loss for words; a simple nod, his only reply.

The Fae princess opened the sketchbook to her depiction of the compass. “Link arms, and whatever you do, don’t let go until I tell you. I’m not sure what would happen if you did. Dedo said they only designed the compass for one traveler, but I’m pretty sure as long as we are all touching, we can move through together.” Her voice trailed off in an echo.

“Move through?” Lennox asked.

“It’s hard to describe. Like traveling through a kind of ghost universe that replicates ours, but is not ours. A different layer. That’s not the best description, but it’s how we move using the compass I saw Dedo access.”

She linked her arms through theirs and touched a picture she had drawn next to the direction on the compass for her destination. The trio hit the shoreline of tumbled agates, a wave washing over them, soaking their clothes. Faith squeezed their arms, hanging on, then touched the colored agates. The sound of the crashing waves faded as they landed in the cavern deep below the Fae castle on the northern shore of Lake Sapphire.

As before, the cave was dim, bits of mica shimmering throughout the cavern, eerie green shadows reflected across the walls and the vast pool. The water was smooth as glass, looking like a mirror that stretched out before them.

"Faith?" Lennox did a three hundred sixty-degree turn, taking in their surroundings.

"Shhh," she pressed a finger to his lips. She dropped her arms, releasing their linked elbows, and opened a small pouch at her waist. The two men stood still as Faith moved to the water's edge. She pulled a black pearl out and tossed it as far as she could into the pool. Ripples moved out to the other side, then back toward her, where she stood at the edge, water touching the tips of her boots.

"Mother?" Faith whispered. The word echoed off the walls. Silence answered. "I don't know if you can answer right now, but I have so much to tell you. I've brought some special people to see you."

Silence.

Robin and Lennox looked at one another. Robin felt sorry for Faith, a lonely girl pining for her long-lost mother. He could barely stand to witness this. Just as he was about to turn away, a glow shimmered across the water, and the mica in the walls reflected it, lighting up the cavern.

Lennox took a tentative step forward, his heart hammering against his chest.

"Ah, there you are. I was afraid I had dreamed about our last meeting. Are you well?"

The drawing Robin and Lennox had seen earlier came to life in full color as the image of Aleta Dawn Stargazer looked out from the surface of the pool. The man kneeling at the side of the pool behind the princess instantly drew her blue eyes.

"My love?" Aleta whispered, her voice catching.

Tears streamed down his weathered face. He reached his arms out as though he could embrace her.

"Oh no, no, no," she cooed softly. "No tears, my love. Just seeing that you are alive will sustain me, no matter the coming trials we both must endure. What a magnificent gift you have given me, Faith Lisbet. A magnificent gift indeed." She projected a smile, and the walls shimmered brighter. Her eyes drifted further back and landed on Robin. "Lancer?" she asked, befuddled. "No. Of course not. How silly of me," she laughed at herself. "You're Robin

Goodfellow. Son of Lancer and Alora. I can't believe how much you look like your father. I must say, you are an unexpected visitor. What brings you to my prison, young Goodfellow? Come now, speak your mind," she encouraged.

"I...I saw a portrait Faith had drawn of you and remembered..."

"Remembered?" Aleta prompted.

"Your face. I clearly remembered your beautiful face when you cast the Trillium spell on me as a child. It was you, wasn't it?"

"Someday, I hope to tell you the entire story. It is enough for now to put your mind at ease, to confirm your memory is true. It was me. I can tell that you are free of the spell now, which means you've found your sister, Valvina Ariana Goodfellow, yes? Let peace rest in your heart. I hope we will meet again face to face."

Robin nodded, stepped back, a thousand questions pushing to the surface. But he recognized that this was not the time to demand answers.

Faith stood and told her father, "Time is short. She cannot maintain the connection for long. It drains her power. She needs all her magic to fight her enemies. Say the words you've longed to tell her all these years before she must leave us."

Faith gently wiped the tears from his cheeks, moved back to stand with Robin, giving her parents as much privacy as possible in the small cavern. The Fae princess leaned her back against Robin's chest, and he wrapped his arms around her, resting his chin on the top of her head. They were witnesses to the sweet, quiet words her mother and father spoke urgently to one another.

Aleta's face faded, and Lennox cried out, reaching his hand out over the water to...nothingness. The shimmer dimmed, and the mica only sparkled here and there on the walls again.

Lennox backed away from the edge. "She said she doesn't know where they have her imprisoned, only that the Gugwe are her keepers. They seek to steal her magical powers, but she has held on. All these years, she has held on. She must hold longer." He ground the words out, and his hands made hard fists.

"We need to go now," Faith said as she linked arms and elbows with Robin and Lennox, then touched a symbol on the compass, as she'd seen Dedo do. Her voice was an echo in the empty chamber as they disappeared. "I think there are two others you need to take counsel with, Father."

WHAT STARTED AS A KIND gesture turned into a food fight and peals of laughter. Lenny had found a bush thick with ripe autumn raspberries. Without thinking, eager to share the bounty, he tossed one to Lester, but his brother was looking in the opposite direction. The juicy berry hit Lester in his ear. Lester put his hand up, swatting at what he thought was an insect. The berry juice spattered across his face, and his fingers came away stained red. Lester stared at his fingers, then looked at Lenny, who tossed back a handful of raspberries into his mouth, eyes closed, savoring the flavor. "Hurry, Lester, before I eat them all!" he called happily to his brother.

Lester had worked his way to the other side of the berry bush, picking berries as fast as he could. "Here, Lenny, let me help you," Lester called out. "Open wide!" Before Lenny could follow the command, Lester pelted Lenny's face with a handful of overripe berries, hitting it in a dozen places. Juice splattered, running down to stain the clean tunic Lenny had donned that morning. Still, he felt laughter bubble up and out of himself. The two brothers held their mouths open as wide as they could, each taking turns tossing berries to see how many they could get into the other's mouth. Most hit the target, but lots splashed across skin and clothes. The two gargoyles were a sticky mess by the time they'd picked the bush clean.

Rolling on the ground, tittering with laughter, they finally noticed the Princess had arrived back at Stone House Camp. She stood a few feet away, her foot tapping the ground with impatience. "Kings," she greeted them coolly when they made eye contact. "I see you are busy taking care of your people's problems and issues. Perhaps I should come back at a time more convenient for you?" Her eyebrows rose at the question.

Lenny answered by pelting her with the last berry he had in hand, which he regretted a moment later, as he'd intended to relish the flavor of it. It delighted him when the juicy berry hit his target, landing smack between Faith's eyes. Lennox broke out with a great guffaw and bent over, slapping both hands just above his knees. He hadn't had a good laugh in years. One look at Faith's face and he immediately tried to rein in his amusement, but another chuckle slipped out. The next thing he knew, Faith was holding her sides, joining him in genuine laughter. Robin stood ten feet away, leaning against a willow tree, separating himself from the shenanigans.

"You three should get along just fine, yeah?" Faith said to her father and the Gargoyle Kings. "Your sense of humor runs along the same lines," she said flatly. "Too bad you didn't harvest those berries and have Delainey bake you a pie," she sighed at the loss.

"King Lenny. King Lester. Meet King Lennox. Fae King of the Northern Lands. You have some history you can share with him, and I think he could use your counsel. I figured you two were best for the job. Enjoy the afternoon, gentlemen," she smiled. As she passed Robin, heading toward the Dream Weaver's Stone House, she took his hand, pulling him along. "Maybe if we're lucky, Delainey will have foraged berries herself and baked a pie, yeah?"

"You're a positive thinker, lass. I like that about you." Robin told her.

There was no pie.

But, as luck would have it, they reached the Stone House in time for tea. Delainey found it ambrosial to find Faith and Robin at the door, with a rum raisin cake cooling on a wire rack in the pan. She settled them at the table and put the kettle on. It wasn't long before Ari came through the door, his nose leading him to a freshly baked cake. Clearly, he'd gained quite a few pounds over the past month and a half, likely from eating Delainey's baked goods every day.

Robin asked for the news. The Dream Weaver told them that Carlisse, Raven, and the lads had been through only two days before, now headed for the moot. "Say," he wondered, "isn't tomorrow the big day of your speech at the big gathering?" Ari asked.

"It is," Faith confirmed. "We'll be back in time," she assured him. "I'm using the Goyle's compass system." She told them her father was consulting with the kings. Delainey shared that Carlisse's role as an ambassador was a success. Over twenty of the Robins' clan had followed them back here. Delainey credited the increase in the Edgewood's population to her sister. Claiming that Carlisse sold the dream of the Village of Edgewood as a place where all the races could live in peace together. The newcomers wanted to be part of building such a community.

"Speaking of the village residents," Robin put in, "I'm going to head down to Rolland's smithy and see how the weapon making is coming."

"Good idea," Faith added. "It could be an impressive addition to my speech if we could show off a cache of quality weapons at the moot tomorrow. It would illustrate to the people that we're thinking ahead and planning. I'll go with you. Thanks for the cake, Delainey. That was a treat!"

SAFFRON SPOTTED ROBIN and Faith before they reached the shop, rushing out to meet them. She offered to lead Robin to where the members of the clan who'd arrived two days before were setting up living quarters. That way, he could get the latest news from his people. Faith debated whether she should go with them or if she'd just be in the way of his reunion. As she turned to continue to Rolland's forge, Robin snatched her hand and pulled her along behind him. She couldn't help feeling good about being included.

It impressed Faith to watch as Robin greeted each individual. He made every one of them feel important as he called them by name, introduced her, and listened to their tales of the adventure to get here. Robin took the time to hear about their dreams as they expressed hope for how life could be in the Edgewood. The Goodfellow didn't rush anyone. He listened with focus and asked engaging questions. As he'd talked with each emigrant, he'd expressed his thanks for all their information and support. Finally, he told them he had to go check on Rolland's weapon production. One lad jumped up. "I'll take you to the smithy, Robin. We've been working in shifts. Started the day we got here. After our daily shift with the blacksmith is done, we work on our living quarters as a team." The lad beamed with pride and gestured that they should follow him.

Saffron held Faith back a few steps, letting Robin and the lad move off ahead. "So?" Saffron raised her eyebrows.

"What?" Faith scrunched her eyes, her forehead wrinkling, unable to guess what Saffron wanted.

"You," she pointed at Faith, "Robin," she pointed at him. "Traveling together?" She insinuated it meant they were a couple.

"Yeah, Saffron," Faith responded. Saffron rubbed her hands together, a smile spreading across her face. Faith added context. "Robin, *my father* and I are traveling together." Saffron's face fell in disappointment. "Nothing's changed," Faith admitted. "We're still just friends. Frankly, I've decided that I've got my hands full. I'm still trying to figure out how to unite all the races to the common goal of fighting an enemy that wants to enslave us all. I can't even think about whether Robin and I...well, you know what I mean, right? There's just no time for anything but figuring out how we beat those monsters."

"You've got your priorities straight, Faith. I'm kind of insulated from everything that's happening, but I promise to keep that goal at the forefront of everyone here from now on."

"Thanks. I need all the support I can get."

Faith's eyes goggled when she entered Rolland's shop. The big goblin wore a heavy leather apron and held a red-hot length of iron in a gloved hand. He moved with a kind of grace for such a large man. She watched as he took the glowing rod to his anvil, lifted his hammer, pounded the hot iron, shaping it to his liking, sparks flying with every strike. The far wall in the shop contained wooden crates, stacked three high, the topmost still open. Robin showed her that Rolland and his crew were filling the crates with knives, swords, pikes, and axes. Two were almost full of shields.

"Rolland," she turned, a radiant grin spread across her face, "you and your team are amazing," she praised him. "I never dreamed..."

Rolland plunged the blade he had been working on into a barrel of water. A loud hiss sounded, steam rising from the vat. "You do the dreaming, Princess, and we'll help you make those dreams come true, right lads?" His team pledged their best.

He put the new piece aside. There were others in the smithy working on finishing the weapons with handles and such. A long bench on the opposite wall held males and females alike. Each of them was busy crafting sheaths, stamping designs onto the leather, or stitching matched leather pieces together using an awl.

Faith looped her arm in the crook of Rolland's, turned him away from the group and whispered, "I have a favor to ask, Master Rolland."

He shook his head in understanding and motioned her over to his private work stall. "It takes some getting used to," he confessed, "but sometimes it is convenient to have a seer know about things that are going to happen before they actually do." Faith cocked her head in question, and he continued, "I didn't expect to see any of you again until well after the moot. I imagine you'll all have missions to follow to prepare for war. In addition, I'm told you'll continue to gather people all across Sharas to your campaign, but the Dream Weaver assured me you'd be here this week. Not only that, but that you'd be wanting one just like I made for Saffron."

A look of surprise bloomed across her visage. "Ah, would you mind taking off your right boot?" Rolland asked shyly.

She leaned against the wall of his private workspace and fought her right boot off, cheeks turning pink as she handed it to him.

Rolland shuffled through several pieces of leather on a shelf, pulled one, and held it to her boot. Satisfied with the match, he used an awl to punch holes in the boot, matched to the strip of leather he'd chosen, and sewed the strip inside. Faith watched with keen interest. When he finished, the fresh addition looked like it had always been a part of the footwear. Rolland pulled open a drawer and produced a stiletto, the handle inlaid with mother-of-pearl. "To match your wings," he winked, holding it out for her to see. Then he slid it home, fitting safely inside the new hidden scabbard inside her boot. "Best you keep that as your secret, Princess."

"It's beautiful work, Rolland. I don't know how to thank you. I've wanted one ever since I saw Saffron's."

Robin called out, "Faith? We should get going. The lads have rigged up a special backpack for me so we can take a small sample of Rolland's weapons to display after you give your speech at the moot. Starting next week, a crew will make regular deliveries just as soon as you decide where we want to store weapon caches."

Faith laid her hand on Rolland's and squeezed, mouthing a silent "thank you" as she slipped out of his workspace into the main of the smithy. "This is just what we needed," she nodded to the pack of weapons Robin was settling across his back. She did a full 360-degree turn. "My thanks to all of you. One for all," she said, and they took up the chorus, "and all for one."

Robin took her hand and waved his other as they left the shop. "We'd better collect your father and get going. Val's probably worried sick. We should have been back a couple of hours ago, but this side trip was well worth the extra time, yeah?"

They found her father in the King's shed studying the compass she'd painted on the floor months ago. He was also memorizing the map surrounding the compass that depicted the Lands of the Gugwe in Adana.

"The Gargoyle Kings have helped me come to a decision." Lennox told her without looking up from the artwork.

"You can tell me later, Papa. Robin is eager to get back. The moot starts tonight, and I have a big speech to make. You both have parts to play as well."

"Just a moment." He stopped her. "This is important. You were right when you said I had abandoned not only you, but..."

"That's water under the bridge, Papa, please..."

"Let me finish." He touched his finger to her lips. "Not only did I desert you, but I was derelict in my duty to our people as their king. You said I had forsaken our people, broken their trust. It's true. I put my selfish pride and wants before everything and everyone else, without an ounce of guilt or regret. So, I'm abdicating my sovereign power. As of this moment, I formally renounce the Fae throne and name you, my successor. I promise to do everything I can to support you. After, and only after, I fulfill my duty to you will I take up my search to find your mother once more. She bade me help you first, and I could not refuse her request. I pass the reign of the Northern Fae Kingdom to my daughter. Each of you here is a witness to my abdication of the Fae throne." Lennox fell to one knee in front of Faith.

Her mouth had fallen open. She held the back of her hand to her gaping maw and looked to Robin, then to the two gargoyles for help, but found none. They silently agreed with Lennox's choice. Reaching down, she pulled her father to a stand, sighing heavily. "Great timing, Papa. No extra pressure, yeah?"

"Thanks for *your* help," she delivered her words with a heavy dose of sarcasm to the two Gargoyle Kings.

Linking her arms with Robin and Lennox, she bent to touch the location of a cave that was close to the moot. The three travelers disappeared, with little bits of sparkling dust floating where they'd stood a second ago.

The kings looked at one another, shrugged their shoulders and went back to playing their game of stones.

Robin fought the spinning of his head and the nausea rolling in his stomach as the trio raced through a black hole, sparkling lights surrounding them. He felt hot, and the heavy weight of the pack didn't help. He thought if he could just shift the pack to let some cool air against his back, it would give him relief. Struggling with the straps, he got the pack loosened. Just as he and Lennox touched down on the cave floor, the pack slid off his shoulder and hit Faith's arm where it linked with his, knocking her hold loose. Her feet hadn't touched down yet, and Robin felt her rip away from him back toward the dark hole. Faith screamed in alarm. Robin tried to grab hold of her. He latched onto her backpack, but it slid off her shoulders.

A vortex of powerful wind pushed against her as he fought to hang on.

"Robin!" she cried, "Don't let go!" The maelstrom twisted her slender body. Her own weight jerked her into the whirlwind. Robin watched with dread as her essence disappeared into the tunnel. The Goodfellow looked down in disbelief at Faith's backpack still clutched in his hand. When he looked back up, he shouted Faith's name, but the black hole they'd traveled through had closed. There was only the rough stone of the cave wall to meet his reaching hands. All he could think of were her instructions when they'd started this little adventure. "Don't let go until I tell you to. I'm not sure what would happen." He dropped her backpack and looked down at his empty hand. He'd let her slip right through his fingers. Lennox's expression was a mask of horror.

Chapter 6: What's What?

Val had asked Garrett and Aliah to keep watch at the cave, awaiting Faith's return. Overseeing the final setup of the stage, she directed others to finish last-minute details. All she could think to do was to make herself available during Faith's absence, answering volunteers' questions. Val's strategy was pretty much to make everything up as she went along. They had a team of ushers; each person identified with a red strip of cloth tied around their upper right arm. Their job was to guide people to any open seats that were still available. Attendees and early arrivals had been staking out places to sit for hours. Amphitheater seating was pretty much at capacity, as was the grassy space between the stage and the first theater row. The engineers on the arena building project had cut in thirteen rows of natural dirt seating. The space circled out, surrounding the stage. Each level rose like steps, one row above another. Directly behind the top row was an open meadow. Summer's wildflowers, now seed heads and fuzzy tips waiting for the wind to spread them for next year's growth, covered the ground. Less than an hour before the moot was to start, people were still spreading out blankets in the field, staking their claim on the space. They couldn't have hoped for a better turnout.

The stage sat back far enough that everyone, no matter where they sat, could see and hear the scheduled speakers. A mixed group of musicians was casually jamming together center stage in an unplanned concert. When she wasn't directing someone or answering questions, Val was walking back and forth behind the musicians. By this time, she didn't care if anyone could hear her whispering curses under her breath; Faith's revised speech, neatly re-written, clutched tightly in her hand.

GARRETT WAS ON HIS feet as soon as he heard the first noises coming from inside the cave. He ran for the opening, ready to give Faith a piece of his mind over returning so late, mainly because Val had given him a piece of hers.

Reaching the arch, words ready to spill out, he looked around for the target of his intended dressing-down. But he only found Lennox, who sat with his head between his hands. Robin stood gaping at his open palms. Taking in the details, Garrett could see Faith's backpack at Robin's feet. There was a large canvas carrier hanging off Robin's shoulder, the weight dragging his body off balance. "Where is she?" Garrett turned full circle again, looking for Faith.

"She slipped right through my fingers," Robin whispered to himself. Faith's scream echoed over and over in his mind.

"What are you talking about, Robin? Focus!" Garrett shook him by the shoulders. "Where is Faith?"

Aliah arrived at the cave entrance. "What's going on?" she asked, looking round wildly.

Robin looked at Garrett, then back at his hands and down at Faith's backpack. "Our link broke just as we got back, but Faith hadn't touched down yet. I lost contact with her. A powerful vortex pulled her, sucking her back into the...I don't know what to call it, other than the space we traveled through. Then, the doorway Lennox and I came through closed. She's out there somewhere." He waved his hand toward the back wall of the cave.

Garrett snapped his fingers, his idea solidifying. "She'll use the compass she drew in her sketchbook."

"Can't," Robin shook his head. "Her sketchbook is in her pack here." He nudged it with the toe of his boot.

"She'll probably just draw another," Aliah suggested.

"Yeah, probably," Robin agreed. "As soon as she figures out how to stop floating through the black hole, gets drawing supplies and can recreate it. The moon's almost up. The moot starts shortly."

Garrett grabbed Faith's pack and rifled through it, pulling out her sketches. Flipping through, he found the compass and studied the pictured locations surrounding the directions. "Robin, where did you come from?"

"Our last stop was a visit to Stone House Camp," the Goodfellow responded, his crestfallen face lined with worry.

"Lennox," Garret's words tumbled out fast now, "you need to go with Robin to the stage. I was going to act as the Master of Ceremonies to introduce speakers, but you'll need to do it in my stead. Val will keep you on track."

The former Fae King nodded his acknowledgement and came to his feet. Garrett looked at Robin. "Get to the podium and take charge. Put every speaker on stage that you can find to stall until I can get Faith back here."

"What?" Aliah shouted. "Are you crazy? You know nothing about using that compass. She uses magic! Magic you don't have. Garrett, you can't go!" She pleaded, eyes filling with tears.

"I have magic," Garrett assured her.

"Not the same!" her voice rising shrilly.

"Aliah, I have to go after her. She'd do it for me. Go. Val will need your help to keep things rolling for the presentations. Think! This is the most important gathering of all the races in Sharas ever to take place. Don't you see? There's only one shot at this. It's critical that we get it right the first time to even have a chance of bringing together all the people to fight for a common cause. We cannot fail. I'll do my best to find her, but you know as well as I do, Faith would expect us to carry on, yeah? So, you will all have to do your best to carry out the original mission. If we can't even pull off the moot after everyone traveled here, they certainly won't have any confidence in us in forming up a united army. Focus on why we organized this moot. All for one and one for all."

Garrett gave Aliah a sad smile, then reached his hand out, touching the symbol representing Stone House Camp Faith has rendered on the artistic compass. A slash appeared in the wall behind him. He tore the drawing out of the book, rolled it up, and secured it under his vest. He winked at Aliah, shifted into his fox form, snapped open his wings, and shot through the opening. Aliah hollered his name. But just as fast as the travel portal opened, it was gone, and Garrett was gone with it. Her hands rested against the hard rock of the cave wall where the portal had closed.

FAITH DIDN'T KNOW HOW long she had floated aimlessly before it occurred to her to try her wings. Maybe if she were flying, she could pull away from the strong vortex that continued to draw her further into the black hole. Tiny sparkling lights flickered all around her. The feeling of weightlessness, of peace, engulfed her. All the pressure that had been plaguing her for weeks was gone. She wished Val were with her. Val would love this feeling. Thinking of her sister-friend brought another consideration. Faith knew how angry her friend would be if Faith was late or didn't show up at all for the moot. So many people had done so much planning and hard work to bring this off. Not to mention all the people who would have traveled long distances to be at the gathering. That made her wings snap out!

She found she could make progress against the vacuum. It was slow, but at least she was working her way back in the direction she had come from. She studied the surrounding lights, discovering that the shimmering across the astral plane was the negative of the star-filled sky in the real world. The Fae Princess searched for the Big Dipper and the North Star while she paced herself with the physical exertion of pumping her wings. She could feel soreness in her shoulders already. It took her a while to find what she referred to as 'her Big Dipper'. Faith didn't see it at first because of the mirror effect of all the constellations being reversed on this plane. But when she found it, she smiled at a memory, causing her to feel warm all over. Recalling the words that Garrett told her every year on her birthday, "If you're ever lost, find the North Star. I'll always be there waiting for you." With renewed energy, she adjusted her trajectory, lined her body up, pointed toward the Big Dipper, pumped her wings harder, and focused on a goal.

VAL TOOK THE NEWS BETTER than Aliah thought she would. At first, Aliah wasn't sure because she was at a loss when her sister's immediate reaction was to walk away without a word. But Val returned thirteen minutes later. She'd changed her clothes, dressed in leather pants, ankle boots, and a dark maroon velvet tunic. Val wore the silver ring the old nurse had given her. She twisted the silver circlet three times around her finger, as the old nurse had taught her. Val found she could feel Faith suspended somewhere, but not in this world. Her stomach clenched with worry. The silver ear cuffs she sported featured a cluster of butterflies in flight. She'd rubbed her lips with berry juice, giving them a deep red color, the way Saffron had shown them.

"Val...," Aliah stammered, "You look..."

"Determined?" Val finished for her sister.

"Well, yes. That's actually an appropriate description, but not the one I was going to use. What are you planning?"

"We will not blow this chance. Faith would want us to do everything we could to unite the people if she can't be here to do it herself. All I know is if we fail now, we'll lose the people's trust, lose any semblance of confidence that working together could be possible. There's still hope she'll make it on time. The moon's almost up. The prophecy didn't specify how the 'princess of them all' was supposed to unite the races, but I believe in her cause. I'm going to get this show rolling." Val gave Aliah a quick hug, walked up the stage steps with purpose, and marched over to Lennox. Looping her arm through his, Val placed a beaming smile on her face and walked in tandem with him to the podium. The musicians laid down their instruments. Cheering rose from the crowd.

Moonshine created a spotlight on the stage. Val stepped forward, taking advantage of the light. "Welcome everyone! Welcome to the first moot of Sharas' citizens!" Val opened her arms wide as if she could embrace all the attendees. "My name is Valerie Victoria Pureheart." Another cheer. "I'd like to start by thanking all those who worked so hard to make this event possible. I'd also like to extend my thanks to everyone attending. Thank you for taking the time and making the effort to travel here for this important occasion. We have many fine speakers lined up for you. Speakers from every race, every walk of life, from all across Sharas. Remember, we also welcome your input. All we ask is that each of you be open-minded. We all have a voice. Troubled times, dangerous times, are at our doorstep." She moved her head back and forth to make eye contact with the crowd. "Lennox Stargazer will be your Master of Ceremonies tonight. He's here to introduce our first speaker."

Val turned from Lennox's side, did a half bow, waved to the crowd, snapped out her wings, bounced three times on the balls of her feet. One of the flute players quickly blew a tune, just as if the two of them had choreographed it. The music matched Val's flight as she flew up and out over the amphitheater. His flute reached a crescendo at the same time she reached the meadow on the ridge above, the last note fading to silence as she touched down. The entire crowd had craned their necks to watch her exit from the stage. The assembly loved the stunt, clapping enthusiastically.

Lennox moved to center stage, applauding with the audience. He held up both hands, palms out, to quiet the assembly, announcing, "It is with great pleasure I introduce you to our first speaker, Garth Gladheart. Garth hails from the mid-South area of Sharas. He's served as the stable master for Sir Robert Watson of Bayside for the last twenty years. Please give a warm welcome to Master Garth Gladheart." Lennox led the masses in applause and moved out of the moon's shine as Garth stepped into the spotlight. Looking out across all the people assembled before him, Garth took off his hat, brushed it against his leg, and ran a hand through his hair. He stood with his feet forward in an open stance, gripping his hat with both hands. A hush fell over the crowd.

"Hello." Nervous, Garth cleared his throat. "I don't profess to have any special qualifications to be on stage here, talking to all of you good people. I've always lived my life as a simple human man. Don't have any magic powers. Been to a few places around Sharas. Like many of you, I've seen my share of good times and my share of bad ones. Every day in places all over our land, my experiences have varied. Thankfully, there have been occasions when I have found that someone can amaze me with incredible kindness. I've seen evidence that people of every race who are part of our communities show kindness regularly to others. They offer kindness to friends and strangers alike."

Garth twisted his cap in a continuous circle as he talked. "The unfortunate thing is that I also have seen cruel acts, heard cruel words from our own to our own. Shameful words that were flung about without thought or care. More times than I care to count, been a witness to despicable behavior. Not behavior that threatens your life. But damaging conduct that hurts feelings and helps build invisible walls between people. Why does that matter? We are facing a dangerous enemy. An enemy who is not part of the citizenry of Sharas. It's not just feelings that are going to get hurt. This is an enemy who is a threat to every single one of our lives. A common foe among us, some of you know them as the Gugwe. I've heard them referred to as the Beast-men. These monsters don't threaten just you or just me. The Gugwe threaten your mothers, fathers, aunts, uncles, brothers, sisters, children, friends, and neighbors. This adversary threatens our very freedom. The Gugwe, our common enemy, has plans to take us all. If they don't kill us, they will use us as their slaves! Slaves to plant and harvest the fields for them and theirs. Slaves who will work in their mines. Masters who will make you do their work, while they starve us and control our lives. They intend to own us like livestock!" Garth shuffled his feet, twisting his hat, boot toe moving in a circle. "Well, I don't know about you, but I will not stand for that! WILL YOU?" he shouted out at the crowd, thrusting out his neck, face beet red with anger.

The audience roared, more than half coming to their feet, shaking fists. Garth pumped his fist in the air three or four times, then put his cap under his arm, held his palms up to quiet the people again, as he'd seen Lennox do.

"I'm glad to see you agree with me."

They cheered.

"Thing is, as I'm looking out at the faces in this crowd, I see your honest, emotional reaction to the thought of *any* Sharas citizen becoming a slave to the Gugwe tribes. AM I RIGHT?"

More cheering, whistling.

"We have many people from different ethnic backgrounds who live in Sharas. Let's be honest. We haven't all gotten along with every citizen, even though they, too, are part of the population of our own lands. Sometimes the goblins are angry at the Fae, or the Fae at the goblins, or humans. Lord knows there are arguments between us all. Seems like arguments and hate have been growing between the racial groups that make up the citizens of Sharas. That is the point of my talkin' to you all tonight. I stand here as a simple man to tell you the simple truth. We can't beat the Gugwe fighting as separate groups against those monsters. If we don't put our differences aside and unite, we'll never beat the Gugwe. Surely, we cannot win if we can't be tolerant of one another's differences and work together. There is no doubt we will lose if we don't unite to fight our common enemy! If we stay in our segregated groups, all hope is lost. Unite, and we have a fighting chance."

The crowd quieted. The heavy silence was eerie over the amphitheater as the audience weighed Garth's words.

"Let me say that again, so it sinks in. WE WILL LOSE IF WE DON'T UNITE TO FIGHT OUR COMMON ENEMY!"

Cheers. Shouts. Whistles. Cat calls. Hoots and howls.

"Make no mistake or miscalculation." Garth looked out across the audience. "Every. Single. One. Of. Us. It does not matter whether you are human, Fae, goblin, gargoyle, whatever ancestry or stock you come from, UNDERSTAND THIS! THE GUGWE DON'T DISCRIMINATE WHEN THEY TAKE SLAVES. Every individual here fits their criteria to become a slave to their nation." Garth cupped his hand behind an ear. "What criteria, you ask? The only criterion the Gugwe needs. It's as simple as the fact that we are not of the Gugwe race. They believe themselves to be superior to all our kinds. Well, I'll tell you what! I'd rather fight for my freedom and die, then become a slave! YOU?"

The response from the crowd was so overwhelming, Garth had to cover his ears as he shouted over the cacophony. "WHO AMONG YOU WILL PUT ASIDE OLD HATES AND GRUDGES? WHO AMONG YOU WILL BAND TOGETHER AND FIGHT AS ONE PEOPLE, THE PEOPLE OF SHARAS, AGAINST OUR COMMON ENEMY?"

Garth let the noise and chaos rage as he walked off the stage, fitting his hat back on his head as he went. It took Lennox at least ten minutes to calm the audience so that the next speaker could start.

Luna shone down, lighting up the stage, casting moon-shadows all across the woods. There was a crew that worked in and out, circulating around the crowd, offering ale, whiskey, mulled wine, and hot tea. Zeeka kept turning out warm hand pies, both sweet and savory, to be distributed, while those with a message to share took the stage in turn. Loud goblins, shy gargoyles, gruff men, determined women, and proud Fae took turns in the spotlight. Some spoke for ten minutes; others, for an hour. A few came up just to voice their offer of support for uniting against an enemy that wouldn't blink an eye at stealing their lives, homes, and welfare.

There were some tense moments. Old arguments broke out over who was responsible for this or that old grudge, but Val always soothed the assemblage again with her natural charm. The musicians took up their instruments whenever she announced an intermission. Zeeka did her part by offering roasted chestnuts, maple candy, and caramel apples on sticks.

WHILE THE MOOT WAS in full swing, Garrett flew smoothly through the twilight sky of the other world. He identified the backward pattern of the constellations as soon as he'd come through the travel portal. It didn't take him long to orient himself. He immediately headed toward the only star cluster he considered his goal: the Big Dipper. Faith had to be there. She just had to be, he told himself. If she weren't, he would have to figure out his next move. But until he determined his instinct was wrong, he would remain stalwart, pushing toward the North Star. Time passed oddly here. Garrett couldn't get a sense of how long he'd been looking for Faith since he'd come through the slash between their world and this one. At least that was how he came to think of it in his mind. The muscles that worked his wings were aching. It felt like he'd been flying for hours and hours, but that didn't have any effect on his determination.

Garrett had to admit it was beautiful here. The surrounding sky was a palette of soft slate gray, accented by shimmering stars across the horizon, glittering like the Milky Way, but in a silver color. He didn't feel anxious or afraid. In fact, he felt so relaxed that he considered whether it would be alright to take a break and rest a bit, searching about for a comfortable place to light. Just as he was about to perch on a rather dull star, its surface attractive for a peaceful repose, out of the corner of his eye, he saw Faith's wings. Opalescent shine reflecting off the North Star. There she was, waving at him.

When the Foxfire touched down next to her, he shifted to his human form and wrapped her in his arms. She clung to him for a few moments, then, half crying, half laughing, relief at war with joy, she pushed him to arm's length and said, "You came for me. Just as you promised me all these years. Remember? You said that if I were ever lost, I was to find the North Star." She blinked her eyes, dipped her head shyly, grateful to have such a good friend to count on.

He gave her his best smile, bowed and said, "At your service, Princess."

She cuffed his arm, snorted, "Don't be so formal, Garrett Emmon Gladheart! I thank you with all my heart, but I'm afraid you've put yourself in a terrible situation!"

"Calm down. Tell me what you mean, Faith. What's terrible? I came to find you, and here you are. So, I'd say, all is well." A satisfied smirk crossed his face.

"I agree that part is good," she allowed. "The bad news is, I don't know how we're going to get back. Robin has my backpack with my makeshift compass. I suppose we could find a dead star, and I could try carving a compass, but it's going to be difficult and take time."

He watched the Fae Princess pacing back and forth, back and forth, as she talked.

When she came close again, Garrett grabbed her by the shoulders. "What kind of rescue would it be if I had no plan for a way to get us back?" he asked, winked, as he dramatically pulled the rolled-up sketch he'd taken from her book, presenting it to her as though he offered her a jewel.

"Garrett," she whispered and looked at him with wonder.

"I also grabbed a chunk of coal in case you needed to add anything," he suggested.

"Wow, we've both changed so much since this whole thing started. You're so responsible now."

"Speaking of responsibility, I don't mean to rush you. It is very peaceful and stress-free here, but I'm afraid you're needed back in our world. Val's stress level is probably through the roof by now. I can't guess how much time has passed since I came through the portal to find you, but when I left, the moot was close to starting and..."

"And Val's going to kill me!" she finished for him. Faith linked arms with Garrett. "Don't let go. That's what went wrong the last time," she explained as she reached for the drawing of the compass.

"Wait!" Garrett cried out. He shifted into his fox form. He pulled a long leather strip from the pocket of a green velvet vest Aliah had designed and sewn for him. The vest fit his human form, but left plenty of room for his wings when he shifted. It allowed him the ability to carry things with him in his fox form. And vainly, he thought it a rather rich look, the way the green velvet accented his red fur. His bushy tail flicked side to side as he looped one end of the leather around Faith's belt, securing it. Then he attached the other end to the leather chest harness that held his vest on. "We can move faster if we both use our wings. I'm not taking any chances of losing you," he winked at her.

Her Fae opalescent wings and his foxfire thick fur and feathered, copper-colored wings snapped out simultaneously. Faith put her palm squarely over the compass symbol that she'd drawn a moment before. The two friends moved like shooting stars through the pewter sky.

VAL TUGGED AT ROBIN'S sleeve. "What are we going to do? There's still no sign of Faith or Garrett." She wrung her hands in worry. "You're lined up to speak next, then Faith was supposed to be the finale. She's meant to deliver a rousing speech to unite everyone, bring them together to prepare to defend Sharas." Val's voice reached a high pitch. She felt lightheaded. "Plus, you know...the big reveal."

"Shh," Robin put his forefinger to his lips. "We'll figure it out. Listen! That Fae male who just took the stage to speak right now? He was one of my earliest friends. The young goblin female on stage with him? Her name is Tula. They have a powerful message to share. Listen." Robin pulled Val in front of him, facing forward, wrapped his arms around her and rested his chin on the top of her head. He felt her muscles relax and the strain go out of her as they attended the speaker.

"Greetings, citizens of Sharas. My name is Badger Bartholomew Brogan." Badger reached down and gently took Tula's hand, visibly startling the girl. Her eyes were wide and unblinking. Tula's chest constricted, breath coming in short huffs. She broke out in a cold sweat; the crowd gave her stage fright. Badger lifted their clasped hands straight up in the air and continued.

"Tula is this young lady's name." Badger made an encouraging motion, and Tula offered the assemblage a sweet curtsy. The people laughed, enchanted, and smiled at her.

"I met Tula seven years ago. I wish I could tell you our meeting was a joyous experience." Tula turned her head up to look at Badger's face. "On a trading mission, I had been gone from my village for several weeks. When I returned, I found everyone slain. Bodies of my friends and neighbors ripped apart. The dead lay everywhere. My younger brother was among them." His voice cracked. Badger allowed his words to sink in as he made eye contact from one end of the theater to the other. "I followed a trail that my people's enemies did not bother to conceal. The attackers did nothing to hide their tracks because they had no fear of us. They think we are weak. I followed their path. The next village I came upon held the same horrors as my own. The stench of death hung in the air. Blood soaked the ground. I followed the eastern shoreline of Sapphire Lake to the next settlement. Whether Fae, goblin or human inhabited the villages, they spared none. Regardless of race, gender, or age, brutal deaths were doled out everywhere the Gugwe had raided. Tula was the only survivor of her clan. They killed her family, friends, and neighbors. The elders of each village were slain. Every mature male slain. Females all taken for slaves." Badger kneeled down and gently turned Tula toward him and asked, "Who took them, Tula?"

The crowd was so quiet, you could have heard the movement of a butterfly's wings. Badger looked back out at the audience, still on his knees before Tula as he explained, "Tula has only spoken one word in all these years. One word, since she witnessed the Gugwe raid her village, slaughter her family, her people and steal her mother away to become a slave."

"One."

"Word."

"In all these long years while the two of us have lived like animals in hiding, spying on the Gugwe, gathering information. Learning about this enemy, so that one day we could avenge those that were taken from us either by vicious, senseless death or to become slaves."

"One."

"Word."

"Who took them, Tula?" Badger shouted out to the crowd.

Tula turned to face the people who stared at her in silence and said her one word. "Monsters."

Shivers ran up the arms and necks of everyone in attendance.

Badger stood holding Tula's hand. "Monsters," he repeated. "We have seen many places over the years that have been the target of the Gugwe's ruthless, inhumane strikes. The two of us have gathered information to fight this enemy." The crowd cheered. Badger went on. "But I warn you! Even united against a common enemy, this will be no easy fight. MONSTERS!

Tula told you true. The Gugwe are monsters, and you have no chance at all if you stay in your own little factions. No chance whatsoever. We must become one people. The people of Sharas, to fight against our common enemy."

Badger's face was stern as he turned to leave the stage. Tula opened her arms to the crowd. A silent plea, then gave a quick curtsy, running to brush past Badger, leading him off the stage.

Silence hung in the air.

Robin held his breath.

Val squeezed his fingers. Then, of a sudden, the throng exploded to their feet, applause echoing across the stage, joined by hoots, howls, whistling, and shouts of Badger and Tula's names. Stomping of feet. Begged to hear more!

The people were so worked up, Lennox rushed forward and labored to pacify the audience before things turned into a riot. Val pushed Robin out onto the stage. "Go, go!" she told him, shoving a flute into his hand.

The Goodfellow put the instrument to work. The other musicians joined him, and they played a lively tune to match the energy in the atmosphere, slowly changing the tempo to bring the fever down. Lennox backed out of the limelight. Little by little, the crowd took its seats once again.

Robin put his flute inside a deep pocket in the breast of his coat. Standing front and center on the stage, moonlight casting his shadow large behind him, he stared out at the audience, and they stared back.

"Robin Wilum Goodfellow at your service," he announced, followed up with a curtsy. The crowd laughed. "You can't blame me," he told them, with a quirk at the side of his mouth. "It worked so well for Tula. I would have been a fool not to try it, yeah?" Soft laughter echoed around the amphitheater. The atmosphere relaxed.

"My father, Lancer Ian Goodfellow, has been missing these last six years. I often wish I could call on him for advice, but that isn't in the cards."

A heckler yelled out, "We don't want leaders like your evil Queen Morveena!" Other voices rose to support the statement.

Robin held his hand up for quiet. "You'll get no argument from me on that account," he told the people in earnest. "But I have no intention of taking the goblin crown or trying to step into my father's shoes, so to speak."

The crowd roared in amusement again, because everyone knew gobs didn't wear shoes.

Warming to his audience, Robin physically worked the stage front, moving back and forth before his votaries. "There are many things we don't know about each other. Secrets perpetuated that the next and last speaker will make clear to you, though I cannot in this moment. I will tell you this," he paused, making a slow circuit to have eye contact with everyone. "If there was one thing my father taught me true, it was that squabbles, hatred and fighting among the people of Sharas only leaves the door open for invasion. Our in-fighting invites our own destruction and enslavement."

"We do not need to choose to follow a king or queen of the goblins." He strode purposefully across the stage and shook his fist. "There is no need to choose to follow a king or queen of the Fae." Robin's voice rang out across the theater. "Sharas does not need a king or queen of men. Kings or queens of gargoyles or selkies or any other race." Robin's voice boomed out at the onlookers. Then, he let silence ride across the space before he spoke again. Using a quiet tone, the atmosphere so hushed, his gentle pleading reached every ear. "What we need," Robin raised his eyebrows, "What we do need is to follow a leader who has our collective well-being in mind. A leader who represents us all. Not factions. Not factions of Fae, goblins, gargoyles, men, selkies, or others! A leader who represents us all as equal citizens of Sharas."

The crowd roared in approval. Some previous nay-sayers were nodding their heads in agreement with Robin's words. Some faces expressed surprise, where hope was written on the features of others. A few still wore skeptical frowns, but mostly smiles. Robin looked to the side of the stage where Val stood. She shook her head in the negative to let him know there was still no sign of Faith.

Holding both hands up to quiet the people, Robin swallowed hard. His mind was racing. How was he going to announce that the person he'd primed them all to hear wasn't able to make an appearance? "Ladies and gentlemen," he stammered, then his face crumpled, not sure what to do or how to go on. All this work, all this effort, and no grand finale. The big moment had finally arrived, and there was no Faith. No, princess of them all. They'd failed. There was no one to lead them in the concept of 'all for one and one for all'.

At his darkest moment, an idea popped into his head of a sudden, and he moved with quick grace across the stage to where Val stood behind the sideline curtain. His hand snaked out and locked onto hers. He pulled her onto the dais with him. Caz was sitting in the front row. He stood and began clapping as Robin gently pulled Val to the center, into the limelight. The applause caught on, rippling through the crowd.

Val was whispering hissed words at Robin, her face burning red. She had a death grip on Robin's hand, not about to be left standing center stage alone. The audience held its silence, waiting.

Valvina Ariana Goodfellow's mind raced. She felt sweat dripping down her back between her shoulder blades. There were flashes of light at the edge of her vision. Then, just as she was about to move into a full-blown panic attack, she saw a shooter cross the skyline. A shooting star had always been a talisman of good luck to her. Val took it as a sign.

One talent that few people knew about was that Val had an angel's singing voice. She had only heard her friend Saffron sing this song once, but it had moved her so personally that she had been singing it privately for months now. A hush fell over the crowd as Val sang 'Our Return'.

The fires burn and burn and burn,
Forever awaiting our return
To home; to hearth;
And all along the road
Our people walk in search of self
And family lost – too high the cost.
The fires burn and burn and burn,
Forever awaiting our return.
Home is where we long to be –
On the northern shore along the sea,
Free to wander long among
Our forgotten ghosts –
Our history erased by evil hosts.
The fires burn and burn and burn,
Forever awaiting our return.
Forgotten war and rage
Have brought us to the center stage.
But we have not lost memory
Of those we loved,
but lost the key -

The door closed fast;
Our dreams a nightly reverie.
Some sweet day,
One shall come, one to lead us
Back the way we've come;
Our tears will never build the bridge,
The very one we need to cross.
A path that we must travel to find the history lost.
The fires burn and burn and burn
Forever awaiting our return.
The clans forgotten,
The clans reborn,
Cursed to travel from dusk till dawn as
The souls we mourn, the ones we lost;
Now will find their way when a leader takes their hands
And guides us back to our homeland.
Until that day;
The fires burn and burn and burn
Forever awaiting our return.

WHEN SHE FINISHED, she saw people crying and hugging. Goblin, Fae, human, goyles and all the others in attendance. She brushed the tears from her cheeks.

"Sometimes," she started, her voice cracking. Robin squeezed her fingers. Val cleared her throat and spoke out stronger, louder. "Sometimes, everything isn't as it seems. We get fooled. Someone who wants the authentic version of history hidden twists the account of history they want us to learn. Then, there are times we just lose our way. Each of you probably has at least one person who means the world to you. My best friend is that person to me. Faith Lisbet Stargazer. She's like a sister to me. Faith was the person meant to be standing here. Now. She was the one who was supposed to be telling you the secret truth we've recently learned. Faith had so many things she wanted to share with you. She wrote a speech," Val held up the papers crumpled in her fist, "but circumstances turned the tables on us again, so she couldn't be here. Couldn't be with you now. A twist of fate, if you believe in such things."

Val stopped, stood tall, unfolded the papers that contained her sister-friend's thoughtful words, smoothing it against her velvet tunic and then held the handwritten speech in front of her, "If Faith Lisbet Stargazer could have been here, she would have told you that sometimes the truth, the past, was deliberately hidden, buried. She would have wanted you to know that we are, all of us, more alike than we are different. Faith would want us all to choose to live by our own choices, not by chance or happenstance. My best friend dreams of our lives being the finest they can be. We both dream of all the people of Sharas choosing to be motivated, never manipulated. Your lives should be purposeful, not lived as slaves without purpose or free will; our greatest prayer is that we will all do our best to make changes and improvements. Not just for ourselves, but for our neighbors as well, with no excuses. Faith Lisbet Stargazer takes steps every day to pursue the dream she holds in her heart for all the citizens of Sharas."

"Carrying a vision in her heart like a beacon to light the way for all who will listen and follow. *All for one and one for all.*"

"Keeping the dream alive that the people of Sharas will forgive and forget their differences and instead focus on all the ways we are alike."

"We have kept a great secret from some of our people. Faith should have been the one here to share this truth with you, but she's not here to do so. I know she would want me to give you this knowledge to help heal the hatred among us. If you'll indulge me, I have a secret, too. It has just occurred to me—became crystal clear to me, really—that the time for secrets is over. I thought I needed to keep my secret all to myself, but I don't think that's the right decision now. I think you have the right to know. Yes, I believe you'll agree that revealing my secret is the right thing to do, for all our sakes."

Robin stood off to the side, still on stage, but giving Val her moment in the limelight. Shock raced through his body as he realized what she was about to do. He reached out to stop her. Too late. Her black, luminescent wings snapped open. Val turned to her brother, waved her arm at Robin, and pointed. Then announced, "I recently learned I am the long-lost daughter of Lancer Goodfellow, thought to be dead all these years. The truth is that I was fortunate to be fostered in secret by a good, loving family."

Her eyes moved across the audience, from one end to the other, making eye contact with as many people as possible. Making a connection. "I can see you're wondering what that means? What it means is that I am not a Fae, as I was raised to believe. My foster name is Valerie Victoria Pureheart. ***My real name is Valvina Ariana Goodfellow***. Though many of you know me as a Fae, I am really a true-born goblin."

Val pushed her wings into motion, lifting from the stage and flying back and forth in front of the onlookers. Gradually, the people realized Val was claiming to be a goblin. Her revelation confused them because they knew goblins didn't have wings. The audience had only ever been told that fairies had wings and could fly! Murmurs turned to shouts, some angry; some in disbelief; some accusing her of lying. Robin could envision everything going south from here, as panic seemed to froth up in the crowd surrounding them.

He stepped forward, shouted, "It's true! What Valvina says is true! She is my sister. She's sharing the truth with you. Our Queen forced goblins for a generation to hide our wings. Our history was deliberately distorted. Rewritten. The Fae and the goblins are related. We are of one race that split into two. Over time, we developed different customs, but we are the same people."

In a desperate measure, Robin pulled off his jacket and threw it on the floor. He squared his shoulders, pushed his chest out, a fierce look on his face, and allowed his great leather wings to snap out. The crowd reeled, drawing in a collective gasp. Hands flew to cover mouths in surprise. Fae, surprised at the declaration and physical show of proof, were stunned by the race connection. Goblins panicked, shocked at Robin's exposure of the secret that they were all meant to keep hidden in shame and fear. Then, like a row of dominoes lined up, the first fell, creating a cascade of goblins who stood and allowed their hidden wings to emerge. For some, it was quite painful, having kept them closed for so long. Others had to remove a binding around their wings before they could snap theirs open. A few revealed they had them, but their muscles were no longer strong enough to push them out.

Val came back to Robin's side, taking his hand again. It looked as though they had lost control of the moot. Val raised her and Robin's hands fisted together into the air and cried out over and over, "We are all one people of Sharas. All for one and one for all!" Over and over, the two stomped across the stage, repeating the words. It wasn't long before all the other speakers joined Val and Robin on stage, chanting, "All for one and one for all!"

The message took hold. Soon after, the horde took up the words. The entire throng began shouting the mantra, "All for one and one for all'.

Out of nowhere, a bright green light slashed across the stage, blinding the audience.

Faith flew in alongside Garrett in Foxfire form, landing center stage.

"Am I late?" she asked her best friend.

Val sank to her knees. Laughter and tears bubbling out of control.

Baffled, Faith whispered, "What's what?"

Chapter 7: Solidarity Secured

Three days out from Vattusk, traveling northwest to the BloodKnife village, Zilla was losing control. The albino woman consumed his thoughts. He slept badly and could barely eat. It was as if a sickness had overtaken him. He knew it was suicide to lust after the Thana's betrothed, but nothing he did to distract himself made any difference. Zilla had taken on double shifts scouting for the Thana's entourage, making sure he was absent from group meals where he was likely to see Abaddon. Nevele kept a constant watch on the Gugwe KuRuk.

That evening, the camp was quiet, with a full moon overhead when Zilla returned. He reported to Seeker Vutova that he had neither seen nor found any evidence of enemies in the area they had assigned him to cover during his shift that night. The Seeker sent him to the cook's fire to get a hot meal and suggested he get some rest.

"Why don't you take tomorrow off?" Seeker suggested, "You've been pulling two shifts for days now. There are others who can stand you for a couple of stints."

Zilla stared at the Scout Leader with bloodshot, dead eyes.

Finally, with an uncomfortable feeling crawling over his skin, Seeker released a low growl. "Very well. Be here at sunrise for your assignment. If you are late, I will give the task to another."

Proffering a mocking bow, Zilla turned toward the cook's fire, his steps slow, weighed down with his self-inflicted malady.

The Bear Ridge KuRuk took a bowl of stew from the assistant cook manning the fire. There was always someone on duty to serve meals. Zilla's eyes looked out across the plain, a vacant stare ambivalent to the moon shadows cast upon hundreds of small ponds and lakes that riddled this land. He finished the contents of the bowl, never registering the taste of even one bite. Absent-mindedly pushing the empty vessel back toward the cook, who wasn't even nearby, the hollow wood clattered to the ground.

Zilla stood, and fate cast a shadow upon him.

Straight out from the cook's fire, backlit by the moon's silver shine, Zilla could clearly see Abaddon. Silky white hair hung to her waist; arms raised in supplication to the mother moon. The albino female stood atop a small hummock amidst the waterholes that stretched as far as one could see. A fever swept through his muscled body, and a voice in his head told him there was no harm in taking a closer look. Carefully, he twisted full circle, but saw no one about the camp. Zilla moved into the shadows, working his way toward the only knoll in a five-mile radius.

Zilla Bear Ridge belly crawled around the edge of a large pond, cattails giving him cover. His breath came in sharp huffs. It felt like his heart, beating like a drum, lodged in his throat when he skirted around the water's edge to catch a full view of the white goddess. Zilla knew he should pull back, get away from her. But a madness had taken over, and the voice in his head argued that he only needed to have her, taste her, just once. Surely, that would sate him of his bewitchment of her. After all, the voice suggested, it was her fault he was losing control. Yes, definitely her fault. She must have cast a spell on him. Must be a witch. Of course, that had to be the answer. She was a witch. The thought stupefied him. No wonder he seemed to have lost control of his senses. Why else would a woman be out here alone worshiping the moon, the voice reasoned, if she wasn't a witch?

He stood abruptly, intending to rush her, clamp his hand across her mouth to keep her quiet until he could explain, could convince her he had answered her siren call.

Zilla extended his right foot to run toward Abaddon when a thin garrote looped over his head and tightened across his neck. A threadlike ring of blood flowered beneath Nevele's tool, and he whispered in Zilla's ear, telling the Bear Ridge KuRuk, "She is pure. The future empress is not for the likes of you. Abaddon is betrothed to Thana NukPana, fool." Hissing out the last word, Nevele twisted the garrote tighter, and Zilla's face turned blue, blood running in thin rivulets down his chest. His knees gave out. Nevele let the body drop to the ground. He pulled his long knife from its sheath, stabbed the dead KuRuk in the sternum, twisting back and forth. Nevele grabbed the tip of the damaged bone, ripping flesh, cracking the chest bone to expose the heart. Having cut out the organ, Nevele carried the bloody mass to his master, leaving the dead body behind.

Abaddon, unaware of the violence done in her defense, continued her supplications, a mantra repeating in a whisper from her lips.

Thana knew when he saw the heart in Nevele's hands that it was Zilla's. The KuRuk had been unstable for days. Nevele watched as Akama ate his enemy's heart. When he had choked the last of the bloody muscle down, Akama ordered Zilla's body staked out after Abaddon returned to her tent. Returning to the corpse, Neville slit its belly open, spreading out its guts as an invitation for an easy meal to whatever animal discovered it first.

When the company moved out the next morning, a startled flock of crows flew up, circled the hillock, before landing back where they had been feasting.

"The black ones must be on a dead thing," Seeker commented to the man mounted next to him. "See if the Thana wants us to check it out." Following Seeker's request, the next man in line came forward.

"You asked for me, Scout Leader?"

"Yes, it appears Zilla Bear Ridge finally took my advice for a day off. I need you to cover the eastern section. Return to us at sunset with your report." The scout saluted and moved out. The 26/66 slowly traveled northwest, leaving the Bear Ridge KuRuk behind.

A DAY'S RIDE FROM THRALL Lake, the consociation turned due west to go around the immense lake. Thana and the 26/66 had one last tribe to meet before the Gugwe gathering. The BloodKnife tribe made their home along the northern river that fed into Thrall Lake. An hour later, Akama's host came face to face with a small contingent accompanying the BloodKnife KuRuk. The Thana aggressively inquired if his representatives had made the KuRuk aware that he would visit their village before the 13-tribe conference. Borta confirmed they had known, had been waiting for his arrival. He explained they were on their way to meet with a tribal scout to see if there was any word of the Thana's coming. Borta informed Akama that his village was only another hour's ride away. He assured the emperor that the BloodKnife tribe was looking forward to welcoming the great Thana NukPana and his entourage.

Weary of travel, the Thana took advantage of the chance meeting, informing the BloodKnife leader that they would make camp here for the night. He assured the KuRuk he still intended to visit the BloodKnife village. But the journey had taken them longer than expected. He had changed his plan to accommodate the coming winter solstice. His visit to the BloodKnife village would have to wait until after the tribal parley. He assured Borta that as Emperor; he wanted to know all the people of the Gugwe Nation.

Borta considered the Thana NukPana's statement. Nodded his head in acquiescence. Thinking to himself, it was more likely that the Thana wanted the BloodKnife people *to know him*. The emperor wanted to be recognized as leader over all 13 Gugwe tribes, and not necessarily in his desire to know the people.

With the decision made, the 26/66 set about organizing camp right there on the southwest portion of the lake. After the Thana and the KuRuk held private meetings, they agreed to proceed together to Thrall Lake for the great gathering.

Borta brought his advisors, Neehna, and Vigga, to meet with Akama, Neetriht, Taramat, along with the rest of the 13 while the camp was being set up. The other KuRuks with Thana's entourage organized the set-up. They arranged the boys into a human chain to bring buckets of water to the camp and cook's fires efficiently. Two lines formed back-to-back. They handed full buckets up the line; sending empty buckets back down to the water's edge to be refilled. The cooks got their fires started and began preparations for the evening meal. Hunters had brought down a moose in the marshes the day before. It had been gutted, skinned, and cut into sections that several hunters could carry. The meat would make a fine welcome for Thana's guests, the last of the tribal visits.

Borta listened with interest to Neetriht's leadership ideas. Neehna committed her words to memory, in case the KuRuk inquired about it later. They introduced Vigga to Akama as the BloodKnife War Chief. The Thana immediately called for his mapmaker. Taramat rolled out several artists' renditions of her charts. As the War Chief talked, she occasionally added additional detail to the depiction described by the well-traveled KuRuk.

The BloodKnife KuRuk informed the Thana about the Goblin Queen and Prince Rupert's recent visit. Vigga didn't bother to hide his disgust of the goblins. He shared his belief that their gang (his slight intended) headed to Vutova, Akama's home village. They had hopes of having a meeting with the Thana after the Great Gugwe Alliance was over.

Abaddon made her entrance. She had her role in the theater down pat whenever Akama or Neetriht introduced her to a new tribal KuRuk. Riding her albino elk, she rode into the meeting space. She had trained the animal to bugle with a squeeze of her legs. Next would follow a signal from her to drop its front knees to the ground, so she could slide off his back gracefully. The majestic animal rose after she dismounted, to tower over her. Their white hair and ice-blue eyes shone under the early morning sun.

The female albino strode to the Thana and kneeled before him. He pulled her to her feet, chiding her affectionately. "You kneel to no one, Abaddon." She turned to meet his guests.

Abaddon stayed for the debates and discussions and attended Neetriht's presentation with her leadership group. When that concluded, Abaddon shifted to sitting in on another discussion with the BloodKnife War Chief. She rarely uttered a word, but spent her concentration analyzing every word Vigga uttered to Akama. Abaddon quickly decided she did not like this man. The talk turned to slavery, and Vigga bragged about how his KuRuk had embraced the practice of taking and keeping slaves in the BloodKnife village. Vigga was eager to show Thana NukPana how the Tribe put slaves to use. He promised a future demonstration to show off his skills in leading a series of raids to gain more slaves in his role as War Chief.

Abaddon did not hide her disgust. Worse, she was distraught by Akama's enthusiasm for Vigga's ideas about slavery. She excused herself, saying she felt ill. Akama barely noticed, so intent was he on Vigga's description of a Fae and human village raid. The man boasted about the bloodbath they left in the wake of their long knives, teeth, and claws.

Taramat caught up with Abaddon when she noticed her leaving the meetings. "Aba, wait," the Map Maker took in her friend's face. It was immediately clear the girl had turned an even lighter shade of pale, looking like she was about to be ill. "Aba, what is wrong? Are you all right?"

"Oh, Tara," the small Gugwe cried, "the closer we get to the Tribal Congress, the more talk there is about taking slaves. The practice of slavery is sick. I hate it. My mother was a slave. It's wrong to take others and make them into slaves!" She stamped her foot to make her point.

Taramat put her arm around Abaddon, looked around to see if anyone had heard the outburst. She pulled the girl close, whispered in panic, "You must never, ever speak out loud against the Thana's plans. That is a sure way to meet your death. You must keep those thoughts to yourself. Do you understand?" Taramat demanded, shaking the albino's shoulders.

Tears slid down the pale, translucent cheeks, and Abaddon nodded. Taramat herded the female forward. "Come on, let's get your face cleaned up before dinner."

ABADDON BARELY SAID half a dozen words at the meal. Again, Thana didn't notice, so engrossed was he in discussions with the BloodKnife War Chief and KuRuk. The next morning, the camp was breaking up, and the entire group journeyed northeast to meet at the opposite end of the inland water. There, where the BloodKnife River flowed out of Thrall Lake, was the location they would meet up with all the other tribes.

Riders heralded the coming arrival of the Thana NukPana. The cooks left early so they could team up with others to prepare a grand banquet for the festivities.

Thana's 26/66, along with the other KuRuks and their companies who had traveled with him since Vattusk, garnered an audience. Their numbers created a great deal of noise and clatter. They gave orders to set up each of the KuRuk's camps. Guides led Thana NukPana's entourage to the best location to settle in. Abaddon was nowhere to be seen. She would make a formal theatrical entrance later that Taramat and Neetriht had orchestrated. The women had sequestered her in their tent and were getting the albino ready for the big event. The three females took a private meal together, the food delivered by Nevele, so they could stay out of the public eye until the event began. After eating, they prepared Abaddon.

Neetriht was brushing Abaddon's long hair. She sat behind her, talking excitedly with Taramat, who was carefully applying her paints to Abaddon's eyes.

"Did you see the marketplace created by the first tribes that had arrived? It was just as we had envisioned it would be, Taramat. They filled stalls with the goods each tribe brought to sell and trade. The Kuktuk tribe had brought salt and sun-dried fish. They provided demonstrations of how they shave the dried fish eggs over the flatbreads they bake."

"Women piled the Vulita stalls with the clothing they embellished using their special metal pieces and beads. Remember those? I'm amazed at how many pottery vessels, cooking pots, and dishes the Wildhorse Tribe had packed and brought to display. It's hard to believe they could make so many in just the few months since we left them."

"There wasn't time to look at their wares, but the Grey Fox Tribe displayed stacks of furs and hides they'd made into clothing, pouches, hats, mittens, rugs, and bedding. Beautiful work, exactly as they had shown us when we were there. The Alabasters had baskets full of dried mushrooms to trade. Even the Bear Ridge and Silver Valley women were displaying their silver and cobalt beads. The market is going to be a success. I'm sure of it."

"Will you take me to this market?" Abaddon asked, curious about her friend's enthusiasm.

"Of course. But not until tomorrow, sweetling. First, you must play your significant role tonight," Neetriht promised her.

Taramat rose and went to a large trunk, pushing up the heavy lid. She struggled with a large canvas-wrapped package and took it to the entrance of their tent. Nevele was waiting just outside, and she handed it off. He winked at her, and she let the flap fall and went to get another package from the chest. "What was that?" Neetriht asked.

"I had an idea for some special costuming. That was for Akama," Taramat told her. She placed the wrappings in front of Abaddon. "This is a gift for you. Open it."

Abaddon allowed the questions in her eyes to go unanswered and tore at the hemp twine, unfolding the canvas wrapping. Her mouth fell open at the contents. There was a small stack of white items in front of her. On top was a four-inch-tall cap made of polar bear fur. Beneath the headdress was a vest of white leather, sewn with patterns of the moon phases, made from thousands of cobalt and diamond beads. They had decorated the vest with a collar, a polar fur that circled her neck, making her sharp chin and ice-blue eyes stand out. The last items were fur cuffs that Neetriht fastened around her wrists.

Taramat helped her put on the vest. Neetriht produced a small, round, silver mirror she had acquired during a tribal visit months ago. She turned it so that Abaddon could see the image she presented. A tear splashed onto her cheek in the reflection.

"Oh, no, no, no," Taramat wiped the salted water away. "No tears. We don't have time to do your makeup again. Don't you like it?"

"No one has ever given me such finery." Abaddon whispered and kissed Taramat on the cheek. As if on cue, someone struck a huge gong. A deep chime rang out across the tented temporary village on Thrall Lake, signaling that the Gugwe Tribal Concord was about to begin.

Jutting out in front of the lake was a natural rock stage that butted up against a curved rock wall. The acoustics created a cave-like echo that pushed sound out to the crowd, enhancing the speaker's voice so all could hear. They had strung a caribou-hide curtain up on one side to hide those waiting in the stage's wings. Drums pounded in perfect rhythm as the audience took their seats. A long aisle led to the dais, splitting all the tribes in half. Placement of the tribes' representatives, carefully arranged, left some space between certain factions known to clash.

Nevele appeared on stage, took up a heavy club, and struck the gong once more to start the show. The drumming ceased. The votaries quieted, and Akama Vutova, the Great Thana NukPana of the 13 Gugwe tribes, swept out from behind the curtain in all his glory.

He had marveled when Nevele had presented him with Taramat's gift. Swaggering to center stage, the weight of a great floor-length polar bear fur cape swinging behind him. Taramat was a master of showmanship. The crowd roared as he strode back and forth before them, vacillating his arms in circles to encourage their bellowing.

Akama loved the stage. He held up his hands, palms forward, and stamped his foot. Silence fell across the audience like a shroud. The Thana went down on one knee, stretched his arms out toward the aisle, and hundreds of heads turned to see Abaddon seated like a goddess upon Frost, her albino elk. She wore a polar fur cap on her brow; white fur circled her neck and wrists. Her white leather vest shimmered with every move, enhancing her white skin and hair. Abaddon did not look like an abomination now. She looked like someone to be worshipped.

Akama rose and danced down several steps. Coming to Frost, he lifted Abaddon off her mount, led her up to the dais and proclaimed to the crowd, "I give you your empress, Abaddon of Alabaster."

The assemblage as one bent their knees, and a cacophony of voices cried out, "The Empress, the Empress!"

Thana NukPana led Abaddon to a carved chair that sat raised behind him, where she was to sit on display as he spoke to the people. His great white cape was a visual to be mentally associated with the white purity of the albino. That's what they were selling. Thana was as pure as his new empress. He used his thespian skills to weave a dream of how he envisioned the Gugwe nation would thrive. Embellished how the changes that were to be embraced for the betterment of the Gugwe race would change their lives. He signaled the drummers; they took up a beat. The stage swelled with his original 13/31. Abaddon, as Taramat had instructed her, danced alone, wielding her spear, down to the head of the 13/31, all eyes riveted to her as the drums rolled. Then, the entire 13/31 group began their pattern again across the stage. The Gugwe Empress stomped out a series of complicated movements. Akama copied her, followed by the 13/31, who mimicked the Emperor and Empress. This performance showed off the strength and spear training dance that they had all done twice a day for months now. It was an impressive choreograph. When the cast finished, the crowd went wild.

Thana gracefully guided Abaddon back to her perch. The emperor called for the Youngbloods to take the stage. Callen Vutova led the Youngbloods through an extraordinary routine. The performance included military maneuvers and dances that caught Vigga's attention.

Summoned to the stage, Taramat instructed the 13 KuRuks to repeat together an allegiance to Thana NukPana. The adrenaline was running high. Oath-swearing seemed the natural thing to do, caught up as they were in the moment's theater. No questions were asked, not that any would have been allowed.

The Thana proclaimed that over the next three days, each tribal leader would address the crowd. The free market would be open for trade, and they would feast together to celebrate their solidarity.

Finally, the theatrics concluded for the evening. The Thana closed the performance with an announcement. All the tribes would be required to send their warriors in the coming spring of the new year to meet at Bear Ridge at the equinox. From that location, Akama told them he would lead the Gugwe Nation's warriors south. The new year would begin with conquering the lesser populations of Fae, goblins, gargoyles, and humans. Nothing could stand in their way, he told them. The Gugwe were born to rule. It was the destiny of those lesser than them to serve the Gugwe nation as its slaves. The cheering went on and on. The KuRuks all raised their fists, shouted, "Thana, Thana," repeatedly. No one noticed as Abaddon turned to the side of her perch and vomited, sick that she would be a part of this plan.

Chapter 8: Don't Get Lost in the Vortex Again

Raven stood in the shadows, watching with pride as Carlisse entertained a group of goblins. All of them were in line to get a tattoo. She regaled them with stories of the trip she'd been on with Raven and the lads. Carlisse carried a small bound journal containing her tattoo designs, a gift from Raven. Now, her customers could actually see what the artwork would look like before she inked it. When the person chose one, she carefully closed the book, wrapped the thin cords around the leather cover, and replaced the small tome in her waist pouch. Without skipping a beat, she sat the current customer down. She started another story for the ready-made audience while mixing her inks and putting a flame to her needle to sterilize it.

"She's always been good with people," Val said from behind, startling Raven from his reverie.

"A natural," he agreed. "Carlisse's perfect for the role of emissary. She won the hearts of the clan in half a day. Of course, it doesn't hurt that she's a talented tattoo artist." He gave Val a smile and winked.

"That's what the cook, Zeeka, told me, too. Thanks for watching over her."

"My pleasure," Raven said.

"Yeah. I can see. Have you told her yet?"

"What's what?" Raven turned toward Carlisse's sister, his face serious.

"Oh, come on. It's written plain as day on your face and in your gaze when you look at her." Val punched him playfully in the arm.

"What are you...oh...ah..."

Val stood back from Raven, a look of wonder appearing across her features. "You didn't realize..."

"Guess you've given me something to think on," he quipped. "By the way, a very effective speech you gave as a stand-in for Faith. You did a great job of rousing the crowd," he complimented her. "You Pureheart girls sure have a knack for surprises." Blood rushed into Raven's cheeks, and he stammered,

"Sorry, I wasn't thinking. I...I guess you're not a Pureheart, based on your big reveal last night," he bowed. "You're our very own Goblin Princess."

Raven Renzo Rolando went down on one knee, took Val's hand and said, "I swear on my life to always protect you, Princess Valvina."

Mouth falling open, Val's own cheeks turned red. "What are you doing?" she hissed. "Get up!" Her eyes looked around wildly to see if anyone had seen, relieved that those in line for Carlisse's talent completely focused on Val's sister. "There will be none of that!" she scolded him. "I expect you to treat me as you always did, Raven Rolando, understand? Oh, and by the way, I'll always be a Pureheart, just like Carlisse, Aliah, and Delainey will always be my sisters. No one can ever take that from me." She realized she had been poking him in the chest with her forefinger, giving punctuation to each of her words. She flushed a deeper shade of crimson.

Val ran her hands over her tunic as if to straighten it, though it didn't need it. "Now," she said formally, "if you can get the Fae Ambassador away from her admirers, Robin, Faith, and I are holding a private meeting down at the bonfire on the beach. We'd like the two of you to be there. There's a mission we want to discuss with you."

"When?"

"One hour."

"We'll be there, um...Val." Raven quirked the corner of his mouth up at her. Her shoulder brushed his arm as she marched away.

ALTO HAD PULLED FAITH aside when he'd found her on the trail leading to the beach. "Faith, can you spare a minute?"

"Sure, Alto, what is it?"

"Let's move off the path so we're not blocking it and have some privacy." He led her to a small copse of pines. Faith took a seat on a large rock that jutted out of the sandy ground. "You asked me to observe everything at the moot." Alto began. "Speakers. Audience. The reactions. You wanted my feedback on how all the different factions reacted to your speech."

"I did, Alto, but I didn't give a speech."

He rolled his eyes at her. "Still, I watched from before the moot even started, observing all the way through to this morning, looking for a latent reaction. After a night of sleeping on everything that had happened last night, I woke up curious. All the speeches enthralled the attendees last night. It intrigued me to see if anything had changed in the light of day, yeah? A new day can have that effect sometimes. Well, I've come to a solid conclusion, and I think it's important to tell you about it." He licked his lips. Alto put his hands behind his back so she wouldn't notice them shaking.

Faith blinked a few times, recalling how Alto had felt so strongly against her when she'd told the group at Stone House Camp about the Dream Weaver's foretelling. Memory brought back how he had bristled at her philosophy—all for one and one for all. Not to mention how angry he had been about her suggestion that goblins and Fae were really all people of one race. Months had passed since his anger had retreated. It was hard to forget he'd actually attempted to kill her, even though she had forgiven him. She'd taken the opportunity when she saw a way to bridge the gap between the two of them. He'd become a travel companion. His job was to have discussions with her, even if he was at the opposite end of the spectrum on a topic. She benefitted because it allowed her to learn about other people's opinions. The ability to communicate opinions, thoughts, and feelings in a healthy debate had helped her grow as a person. Since that rough start, Alto held up his part of the bargain, giving her the benefit of his doubts and sharing his thoughts with her from time to time, even if he didn't see eye to eye with her. Now, he found himself in front of her again, offering her a dose of his honesty. She'd told him once that she could learn from their conflicting positions, as long as they were honest with one another.

"I'm listening," she breathed.

Alto heaved a heavy sigh, as though he were in pain. "First off, I've learned a lot since Stone House Camp and the huge mistake I made there. I've told you before, but I am sorry. I appreciate the second chance you gave me." She protested, but Alto held up his hand. "Please let me finish." Faith nodded.

"I still don't have my arms wrapped around your whole prophecy, but I admit I was wrong about the gobs and Fae being one race. Hard not to believe when I'm afflicted with evidence attached to myself." He turned and pushed out his own leather wings to show her. Faith bit her knuckle to keep from interrupting him.

"Anyway, everything I witnessed yesterday and this morning sold me on the 'all for one and one for all' thing. There was a powerful movement among the people last night. It was physical and visible if you were watching for it. And the important part is that it was not just the Fae and goblins who felt moved. It was *all the people* in the audience. I thought you should know that's all." Alto raised his eyebrows to see if she understood.

"Thanks for sharing, Alto. But I don't see how this relates to me, except for your change of heart on some issues. I'm glad about that. Still, I didn't give my 'all for one and one for all' speech. Val did. See, what happened was, I was late because I got trapped." She cut away from that explanation. "Oh, it doesn't really matter the reason I didn't get back in time to give my speech. Val made the big announcement, revealing the truth. Not me. So, the people's reaction has nothing to do with me." She wrinkled her forehead quizzically. "Right?"

His body tensed. Clearly, she didn't understand what he was trying to tell her. He forced the words out, wanting to get this over with. "That's exactly my point," he said passionately. "*You* didn't enlighten the people about the truth of the past. Val did. Well, and Robin too. *You* didn't give your 'all for one and one for all' speech. Val did. *She* roused the people. *She* inspired them to work together. Have you seen the crowd this morning? They're lining up at the different tables manned by your cousins, who are taking names and putting them on lists. People are committing themselves to working together on things like making weapons, for example. Robin put out a big display of Rolland's best wares. The people are volunteering for weapons training, supplying and making materials we'll need for war. There will be those who will offer support for warriors on a campaign as cooks and such. There's a lot of workers needed to keep an army supplied, fed and cared for. I admit I didn't think it could be done, but it worked."

Sorrow filled his eyes. He cocked his head as if in apology. "It worked, but I think it's important that you recognize it was Val who made it work, who made them believe. I don't know?" He cringed, running his fingers through his hair. "It's like the Dream Weaver's prophecy you got mixed up with Val. Almost as if the weave she wove wasn't for Faith Lisbet Stargazer. It seems like you somehow got Valvina Ariana Goodfellow's weave. Does that make any sense?"

Faith's lips were slightly parted. She stared right through Alto, letting his revelation soak in.

Alto toed the sandy ground with his boot. "Anyway, that's my honest feedback. One other thing. I'd like to close this chapter between us. I support this effort, but I'm planning to go with the cohort that's rumored to be discussed at that meeting down on the beach shortly. Word is that it'll be your cousins who will be in command of the reconnaissance on the Gugwe. Time for my role to change. I just wanted you to know that I hope our paths cross again sometime." Alto nodded to her, hurrying to the path, heading to the beach to join in the planning.

Faith looked down at her hands as if they belonged to someone else. *Well, she thought, I just got served a great, gigantic piece of humble pie. Alto was true to his word. He gave me his complete honesty, even though it clearly pained him to do so. I gave my word that I would try to learn from his frankness. Bloody hell, I even claimed it was something I needed. So, looks like somebody has some serious soul-searching to do. Before I jump off that cliff, guess I better get myself down to the meeting. Something niggled at her memory, but she couldn't put her finger on it.* She joined some stragglers heading in the same direction, eager to hear Robin's plan.

THE GROUP DECIDED BADGER and Tula would accompany Travis and Shaun north to see what intel they could gather. The plan was that they would return within three months to report. In explaining how they could speed their trip, Badger drew a rough diagram in the dirt of a device he'd made to travel in winter weather. If they didn't use his invention, he told them they would make little progress in the heavy snow and ice-covered lakes this time of year.

"Huh," Travis commented, scratching his chin. "How's your contraption work?"

Badger explained he got the idea one summer as he and Tula had hidden from a Gugwe gang. The two of them watched the Gugwe use sails on their boats to cross a lake, rather than traverse around the shoreline on foot. When winter rolled around the following year and the lakes and rivers froze over, he added a rack to the bottom of his small boat, affixing two wide skis to it. Tula, he told them proudly, had sewn the sail for their contraption. This allowed them to 'sail' across frozen lakes in the winter. The Gugwe hadn't seen his new contrivance, so the Alliance would still have the advantage in using it to make a quick getaway.

Travis bet Shaun he could beat him across the first lake they tried the ice boat on. Badger shook his head at the two brothers. They gambled on the odds about everything.

Brittany showed up a few minutes later, her gear all stowed in a pack strapped to her back, along with a pair of snowshoes that she'd traded a pair of boots for.

Her oldest brother stepped up to her. "Where do you think you're going, Brit?"

"I'm going with you. Faith said that whatever I wanted to do was fine with her."

"Yeah? Well, it's not Faith's permission you need. You're not coming. We're going to Gugwe country. Too dangerous."

Her face lit up with fury. "You. Don't. Tell. Me. What. I. Can. Or. Can't. Do." She spat the words at him with venom.

Travis threw his hands in the air. Shaun stepped between them. "He's not trying to tell you what to do, Brit. He's telling you he loves you and doesn't want you in danger."

Brittany's eyes opened wide. "Oh. That's so sweet." She shined her fingernails on her shirt. "Why didn't he just say so?" She moved toward Tula and offered her hand to the young goblin. "Nice to meet you, Tula. I just know you and I are going to be the best of friends."

Brittany looked down at Badger's sketch. "That looks interesting. Bring me up to speed."

FAITH WATCHED QUIETLY as Robin and Val explained the plan they'd put together for Faith's uncles and her father. Training sessions would begin in two days. Her cousins were manning the sign-up tables for volunteers. They suggested a list of people to head up and organize methods of communication, supply chains, and the appointment of a weapons master. Carlisse's name came up as a recommendation for Map Maker, her artistic talents put to another use. Word went around that Robin hoped Carlisse and Raven would lead a group north. Faith raised her hand and said she would love to be a mapmaker. Robin and Val gave her a thumbs-up. It bothered her a bit that no one had thought about putting her artistic talents to use, and she had to suggest it.

They nominated Cervil and Weasel to act as statisticians. In developing actuarial information, the two would work with Lehto and Bento. Those two would head up supply acquisitions and disbursements if they accepted the positions.

The discussion was short and sweet about Carlisse continuing her work in her role as emissary. She would go north with Raven and his lads. They would help coordinate volunteers and training. Attendees returning home would share the news about the moot with their villages and clans. Word would quickly spread north and south, east, and west about the skills the army needed.

The plans fell into place. They made decisions. The group disbursed. Val came to Faith, excitement in her eyes. "This is really going well, don't you think?"

"I do," Faith agreed. "You've gotten a lot accomplished, or at least moved forward so quickly it feels like we're caught up in a whirlwind. I don't think we could have hoped for better." Faith smiled at her sister-friend. Val beamed at the praise. "I'll catch up with you at dinner," Faith told her. "I'm going to pay a visit to the Gargoyle Kings, bring them up to date. Maybe they can offer some direction in mapmaking. Get it? Direction? Mapmaking?"

Val laughed at Faith's lame joke and turned to make her way back to Robin. She wanted to solidify some details and share another idea that had just occurred to her. "Give my love to Delainey, will you? Don't get lost in the vortex again." Val called out to her over her shoulder.

The Fae Princess looked around at all the activity. "I wonder which vortex she's referring to?" Faith said under her breath as she watched Val move away.

Chapter 9: My Mission Is Clear

The long-lost king of the goblins spent his first two days of freedom sleeping. It had been a very long time since he had felt safe enough to allow himself such a rest. Besides, there was an intense search for him above ground, ongoing and active since his jailers discovered his escape. Fear of Borta motivated the guards to find their missing charge. Lancer was Borta's favorite slave. He delighted in torturing the old goblin above all others.

After two days, the guards abandoned the search. They resigned themselves to breaking the news to Borta when he returned from the Gugwe gathering. An exhaustive search brought them to the conclusion that Lancer Goodfellow had made a clean getaway. They dreaded having to deliver such a message to the BloodKnife KuRuk. The prison guards argued constantly about who should have to shoulder the responsibility. There was a lot of posturing and a few fistfights over the dilemma.

When Lancer awakened on the third day, he woke with a voracious appetite. Rummaging through the pack Rupert had left for him, he discovered food. Four packages of dried jerky, a dozen biscuits wrapped in rhubarb leaves, a small crock of honey that was sealed with wax, and a wheel of cheese the size of his palm. He looked at his stock and decided it was best to discipline himself. He started by eating only one pack of the jerked meat. Then, conserving food for the days to come, he allowed himself two biscuits. They had starved him for so long that rationing food came naturally. Lancer carefully re-wrapped the rest of the biscuits to keep them from turning rock hard. He washed it all down with water from a skin he retrieved from under the coat Rupert had provided.

Hunger tamped down to a dull ache for now; he became aware of his own stench. Lancer didn't dare use the water in the skin for washing; he'd need it to stay hydrated. Besides, it would take more water than that skin could hold to clean away the filth layered on his body. Deciding it would be safer, he would wait until dark, then make his way to the river to have a proper bath. He knew the stream wasn't far from the prison cave, having passed it every day since his imprisonment there. It had been years since he had given any thought to being able to wash himself in that stream. Lancer felt confident that no slaves or guards would be near the flowing water at night. He knew the penal routine by heart.

Lying down to rest again, he was careful to keep his ruined back from touching the sandy floor. Some of his whiplashes had broken open, seeping blood. A few of the wounds that were infected were oozing pus. Much as he wanted to wrap up in the coat to get warm, he didn't dare until he was clean. Why ruin that nice coat by transferring his current stench to the pelts?

Sleep claimed him again for several hours. Waking, Lancer lay there with his eyes open, studying the intricate tree roots above, replaying the conversation with his damaged son. Finally, he stood and carefully stretched. Reaching up, he took a handful of roots, pulling himself up. Then pushed his face out past the tree's bark, checking the coast was clear before he pressed his body out of the tree sanctuary. Carefully, he marked the location so he could easily find the tree again that held his meager resources. The king moved through the woods faster than the human eye could register.

Luckily, it was a chilly night, but not freezing. When he reached the riverbank, he stripped off the rags he wore, scooped out a hole in the sand and buried the smelly, tattered duds, piling the sand back over them. He rolled a rock to cover the disturbed ground. Using his fingers, he spread the pine needles and leaves around to match the rest of the forest floor, leaving no sign of where he had buried the filthy scraps.

He entered the water gingerly, with small steps, mindful of avoiding a splash that might draw attention. His hands gripped handfuls of long grass, ripping them from the ground by the roots. Lancer submerged himself, quelling any noise from the reaction to the cold bath. The flowing water stung his back like crazy, but he forced himself to rub the whiplashes he could reach. The grass was effective in working off the scabs and infected flesh. After tending his injuries, he pulled fresh greens and scrubbed the rest of his body, working his way up to his hair. He'd need soap to get rid of all the dirt, but this would go a long way to getting rid of the smell and small vermin that plagued every slave in the Gugwe prison.

His skin dried as he moved with swishing speed back to the comfort of his root cellar. The skeletal goblin took the small clothes Rupert had provided and deemed he could do without them. Pouring just enough of the liquor out of the flask his son had forgotten to reclaim, Lancer soaked the material with the spirits. He clenched his teeth down on a thick stick, a scream trying to rip from his throat, as he laid the saturated cloth across his bloody cuts to disinfect them. The burning was torture, but he absorbed the pain, using it to fuel his hate toward the female that had betrayed him. When the worst of the stinging had passed, he dipped two fingers in the jar of honey and spread the sticky substance on his clean bandages, then wrapped his wounds. When his medicinal efforts were exhausted, he forced himself through the motions of putting on the fresh clothes from the pack. Finally, he wrapped himself in the luxury of Rupert's wolf-skin coat.

Warmer now, he ate a miserly portion of jerky, a small wedge of cheese, then spoiled himself with one biscuit, doused with a generous drizzle of the precious honey. Closing his eyes, he focused only on the explosion of flavor and sweetness that coated his mouth. When the last of the saporous treat left him, he finished his feast with a careful swig from the flask. He allowed the liquor to bite his tongue and cheeks before swallowing. After corking it, he slipped the flask back into the inner pocket of the coat. Examining the other pockets, he found one that contained two tightly coiled garrotes, and left the weapons hidden there. Lancer lay down to consider his son, Ruppert, and what kind of male he might have become under the thumb of Montestrell's wicked seed.

Unused to having the time and quiet to reflect on anything but the sounds and smells of suffering in the prison. The sense of the day to day, hour to hour was taken up with the task of keeping himself alive while incarcerated. All other considerations had been missing for years. Thoughts jumped chaotically from topic to topic. Time traveled in memory from the past to imagining the potential future. He fervently hoped that Robin had fared better than Rupert under Morveena's hand. The Goblin King wondered if his youngest son had made any progress in finding his sister through all these years. He regretted not having provided some information to Robin about the girl, but he had none to share. Lennox Stargazer had refused to provide him with Valvina's foster location.

Lancer's imagination ran wild with all the ways Morveena could have destroyed the Goblin court. It was likely the bitch had led their clans astray for her own selfish motives.

Thinking of Morveena brought a very recent memory to the forefront. Hard to believe it was only four short days ago, he recalled hearing it when chained in the cell. He visualized being shackled, hearing the voices in the adjacent chamber. Lancer relived the very moment he had recognized Morveena's voice. He struggled to reconstruct the eavesdropped exchange.

The goblin fugitive bolted upright when he clearly recalled Morveena's words to the adjoining cell's inmate. *"I hope you're not being mistreated, Aleta. I will remind your keepers that you are a queen and should be treated as such. I'm sure the opportunity for me to do so will come around in the next few years."* Her evil laugh echoed in Lancer's mind.

Pacing space in the root cellar only allowed for three steps back and forth in each direction. The Goblin King's hands clasped, one washing against the other in agitation. He came to a standstill, reached without thought for the flask, and took a sip of courage. His voice creaking out to himself, *"That zany witch had taken Aleta Dawn Stargazer, Queen of the Sharas Fae, and handed her over to be kept prisoner by the Gugwe. The same way she had gotten rid of me. Lennox must be beside himself. How many years had she been captive? Certainly not as long as him, could she?"* He took another sip, licked his lips, and sat down. The thought struck him, and declared it out loud, *"Why, that must be the very reason the moon finally turned my luck for Rupert to discover me here and set me free. Yes. I'm sure that's why I've been emancipated again after all these years."* He drained the flask, turning it upside down over his mouth to be sure he got every drop. He sighed, recapped the empty container, and stowed it away.

"My mission is clear; my purpose; my goal. I'm going to plan a prison break and rescue Aleta Dawn. I owe her that much at least as an old friend."

Lancer Ian Goodfellow curled up on the woven roots, warm in his new coat. He thought of exactly how and just what he would need to make this rescue happen successfully. Tapping the tips of his fingers together, he dared to consider. First, he had to confirm that the Fae Queen was indeed imprisoned. Then, once he had safely liberated Aleta, he ruminated on just how the two of them could work together to take down Morveena Morgan Montestrell. Lancer acknowledged he had a mission worth living for.

Chapter 10: Time to Share Some Secrets

Garrett sat on the beach, deep in thought, his back against the boulder, as he studied the horizon. He had chosen the spot because there was little chance of anyone finding him there. Privacy was critical in practicing the mental blocking Mari had taught him. Giving himself a pat on the back, he acknowledged he was becoming quite good at it. Practicing was definitely a key to success.

Before he'd left for the moot, while staying with Faith's Aunt Mari, he'd had his first scare when the Aurora Borealis was in full swing. It was as though that huge Gugwe was right there, looming in his face, sour breath, and asked, "Who's there?" Garrett had told no one but Aliah of the incident, but at sunrise, Mari had peered into the window of the cottage he was staying in and found him wide awake. She smiled, waved her hand and arm, asking him to come out to her. Faith's aunt pressed her lips closed and put a finger to them, communicating her desire that he leave quietly and use care not to wake his roommates.

Garrett placed his feet strategically, moving through the jumble of bodies scattered across the floor, still sleeping. Out of habit, Garrett grabbed his hat, vest, bow, and quiver off the pegs by the door. Mari waited at the gate that opened onto the beach. Whitecaps rolled across the lake, running up over the sand when they hit the shoreline, then receding back. He pulled the brim of his hat down to block the early morning sun hatching above the water level, lighting up the sky with pink, orange, and yellow to herald a new day.

Mari said nothing until they'd trudged through the sand a good five hundred feet from the cottage. "This way, Garrett," she said cheerfully, leading him down a path between tall cedar trees, away from the crashing waves on the shore. Moisture muffled sound inside the cedar fen, as though a blanket covered the lowland. The air was a cool touch on his face.

"So, Mistress Mari," Garrett ventured, but she cut him off.

"If you wouldn't mind, Garrett, hold your questions for a moment or two more. We're almost at our destination, and I see no point in having to repeat words." She didn't wait to hear if he minded or not, but kept on at a sure-footed, steady pace. That he'd been instructed not to ask questions just brought several more to his mind as he trudged behind her.

The two of them reached the base of a steep hillock. Mari took her hat off, using it to fan herself as she trudged up the slope. Patience reaching an end, Garrett decided he would ask his questions at the top of the hill. Breath coming deeper and faster as he scrambled up the last few feet, determined to find out what this was all about. Wasn't Aliah always telling him he shouldn't be shy, that it was important to assert himself and set his words free? He figured now was one of those times. When his last two steps brought him level at the top, the statements, and questions he'd planned to say flew right out of his head.

The view below took his breath away. The tree canopy spread as far as he could see. Spring had pushed new buds open, unfurling bright green leaves all across the valley that stretched before him. The sky was a vibrant blue. He wondered what this place would look like in the fall when all the leaves turned into a painter's palette of color.

Garrett honed in on a movement that caught his eye at the bottom of the ridge where he and Mari stood. There, he could see a large wooden table with benches attached along the sides. A woven basket sat on top of it. He squinted his eyes, not surprised to see Reatha and Evy waiting for them.

"Good morning, ladies." Garrett called out in greeting.

They returned pleasant greetings. "You're just in time for breakfast, young Gladheart. Here's a spot for you." Reatha patted the place next to her. "We've a lovely spread to share. Morning cake, carrot raisin muffins, hard-boiled eggs, fresh biscuits, and honeycomb." Reatha handed him a plate, inviting him to dig in. The three women began serving themselves, not bothering to wait for him.

Just as he filled his mouth with half a muffin, Evy looked him square in the eye, said, "We'd like to hear all about your, um, vision of the Gugwe Emperor. The one that came to you during the northern lights." She held his gaze. "If you'd be so kind as to share it with us, Master Garrett?"

He'd stopped chewing, mouth still full, when she'd made her request. Now, he began chewing with purpose, a question burning to get out.

Swallowing hard, Mari handed him a cup of water. He tried but failed to keep the emotion off his face. "Did Aliah..."

"Now, see here. We needed no one to tell us about your vision." Evy assured him. "There was no betrayal of your confidante. It was the three of us who threw a shield over the contact you had with the Gugwe. Luckily, we did so *before* Thana NukPana got a good look at you and your surroundings. What you experienced wasn't really what we would call a vision, per se. No, what you had was a *connection*. Under those circumstances, both parties can see through the other's eyes, as though they are right there with one another. That type of joining with a powerful being, particularly a being that knows how to use such a connection, provides an opportunity to take control of the party on the other end of the link. It's imperative that you guard against accidental connections and exert control at all times. We doubt that Thana NukPana would hesitate to make you his creature. That would not be good for you or us," Evy and Reatha both nodded in agreement, sewing needles busy again in their hands.

"Thana NukPana? That's who the Gugwe is I'm seeing, uh, connecting with? The leader of the Gugwe nation?" He swallowed hard. "Bloody hell."

"Emperor of the Gugwe nation." Evy clarified.

"How is that even possible? What do you mean you threw a shield over the contact?" Garrett asked.

Reatha stilled her hands, put her sewing on her lap, and sat forward. In a grim voice she told him, "We," she drew her finger in a circle to include Mari and Evy, "have some ability as seers, as well as a bit of magic among us. There hasn't been a Foxfire in Sharas for years and years. When Evy first dreamed of you, we were shocked to find the Foxfire was our own Garrett Emmon Gladheart. We figured there had to be a link between you and Faith. That's your destiny as a Foxfire; it is important that you keep near Faith, to protect her from the three chances for death cast in her future. Why, I believe you've already saved her once, correct?"

"I..." Garrett let his mind drift back to Alto's arrow. "It was just luck that I saw the shooter and blocked her from his shot," he argued.

"Humph," the old nurse grumbled. "Just luck that at that very moment, you made your first shift to your Foxfire form? Not likely."

"Alright. Let's say that what you suggest is true. How did I get adopted by the Gladhearts right around the time Faith came to live in Sir Robert's fortress? Where did the ability to shift into a Foxfire come from? What powers does a creature like me have? Are you suggesting that Faith will need to be saved two more times from the hands of death?" His voice was winding up with irritation.

Mari handed him a biscuit she'd broken open, loaded with a generous clot of honeycomb. He popped it into his mouth without thinking.

"If I might? I'd just like to clarify some things while you are busy enjoying a bit of honey, dear. We aren't experts on Foxfire abilities, but we know you can shift and fly. In addition, you enjoy enhanced hearing, sight, and smelling abilities, as any fox would. We know Vulpes vulpes for their skills in stealth and their ability to adapt to many types of habitats. Aleta once told us about Foxfire's ability to form a connection with others, as I've described to you. A mental connection, but...more. Like the one you seem to have with the greatest enemy of Sharas." She patted his hand in sympathy. "We can assist you in learning to maintain control over that connection—which is an *advantage* to be appreciated." She let the word hang, giving him time to consider it. "We definitely want to help you learn self-control. It could be a disaster if whoever is at the other end of a connection dominates you and has the power to manipulate your actions. The three of us thought perhaps you would want us to instruct you? Teach you unique skills you can use to restrict the link so it benefits you and not the party on the other end of the connection? It may be beneficial for you to manipulate the bond to spy on your enemy while shielding your connection from him. How can you take advantage of the union?" She winked. "The trick is not to allow your opponent to gain any dominance over you." She raised her eyebrows and tipped her head forward.

"That makes sense," he agreed. "I wouldn't want to give him the opportunity to get information about us. Definitely wouldn't want it to take place because I was ignorant of how I could protect myself against such a thing happening or for being too stubborn to learn."

"Good," Mari patted his shoulder. "Eat the rest of your breakfast, and we'll begin your training right away."

THE MEMORY FADED IN the bright glare of the sunset. Garrett had also been drilling himself on shifting. Forcing his body to merge back and forth, back and forth from his human form to his Foxfire persona, until he could make the change at will. It was way easier when the Aurora was dancing, but as he practiced, he found it possible to make the shift anytime. In addition, he had trained his power not to shift as the northern lights danced. Each day, Garrett exercised his ability to open and close a channel to his thoughts, using a visualization of an iron gate to assist the action. He trained himself to settle without movement or sound in Fox form, becoming proficient at listening for long periods. When the chance came, he could gather intel without revealing his presence to the Gugwe Emperor. If discovered, he wouldn't appear to be anything other than a common fox.

Dusk had given way to darkness. Garrett felt his skin pebble, deciding he should probably head back to camp and get a hot meal. He'd been at his drills for a couple of hours. It was time to find out what Faith's next steps would be. Green ripples skittered across the sky, causing an overwhelming urge to shift. The Foxfire didn't fight his gut instinct. The moment his transformation was complete, he found himself vis-à-vis mentally with the Thana.

Magnified, the freakish face appeared as though he were nose-to-nose with the monster. A gruff voice growled, "There is someone here; I can feel it." A snarl rumbled through his body that Garrett could feel down to his bones.

Garrett threw a shield in place. Crab-crawling backwards to move away from the frightening maw, layered in razor-sharp teeth and expelling foul breath. Gladheart took deep, even breaths to calm his heart, bringing his practice into play. Becoming as small and quiet as a mouse mentally, while hanging on to the bond. Slowly, he allowed his mind to creep forward until he could see through the eyes of his enemy. The gaze took in the land surrounding Thrall Lake. Through the eyes of his enemy, his vision lingered on an albino female. She wore a beaded leather vest. It shimmered when light caught the crystals that embellished it, reflecting, sending flashes of silver out, almost like magic. Garrett's breath hitched when he looked through the orbs, revealing over a thousand Gugwe monsters. Someone was speaking, suggesting they all travel back to their villages. Saying it was time to ready their warriors to meet in Bear Ridge for the raids to begin at the spring equinox. The speaker praised Thana NukPana's plan to capture slaves, so that goblins, Fae, humans, and others would improve the lives of the Gugwe nation. Garrett blanched when hundreds took up a chant and pounded their fists in the air in approval.

Having heard enough, he hurried to slam the link shut. Just before his mental iron gate blocked out everything, Thana NukPana glimpsed a red fox. In a flash, the vision was gone. The Foxfire shifted. Garrett stood, brushed the sand off, and immediately set out to find Faith and Val.

Garrett Emmon Gladheart had decided it was time to share some secrets.

Chapter 11: I Need to Think

Waiting six days for the new moon, he spent his time resting, building up his strength. On the seventh, Lancer Goodfellow's dark skin blended into the opaque night as he used the shadows to hide his predatory speed.

He left his hiding spot when he was sure the guards had settled in for the night. The sentries had a bad habit of drinking a predictable amount of homemade shine. They broke the nightly tedium of their jobs with drinking interspersed with dice and gambling. Lancer sped across the open ground from the forest treeline to breach the entrance of the BloodKnife's prison.

Holding his breath, Lancer slipped past the crowded first cell. *Had he stunk like that just a few days ago?* Gooseflesh raced across his skin as he passed his own cell, the memory fresh of his recent whipping. Rounding the corner, he could see a dim light at the end of a deep corridor. Guards' voices and laughter carried back up to him in an echo that reached his ears. Sounds coming from their quarters satisfied Lancer that the watch wouldn't be making rounds soon. He moved swiftly through the opening toward the end of the lengthy cavern. His breath hitched when he stepped into the subterranean grotto. Stopping short of the water that filled the pool in the center of the room, he surveyed the cavern. They had suspended Aleta above, hanging spread-eagle by her outstretched limbs. In the heavy gloom, Lancer couldn't see any dry ground between where he stood and the controls for the pulley system that held the captive. Even in the dark, he could see her muscles shaking with exhaustion.

"Who's there?" she called out. "If you're checking to see whether I've changed my mind, you're wasting your time. I've told you, I'll die before I transfer my powers to you. Go away. You're interrupting my quiet time." She tried to hold back a well of manic laughter, but failed. Lancer recoiled, hating to see the Queen of the Sharas Fae brought low to near madness. She was once the best friend of his wife, Alora. Once. Once she had been the wife of his own best friend, Lennox Stargazer. He pushed down his feelings of betrayal he harbored against his old friend. What Lennox had done had nothing to do with his decision to save Aleta.

His voice, rough from disuse, called to her softly, "Aleta? Aleta Dawn Stargazer? Take heart. I'm here to help you." Lancer licked his dry lips, his nerves on high alert, barely keeping his own fears in check.

"Who are you?"

"Lancer Ian Goodfellow at your service, Queen Aleta." He bowed as far as his ruined back would allow without ripping open his wounds, though she couldn't see the gesture. "At your service," he repeated, the words bittersweet in his mouth.

"Lancer?" He heard his name tremble in her mouth. "How are you here? How did you find me? Do you have any news about Lennox? Are you really there? Am I dreaming? Is this some kind of trick?" Her last question was a whisper, but his goblin-enhanced hearing caught the words.

"I am no dream, no trick, I can assure you." He chuckled to himself. "I was a prisoner here myself for more years than I can count."

"Ah," she said knowingly. "The shamans are using you to bait me, yes?"

"What?" he croaked, horrified that she would jump to that conclusion. "No, no, my old friend. We must keep our voices down. No one must find me here. I recently escaped, and I've no wish to be imprisoned again. I promise to tell you the whole story later. Just now, we are pressed for time. Days ago, I was in the adjacent cell when Morveena Morgan Montestrell," he spat out her name as though it was poison, "came to taunt you. I recognized her voice, her evil laugh. I heard her say your name. After my escape, I had to stay hidden while they searched for their missing prisoner. Then it seemed best to wait until the new moon came out, making shadows for cover. I promise I will come up with a plan and bring you out of this hole. It is critical that I lay my plans carefully and don't act rashly. Rushing the task would risk failure for us. I felt it was important to come tonight. To let you know, I plan to rescue you soon," he paused. "I...I came to give you hope."

"Hope?" Lancer heard her draw a deep breath and slowly release the air through her nose. "Very well. I will hold the hope you bring this night cradled against my heart. Don't take too long in your planning. There is a unique window of time over the next three days. You know how you hear things in here? Guards talk? The Gugwe are having a tribal conclave. The first time a Thana NukPana has brought all 13 tribes together. After the assembly breaks up, they will probably return to their villages, and Borta BloodKnife will come back here."

"I know of the Gugwe rally." Lancer shivered at her mention of Borta's name, fighting to bring his terror under control, having been abused by the monster for so many years. "Time waits for no one. So, it makes sense to use this opportunity to help you get free in the next few days. First, there are supplies to gather; likely I will need to steal them. Soon, Aleta, I will be back for you soon. I promise."

"You must consider the fact that I likely cannot walk or fly. They've had me trussed up here too long. If that makes your task impossible, I understand if you must forgo my rescue. You should save yourself while you have the chance."

"Nothing is ever impossible. Keep yourself well until I next return for you. Do nothing that would cause them to move you. I need to think. When I come again, you will leave with me, Aleta Dawn."

Lancer raced to the entrance, letting the shadows swallow his form. He crept toward the lights he could see in the valley below, where the BloodKnife village lay nestled between two mountain ranges. That is where he would find the supplies he needed. He must become a ghost. Time was short, but the night was young.

KETO AND LUTE WERE under Rupert's command. The two lads had argued after they had snuck away from the hiding place they'd used. Their assigned mission had been to listen to the Gugwe Emperor as he put on his show, disclosing his plans to the leaders of the 13 tribes. Lute had wanted to return to Sharas immediately, to search out Robin Goodfellow and deliver this news. Robin would need to know in advance that the Gugwe planned to take Shara's citizens without racial preference, as slaves. Keto insisted they couldn't leave yet, that it was important to keep up the appearance of being loyal to Morveena, at least for now. He was of the mind that they should report back, as she expected them to. After that, they could slip away when the chance came. Keto thought it possible some of the other lads were still devoted to Robin and might want to go with them. If the two of them didn't return at all, there was no question in his mind what would happen. The Queen would send a search party for them, with orders to bring her their heads. That or hand them over to Rupert for punishment. It would be better if they found circumstances more in their favor to make their getaway.

In the end, Lute had to agree it made sense to avoid having Morveena after them while trying to get out of the Gugwe's territory, whole and alive. He dreamed daily of the time that would come when they could reunite with Robin as their leader.

Lute and Keto found the goblin camp south of Vutova. Apparently, the Queen wasn't confident enough of her status with the Gugwe to waltz into the Thana NukPana's home village, as if she were his honored guest. The troop had set up on the riverbank that ran along a deep ravine, not openly visible from the trail on the plain. Rupert's outlier guards spotted the two returning spies and guided them to the Queen's tent.

Morveena was in an ugly mood, stewing about the turn of events that were beyond her control. The two lads cringed as her hand shot forward like a snake and clamped onto Keto's throat. "Where have you two lackeys been? I've been waiting hours for you to return," she screamed.

Rupert stood behind the Queen, hands clasped behind him. He barked, "Report!"

Keto and Lute jumped. Morveena's sharp nails ripped lines that bloomed with blood across Keto's throat as he pulled away. She turned a grim face to Rupert and informed him, "I'll handle this if you don't mind."

Rupert bristled with anger. He loathed her pulling rank on him in front of his soldiers. Wisely, he held his tongue, as he was as likely as not to lose it if he challenged her when she was in this mood.

The Goblin Queen turned her shining eyes back to Keto and Lute. She tapped a blood-red fingernail on the arm of her chair and, in a near whisper, said, "Report." Standing behind her, Rupert rolled his eyes.

Lute's thoughts tumbled into chaos. He made a quick decision to ignore her first question. He reckoned their circumstances would worsen if he tried to explain. The two of them had to wait hours before they could safely sneak away from the Thana's assembly. There were many discussions among the Gugwe before the crowd moved away to partake in the First Night Feast.

Instead, Lute launched into the list of things he and Keto had decided to report on while making their way back to the troop. Small clusters of lads gathered in the background to hear what the spies had discovered.

"My Queen," Lute began as he bowed before the brazen redhead. "We confirmed the following in our espionage efforts:"

1. "Thana NukPana has truly achieved rule over all 13 of the Gugwe tribes."
2. "He has organized a leadership team to support his rule."
3. "His fist is iron. They slaughter and replace anyone who opposes him or his new vision. He made an example of several Gugwe during his theatrics on stage."
4. "To be fair, it appears the new traditions he is imposing on his people will actually benefit the whole of the Gugwe nation."
5. "The Gugwe have a method of mind control they can use against victims. He plans to teach the Gugwe population how to use it."
6. "Thana NukPana has laid out a plan with the 13 KuRuks to conquer Sharas and take slaves."
7. "Not only does Thana NukPana plan to take humans and Fae as slaves," Lute swallowed hard. "He plans to take goblins into servitude as well. Keto heard the emperor tell one of the KuRuks that you were stupid. It amused them that you were actually waiting for him in Vutova as though you planned to volunteer to be his first queen in bondage."

Morveena's rage boiled over. She struck Lute open-handed so hard across his cheek that it knocked him from his feet, her lethal nails raking bloody lines across his face. She turned to Keto. "Do you have anything to add?"

Keto violently shook his head, taking a step back from her.

"Get. Out. Of. My. Sight." Turning full circle, she was shrieking at the lads who'd gathered round to hear the intelligence. A look from her sent them all running back to their tents, hoping to avoid her fury.

Rupert merely stood still behind her. His own hatred distilled in a slow drip as he compiled a growing list of lies she fed him. Tallying up the false promises she flung at him, like carrots dangled before a horse, he realized all the points were on her side of the ledger.

"First thing in the morning, Rupert, I want you to give orders for the troop to pack up camp. We're heading back to Sharas."

Locked in his own thoughts, her voice sounded far away.

"Perhaps your pea-sized brain can come up with a plan to figure out a way to make a deal with Thana NukPana once we have the Fae Princess as our captive again? That would be a way for you to prove that you are ready to be crowned king. So far, I find your abilities lacking, Rupert. Leave me." She flung her fingers at him, dismissing him as if he were a boy. "I need to think."

As soon as the tent flap fell closed behind him, Morveena pulled a small mirror and a razor-sharp knife from a pocket. She slashed her upper left arm, sheathed the blade, and allowed herself to bask in the throbbing sting the cut produced. Using her right forefinger, she dabbed at the blood running in rivulets down her muscled arm. She fought her desire to lick the bloodied fingertip. Instead, held the tiny mirror so she could see her eyes as she placed a blood-red dot between her blue orbs. Holding her breath, she felt euphoric as she watched her blue eyes turn black and beady. Eyes that stared at her reflection from within. The witch placed additional blood dots below her eyes, and a feeling rose in her to call out a "kik-kik-kik-kik-kik". Instead, she uttered her spell in a gravelly voice to complete her transformation.

"Dryocopus pileatus inside me,
open your wings to fly;
take me with you.
I'll be watching through
our beady eye.
Black and white our
feathers glisten;
our blood-red crest ablaze
under Luna's bright beam.
When we're done,
our flight complete,
I'll wake from this dark dream.
Then you will see the world
through our blue eyes,

but wait within unseen,
until I call upon you next,
my sweet Picidae."

THE BIRD'S FULL WINGSPAN opened. The piliated woodpecker swept up to soar across the sky, crest flaming red in the morning sun. Powerful wings pushed her south toward Thrall Lake. She would see for herself what the Gugwe planned. Content to savor the aerial view while she entertained alternate options to her original plans.

Chapter 12: What's the Name?

Rolland patted Saffron's knee as they sat on the buckboard pulled by two well-muscled Morgan horses. The beasts strained to pull the load uphill. Hiding wooden crates that contained the smith's first delivery of weapons, the wagon bed was covered with rough canvas.

Cazzidy Beaumont Touchstone cracked a big smile when he saw the wagon come level over the rise. He waved a welcome to the two travelers, then continued his demonstration for the soldiers he was instructing on the use of the quarterstaff. Caz was generous with praise and criticism as he moved in a circle around his paired students.

It was Val who spotted the visitors next. "Red!" she squealed at Saffron, dropping the ropes she'd been weaving and running toward the wagon. Robin heard her and gave his own gesture, moving in tandem with his sister. He wondered if the visitors had heard the news about Valvina at Stone House Camp.

Rolland brought the horses to a standstill. Saffron jumped down just in time to open her arms for an emotional hug from Val. The two spun around as they clung to one another. The big male shook the ground when he vaulted from his seat. He stretched his arms over his head and then out to the side, moving his head to work the kinks out of his neck and shoulders.

Robin met him straight on, clamping a hand on Rolland's shoulder. "It's good to see you, Rolland. Pleasant trip?"

"No trouble," Rolland reported. "Glad to be here, though. We'll only be staying tonight and tomorrow night. I want to get an early start back the next morning. Got lots of work to do."

"There are three lads who would like to go back with you. They volunteered to be apprentices. You'll have to interview them before you leave to decide if you think they'd work out on your team, yeah? How are the other prentices working out?"

Rolland gave Robin a twitch at the corner of his mouth, as close as he ever came to a smile. "Come and see for yourself," he said as he turned, leading Robin to the back of the wagon. He loosened the ties at the corner and lifted the canvas to reveal a full load of crates stacked two high. "I would have brought more, but I don't think the horses could have handled the load."

Robin let out a slow, appreciative whistle. "What's what, mate?"

The shy oaf beamed with pride, forgot his modest ways, his enthusiasm overriding his natural behavior. He gave a running confabulation of the weapons he was delivering. "Wait until you see the new design one of Raven's lads came up with to make it easier to set the crossbow. We brought two boxes of those. Saffron figured the females would want them." He'd pulled the canvas up on the other side and pointed to a row of identical-sized containers. "Those are all arrows. We had three new recruits from towns near the Edgewood who'd heard we were hiring weapon makers. Oddly, they all showed up on the same day." There was a twinkle in his eye as he lowered his voice to a near whisper. "All three of them are fletchers."

Rolland looked around, then continued, "I don't want word to get out, or someone will offer them higher pay and hire them away. Anyway, I brought Caz's order for two crates of quarterstaffs he asked for. Some are oak. I made a few out of walnut and a stack of hickory. There's an assortment of shields, knives, swords, and axes. We're working on something special to bring you on the next trip, but you'll have to wait to find out what it is." As if Rolland suddenly realized he had just said more words to Robin in the past five minutes than he had in all the years they'd grown up together, he clamped his mouth shut. An alarmed look spread across his face.

Leaning in close, not wanting to embarrass the lad, Robin said, "It's fine work, Rolland. You should be proud. I'm impressed with you and your team. We can't train soldiers if we don't have weapons. What you've created here can mean the difference between life and death for us when the war starts. In fact, we couldn't even dream about it without your talents, yeah?" Robin pushed away and gave Rolland Rafael Brown a two-finger salute. The big male blushed.

"Alright then, mate," Robin said. "What say we unhook your horses? Assign some lads to unload, while Val and I take you and Saffron to get a hot meal? After you've eaten, I'll give you a tour of the training camp? We can catch each other up on the news."

ZEEKA WELCOMED SAFFRON in a tight hug. The two women laughed with joy as they turned in circles, delighted to see one another. Val went to the big cast-iron stove and lifted the lid on one of the big pots, releasing savory steam, making Rolland's stomach rumble. He kept his eyes downcast as Zeeka planted a kiss on each of his cheeks. "Hullo, Rolland." Zeeka greeted him.

"Hullo, Mistress Zeeka." He pulled a burlap bag tied at the top and pushed it into her gnarled hands.

"What's what, laddie?" She asked as she untied the bag. "Oh, you lovely man." Zeeka said, "My favorite tea leaves." She beamed at his kindness.

"Just something I brought for you," Rolland said, shoving his hands in his pockets.

Saffron babbled the news from the Edgewood as she and Val moved back and forth from the stove to the tables, serving bowls of spicy stew to Robin, Faith, and Rolland. They set aside three for Zeeka and themselves. Saffron described the twenty-six new homesteaders who lived in the revitalized village. The Edgewood now boasted a laundry service, a bakery, the hostel, an ale-house, and Rolland's forge. The nearest four farms were trading milk, eggs, cheese, vegetables, and fruit with them. Visitors were becoming common as traders learned Rolland was buying materials for weapons. Why, Saffron laughed; even a hatmaker had settled in. Whatever would they do with a hatmaker? Everyone laughed.

Caz had come into the food hall and stood back, listening to Saff tell their news, her voice light and happy. He felt a pang of loss, but also gladness that she had found somewhere she could grow and express herself. Her voice rose and fell. Occasionally, Rolland added a word or two. Caz recognized they were in sync with one another. His eyes found and came to rest on Faith. She raised her eyelashes, locking her eyes with his. The group laughed again at something Saffron had said, but he'd missed it.

Val asked about Delainey. Her red-headed friend produced a thick envelope with her name on it, telling her she had one each for Carlisse and Aliah as well. She offered to take letters back to their sister when they set out to return to Edgewood in two days.

Robin watched from the corner of his eye as Faith got up, dipped a fresh bowl of Zeeka's stew, and waved Caz over to eat beside her. With the dishes cleared, Zeeka shooed them off, saying she'd take care of the washing up. Robin suggested a tour of the training grounds they'd created after the moot concluded.

Rolland, Caz, and Robin walked in a line in front of the girls, who straggled behind, sharing whispers and giggles, enjoying the company. Val was pumping Saffron for information about how things were going between Delainey and Ari.

When the girls caught up, they were stunned into silence as Faith's Uncle Jak called out the commands to a formation of 100 bowmen. The soldiers worked in a choreography of movements that rippled like rows of dominoes. The first row loosed their arrows, immediately kneeled to allow the row behind to send a volley, then fell to their knees. Then, the third, fourth, and fifth rows loosed in quick succession above the heads of their fellow troops on bended knees. While down, every bowman had reloaded and stood in a wave, ready to send the next volley of arrows.

"Impressive," Saffron said, squeezing Rolland's hand.

"Wait till you see the next division, Fron," Robin led them on, eager to share their successes.

Robin and Caz took the group to watch sword training and axe wielding. They introduced them to the students in rotating language classes. Caz explained that learning other languages gave the students the benefit of understanding unified members of the new army, as well as enemies. It allowed soldiers to operate efficiently and make better decisions based on what they would hear in a foreign territory. There were classes on cultural differences, as well as similarities. This training was an effort to eliminate lack of knowledge, rumors, and false hearsay from the mix of races among the troops.

Saffron let out a full-bellied laugh when they came across Carlisse's tattoo parlor. The setup comprised a natural rock formation that allowed the artist a great perch to sit on. Her customers could lie back or lie belly down, depending on where the skin canvas was on their bodies that they wanted her to ink. There were seven or eight waiting for their turn, but she took a break to visit with Saffron and Rolland, wanting to hear some news of her sister,

Delainey. Saffron proffered a letter with Carlisse's name. Carlisse promised she'd deliver one to take back to Delainey by tomorrow night.

When they came to the next station, Caz announced, "This is where I'll leave you. My team is back from break, and we're ready to drill again. See you at dinner, yeah?"

They hung there for a few minutes until Caz had organized his people, then watched as the unit moved like a well-oiled machine. The soldiers used quarterstaffs, legs, and arms. They danced a powerful set of moves as he called them out, routines that were becoming second nature, the response automatic.

One by one, the tour group dropped off. Faith waved and returned to a small gathering of artists who were working on reproductions of maps to be distributed when the army moved north. The artists were an odd cast of characters made up of gargoyles, selkies, humans, a handful of Fae, and goblins. Some were talented artists. Others, well-traveled consultants. They provided the facts and tactical geography that the artists turned into topography. Carlisse worked with the group for a half-day every other day. The demand for her tattoo work was high, and Faith felt the symbols she had designed that everyone wanted inked helped them bond, united them in their goals, and mixed groups.

When Val, Robin, Rolland, and Saffron circled back to the cook's hall. Rolland found his horses cared for, hobbled in a meadow of fresh grass, the wagon parked, and a tent set up. Robin pointed out where they could wash up and said he'd meet them for dinner at dusk. Raven stopped by and asked Rolland to play a game of stones. Saffron went off with Val. Likely, he surmised, to engage in more gossip.

"So, what's the name of this camp?" he asked Raven after he placed his stone.

"Name?" Raven moved a stone.

"Yeah. You know. Like the name Stone House Camp," Rolland reminded him.

Raven nodded, "Good question. Everyone's been so busy, I don't think they thought to give it one. At least no one suggested a name that I've heard."

"Gotta have a name," Rolland grumbled to himself as he took his turn, placing the stone that won him the game.

Raven looked sideways at him. “You weren’t even paying attention, laddie, yet you won?”

“Clearly, I was,” Rolland shrugged.

“Was what?” Raven scratched his head and leaned back.

“Paying attention,” Rolland smirked, holding his hand out.

Raven flipped him a silver nugget. “See you at dinner, mate.”

SAFFRON COULDN’T BELIEVE how two days flew by and already they were stowing their things on the wagon, horses harnessed. The three lads who were going back with them had their things already loaded. They were eager to get on the road.

Zeeka was pressing a basket into Rolland’s hands. Saffron knew the old cook had a soft spot for him. Her own eyes teared up when she hugged Zeeka goodbye, begging her once more to come and settle in the Edgewood.

“Maybe when this is all over I’ll come, lass. My place is with Robin and Cazzidy. At least while they are duty-bound. Robin’s a born leader, you know. Save me a place in your village. I’ll make my way there, eventually.” Zeeka patted Saffron’s hand and slipped an envelope into the redhead’s pocket.

“What’s what, Mistress Zeeka?” Saffron asked.

“You’ll have to do your best to keep the goblins that have settled in the Edgewood from getting homesick. You can introduce new, tasty dishes to newfound friends who are not familiar with our herbs, spices, and different dishes. Of course, it is just as important to make dishes others are used to, so the goblin folk sample those too. I thought it might be a good idea to set my best recipes down on paper so you can provide home-cooked meals at your new establishment. Between you and Miss Delainey, you’ll pack ‘em in.” Zeeka granted a big smile and winked at Saffron as she turned to climb up beside Rolland. “It won’t hurt that you’ll be serving Bedwer’s ale, neither.” Saffron’s mouth fell open, surprised the old cook knew where she’d gotten the perfect concoction for her brew.

Robin looked up at the two of them, wished them safe travels, and sent his greetings back to the Edgewood. “Can we look for another load of weapons in two full moons?” He tossed a pouch of coins up, and Rolland snatched it out of the air and weighed it in his hand. He pulled the purse open, dumped half the coins out, pulled it tight and tossed the bag back to Robin, tucking the loose coins into a pocket.

"I need this for more materials and to pay the lads. You keep the rest. You've got an army to feed."

"Are you sure, lad?"

"I'm sure. One favor, though?"

"What's what?" Robin asked.

"A name," Rolland said, taking the reins in hand. He disengaged the handbrake, and the horse's ears twitched, recognizing the sound.

"What name?" Robin's forehead crinkled in confusion.

"We named Stone House Camp. Now you've all built this training camp. There's going to be a war."

"And?" Robin prompted.

"And I want you to give your training camp a name. Bring your team together in another way."

"You have a name you'd like to propose?"

"I do. Actually, a name and a prediction," Rolland nodded solemnly, "Gugwe's Tears."

The huge goblin clicked his tongue and lifted the reins, the horses responding to his signals.

The wagon rolled away. Those who were training at Gugwe's Tears could hear Saffron's voice drifting on the wind as she sang 'Our Return'.

Chapter 13: Friday the 13th

It was Friday the 13th day of the moon's cycle when a strategic idea struck Faith. She'd been alone in the artist's hut for the past hour, the others done for the day, some having other duties. The Fae Princess was just putting the finishing touches on a new map she'd made. Consulting with King Lenny and King Lester on her last visit to the Stone House Camp proved invaluable. She'd been able to take detailed notes on their answers to her questions. Her rough sketch earned their high praise. The result was the creation of the colorful cartographic design of what they once knew as the Kingdoms of the Northern Fae and Northern Goblins.

She put her artist's mark in the bottom right-hand corner and stood back to critique the work. Her eyes followed the contours along the shore of Sapphire Lake. Mountain ridges arched to the base of the Sapphire Peninsula, where the abandoned Fae castle stood. Tracing her finger along a course on the map, she stopped at the point where the arm of land jutted out into the water. It looked almost as if it were reaching across the cold abyss to grasp something. She thought of the pool at the bottom of the castle dungeons, continued moving her finger to the tip of the peninsula at the point. There, she tapped the likeness of the castle she'd depicted, fingertip touching the reproduction of the home she had no memories of. Her eyes were drawn north of the castle, where the Gugwe hailed from. It felt like finding a missing piece of a puzzle. With a plan coalescing in her mind, her trance broke.

Purposeful movement around the makeshift art room provided efficiency. Faith put away the supplies and carefully cleaned her brushes. Gathering the rest of her things that were scattered about. At the last minute, she grabbed the map. Rolling it, she secured it with leather straps to the side of her pack. Long strides took her away from the artist's hut to where Caz's division trained. She noted that the last of his students were heading towards the cook's hall. He saw her approaching, leaning on his quarterstaff, waiting to see what had lit an obvious fire under her. Silhouette backlit by the sun that hung low in the slate-gray sky, spotting him, she increased her speed.

"Afternoon, lass," Caz greeted her. "I think I see steam coming out of your ears. What's what?"

She punched his arm playfully, took off her pack, leaning against a target frame his group had been using for practice. Caz came in so close he could smell the lavender she used to wash her hair. He feigned reaching behind her ear, coming out with a Queen Anne's Lace flower, its stem pinched between his fingers. "My mistake. Not steam. Lace." Cazzidy Beaumont Touchstone gave her his best smile.

Returning one of her own to him, she gracefully accepted the lacy floral. Her smile widened into a grin. "My lace," she said, popping her wings out. "Your leather," she teased, tapping him on the shoulder blade. "Listen, I'm calling a special meeting. I was hoping you would come. I could really use you there for support and to put in your two cents on my latest idea."

Cazzidy didn't ask her a question. He just picked up her pack, snapped out his wings and said, "Lead on. Can't wait to hear what's got you all pumped up, yeah?"

Faith ran several steps and pushed off on her toes, wings working to get her airborne, Caz right behind her.

"Let's find Garrett. I want to ask him to round up my father and Dedo and bring them to where Robin and Val are working."

"Can you share a preview of what's what?" Caz pushed.

"I guess since I've asked for your support, you deserve to know what you're in for, yeah?" She flashed him a smile. "I want to move Gugwe's Tears north to the Fae castle on the Sapphire Peninsula before winter sets in. If there's going to be a war, I want to choose where we meet the enemy."

Caz nodded his approval.

MORVEENA HAD PERCHED on a half-a-dozen trees, occasionally hammering her Picidae beak to keep in character with her cover. She'd been eavesdropping on various groups of Gugwe as they met with Thana NukPana and his 13, making plans, dictating new ways he expected the tribes to adopt.

She'd heard discussions about how the warriors planned to converge on Bear Ridge at the Spring Equinox. Once there, the Gugwe intended to move as one unit to begin their acquisition of slaves. Her two spies had been correct.

It was clear to Morveena's Picidae that goblins were less than nothing to Thana NukPana. It infuriated her that he put goblins in the same category as all the other races. Based on what she had overheard, her plans would have to be adjusted. In the end, she would devise a way to teach the Gugwe Emperor that goblins were indeed different. Taking flight, she headed back to her own camp.

DEDO CALCULATED HE wouldn't be missed until tomorrow. He used the Gargoyle touchstones to travel the great distance. His essence passing through woods, meadows, hills, and valleys rushed past in a blur as he made his way to Sir Robert's fortress. He climbed the stone chimney, dropped through the flue, brushing off his fine coat as he stepped out onto the wide hearth. With a quick look around, he found the coast clear. The small gargoyle touched the blood-red cornerstone and was swept to a small grotto below. A place he hadn't visited in almost thirteen years.

For a moment, fear gripped his heart. He was breaking a very explicit instruction given by his master never to do what he was here to accomplish. It frightened him to consider what the backlash might be.

He pushed his terror down. Surely, the information he had to convey overrode all previous orders, didn't it? Yes, absolutely, he convinced himself. Without further consideration, his small hand reached out and touched the ruby-red jewel set in the center of a circle that depicted an evil spirit's face. The center of his palm sizzled; the smell of burned flesh stank in his wide nostrils. "Take me to my master," Dedo hissed.

The small cave filled with smoke.

When the haze cleared, Dedo was gone.

RUPERT HUDDLED IN A natural rock indentation, out of the wind on the ridge overlooking their camp. He was watching for Morveena's return, morbid thoughts keeping him company. The goblin princeling was near the end of his rope. He couldn't rid himself of the thought that it was high time he was named king, just as his Queen Regent had promised for so long. Rupert was tired of waiting for confirmation that Lancer Goodfellow was dead. Particularly since he now knew his father was alive, if not well. His angry thoughts drifted to his father, remembering the pitiful shape the man he'd looked up to as a boy had become today. *Had Lancer been right? Had Morveena given his father to the Gugwe as a slave, pretending innocence all these years, sending out search parties for the missing king as a ruse? She was dangerous, selfish and cruel, he mused. Once he became king, Rupert thought it might be wise to consider ruling without his queen. Most times, she treated him no better than the royal dogs, and she actually liked the canines. He snarled at the thought that her base treatment of him was growing worse every day. Well, he considered, picking at his fingernails; she was under a lot of pressure. Perhaps he should bide his time. See if things improved once they captured the Fae princess again.*

Out of the corner of his eye, Rupert caught the flash of her red crest as she soared across the sky toward him. Just as he was about to stand, he noticed movement below, to the right of his protective niche. He recognized the squat, demonic gargoyle. Rupert detested gargoyles. A memory pushed to the surface flashed before his mind's eye. He saw himself as a child, looking down from his bedroom balcony, where Morveena met with this very creature. He was sure it was the same one. Confusion kept him still and secreted now, just as it had back then. Cowering down, he ran a looping catechism silently to himself, 'Don't see me. Don't see me. Don't see me.'

Morveena's keen bird sight honed in on the gargoyle waving at her at the base of the ridge. A surge of rage ripped through her body at seeing the unexpected goyle, causing her to nosedive toward the ground, straight at the creature. Rupert held his breath, watching. It looked as though she would crash the Picidae body against the rocky outcropping. Her body shifted so fast that it pulled the breath from her lungs. Her feet hit the ground running. When she reached the goyle, who stood paralyzed by fear, her hands wrapped around his throat, throttling him until he nearly passed out. Dedo tried to say something in his defense, but only a croaking gurgle came out. She shook his body, screeching bloody murder at him, his eyes ready to pop from their sockets. Finally, she cast his limp form away from her, as though he were a leper.

Her voice was hard and dangerous. "I instructed you never, ever, no matter the circumstances, to contact me, under penalty of death. What part of that order did you not understand?"

Dedo had risen to his hands and knees, retching, his body wracked in spasms.

The red-haired witch pointed her finger at him. "You have one chance to explain why you've sought your death today. Indeed, you must have a death wish to jeopardize anyone finding out about the connection between us. I will grant you one word, so weigh your choice. It may well be the last word you speak before you die, fool. You've risked years of planning." She clenched her fists, body shaking in fury, hardly able to keep herself from pummeling him to death.

"Three," he rasped. "I need three words to explain."

Shocked at his impudence, she allowed it. "Very well. Three." Morveena's face turned an ugly purple, rage so great her features betrayed the demon who lived inside. Taking a step toward him, ready to destroy the traitor before her, she visualized pulverizing him.

"Valvina. Ariana. Goodfellow." That was the name he spent his three words on. He held his breath, waiting for her next assault.

Morveena Morgan Montestrell Goodfellow rocked back on her heels as if he had slapped her, shock riding across her face.

"I had to break your directive, mistress. Your daughter is alive. Valvina Ariana Goodfellow lives."

The Goblin Queen swooned. Dedo rushed to her side, eager to steady his master. "How can I serve you, my queen?" he begged of her, supporting her weight.

"Tell me everything," she whispered as she cupped his cheek lovingly.

Rupert leaned back against his rocky cove, heart racing. He belly-crawled as close to the edge of the drop as he dared. He didn't want to miss a word between the two of them. Now that the shouting was done, their voices lowered in conspiracy. Muscles tight as a bowstring, blood pressure off the charts, he listened to Dedo. The gargoyle described Valvina's pronouncements on the stage at the Sharas citizens' moot. Robin confirmed

Valvina's claim in front of hundreds. Dedo told of the long, close friendship between Valerie Victoria Pureheart, who'd come to live in Robert's fortress as an adopted daughter in the Pureheart family around the same time they had brought the orphan Faith to live there. The two girls had grown up together and were practically sisters. It couldn't have been a coincidence. He speculated it must have been Lennox Stargazer who helped Lancer to secret Morveena's babe away. The Goblin King had claimed Morveena's babe had been stillborn at birth. Dedo also reported Lennox lived. The Fae King was working with Robin to build an army in preparation for the coming war with the Gugwe. The gargoyle confessed he had no choice but to come to her with this news. Surely, the knowledge that her only child lived would stay his execution?

"Wise master," he crooned, petting her arm, "all your plans have come to fruition one by one over the years. We rid you of your husband. Made you Queen Regent. We captured your Fae enemy and gave her to the Gugwe for safekeeping. You were successful in disguising yourself as Aleta Stargazer to lay a curse upon the Dream Weaver and her brother. You devised that clever plan, so the Fae Princess would receive the weave you made for her if she ever turned up. But they hid her right before my eyes all these years. You must admit, all went according to your grand plan, yes? Still," the Gargoyle paused, tapping his finger to his lips. "That your daughter is alive, well...you have only to tell me what you wish me to do, now that you know. Please, great mistress, tell me how to serve you best?" Dedo dropped to his knees and kissed the hem of her dress, looking up at her with worshipful eyes.

"Valvina Ariana Goodfellow are three words that have saved your life, Dedo. They have redeemed you back into my good graces. You were right to recognize how important that news would be to me and the future. I promise I shall reward you when the time comes." She brushed his cheek gently and looked at him with loving eyes. "Dedo, ever my favorite loyal servant. Listen closely. Here's what must be done. They still hold Aleta as an inmate at the Gugwe BloodKnife prison. Those worthless Gugwe shamans have had no success in wresting away her powers, and they've had years to try. You must go back and resume your role. Tell Faith Stargazer that you've discovered where her mother is being held prisoner. Do whatever is necessary," she licked her lips, "to get both Faith and Valvina to attempt the rescue of Aleta." She uttered a sinister laugh, rubbed her palms together, "If those two girls come to rescue the Fae Queen, I can kill three birds with one stone, yes?"

Dedo sat with his knees to his chest, chin resting on them, arms wrapped around his legs, nodding his head in agreement. "Delicious, my queen. How will you do it?"

"Once I capture the Fae Princess again, I will have both the Queen and her daughter to trade to Thana NukPana. In exchange for those prizes, the emperor must give me his guarantee that goblins are off-limits as he builds his empire on the backs of slaves. Once I am reunited with my flesh and blood, I will groom Valvina to become the queen I always meant her to be. All in due time, of course. Of course, it will be necessary for me to continue at Queen Regent until my daughter is fully trained, and who knows how long that will take? In the meantime, she will rule by my side. I can guide her and teach her the power of blood magic. Eventually, we'll be able to seize Aleta's power and wipe out the Gugwe nation to rule all of Sharas and Adana."

"But, my Queen," Dedo chewed his lower lip, "haven't you been grooming Rupert Goodfellow for the kingship? Shouldn't Valvina be the successor to the throne after Rupert's rule?"

She backhanded him so hard his teeth rattled as he fell to the ground, body shaking from the strike. "Forgive me, Master. I meant no offence." His leathery body crawled on his knees to her, kissing her shod feet as she kicked him away. "I merely meant to point out that the Goblin people would more readily accept Valvina as a ruler if we observed the normal order of succession."

"A daughter of my blood will be no successor to another, except me," Morveena declared.

"Of course, my queen, of course," he whined, cringing back to avoid another blow.

"Besides," she told him, "Rupert is a worthless worm. An easily manipulated fool. The people think of him as a joke. Only his clown of a brother holds any love, any regard for him, despite his rough treatment he showers on his younger sibling. I would bet Robin will come within my grasp again to protect those girls. If he does, I'll have a plan ready to make both those Goodfellow losers of Lancer's spawn disappear. The throne will belong to me and, when my rule is over, to Valvina. A new era is about to bloom for the goblin people, Dedo. A gilded era."

Morveena stared off into space as she envisioned new plans to bring all her dreams to fruition. She surprised herself when realizing she'd actually choked up, her eyes filled with unshed tears. "My daughter, my baby, is alive. Not dead, but alive. Yes, a new age is nearly upon us. Go at once, Dedo. Put the plan into action."

She lifted his chin with her razor-sharp, red-lacquered fingernails. "And Dedo..." he blinked innocently at her. "Never, ever, under any circumstances, under penalty of death, contact me, risking discovery of our camaraderie again, or I will kill you on sight. There will be no opportunity to say one word in your defense, much less three. Too much rides on your role as a mole in the enemy camp, yes? I will summon you when the time is right." He blinked twice, his body riddled with fear.

Violently slashing her palm, she pressed a bloody print to his forehead, whispering the words to send him back whence he came. Eventually, she would have to eliminate him. He knew too much. She couldn't risk anyone discovering that he had been her creature, her spy, all these years. The fool had not even discovered that the girl raised in Sir Robert's fortress had actually been the Fae Princess. No matter. For now, she admitted he had brought her the best of luck on a Friday the 13th.

LENNY LEANED BACK FROM the obsidian scrying mirror he had been using to watch Dedo's activities. Turning with a grim look on his face, he told his brother Lester, "It is done. Dedo has reported to Morveena Morgan Montestrell Goodfellow that her daughter Valvina Ariana Goodfellow lives."

Lester locked eyes with Lenny, picked his nose, inspected his finger and flicked a booger to the floor.

Chapter 14: A New Beginning

"Let me get this straight. You're telling me you have a magical connection that allows you to spy on the Gugwe Emperor's conversations and actions?" Val's voice spiraled up an octave with each word.

"More or less."

"Can the Gugwe King spy on us through you?" Faith asked.

"Emperor," Garrett corrected. "The Gugwe *emperor.* Theoretically, yes, but your aunts and the old nurse, Evy, taught me how to block him. To hear them tell the story, it seems to be something special a Foxfire can do. The ability is strongest when the Aurora Borealis is in full swing, but I've been practicing. I can make the connection at will now. They trained me always to keep the block in place to protect against linking from the other direction. I don't want to take a chance that he could listen in on any of the Alliance's plans, yeah?"

"Who else knows about this?" Val asked.

"Aliah, Faith's aunts, Evy, and now the two of you."

Faith steepled her fingers under her chin.

"Want to share what you're thinking?" Val poked her arm.

"Just that I'd like to keep the knowledge of this advantage limited to a tight circle of people. The fewer who know, the better. I don't think Mari, Reatha, or Evy would ever say a word about it. Aliah either, but to be sure she knows we don't want it to get out, would you mind asking her to keep it a secret, Garrett?"

"Sure," Garrett agreed, but he looked uncomfortable.

"What's what?" Val searched his eyes, keen on his discomfort, when Aliah's name came up.

"Nothing really. I...um...er..."

Faith cupped his cheek. "We're your best friends. You can tell us anything."

"She's right," Val added, "we've always had your back and you've had ours. Besides, if you don't spill it, I'm going to torture it out of you!" Laughing, Val punched him in the arm.

"Alright, alright. It's just...there's been a distance between me and Aliah since, well, since..."

Faith finished the thought for him. "Since you found out, she knew they adopted Val later than the rest of the Pureheart sisters? Since the old nurse gave Val directly to her? You think it was a betrayal that Aliah never told Val, right?"

Garrett shrugged his shoulders. "I just...I know it's none of my business, but, yeah, it seems like a betrayal. And...and the entire story just made me lose my trust in her." His face looked so defeated, it plucked at their heartstrings.

"I can understand why you feel that way, Garrett. I'm struggling with it myself. But," Val took his hands in hers, "I'm trying to work past it. She'll always be my sister in my heart, you know? Have you tried talking to her about it?"

"Not yet. I've been busy. We all have. The truth is, I've been avoiding her."

"I won't push you," Val promised, "But, I think you should talk to her. Maybe you can work it out. You'll never know if you don't have the conversation. If you can't work through the issues, you can make a clean break. But it's only fair if you put your thoughts out there for her to consider, rather than thinking she can read your mind, yeah?"

"I agree with Val's opinion. You should at least give her the courtesy of knowing what's changed your feelings."

The three of them did a group hug and started joking around. They didn't notice Aliah hurrying away from the treeline.

Faith stepped back. "Hey, we need to meet with Robin and Caz. I'd like you to share your connection ability with the two of them if you're comfortable with that. No one else, unless we've all discussed it first, agreed?"

Garrett gave a half-bow at the waist. "Garrett Emmon Gladheart at your service, princesses."

They both playfully punched him on the arm.

CAZZIDY AND ROBIN LEANED on heavy sticks as tall as they were. If one wasn't poking at the fire, the other was. Shooting sparks flew above the flames as they listened to Garrett's details. He provided the current location of the Gugwe Emperor, information he had gleaned from listening in on Thana's summit. He disclosed the fact that Morveena and Rupert were in the same area, apparently hoping to meet with the emperor.

Robin could only speculate that they likely wanted to make some kind of deal with the Gugwe leader. He glanced at Faith, worried about her safety.

"I think we should all focus on the ability Garrett has—a gift. Let's see if we can come up with some different ways we could put his resources to work," Faith suggested. There was a nattering of one-syllable comments and nodding heads. "Good," she smiled all around. "Since you're feeling agreeable, it seems like a good time to make an announcement."

All eyes were intent on the princess with the fawn-colored hair.

Taking a deep breath, Faith pushed out the words she'd bottled up. "The prophecy told me to go north. It's been nagging at me that winter will be upon us in just a couple of weeks. Thanks to Garrett," she nodded her approval at him, "we now know that the Gugwe plan to amass at their Bear Ridge village at the spring equinox." Faith pulled the map she'd recently finished and rolled it out. Caz placed two rocks at the top corners, and Val put rocks at the bottom corners of the drawing. Faith pointed at what she thought was the approximate location of Bear Ridge. Then, letting her finger slowly trace a course south around Sapphire Lake, the route turned north to the tip of Sapphire Peninsula. She tapped the point twice. "This is the location of the castle of the northern Fae. The rumors say it is all but abandoned. I believe we should move the army there now, so we can prepare to use it as a stronghold when the war starts in the spring. This training camp has served us well, but if we travel north now, we can pick up additional recruits. Those who attended the moot have spread the word as they were returning home." She looked down, toeing the tip of her boot in the dirt, bit her lower lip and said, "I don't want this war to just *happen to us*. I want to pick the place where we'll face the Gugwe, a place that will give us the best advantage. Badger and Tula returned from their mission a few days ago, along with my cousins and uncles. The two of them have offered to accompany us as far as the peninsula arm that leads to the castle. From there, Badger plans to travel to the villages that lie between the Fae castle and the Gugwe lands. He can warn of the impending attack before spring. That would give them a chance of survival. They would be welcome at the Fae castle until they can safely return to their homes. The group will bring back whatever intel they can gather during their travels. The sooner we make the move, the better prepared we'll be and..." Faith looked each individual in the eye before she continued. "We can get back to training. Reatha always said practice makes perfect. I know I said I had an announcement, but each of you has a say. I want your input, not automatic capitulation. We're a team, or we're nothing. We should decide as a team. I value your opinions and thoughts." She hung her head, finishing in a quiet voice, "All for one and one for all."

Garrett lifted her chin. Blue, trusting eyes stared into his. "I'm in. AFOAOFA."

"What?"

"A-foa-ofa. Acronym, get it? A-foa-ofa." He rolled his eyes. "All for one and one for all. A-foa-ofa," he held both hands wide and shook his head at the group.

"A-foa-ofa," Val nodded, "I like it. I agree."

"A-foa-ofa," Robin and Caz said in tandem. Everyone laughed.

"One thing," Robin broke in, "I don't think we should abandon this training camp. The setup has worked well. Maybe keep some of the army here?"

"I think I have a solution to that," Faith told them.

"Share it, lass," Caz said.

"Another advantage we have—well, three really," she smiled, "Seers. My cousin, Kris, let me know that my Uncle Robert was successful in rousing a pretty large army from Sharas' mid-lands and further south. Kris claims they'll be here in the next day or two. He can't be sure, but he thinks it may be near five hundred new recruits. Robin and Caz grinned at the welcome news.

"Sounds like we agree, yeah? This division of the Alliance Army will begin packing up to move. That will make room for Robert's ranks to take over here and ready themselves, training for the spring rout, when they'll join us further north. That's all I've got for now. Anyone else have anything they want to discuss?"

Everyone started getting up, gathering belongings. "We've all got other meetings where we can pass the orders up the line to get ready to break camp. Cross your fingers that Rolland will get here soon with another weapon delivery. We'll take what we already have north with us. Keep an eye out for Dedo. Whoever finds him, send him to Stone House Camp to find out about the next weapon transport. I also want to tell Lennox about the plan myself. I'm not sure how my father will feel about returning to the Fae castle. He may choose to remain here and help Robert with training the new recruits."

Val rubbed Faith's shoulder in sympathy, then walked off with Garrett and Caz. Faith called out as she was rolling up her map, "Robin, a word?"

When the rest of the group had passed out of earshot, Robin said, "Are you sure it's me you wanted a minute with, lass, not Caz?"

She winced at his tone, answering, "You're angry."

"I'm frustrated," he confessed. "Sorry. I didn't mean to sound like a bloody bore; it's just that Val told me she shared with you that there was nothing going on between the two of us. I wish she had told you long before the shock of finding out she was my sister. Still, I haven't been able to get five minutes alone with you to...um...to figure out what's what between us. I don't get it, that's all." Robin peered up at her from under his thick black eyelashes.

"It's complicated, Robin. Look, I'll be honest. When we first met, I shared with you the shock of discovering I was Fae, how strangers had shown up at my home, claimed to be family I hadn't known about. We've been through a lot together. The surprises keep coming, you know? Now, my best friend turns out to be a Goblin Princess, not my fairy sister. But she's your actual sister. Val's still just like a sister to me and my best friend, but it just seems there's one thing after another. To add to the confusion, my father showed up out of the blue. I only recently learned that I wasn't an orphan adopted by Reatha and Robert, who are really my aunt and uncle. I know you can relate to that, since your own father has been missing for most of your life." She threw her hands in the air. "Then there's the pressure from the prophecy. Not to mention All. These. People. counting on me to pull off some miracle because some cursed Dream Weaver rattled off a fairy tale prediction. Have I mentioned that fortune was really a nightmare from my perspective? Anyway, I've realized that I felt like I was rushing into something special with you. And just as I was getting comfortable with it, I found myself overwhelmed with all the things that had happened over the last few months." She tipped her chin up to look at his face. "It's important for me to figure out who I am, and come to terms with who you are. Admit it. You've had some big surprises too. Like your creepy stepmother's behavior, the way your brother Rupert has treated you. Not to mention suddenly finding your long-lost sister, whom everyone thought was dead. There's the bit you need to get your head around about the Sharas' goblin clans looking to you to become their leader."

"I hear where you're coming from," Robin assured her. "But remember, we've been through a lot of those revelations together. So, where do we go from here?" he asked.

"Right now, I need you to be my friend, an adviser, and my confidante. We both took on a lot of additional responsibilities. I think those obligations need to be our focus. I don't have all the answers, but I can tell you how I feel right now. Let's take some time for ourselves and give our best to the commitments we've made to people. We'll see how things turn out later. You must know you're very important to me, Robin, and one of my best friends. I care deeply about you. You're one of a handful of people I trust completely. Your help and support mean everything to me."

"My help and support are always yours, lass. You're important to me as well. If that's how you feel and friendship is what you need right now, I respect that. Just know that I'll be waiting for the day when you give the signal that you're ready to explore what more than friendship might mean for us, yeah?"

"Oh, Robin." She gave him a hug. "Thank you for understanding." She skipped backward, a huge grin stretched across her face, feeling as though a tremendous weight had fallen off her shoulders. "I've got to find Lennox. I don't want word to reach him before I tell him myself about moving the army to the Fae castle. See you at dinner?"

Robin nodded and waved. "Seven sharp, yeah? Zeeka will expect us."

He startled when she snapped her wings open, leaped into flight, calling over her shoulder, "Hey, if you see Dedo, let him know I'm looking for him, would you?"

VAL WHISPERED, "GOOD luck," in Garrett's ear, crossed her fingers, and put them behind her back. Then, for good measure, she gave him a little shove with her other hand and tip-toed off in the opposite direction.

Aliah stood at a chopping block at the far end of the cook's hall, with a pile of carrots, onions, and potatoes in front of her. He could see she was finishing the last of the carrots, scraping the thin orange circles from the cutting board into the pot below. She scooped a dozen onions closer and used her belt knife to peel the papery skins off. He approached just as she began roughly chopping the pungent bulbs.

His tongue felt thick, mouth dry. Garrett's stomach felt like it was doing a series of backflips as he came into Aliah's view. "Hullo," he greeted her.

Aliah's eyes opened wide, onion tears forming at the corners as the juices hit. "Hullo, yourself." She brushed the back of her hand against her eyes to push the stinging tears away.

"Um...ah..."

She rolled her eyes at him.

"That's um...I mean, those tears are from the onions, yeah?"

"Mostly," she answered.

He rolled up his sleeves, stepped up to the side of the chopping block, produced his own knife, jumped right in, dicing the onions with her. It was only seconds before Garrett produced his own onion-juice tears. When those let loose, so did his tongue.

"I've been wanting to talk to you," he told her.

"You could have fooled me," she shot back, tears burning freely.

"I know. Sorry, I've been avoiding you. I guess I really needed to think for a while and understand my feelings. Things seemed confusing."

"Things?"

"Look, I just want to be blatantly honest with you. When Val confronted you about how you didn't have a vision about her, because you knew how she became part of the Pureheart family, I just couldn't believe it. She accused you of always knowing and never telling her all these years. It just...well, it just made me feel like I could never trust you. Not if you kept a secret like that from someone you've loved as your own sister." He was silent until the count of ten to see if she had anything she wanted to say, but she just kept chopping onions. "Anyway, I wanted to tell you myself why I've been keeping my distance, evading you. I know you must have had your reasons for keeping the truth from her. Or maybe the old nurse put a spell on you, or you made a promise, or you thought it would put Val in danger, or I don't know! Aliah, please say something."

She laid her knife down and pulled up her apron and wiped her face, smoothing it back down over her clothes, and moved her shaking hands behind her back to hide them.

"I wish I could claim any of the reasons you suggested, but I can't. There was nothing sinister or selfish in my inaction. Val was a baby when the old nurse handed her to me. That woman has always been a scary old biddy. Still is. She placed an enormous responsibility on me while keeping everything mysterious. Then, the years went by, and we were a family. Sometimes I could tell that Val was analyzing minor details about how she differed from Delainey, Carlisse, and me. But also, I could tell she noticed how the three of us were alike in looks and mannerisms. Once in a while, she'd be on the brink of saying how she didn't fit in. But she always bit back the words, saying nothing. Maybe she confided in Faith, but never to any of her sisters. She left all her questions locked up inside, asking none out loud. So, I let my words lie at the bottom of the cauldron. I didn't want to be the one to make her feel she was anything less than our full sister. I would never have lied to her if she had asked, but I never had to. It just never came up. I didn't really consider the consequences of keeping the secret to myself. To be honest, I never contemplated that it might be important to her. We lived in our own little world, and we were a happy family." Aliah heaved a heavy sigh. "I am sorry if you don't feel you can trust me anymore. I can promise you I would never, ever divulge any of the secrets you have entrusted to me to another soul. Do you..." she swallowed hard, but the question had to be asked. She just couldn't torture herself any longer with harmful emotional speculation. It was driving her crazy trying to guess what his avoidance of her meant about their relationship. "Do you think there's still a chance we could work things out and be together?"

Garrett pushed the chopped onions into a pile, swished his blade in a bucket of water to clean it, wiped it on his pant leg and sheathed it. "There's always a chance," he told her softly. "But I guess I feel like we need to start over. I'd like to understand how you came to your decision to hide the truth from Val. Maybe over time that will happen, but for now, I'm hoping we can start over by just being friends and work on that relationship first. Would you be willing to start there?"

"Garrett Emmon Gladheart," she curtseyed, "how do you do? My name is Aliah Bethany Pureheart. Pleased to make your acquaintance," she smiled shyly at him.

"Meet me for dinner at seven tonight?" he asked.

"I will. By then, these onions will be cooked, and I promise there'll be no more tears. Just a new beginning."

Chapter 15: You Disappoint Me

"You asked to speak with me, Thana NukPana?" Vigga greeted his emperor, leaving all the bowing and scraping to others. War chiefs did not bow, did not scrape.

"Vigga. Come. Sit," Akama held his hand, pointing at a spot across from him. "I need your expertise."

Vigga's smile slid into place. He liked it when others asked him to apply his special skills.

"Borta tells me that the Goblin Quean, Morveena, and her Prince consort were at the BloodKnife village. The KuRuk believed they were seeking an audience with me before we held our historic tribal congress."

"Yes. I saw them there. I suggested they might want to await your return to Vutova. The Quean wishes to make a deal with you in exchange for a Fae Princess. It is my opinion that she is one who cannot be trusted, Thana NukPana."

"What do the Gugwe need from goblins, Vigga, except to build our empire upon their backs?" Akama laughed at his own suggestion. "Since the goblin witch is foolish enough to sit waiting for me at my doorstep, I ask that you grant the Quean her wish. Take a war party and capture the Quean and her gang. Bring her to me. I will make an example of her. Perhaps she can be my personal slave, hmm?"

Vigga rose to leave, granting his leader a tiny bow of his shoulders. "Taking that haughty gob prisoner will be my pleasure. I'm sure it won't disrupt or spoil your plans if she's alive, but perhaps a bit broken when I turn her over to you? I will take my warriors and leave at once. Personally, I think you would be better off with that one dead, rather than as your slave. She's crafty, like a demon. Practices blood magic, but you will see. Rumors have circulated that she had previous dealings with the former Thana NukPana. Perhaps she does not know that she deals with a far cleverer adversary than your predecessor."

Thana NukPana could hear the war chief laughing as he crossed the camp.

Akama was studying the latest map Taramat had created for him. He heard Nevele arguing with someone outside his tent. He called out Nevele's name. His twin-like bodyguard stuck his head inside. Akama asked, "Who is it?"

"Borta BloodKnife," Nevele reported.

Akama heaved a deep sigh. He had not taken a liking to the BloodKnife KuRuk. "Let him in so I can get this over with and get back to my planning."

Nevele nodded, his head disappearing. Borta slapped the tent flap out of his way and entered. The BloodKnife looked around as though he expected a throne room rather than the sparsely outfitted shelter.

"You needed to see me?" Akama asked. "I am in the middle of something." He waved his hand over the charts spread around him. "But...I always have time for my KuRuks," he offered the visitor a disingenuous smile, did not invite him to sit.

"I had an idea I wanted to run past you. But I can come back another time if you wish it." He held a growl tight in his throat, not wanting to show his irritation.

"You are already here and have interrupted my task, so you might as well speak your piece now," the Thana invited in a flat tone.

"There is an obscure human village about two days south of Thrall Lake. It might be beneficial to take a select group of warriors, some from each tribe. They would accompany BloodKnife warriors, who have experience in raiding villages for the taking of slaves. My thought is to provide an opportunity for those who have no experience with such encounters to see how it is done. That introduction would be an excellent basis for training others. Words are no substitute for experience. If you wish it, I will organize the raid and lead a campaign to raze the hamlet." Borta could feel the Thana's hard gaze. Sweat trickled down his back. His killer instinct was on full alert. He was not sure he could win a fight against this Gugwe. It was rare for Borta to make such an assessment, as he considered himself superior to all other Gugwe warriors. But this time, he trusted his gut, his sixth sense. He forced himself to stand still, with a look of infinite patience plastered on his face.

Finally, Akama spoke. "A fine idea, Borta BloodKnife. A superior training exercise of merit. I'm impressed. Make it so, Borta. Make it so." Then the Thana NukPana looked down, studied his maps again, as effective a dismissal as Borta had ever had. He turned on the ball of his foot to exit the tent. Akama called out, "When you have everything organized, send word. My 13/31 and my future wife, as well as myself, will join you on this raid. We wish to witness for ourselves your method of taking new slaves. Perhaps we can offer a fresh perspective? Maybe suggest efficient changes that would enhance your method of operation?" He snapped his fingers at the BloodKnife KuRuk, signaling an end to the conversation.

Borta's face was beet-red, his blood pressure making his massive heart pump at the edge of its full rate. Wonderful, he thought. Now he would have a circus to accompany him on a slave run. It would be a miracle if they could get close enough with the clatter and noise of a large group of inexperienced raiders, much less Akama's usual spectacle. Borta knew that if the raid failed, no common sense or excuses would take the blame off his shoulders. He would likely forfeit his life for the Thana's little show.

Of a sudden, he stopped in his tracks and snapped his fingers. A show. If that is what the emperor wanted, that is what he would give the Thana NukPana. He and his warriors would be the star attraction. Yes, he smiled at his own cleverness. A show is exactly what was needed.

THE BLOODKNIFE KURUK had watched as his best special forces shifted, some to human form, others to goblin bodies. No need to let any survivors that might escape spread word that the Gugwe had raided. It was better to disguise the marauders in human and gob concealments. They moved into their positions under the cover of night. Borta directed the Thana, along with his 13/31, to set up as a temporary outlier force. He suggested they form a perimeter above the village to observe from a ridge-top on the outskirts of the targeted hamlet. He tried to make the placement sound very important; he instructed them to hold a formation ready on the outer perimeter. One could never be sure how a raid would go. It was possible that some of their prey might escape. Those protecting the outskirts of the village must be ready to capture or kill any escapees. Further, he put forward that they were to watch for a signal that the mission had started. He left them waiting there, effectively keeping them out of his way.

Nheena, Borta's shaman, followed the KuRuk like a shadow. Someone had painted her face blood-red. She had made wide, white circles around her eyes. Though she wore many strings of amulets, teeth, small bones, and tiny animal skulls around her neck, the charms made no noise as she moved.

The human village's night guards had already had their throats cut. Death delivered by drowning in their own blood. A fire in the center of the hamlet, hot coals from the earlier cook fire, waiting to be stirred up to start a new day.

Nheena spoke gibberish to herself. Borta watched as the embers were coaxed into a heavy fire, flames licking hungrily toward the stars. The shaman formed invisible balls with her hands, and Borta's ghost force moved throughout the village. Nheena mimed throwing balls of fire at each hut and building. Her magic became reality, and the imaginary balls burst into flames, lighting up the burning hamlet. Akama and the 13/31 could see the flickering light from their position on the ridge above.

Chaos ensued. Screams filled the silence. Terror took the inhabitants under its power. The disguised Gugwe team herded the women and children away from the men, whose throats they ripped out. Claws and powerful muscles dismembered victims, smoke gagging the humans. Some tried to avoid capture and burned alive inside their shelters. Others tried to crawl away, using the smoke to hide their escape. The Gugwe roared, causing the humans to cringe in fear. Their blood soaked the ground. When the screams stopped, only crying and moaning filled the air, music to Borta's ears. He ordered those left alive bound at the wrists and ankles with just enough slack so they could shuffle before their new masters. Last, the new slaves, tied at the neck so each connected to the one behind, marched out before the warriors, their bounty to parade before the Thana NukPana's host.

When the fires had lit up the village below, the Thana, Abaddon, Nevele, Taramat, Neetriht, and the rest of the 13/31 had seen most of the slaughter from their bird's-eye view. Abaddon had turned aside. Taramat held back her white, silky hair as she retched at the scene. The empress was incapable of attempting to hide her abhorrence of the death and violence that had played out before them.

Neetriht could tell that Abaddon's reaction irritated Akama. His sister whispered she would take care of his future wife's blatant angst against one of his new policies, namely, the taking of slaves. Taramat and Neetriht pulled the empathetic albino off to the side, both whispering harshly to the girl. They reminded her she should show no opposition to Thana's sagacity in public. He left them to deal with her and moved down to meet Borta as the KuRuk pushed his captives before him, proud to display his prowess before the emperor.

Thana NukPana waited at the bottom of the ridge, letting his subject come to him. He felt a sharp snap inside his forehead and flashes of light at the edges of his vision, making him stumble. The moment passed, and he reached up to pinch the bridge of his nose, closing his eyes.

"Thana," Nevele moved close so no one else would hear, "Are you alright?"

Akama waved him off. "Yes, Nevele, fine. Just a headache coming on. Speaking of headaches, here comes one now," he told Nevele as Borta approached, preening like a peacock with a swagger in his walk.

"Most instructive, Borta BloodKnife. Let us travel back to Thrall Lake to hold war councils. We must plan new ways to improve the enslaved people's survival rate. You've killed all your potential hard-muscled slaves and kept only the softness of women and children to serve you. Surely, you see the value of harnessing the abilities of the males as slaves? We have arduous work for slaves to do. You will spend your slaves' lives less quickly if you make the highest and best use of strength. Perhaps the Youngbloods could capture the women and children, while you and your special forces capture the males next time?" Thana NukPana patted Borta on the shoulder in a consolatory fashion to convey his pity that the weak were the only bounty gained on this raid.

FLASHES OF COLORED auras added to his reaction. Garrett pulled back from the connection. He gagged, having witnessed the bloodbath through Thana's eyes. His stomach roiled and threatened to release his breakfast.

Faith put a gentle hand on his shoulder. "Tell me."

NEETRIHT STOOD TWENTY feet away from Abaddon and Taramat, watching as Akama and the 13/31 moved back toward Thrall Lake. The prisoners were tied together like animals. She went to her companions. "They are moving out. We'll catch up," she told them. "Better Akama has some distance from you right now, Abaddon. What were you thinking?"

"I know you told me not to defy him in public, but I couldn't control my reaction to such butchery. Can you understand that?" The translucent-skinned female looked back and forth between Neetriht and Taramat. "Those captives. Slaves," she corrected, drawing the word out, clearly disgusted with the concept. "One day, living a quiet, hard life. The next? Raiders invaded their homes. They watch helplessly as they see the invaders kill their husbands, brothers, grandmothers, and grandfathers." Her voice hitched. "Watching them butchered right before their eyes, while their village burns to the ground. After, to be carted off like animals? Do not ask me to be a part of this. I was a prisoner living in my village, hidden away like a dirty secret, only allowed to do menial tasks and dirty jobs out of sight, out of mind. I have knowledge of how it feels to be nothing. Less than nothing. My mother was a slave and I can't..." Abaddon's voice catches and she breaks down into sobs. Taramat stands, holding the distressed female in her arms, looking hopelessly at Neetriht.

Taramat silently mouths to Neetriht, "What do we do now?" Neetriht shook her head and sat down next to them.

"Listen, Abaddon. We will help you. But you are going to have to play a role until we can figure this out and come up with a plan, understand? He will kill you if he thinks you will defy him in front of the tribes. He will kill all three of us. And my grandmother," she added as she analyzed the situation.

"Can you play along until we come up with a solution either to get him to change his mind about taking slaves or until we come up with a way to get you away safely? For all three of our sakes, can you try?" Taramat lifted the pale chin to look into the ice-blue eyes.

"I would do anything to help the two of you," Abaddon said.

Neetriht breathed a sigh of relief, surprised when tears sprang to her own eyes. "Thank you, Abaddon. Thank you," she squeezed the albino's hand in gratitude. "My grandmother thanks you as well."

Abaddon gave Neetriht a quizzical look, and Taramat said, "We'll explain about her grandmother later. Now, here's what you need to do. There is no room for mistakes." The three Gugwe females quickly discussed their strategy before they left the smoking remains of the human settlement behind. Hurrying, they needed to catch up to the others for the trip back to Thrall Lake.

WHEN THE 13/31, BORTA'S troop and special forces arrived back at Thrall Lake, it surprised Akama to find Vigga waiting.

Thana NukPana clasped his huge hand on Vigga's shoulder. "Ah, Vigga. Have you brought me a prize already?" He laughed, excited to confront the Goblin Quean. Who better to take his frustrations out on?

Vigga twisted, hoping to distance himself from the emperor, but Akama gripped him in place. "I, ah..." he swallowed hard, "I have some bad news, my emperor."

"Don't make me wait for your report, War Chief," the Thana squeezed harder.

"When we reached Vutova, Thana NukPana, your kin, said they had seen the goblin camp south of the village. But the gobs had packed up camp in the night and disappeared two days before our arrival. The Quean bitch is gone. I questioned everyone, but no one saw which direction they went. I thought it best to return as soon as possible to let you know."

"You disappoint me, Vigga BloodKnife," Thana NukPana said in a flat tone.

Akama spoke the words to take control of Vigga's mind. Once he had gripped his soul, the emperor pushed him to the ground and commanded, "You are a worthless worm, Vigga BloodKnife. Get down at my feet and slither like the worm that you are."

Vigga's eyes rolled back in his head. With his arms plastered to his sides, slithered around in the dirt. The revered BloodKnife war chief, brought low before all. Thana walked away, leaving the once great Gugwe to slobber, his tongue hanging out. Dirt streaked his face; everyone moved to escape from the aberration who had once been a feared leader among them.

Chapter 16: Good Luck Talisman

Garrett provided his description of the Gugwe raid to Robin, Caz, and Val. Faith stood rubbing his back, empathizing with the fact that he had to re-live the gruesome attack.

Caz let loose a low, slow whistle. "So Lennox was right. That's how the Gugwe get so close or into a village without being detected. They're bloody shifters. Not only that, but they can shift into two different forms: goblin or human. Maybe others, for all we know." Caz leans toward Garrett. "Sorry, mate. I didn't mean any offence by that, yeah?"

"Let's not forget about their ability to use mind control," Robin reminded the team. "Val, can you make sure everyone is practicing the blocking techniques daily that Garrett taught us?"

"They are, but it won't hurt to emphasize that mastering the mind-blocking could mean the difference between life and death."

"What could mean the difference between life and death?" Lennox asked them as he walked up to the group.

"Mind control blocking techniques," Val answers.

"I can verify that for you," Lennox said. "Not only do we do daily basic blocking, but I asked Jak and Timmon to add the blocking practice when under more pressure. They've been applying it during weapons training and exercises."

"Good thinking. I like that application," Robin complimented Faith's father.

Silence seemed to hover over the leaders.

"Did I interrupt something?"

"Not at all, Papa. We were just discussing the Gugwe's ability to shape-shift you told us about. By the way, have you seen Dedo today?" Faith asked, "I've been looking for him since yesterday, and no one seems to know where he's gone off to."

"Probably up to no good," Val mumbled under her breath. Faith shot her a look.

"Come to think of it, the nosey bugger hasn't pestered me at all for the last couple of days. He's usually a thorn in my side, if you know what I mean." Everyone gave a sign that they'd had similar experiences with the gargoyle.

"I know what you mean," Val agreed. "He's the sneakiest of sneaks."

"Thought you'd gotten beyond all that, Val?" Faith said.

"I've just been quiet about it. I'm still holding my opinion in abeyance until he's proved himself."

"Anyway," Lennox said, "I came here to tell you Rolland just arrived with another load of weaponry. He says he crossed paths with Robert on his way here, that he's leading a force of hundreds from the mid-lands."

"That's welcome news, sir," Robin smiled.

"Young Gladheart, Valvina Goodfellow, the two of you might want to come back to camp soon. It seems Rolland isn't even going to stay the night. As soon as he finishes unloading and Mistress Zeeka feeds him a hot meal and provides him a travel basket of food, he plans to head right back to Edgewood. Seems Miss Aliah has asked to go with him to see her sister, Delainey. Thought you'd like to know."

Val and Garrett locked eyes.

"Thank you, sir," Garrett said kindly. "We're done here, so we'll be along shortly. I appreciate you letting us know. Aliah's decision comes as somewhat of a surprise."

"Well then, I'll take my leave. I'm eager to see what new weaponry the talented smith has for us in this load." Lennox moved back down the trail toward the camp.

Val sat down on the other side of Garrett. "I thought you said you talked to her?"

Robin and Caz acted as if they were busy looking at the map Robin held.

"I talked to her. Guess it didn't go as well as I thought, yeah?"

The team readied themselves to get back to camp. "Oh, one more important detail I wanted to share with you." Everyone stopped in their tracks to listen to Garrett.

"What's what, mate?" Caz prompted.

"The Gugwe can shift into human or goblin form, but if you look closely, you can still tell they're Gugwe because their eyes don't change. They still have a red glow. The other detail I noticed is that they don't know about goblins having wings. Their avatars didn't have any. I guess that's because goblins have hidden their wings for so long. But when the Gugwe shift using a goblin guise, they don't produce wings, making our ability to fly a major advantage."

ROBIN, CAZ, AND GARRETT hurried down to inspect the cargo Rolland had transported. They told the big smith about their plan to move the army that had been training at Gugwe's Tears north to the Fae castle on Sapphire Peninsula. Robert's new recruits would settle in here to complete their first phase of training until spring. Robin suggested Rolland still make his deliveries at this location. They wouldn't be taking advantage of his highest and best use if he spent any more time traveling than he had to. Making weapons was what they most needed him to concentrate on. There wasn't anyone who could fill his shoes. Rolland's skills were too valuable. Caz said they would assign a second team to bring his works further north to the new base.

"Guess the lads will need to build us another wagon before the next cache is ready." The big goblin looked at Garrett. "You, ah...did you know, um..."

"Thanks for your concern, Rolland. We heard Aliah was planning on traveling back to the Edgewood with you. I think Val's with her now.

Caz caught Rolland's eye. "We'll have Robert's troops build you a new wagon. That way, when you arrive next time, no need to unload. You can just trade out for the empty one each time and you won't need to put weapon-making resources on a wagon-building job, yeah?"

"I like that idea, Cazzidy. I'll probably want to keep my horse, though. There's one last thing to show you before I head out. It's the special-order Garrett asked for."

Rolland dragged a big crate across the buckboards and cracked open the top with the crowbar he carried under the driver's seat. His meaty hands lifted a smooth board out. Caz and Robin could see it had two sharp metal blades running the length of the board.

"What's that?" Caz pointed to a kind of white spectral artfully painted on the board.

"Oh, that," Rolland laughed. "Seems Miss Delainey has some artistic talent besides her cooking skills. She asked what Garrett wanted these made for, and after I told her, she dubbed them 'ghosts'."

"Garrett? Care to enlighten the rest of us?" Faith asked as she sat on the end of the wagon, swinging her legs back and forth.

"I got the idea from Badger. First, he drew a picture for me of a small boat he and Tula had fitted with runner blades and a sail. Told me a story of how the two of them could make fast getaways if the Gugwe were hot on their trail. Then, he described a small, lightweight, missile-shaped board he attaches a pole and runs a sail up like a flag. Badger said he harnesses the wind with the sailcloth and steers the board over open water in the warmer months, using ropes connected to the sail. It even has a small rudder, like the one Rolland has put on this one, see?" Garrett flipped the board over to show them.

"What are those blades on the bottom for?" Robin pointed to the two thin steel blades Rolland had fitted along the length of the 'ghost'.

"Badger said he made his rig after observing the large boats sailed by the Gugwe. Then he adjusted the design to be a one- or two-person vessel. The idea here is similar, but on a much smaller scale. Badger told me he and Tula could really move fast, gliding on top of the water, making it easy to get away from Gugwe raiders."

"So, I don't get your new design, Garrett. If Badger had one that worked well, why change it up?" Faith ran a finger down one of the sharp edges.

His cheeks blossomed red, confidence shaken. Garrett didn't want to embarrass himself if the idea was no good, and he still didn't know if his idea would work. It was just a theory.

Rolland jumped in, recognizing Garrett's unease. "Hope you don't mind, Garrett, but DeLainey was so taken with the idea, she ran a partial test on it."

"Yeah, how? Winter hasn't set in yet."

"She said she was just testing the concept of how it would work. Anyway, she and Saffron sewed a sail. They had the lads dig an inch-deep circle and haul water up to fill the indent, and Delainey put her head together with the Dream Weaver. Ari froze the water with magic, making a kind of ice pond. As a one-person plank, it worked great. The girls were so excited about it. We've got twenty boards here for you with sails to match. Saffron and Delainey designed the sail to fit tightly over the nose of the board when you're using it. But the clever thing about the design is that when you're not using it, the sail stays over the nose and wraps over your shoulder, so you can easily carry it on your back. It's ready for a quick hookup for a getaway whenever needed. Delainey said you can just disappear like a ghost. The day after the experiment, the pond was a muddy mess, but everyone in Edgewood Village was talking about your invention." Garrett was grateful to Rolland for easing the tension.

"Would you tell Delainey and Saffron I appreciate the improvement in the design? Being able to strap it on and carry it could mean the difference between becoming a captive or getting away to fight another day, yeah?" Garrett cleared his throat, about to describe the rest of the features of his invention, when Aliah and Val walked up, carrying Aliah's pack.

"Did he tell you his secret feature?" Aliah called out. "The runners on the bottom are like skates to run on ice. Part of this war will involve frozen waterways and lakes. With Garrett's 'ghosts', you'll be able to sail across the frozen water, leaving the Gugwe to travel on foot. At least in the winter. Clever, huh?" Aliah tossed her gear in the back of the wagon, hugged Val and Faith, and stood in front of Garrett.

Mumbled excuses sent the rest of their friends scattering.

"So," Garrett said.

"Yeah, so...I decided it might be a good time to go visit Delainey for a while. Don't tell anyone, but I sketched out the design of the sail for the ghosts and sent it to Delainey last time Rolland and Saffron were here. The plan is for me to oversee the production of the sails while I'm there. It might please you to know that I had a vision of how well your invention is going to work for our soldiers, Garrett, so put your mind at ease."

"Aliah, I don't want you to go. That wasn't what I had in mind when I talked about some distance between us."

"I know. But this isn't about you, Garrett. It's something I need to do for myself. I've put a lot of thought into this. My whole life has been about looking out for my sisters, especially Val. I overcompensated as they grew older, and they started slipping away from me and out of my control this past year. Delainey is staying at Edgewood. Carlisse is off with Raven as the first Fae Ambassador. Now, Val, as Robin's sister. God, Val's a Goblin Princess! That's hard for me to wrap my head around. Anyway, I think I grabbed onto you like a lifesaver and just smothered you. I want you to know I'm sorry for that."

"Aliah..."

"Wait. Let me finish. I think the time has come for me to find out what *I* want. What direction *my* life could take? I think that's a journey I need to take on my own. I hope we'll find one another again. When we do, the chances are good that I will have found myself by then. Figured out some things. Understand?" She wiped her tears away. "You had better stay safe, Garrett Emmon Gladheart. You hear me?"

He took her hands and pulled her close, kissing her on the forehead.

THE TROOPS AT GUGWE'S Tears were packed up, ready to move the following morning. Val and Faith were out on the beach, poking at a small campfire.

"Aliah's decision to leave today surprised me," Faith said.

"Guess she's got some things to work out for herself. I envy the fact that she decided and had the courage to follow through. Sometimes I wish I could do that. I definitely have issues I need to figure out. My head feels like I'm split into distinct personalities. It's difficult figuring out who you are when you thought you were one person, only to find out you are actually someone else."

Faith fixed her with a deadpan stare.

Val covered her mouth as she realized what she'd said. "Oh. Sorry. I didn't mean to have a pity-party all alone. You're invited! I guess we both have the same enigma to figure out." Val reached out and squeezed her best friend's hand.

Faith stood, brushed off the sand, and put another log on the beach fire. "I've been thinking about what Garrett told us regarding the Gugwe Emperor's albino female and her two friends."

"What about it?"

"Well, Garrett said the butchery of the salve raid horrified the albino female. He heard snippets of the three females' conversation and described her disdain for either the attack or the taking of slaves. Maybe both."

"So?"

"Val, I'm thinking maybe we could take advantage of her empathy for people. She might be an inside path we could take advantage of. A chance to see if the diplomatic route might work, rather than the death route? If the females are against the Gugwe doing raids and taking slaves, maybe we can figure out a way to meet with her. She could have some influence over peace versus war. I don't have a plan or anything; it's just a wild thought I had. Maybe the whole Gugwe nation doesn't want the same thing their emperor does, yeah?"

"Interesting idea to consider. Definitely worth seeing if we can find out more. Give some thought to how we could set up a secret meeting with her. I wonder if a Foxfire can choose other connections?"

THEY MOVED THE ARMY from the moot location to Sapphire Peninsula in a full turn of the moon. The weather cooperated.

Tuk, Zud, and Drako had done a successful job as they'd spread the word to all the villages and communities they'd visited. Their efforts resulted in many representatives attending the moot. The three lads crossed paths with Robin at the armpit of the peninsula. They told the Goodfellow that in the future they would direct any newcomers to the northern Fae castle. Robin was pleased to hear that the lads had let anyone know who inquired; soldiering wasn't the only need in the Alliance. They assured interested parties that there would be plenty of jobs available to support the army.

The Alliance Forces adopted the name 'Gugwe's Tears' to apply to themselves as soldiers versus the name of a place, a training camp. As the army had traveled north, such a sizable force on the march attracted attention. The result was that 'Gugwe's Tears' gained new recruits along the way.

Faith's cousins, Mariella, and Kris, roped Tuk, Zud, and Drako into helping them set up tents at the base of the peninsula's arm. The pavilions would serve as a station where they welcomed newcomers. There, they could sign up and register volunteers for many necessary jobs that would contribute to the military operation.

Faith and her companions stopped dead in their tracks when they first sighted the sandstone structure. The castle was massive, and though it looked worn down and unkempt, it was still magnificent. Faith had never seen the outside that she could recall. Her only visit here comprised landing at the lowest level, arriving by using the Gargoyle travel stones and the compass to access the scrying pool her mother had enchanted.

It was easy to let the feel of the place take you in. Built into the natural rock outcroppings, Sapphire Lake surrounded the castle on three sides, a natural defense barrier. That didn't mean an attack couldn't come from the sea, but your enemy could be seen coming from a long way off. She was impressed standing on the shore. The water seemed to go on and on, with no end in sight. No land in sight, either. She held her hand above her eyes, shading them from the sun.

As they approached the castle, Faith felt relieved her father hadn't come with them. He would have been distraught to see his home's neglected condition.

Movement caught her eye. Faith spotted small clusters of people camped in squalid lean-to structures that barely offered protection from the weather or sun. She wondered if there would be more squatters inside the gates.

Robin had come up behind her. "Should we keep on, lass, or have the troops take a break?"

"Sorry, Robin. I didn't mean to hold everyone up. I got lost in the view, trying to see if I could drag up any memories."

"Any luck?"

"None. Seems odd that I wouldn't recall something about this place, but I guess I was too young, just a babe, when Papa sent me to Reatha and Robert. Anyway, in answer to your question, let's keep moving. The sooner we get there and settled in, the better. I noticed some squatters down there," she pointed. "See? Along the outer wall. Looks like rough living. We'll need to help them, yeah? Could be others inside, but we won't find out standing here."

Robin signaled Caz and the body of the Alliance Army. Gugwe's Tears, moved forward.

KRIS'S BODY FROZE, eyes glazing over. Mariella rushed to his side. When the spasm released him, he fell into a coughing fit. His sister produced a water bladder, offering a drink.

"What is it?" she asked, keeping her voice low.

"Faith. She's in danger. I need to get to her now and warn her."

"Kris, Faith has an entire army at her back."

"I know, but it's what's right in front of her she can't see."

WEARY BY THE TIME SHE reached the drawbridge, Faith wiped the sweat from her brow. She felt dirty, hungry, thirsty, and foot-sore. Still, she got a pretty good lead on the rest of the troops, in a hurry to get a first glimpse of her parents' castle. There was a dozen beggars seated along the archway across the bridge, clothes filthy, wearing little more than rags. She strode toward the trespassers, thinking about offering them a hot meal, a bath, and better clothes. Just as her left foot stepped off the bridge, pulleys creaked and the platform was being drawn up, cutting her off from the rest of her companions and the army.

The Fae Princess turned to look at the curious motion, mouth falling open. Toward the arched entry, she could see that those she had taken for beggars were armed and had risen to their feet. Wasting no time, they moved into a formation, surrounding her. She could hear Robin, Caz, Val, and Garrett screaming her name on the other side of the drawbridge. Instinctively, her wings snapped out.

"I'd advise you not to take flight, Princess, unless you don't mind having your pretty opalescent wings pruned from your back. Two of my cohorts have scythes at the ready."

Her eyes were wild as she took in all the goblins surrounding her. "You're making a mistake. I'm friends with the goblin people. Robin Goodfellow is traveling with me. You..."

Her adversary cut her off. "Take her. Bound her hands and those wings." He tossed a filthy burlap bag to one of his gang members. "Put that over her head and let's move out."

Faith screamed as they moved in closer. She noticed some of their eyes. These weren't all goblin thugs! She realized some were actually Gugwe in goblin form. Immediately, she threw up a mental block against any attempt to grab control of her mind. Faith dropped to the ground and scooped up two handfuls of sand. Coming up in a spin, she opened her palms, letting the gritty particles loose, hitting those red eyes. Twisting in a full circle, she gained a few precious seconds for another chance to open wings and take flight. Robin, Caz, and Val rose over the top of the drawbridge, using their own wings. Garrett was seconds behind as he forced a shift. The others had descended on Faith's would-be captors. Garrett shouted Faith's name when he cleared the bridge. Suddenly, it seemed everything moved in slow motion. The Foxfire did a nose-dive toward her, somersaulting to face her in mid-air, a dart striking him so hard in the back that it slammed his body into hers.

The shooter had blown the poison dart using a hollow bone. Then had shifted back to his Gugwe form, loosed his mind control from the goblins he had abducted to stage the kidnapping. He immediately threw the full force of his mind control power directly at the Fae Princess and the Foxfire. That energy did a boom-a-rang right back at him as they both had mental blocks locked in place. It confounded the Gugwe as he slammed his targets again and again with mind control. He failed to figure out why it wasn't working. Val flew up behind him, knocking him out cold with the butt of her quarterstaff. A favorite move Caz had taught her. Though she never could put the move to a proper test during practice, she was quite pleased to find how well the maneuver worked.

They lowered the bridge. The rest of the army filed over the drawbridge, moving into the wide meadow between the two sides of the peninsula point. Robin dispatched a unit to take control of the prisoners. There were four Gugwe, along with the goblins, that had been entranced. Faith directed that the Gugwe be taken to the castle cell block and put under heavy guard. Robin and Caz were questioning the gobs, who appeared to have been victims of mind control, but they wanted to be sure before releasing them.

Kris and Mariella arrived shortly after the chaos had turned to calm, found Val comforting Faith, Garrett sitting at her side. "Looks like the danger has passed," Kris nodded at his cousin. "You're well?" he asked.

"Thanks to Garrett." She thought for a moment, then added, "Val, Robin, and Caz, too."

"Sorry, I couldn't warn you sooner. The vision came on as soon as you stepped onto the drawbridge, but we couldn't get here fast enough. I guess the Foxfire fulfilled another part of the prophecy."

"What do you mean?" Faith tipped her head to the side.

"The prophecy has a couple of references that fit the scenario," Mariella added.

"That's right." Kris cleared his throat and spoke solemnly. "Thrice death will find you, and thrice you will cheat it. Each time, the price will claim a debt, which you shall pay in time. To gain, you must lose, and lose you shall. Those you trust are like coins with two different sides."

"So? What's your point?" Faith asked, not catching the connection.

"The Foxfire has two different sides, yeah? And..." Mariella said.

Kris finished for her. "And the Foxfire has saved you from death three times now. The first time was from Alto's arrow, the second when we lost you to the backward space, using the gargoyle's compass for travel. Now, a third time, from a Gugwe assassin's poison dart."

"Well, that is good news." Faith laced her words with sarcasm. "That means, according to the prophecy, the three potential deaths the Dream Weaver proclaimed for me have happened. Luckily, Garrett saved me three times. I should be safe in the future, right?"

"Theoretically. At least until the next death comes and you can't cheat it."

Mariella blanched. "Kris!"

"Never mind, Mariella. I get it."

"Garrett, you weren't hurt this time?"

"No. My ghost protected me."

"Your ghost?"

Garrett lifted the sail strapped across his chest and shoulder and held up his ice board. The shooter buried the dart neatly right between the metal strips.

AFTER A COLD MEAL OF cheese and jerked meat, Faith sought Garrett in one of the enormous castle halls. He was sitting cross-legged on the fireplace hearth, using the firelight to see by as he worked at digging the dart out of the board. He had already removed the fletched end with the feathers and wore that piece around his neck, pierced through and strung on a leather thong.

"To what do I owe the pleasure of your company, princess?" he said, greeting her.

"I came to thank you again."

"Promised I would always be there for you, yeah?"

She gave him a smile that he knew so well as he continued his work.

"What are you doing?"

"You'll probably think it's stupid. I figured I'd keep part of the dart for good luck. A talisman of sorts."

"Why would I think that was stupid?"

"Don't know. Guess it just seems like something we'd do when we were kids."

She laughed, opened her pouch, showed him her lucky rabbit's foot and the lucky feather she'd had since they were little.

"Guess some things never change."

"Guess not. I'm glad I've been able to keep a few things that are precious to me," she squeezed his hand. "Just make sure you clean any trace of that poison off the dart when you get it loose."

"Hey, where's our third musketeer?"

"Oh, let me think." She closed her eyes. Then casually said, "Seems like she's in the kitchen. Probably helping Zeeka."

"What do you mean, 'seems like'? Did you see her there before you found me?"

"No."

"How do you know then?"

"Oh. Um, I guess I can sense her through my ring. She has one just like mine, you know. Val told me Nursie gave it to her. The story is that my mother made them. Infused with a little magic." She waggled her eyebrows at him.

"Just a random idea, but maybe you should take this seriously and experiment with it. I thought those rings were trinkets you could pick up like the ones at the booths during the May Fair or something. I noticed your cousins wearing silver bands. Come to think of it, your aunts, too."

"There might be merit in experimenting to see what's what about them. I'll take your advice and get Val to check it out with me. She seems to enjoy experimenting with magic."

They exchanged smiles. Garrett popped the dart point out of the ghost board. "Let's go find a punch to make a hole in this so I can string it with the fletchings." The two of them left in search of the tool he needed, firelight casting dancing shadows across the rock walls.

Chapter 17: Silence is the only Response

Lancer observed the BloodKnife village for a full day, hidden in an abandoned barn that seemed to have been a dumping ground at one time for the locals. The junk in the dilapidated building provided excellent cover in case anyone poked their head in. He'd arranged a reasonably comfortable spot up in the loft. From there, he could look through a large crack between boards, giving him a bird's-eye view straight down the main track through the village proper.

First, he saw morning lights, candles, or lamps that shone out from small openings in the village hut walls. Shortly after, smoke rose from cook fires, the night's coals rekindled to morning flames. The males gathered early morning, then moved west as a group along the extended arm of the water, where he knew the mines to be located. He'd worked inside them for years.

Not long after the males had set out, several BloodKnife females gathered in the center of the village. There, a natural spring ran free. Most carried baskets filled with cookware and bladders. They stood in small clusters, sharing gossip as they used the spring to wash containers and cooking utensils. A few ducked under the cold-water flow and rubbed their bodies vigorously, then held up water bladders to fill them. When the work was done, they moved off into small groups. Some went to the meadow. Others hunted along the wooded edges to gather plants, herbs, edible, and medicinal mushrooms, and, if they could find them, to dig tubers. At dusk, the males returned. The females had been cooking for a good hour before taking food from their caches to add to their cooking bags hung above their fires.

On the second day of reconnaissance, Lancer watched the pattern from the day before repeat itself. The men had gone to the mines. He made a quick decision to make his move while the women were engaged in daily chores. He reasoned this place was likely the BloodKnife's summer camp, based on the flimsy construction of the living spaces.

Lancer Ian Goodfellow had taken some time to camouflage himself. Moving at incredible speed, he went from hut to hut. In the first, he took a large blanket made from a caribou hide. He placed it by the bushes near the abandoned shack he was using as his base. Then, he hit two consecutive huts. One little more than a lean-to with a roof barely large enough to cover the owner's treasures. He collected two additional water bladders, some sinew, a needle, and an awl. Each time he came out with booty, he took the goods and laid them inside the blanket. The last four dwellings provided some herbs he found hanging upside down in bouquets from the rafters to dry. In addition, he collected two bunches of wild onions, a woman's knife, another recently scraped large caribou skin that was stretched on a rack. It looked as though the hide had been drying for some time.

From time to time, he checked to make sure the women were still intent on their work at the village spring. His heart thundered when one of them came around the corner, then moved to the other side of the track and loped up the hill. He could see that she was checking a trapline. That close call was all the incentive he needed to fold up the hide with its contents. With sinew straps, he secured the contents closed. The straps also provided loops he could slip his arms through to carry his haul like a pack.

The Goblin King moved at a speed indiscernible to the human eye. He stashed his pack at the base of the trail that led up to the ridge, his hideout near the prison caves a good hour's walk away. Before he returned, Lancer had one more chore to complete. He didn't want the pack with him while he did it, afraid it would slow him down should he need to escape quickly. The sun was on its afternoon descent. He felt his anxiety increase as time was running out. Soon the females would come to the food caches to get meat or fish to begin the evening meal. He planned to be long gone before then.

Luck was with him. Climbing up the wooden rungs of the ladder attached to the first cache he checked, he couldn't believe it was almost full. This cache must belong to one of the best hunters in the tribe. He wasn't greedy. There was always the possibility of coming back for more. Better to take a small amount and rearrange things, so the theft wasn't as noticeable. He ensconced four dried fish and two bricks of smoked meat, placing them in a woven net bag he'd taken from one hut earlier. Gingerly, he scrambled down, muscles still shaky from years of abuse and malnutrition.

Doing a quick sweep with his eyes, he made sure he had a clear route of escape, making all haste to the trailhead where he had left his pack of stolen goods. As Lancer trudged back to his root cellar, his mind raced. He'd visited the mine the day before, scrounged up the tools and things he'd needed from there to assist him with the rescue. Aleta said it wasn't likely she'd be able to walk, much less fly, when he came for her. He hoped his own strength wouldn't fail them both. The idea of becoming Borta's prisoner again almost brought on a full-blown panic attack. Now that he had a means of feeding Aleta and clothing her, he gave some thought to the need to bathe her. She probably had wounds or some sort of sickness, like most of the Gugwe prisoners. If she didn't survive, he would at least make sure she died with dignity. He would want someone to do that for him.

Tears leaked down his rough cheeks. Rupert flashed before his mind's eye. He had to stop for a moment so that he could clear his vision. It would be foolish to trip and fall at this stage of the game. Again, fate was knocking on the door. If he had not stopped at that very moment to wipe his eyes, he wouldn't have seen the bird. A small sparrow had flown out of what looked like solid rock, vines nearly covering the granite face of the prominent ridge. Lancer blinked, sure he hadn't imagined the bird. He decided it might be worthwhile to check out the mystery of the illusion. He moved off the trail toward the place he'd seen the bird exit. There was solid footing to work sideways along the base of the elevation. Maybe the bird had nested in the vines? If he were fortunate, he could steal some eggs.

When he reached what he thought was the right location, he grabbed at the vines, careful not to get his feet tangled. Shocked, Lancer found an entrance that led into a deep cave. His goblin sight, though not as good as it once was, allowed him to see the vacant den, even in that deep darkness. As he explored further in, he detected the sound of water. He lifted his pack off and set it down. With all the water bladders slung around his neck, his thirst was a focus as he set off to find the source.

The cave looked to have had a few different occupants over the years, but none any time recently. There was a natural inner spring that emptied into a bowl-shaped rock, smoothed from hundreds of years of the water's eroding power. He swiped his hand beneath the water and tasted; found it sweet and clean. That decided him. This was the perfect hideout. Once he rescued Aleta, he would first take her to the root cellar until the search parties stopped looking. Then, when the heat was off, he could move her here. The cave—well concealed—had an excellent water source. He reasoned it to be far enough away not to be detected by those who operated the Gugwe prison. Still close enough to the tribal village that he could ghost in when necessary to replenish supplies and food. This was a place they could stay until Aleta was well enough to travel.

Pleased with his find, decision made, Lancer made quick work of opening the pack, sorting through his booty. He stacked the items he would leave here, only lugging what was necessary for the few days that they would need to lie low in the root cellar. He left with a lighter load and an easier heart. Now, if only his luck held, he would make his move to rescue Aleta the following night.

THE MOON WAS WAXING. A shimmering sliver gave Lancer some additional light to see. The moonlight made just enough shadows to let him slip between them as he made his way to the prison's arched entry. There was a steady wind rattling tree branches, giving leaves flight to dance across the ground. His nerves taunt, muscles tight, as he worked at keeping his fear of recapture out of his mind. A small amount of fear could keep a man alive. Too much fear would paralyze a man. His jaw grinding, determined to finish the task he'd set himself, he reached the arch and stood struggling to hear over the wind. He went in, then realized there were two guards, their shadowed outlines preceding them across the cave walls where the torches were still lit. Lancer tore away to hide, heart thundering in his chest.

Keeping his breathing quiet, he watched as the guards went to a wagon parked alongside the cave opening. The sentries were twice his size. Lancer watched as they reached into the back, dragged a heavy object across the wooden bed. Each of the watchmen took hold of a handle on both sides of the object. Working together, they carried the load inside and on down the long cavern that led to the guards' quarters. He could hear liquid swishing in the wooden container they held between them, figured it was likely a fresh supply of sour mash. He hoped that would keep them busy for a while.

Lancer thought he was moving in complete silence, but when he rounded the corner into Aleta's cell, she hissed out, "Who's there?"

The big goblin shushed her, told her it was him, rattled off his name, ordering her to keep quiet as he worked his way over to her. The way they tied her up over the water would not allow him a simple job to get her down. Putting negative thinking aside, he bent to his work. There was a series of spike-driven holes that miners had made years and years before, when this prison had first been a mine. He hung chains around his neck like strings of shells the women sometimes wore, pulled on the hard leather boots that he'd stolen. Specially made for the miners, they fixed the boots with spikes along the edge of the toes. He had a worker's apron on; the front pouch filled with spikes. Using leather strips, Lancer had tightly wrapped them around the spikes the night before. It would make them easier to grip and hold. Lancer climbed along the wall like a spider, placing the hand-held miner's spikes and toe spikes in the holes to hasten his body over the water.

When he reached her, she whispered, "Oh, Lancer, you came. I thought I had only dreamed of you."

"I'm here. Silence now, lass. We'll have plenty of time to talk about it all later." She nodded. He could see the shimmer of unshed tears in her eyes.

Next, he hooked one end of his chain to the biggest pulley that was attached to the wall behind her. Unwrapping a few loops from his neck, he patiently went about connecting those lengths to the chain on the pulley. He used links from his pocket and a pincer tool to close them. He dropped one link, cursing. They both heard it splash into the water below. He held his breath for a tense moment, but after hearing nothing, turned back to the job.

"Lancer..." Aleta said softly.

"Stay quiet," he warned.

"There's something moving in the water below."

The Goblin King looked down to see a large shadow gliding in the pool beneath them. His panic ticked up. Still, he stayed focused on his plan, continued hooking all the chains together. Once that was complete, he connected another pulley, which he locked in place. Using the spike holes as before, he slowly made his way across the hall, keeping a close eye on the pool's inhabitant. Finally, his left foot touched the rock floor. He had made it back without disturbing the water again and heaved a sigh of relief. Moving to a huge stalagmite, Lancer looped the end of the chain he'd attached to his belt around it, securing it to the tackle he'd left waiting there.

"Aleta," he called in a quiet, soothing tone, "you need to let your muscles go limp, let your body weight fall. I've got you."

"What? Lancer, I can't. I'm afraid I'll fall into the pool. My muscles will tear. I've been strung out like this for too long."

"Trust me. I won't let you fall. I promise."

Aleta Dawn Stargazer cast off her fear, letting her muscles relax. She almost passed out when her body weight fell, jerking on the chains, her whole body swinging forward as the chains ripped through the pulley. Her silver ring slipped off her finger, dropping into the pool below. It was a noisy process. Lancer used its end of the chain for leverage, winding it up with the second pulley. Leverage fortified by the stalagmite, Aleta's spread-eagled body swung down, over and across the pond. Her limp body ended up swinging gently back and forth at the edge of the water, where he could reach her. Hanging mere inches from the surface, Aleta found herself eye to eye with a fat, pale, wormlike creature, bulbous orbs that looked blind. The thing must have come from a deep place. She couldn't get any sense of how long the thing's body was from this angle.

"Lancer? Do hurry, won't you? I think there's something here that has probably been dreaming of eating me for some time now."

The king looked down after he secured the chain in place, horrified at the size of the water creature. At least the part that he could see, the dark water hiding the rest of the body. Bloody hell, he thought, he didn't even have a decent weapon to fight it with, only the women's knife at his belt and the pincers he'd used on the chain links. Locking his eyes with the giant worm's rheumy pink eyes, he reached out with the pincers, grabbed hold of the chains still holding Aleta in place, and yanked her forward in one swift motion. The worm coiled and dove. Relieved to see it disappear, Lancer wondered if he had frightened it.

Holding her skeletal frame against his chest, Lancer used the pincers to remove the chains from the heavy cuffs on her wrists and ankles. The cuffs themselves would have to wait until later. He couldn't risk taking the time to cut them off now. She lay like deadweight in his arms, agonizing pain riddling through her body as her limbs reacted to being released from that torturous position. She felt dizzy, sick to her stomach. He slipped her feet and legs through loops that were attached to a harness he wore over his shoulder.

"I know you are in pain, lass, but can you hook your arms around my neck to hold tight? I've got the rest of you." She did as he asked, concentrating on holding her arms snugly around his broad shoulders, muscles quivering. She felt safe, even though she knew real safety was likely a long way off.

He'd moved to the doorway, stopped to listen, and detected the sound of a couple of guards coming along the hallway. He must have made too much noise. Hanging on tightly to his charge, he darted to the right of the opening, barely out of sight. The cavern offered little in the way of a place to hide. Two BloodKnife guards burst into the cell, past them.

The chains hanging in a jumbled mess at the edge of the water were the first thing they saw. Both Gugwe ran to the edge, grabbing hold of the chains, causing the whole contraption to come spinning off the pulley above, pummeling into the dark water. Aleta and Lancer held their breath. As the water bubbled up from below, the rock cell shook, and pieces of stone broke off from above, pelting down. The giant white-worm broke through the surface, hurling straight up fifteen feet in the air, bellowing out a screech that numbed the eardrums. Its mouth stretched wide, rows of razor teeth running in circles around the orifice. The guards were terrified, frozen to the spot. Mesmerized at the sight of that mouth as it shot downward, both men screamed as the orifice closed right over the top of one guard's head. Lancer could hear squelching, crunching noises as the giant worm bit the Gugwe's head off in one chomp, cutting off the scream of the now headless guard. The dead guard's partner scrambled back. He fell on his ass, tried to crab crawl away from the water when the worm's head shot out a second time, able to smell its prey, and took off the entire torso of his body.

Gathering his wits, Lancer raced through the doorway to escape, passed the guardroom hallway and rushed out of the entrance. Their comrades' screams had brought the other guards boiling out of the guardroom seconds later, like someone had poked a hornet's nest.

Aleta clung to Lancer's neck. The Goblin King was relying on his preternatural speed as he raced through the woods before any Gugwe even poked a head out of the prison entry. When they reached the safety of his root cellar tree, he put his back against the trunk. Ignoring the pain of his still-tender wounds, pushed, melding into the tree. He bent his knees to absorb the force of the drop and landed gently on his feet, Aleta tucked tight against his chest.

Breathing heavily, heart in his throat, Lancer held the Fae Queen close, stroked her matted hair, and whispered over and over, "You're safe now. Safe."

THE NEXT THREE DAYS were quiet and uneventful. There were regular search parties out looking for the Fae Queen, but the details of the escape were a mystery to her captors. Borta was due back soon. Realizing their fate, the guards deserted their posts one by one, sure that the escape of Borta's two prize prisoners would mean a death sentence for each of them.

FAITH, FINALLY SENSING she could sneak away with no one noticing amidst the chaos of setting up the new army camp, made her way down to the lowest level of the Fae Castle. She stood before the pool she had visited twice now to communicate with her mother. Putting her lucky feather in her hair, she tucked it behind her ear. Her hand closed tightly around her lucky rabbit's foot. She made a silent wish and sent a smooth agate skipping into the pool, calling her mother's name softly.

She gave up after waiting for two hours. Silence was the only response. Carefully, she tucked her childhood treasures back into her pouch, retraced her steps back up to the castle-proper, in search of a place to sleep. Exhaustion overtaking her, a final thought floated through her mind before sleep cradled her in its arms. She wondered what it meant that her mother hadn't responded to her at the enchanted pool.

Chapter 18: Not So Stupid After All

Morveena was in a foul mood as the troop moved stealthily to return to the BloodKnife prison. Her anger found its way out through her mouth. Unfortunately for Rupert, he was the closest target for her stinging barbs. The goblin prince endured her belittlement and insults in silence, but his mind raged against her callousness.

She reminded him over and over that he was a weakling, a fool who would be nothing if not for her. Recanting his stupidity became a boring chaunt, and he tried to shut her cutting tongue out, instead allowing his mind to retreat and hide in his own quiet place. A practice he'd perfected since he was a boy.

Rupert Gregor Goodfellow recalled his childhood, the gentle touch of his mother, Alora, though he had lost the memory of her face. He recalled his father laughing often in those days. Lancer had been patient with him as a boy while his mother was alive. He reminisced about the first time the goblin emissary had visited his father. The ambassador had brought his daughter, Morveena Morgan Montestrell. Rupert recalled how kind she had been to him as a boy. His mother had been pregnant with Robin. Rupert worried about how the new baby would take his place, though his mother reassured him often that they loved him. She told him how wonderful it would be for him to have a brother or sister.

Then, before he'd found out if his mother's words were true, she had died giving birth to his brother. He had known even then that Robin wasn't to blame. Rupert had even felt sad that his baby brother would never know the love of their mother. Still, he blamed Robin for her death, his loss. Even worse, their father could find no room in his heart for anything but sorrow, stricken with grief over the loss of his wife. After Alora died, Lancer spent his days and nights like a dead man. The king was barely aware of the Montestrell girl, who had stepped in and taken over the care of the two princelings.

Rupert, being older, became close to Morveena, craving attention. He didn't bother to hide his feelings toward the new child. He viewed the baby,

Robin, as something that ate away at the time Morveena could spend with him. She noted how he felt; he thought with resentment. It took him years to recognize that those were the kinds of things she looked for in the world. Once she discovered them, she calculated how she could best use them against people. Morveena used Rupert's anger and insecurity as a tool. She did not encourage Rupert to love and care for Robin, or to help build a bond between them. Her goal had been to drive a wedge between the Goodfellow brothers. Simply because a wedge would serve her best.

"It wouldn't be right for you to hurt the baby because he caused the loss of your mother. But because I love you," she told Rupert, stroking his hair. "I can help you get back at him, a sort of revenge for what you lost." Morveena would wink, then whispered, "Would you like me to do that for you?" She never waited for his answer. Suddenly, she would viciously pinch the baby four or five times, causing him to wail. Turning her back on the infant, she would pull Rupert into her lap, gifting him a smile and a gentle embrace. Acting as though they were in cahoots together when causing the child pain. Morveena had an uncanny sixth sense that forewarned her when someone was coming, Rupert recalled. In seconds, she would untangle Rupert's arms from around her neck, take up the baby so the castle staff would only see her lovingly trying to calm the squalling child. Easy lies escaped her lips, professing no knowledge of the cruel treatment that caused the babe's distress.

A short while after she had somehow seduced his father, Lancer married Montestrell's cruel daughter. It was then Rupert saw her delight in sharing out abuse equally between the princelings. Robin was no longer the only target. As her callous streak developed, the Goblin Queen promised Rupert rewards. A pattern developed. She showered him with affection if he pleased her by performing some base behavior or cruel acts she suggested.

Rupert's mind lingered on Robin. No matter how badly Rupert treated his brother as they grew up, his younger sibling always offered him kind words or a hand to help. Rupert shunned it more often than not. As the Robin grew, he used humor and jokes as a kind of armor against the unkindnesses done to him. Robin sought laughter in his jests to offset his sadness. Over time, he became best friends with Cazzidy Beaumont Touchstone. It wasn't long before they were inseparable, like brothers, which became another thorn in Rupert's side. His jealousy ate him from the inside out. He should have reached out to his brother, cultivating the relationship he desired between them. Envy of Robin and Caz's closeness only made the hate inside him fester. Yes, Rupert knew deep down that Robin wasn't responsible for their mother's death. But with the help of his evil stepmother, he cultivated his hatred for so many years that now it had become like a living thing inside him. Morveena had nurtured that inner fire every chance she had.

When their father disappeared, she turned her eye to him, promising that they could eventually rule together. The Queen Regent took Rupert into her bed. He wondered now how she would try to get rid of him once she had her natural-born daughter, his half-sister, in hand. Someone new to sculpt and mold beneath her evil ministrations. Was his sister, Valvina Ariana Goodfellow, like her mother or more like their father? He finally allowed himself to acknowledge that Morveena would never deliver on her promise to make him king. Still, he didn't want his sister to endure what he and Robin had. Valvina would only become Morveena's doppelgänger if he allowed that to happen.

It surprised Rupert to discover that he still felt a deep love for his father when he had gone back to free him from the Gugwe prison. Looking back on it, his anger had seemed childish when Lancer had asked him about his brother. Any parent would have done the same.

Ruminating on the past, Rupert thought it unlikely he could ever make things right between himself and Robin. But he resolved to let his brother know their father lived. That would be his mission before Morveena struck him down. There was no question in his mind that she would. The only question was when? Until then, Rupert would need to exercise extreme care, ever wary of rousing her suspicions, guarding the fact that his feelings had changed. That his mind had woken to her true intentions. The goblin princeling was fairly sure she wouldn't kill him until she had her daughter in hand, at least not if he remained useful to her. That meant he would have to go along with any of her schemes until Morveena could tuck Valvina firmly at her side.

"Rupert? Did you hear me?"

"Yes, yes, of course," he replied in a sulking voice. "You were reminding me how stupid I am, yes?"

Morveena batted her eyelashes at him. "Mummy has been bad, darling. You shouldn't be the one to endure my anger. Forgive me?"

Sweat beaded on his forehead; the hackles rose on the back of his neck at her sudden change to niceness. "Always, my love," he answered carefully.

"I've been thinking. We're not very far from the prison now. I mistrust any direct contact with the Gugwe, based on what Keto and Lute reported about taking goblins as slaves. Let's make camp at the small lake we passed, just west of the BloodKnife village. The lads can set up camp, while the two of us sneak into the prison and take control of Aleta. We can work out the details of how we will use her as bait to lure that stinking Fae daughter of hers to us. Once we have the two of them, our fortune is all but secured."

"You are a genius, my queen. Tell me how I can serve you?"

She smiled coyly at his acquiescence, reminding herself to be kinder to him until she could reunite with Valvina. Might as well make use of Lancer's spawn until then, but she would suffer him no longer once she was able to groom her own flesh and blood to rule in her stead. Of course, it would be years before Morveena would give up her power to rule. After all, she would need to remain Queen Regent until she could train her daughter properly.

A few hours later, they gave the lads orders to make camp. The Goblin Queen and prince left, traveling with goblin speed to reach the outskirts of the Gugwe prison. The two royals would have turned back immediately had they known. As soon as they left on their mission, the lads kept only what they needed to travel. They wasted no time in abandoning camp, deserting the evil pair while they had the chance.

Rupert was careful to pretend he did not know the prison's location, letting her take the lead. His gut ached at the thought of what her reaction would be when she found his father had escaped. At least she would be likely to take her anger out on the Fae Queen, rather than on him.

Morveena led him to a rocky outcropping a quarter mile from the entrance and bade him wait for her there while she did some reconnaissance. Rupert watched in silence as she laid aside Narrol's cane. She slashed her thigh, preserved enough of her blood to put the markings on her face and recite her spell. Then, she packed the cut with moss, tied a thick strip of material over the wound to stop the bleeding. He felt a revulsion as she shifted to her Picidae form, gave his hand a peck hard enough to draw blood, her beady eyes dancing with mischief, and took flight.

She found the prison entrance a beehive of activity. Though Morveena didn't like the disruption, it gave her the opportunity to glide silently into the cave under night's cover. Landing on a natural rock shelf inside the main hall, she watched. Guards were scrambling to-and-fro, three were on their knees before Borta, their KuRuk. The trio had their hands tied behind them, heads bent down. She could smell the metallic tang of blood that issued from their backs, a gory mass of sliced flesh from a whipping. She cocked her head to listen as Borta ranted and raved, screaming curses at his prison keepers.

"You worthless dogs! You will pay by taking all the beatings meant for my favorite goblin prisoner that you allowed to escape. Your idiocy is astounding! After such a breach occurred, you did absolutely nothing to increase security? Because of maladroit bungling, upon my return, I find the Fae Queen has also slipped away!" Borta's rage kindled anew. He was so intent on resuming his lashings on the victims kneeling before him, he didn't notice the shadows cast on the walls by the woodpecker's wings. Morveena flew close to the top of the cavern ceiling and down the long hallway to where she had last spoken to the Fae witch.

Arriving at Aleta's cell, she found the pulleys and chains were in a heap near the edge of the pool, two rotting, headless corpses stinking nearby. Fury rode across her features. Her first thought was to visit death on the Gugwe KuRuk she had paid all these years to keep the two missing prisoners for her, but a cooler head prevailed. It was more likely in this domain that she would become the KuRuk's focus based on the emperor's decree that *they could take any race* as slaves, even goblins. She would give him no coin to buy the good graces of the Gugwe Emperor by turning her over to him as a prisoner. Morveena trembled with the effort of reining in her anger and swooped out of the prison. It kindled her fury hotter when she found Rupert sulking like a child where she had left him.

Surveying the scene from above, she could see the contents of her pack lying in a pile on the ground. Incredulous at his breach of her privacy, she gaped at finding him reading her most beloved book, 'Blood Magic and the Spells to Defeat Your Foes'. He had it turned sideways, reading the notes she'd written in the margins. That sent her over the edge. Heedless of how close they were to the BloodKnife cave, Morveena let out a kik-kik-kik that turned into a raging death cry. Contorting her face as she shifted, stalking toward her stepson, a madness ignited inside.

Alarmed, Rupert looked up from studying her notes and could see his death in her eyes. She stomped menacingly toward him, screaming at the top of her lungs that the Gugwe had lost the prisoners. Spittle flew from the corners of her mouth, shrieking that Aleta had escaped. Her face had turned blotchy red. His peril became clear as the red-headed she-devil spewed the news that Lancer had disappeared as well. She no longer cared Rupert would know his father had been a prisoner as well.

"Lancer? A prisoner here?" he growled back at her.

Her fury was so great that she pulled a long dagger from its sheath, raised her arm, ready to stab. Her eyes opened wide in astonishment. Stunned, she watched Rupert slash his palm open with his own knife, blood spattering across her face. He cocked his head at her, took Narrol's cane in hand, allowing his blood to run down the length of it. Releasing his hold, thrusting the oak stick toward her yelled a command: "BLUDGEON!"

She dropped like a stone when the thick, wooden cane cracked her head open. Rupert Goodfellow watched in horror, blood running freely from his sliced palm, as the walking stick continued to bash in the queen's skull. Almost as if her blood couldn't quench the magic's thirst until there was nothing left but a bloody pile of pulp. He heard voices in the distance, bringing him out of his trance and back to himself. He whispered, "Stop." The cane clattered to the ground.

Morveena's face was unrecognizable. He could summon no feelings of sorrow as he looked at the bloody mess heaped on the ground. There was only relief at the end of a long nightmare. "See, Morveena," he spoke to her corpse. "I listened and learned from you. Took stock of your precious, selfish wisdom. Guess I'm...not so stupid after all, yes?"

The sound of voices moving closer roused him to action. He grabbed both their packs, stuffing the little book into one, and disappeared into the woods before the Gugwe saw him. The only trace left that he had been there was the dead body of the Goblin Queen, along with the murder weapon used to end her wicked reign.

Chapter 19: Guardian Angels

Repairs to the castle took up most of the Alliance Army's days while the weather held. The surrounding outer walls were patched and shored up. They constructed multiple pavilions to furnish the army with temporary roofs over their heads. Rock and timber walls soon followed to provide the Alliance force with barracks, though it wasn't in the preliminary plan. Winters on the peninsula could be hard. Luckily, Brittany had battered Lehto with her curious questions all day, every day. She discovered that several of the lads had years of experience in construction. A few were even skilled in fireplace masonry, able to create grand hearths and chimneys. Faith congratulated her cousin on having unearthed this great resource. She rewarded Brittany with the honor of also being in charge of the construction oversight. Faith assigned her cousin the responsibility of deciding whether to repair or undertake new construction to meet the many needs of the army.

Travis and Shaun made the mistake of teasing Brittany about her success one day. That same afternoon, the two of them found themselves with their own management responsibilities. Britt put them in charge of rock crews and timber harvesting, as well as the hauling of those resources to the areas she designated. The three of them did as much as they could before heading out on a reconnaissance mission with Badger and Tula. Brittany left very specific instructions and lists in the hands of Lehto before she left.

Zeeka took over the castle's kitchens. Her power extended to the overall running of the keep. She organized cleaning crew shifts and had schedules drawn up to help with food gathering. Preparation to feed the Alliance daily meals required many hands. Caz made sure they delivered the cast-iron cookstove and properly set it up. There was a team assigned to keeping the cook well-stocked with firewood. Caz was quick to move on to other jobs, so as not to get caught up in the kitchen drama. He and Robin rounded up a band to help them build training grounds, targets, and a weapon armory. They even assisted a young metalworker in reviving the smithy. He didn't have Rolland's skills, but the man could do a fair job on repairs or making a special piece to replace broken hardware, which created a steady business. In addition, sharpening knives and other small weapons soon became a daily request for the young smith. A fletcher had three crews. His shop worked twenty-four hours in shifts, turning out arrows and stockpiling them.

Volunteers combed the woods for wild edibles, ran trap lines, and hunted. They contacted the inhabitants of many villages, recognizing the importance of taking the time to let farmers and skilled workers know of the castle rehabilitation and coming war. Word spread like wildfire. As well as the trading of useful products by the locals, it encouraged food trade, as well as the trading of useful products. The need for people who were adept in any skills of craft brought a warm welcome to both visitors and newcomers who were taking up the offer to live at the re-inhabited castle.

It pleased Robin when a few of the barracks were finished. The first occupants weren't separated by race, but a mix of goblins, Fae, and humans took up residence. There were others, of course—selkies, gargoyles, sprites, and nixies—just fewer in the overall census.

Training groups were organized according to the level of experience, strength, and skill. Those who ranked highest found themselves immediately recruited to act as mentors to help with daily teaching and combat drills. The rule they had established was that at least three leaders had to sign off before a soldier could move up to the next level. If they discovered a person had a particular specialty or superior skill with a certain weapon or type of knowledge, like tracking or map reading or healing, they took those individuals out of basic maneuvers. Then, pressed them into bringing others along who shared the same proclivity.

Val loved flying more than anything. She was a natural at getting the goblins, who'd hidden the ability for so long, to reveal their wings ("I'll show you mine if you show me yours."). From there, she moved them to flying lessons. She also had a knack for figuring out how the gift of flight could be used to their advantage. Val recognized each person had a certain style when winging it. Body shapes and sizes created a divergence from the basic winged maneuvers. The goblin princess developed different tricks and tactics that they could use from above. She formed specialized forces to employ the drills she imposed. Caz was always happy to do demonstrations with her. Their camaraderie also served as an example that the ability to fly was no longer taboo for the goblins. Old, ingrained habits were hard to dispel. They encouraged Robin to be seen flying as often as possible to help destroy the stigma that lingered with the use of wings.

Robin and Faith were flying one afternoon down the length of the Sapphire Peninsula. Many on the ground below pointed up at the Fae and Goblin as they passed overhead. Robin's keen eyes spotted a large group of lads walking along the road that led to what was now called Alliance Castle. He shouted to Faith, "I think I recognize those lads! They're a long way from where I would expect them to be. Let's go down and see what's what."

They circled around, landing smoothly twenty yards in front of the ragtag group. Most of the lad's jaws hung open in surprise. Seeing the Goblin Prince, the very person they were on their way to find, had been flying. They tried to overcome their disbelief that Robin himself was openly defying a long-standing law to keep their wings a secret. Something they'd been shamed into doing as youths.

Robin strode up to where the company had stopped. The lads could see his companion was the same Fae princess who had been a prisoner of Morveena's in their camp last year. Raven and some of their mates had helped the two of them escape. Many wished they had gone with them back then. Robin called out a greeting, acknowledging several of the lads by name. He clapped Keto on the shoulder, reached out to Lute, grasping his forearm in welcome.

"This is a surprise, Lute. Must be quite a story you have to tell to find you all here, headed to Alliance Castle, yeah? Care to share it with me? You don't have my brother or my stepmother hidden in the center there, do you?" Robin rose on his tip-toes, pretending to look, and the gang laughed.

The forty lads dropped their packs, sat on them, resting. Faith greeted the lads and waved. Keto scratched his head, not sure where to start, but Lute, who'd been close with Robin in their military training, spoke up, saving Keto the trouble.

"Robin, no point in mincing words. We deserted. All of us. The queen was more and more irrational with every day that passed. Prince Rupert appears to be doing a slow burn over her treatment of him. Of the two, a major explosion was about to happen. It was likely to get all of us killed. The queen sent me and Keto to spy on a big Gugwe assembly. From what we could gather, this was the first time their emperor had ever brought representatives together from all 13 tribes. We reported back to the queen that the Gugwe have a plan to attack Sharas, conquer and take slaves next spring. She completely lost control when we disclosed the emperor included taking goblins into bondage as well. Whatever power she thought she had among the Gugwe has turned out to be less than dust. I earned a good beating for that honesty, I can tell you."

"We both did," Keto added. "After that, we were careful and talked quietly among ourselves," he nodded at the entire troop. "Decided it was time to stop serving that evil wit...oh, sorry, Robin. Anyway, our plan was to find you. Hoping you would take up the leadership of the gobs. See?" All the lads nodded, affirming Keto's plan.

"Have the laws changed, Robin? The last blow I took to my head from that woman must have scrambled my brain. Seeing you display your wings, riding the wind currents. I always wanted to do that myself," Lute admitted. Murmurs, confessions, and small comments moved through the company like a wave.

"A lot of things have changed, Lute. Not necessarily by my hand, yeah? You remember Faith? The Fae princess held prisoner in Morveena's camp?" Forty heads bobbed up and down. A few who wore hats tipped them to Faith in acknowledgement.

"You can get all the details later, but Faith here is the leader of the Alliance Army. We've banded together. Uniting is the only way we'll have any kind of chance when the Gugwe invade and it comes time to fight. The castle out at the point of Sapphire Peninsula," he pointed behind him, "is our base. We're running an active training camp. You lads will be welcome with all your experience."

Keto pulled his cap off, stepped forward, and spoke directly to Faith. "We all thought you brave, lass, the way you stood up to the queen. I have some news you should know about, I think. Queen Morveena and Rupert hatched a plan to go to the Gugwe prison north of Thrall Lake. That's where she'd met up with the BloodKnife KuRuk before the 13 tribes of Beastmen convened. As soon as the two of them left on their mission, we took advantage of the opportunity to desert and make our getaway. Before they left, we overheard her scheme as she told it to Rupert." He swallowed hard, looked around at his companions, his confidence shaky.

Lute poked him in the arm. "Go on then, finish telling her."

Faith looked at Robin, who shrugged his shoulders.

Keto turned his cap around in circles between his two hands, the action meant to keep his nerves in check. "We heard her tell Rupert they would sneak a prisoner out from under the Gugwe's noses. Once they had her, they planned to use the inmate as bait to lure you in and capture you again. The queen was madder than a wet hornet when you and Robin escaped. Anyway, she plans to use the prisoner to get you."

"Did you hear her say just who this prisoner is?" Faith asked softly.

Keto looked at Lute, and Lute answered the Fae Princess's question. "The prisoner is Aleta Dawn Stargazer, your mother."

The two goblin lads quickly stepped back, flinched, expecting her to hit them. It surprised them when she dropped to her knees. Taking one of each lad's hands in her own, squeezing gently, she said, "Thank you. Thank you both for bringing me this news. You can never know how much it means to me. You've confirmed where my mother is being held captive." A smile bloomed across her face. Both goblins were left speechless.

Robin pulled her to a stand, gave the lads directions, then instructions to ask for Raven or Caz when they got to the castle. He and Faith moved off, wings snapping out, which resulted in jaws dropping open again. Robin called back, "It will please you lads to know that Zeeka is here and a home-cooked, hot meal awaits you. I'll check in on you when we return. We're headed to the volunteer stations to see how recruiting is going."

The goblin squad watched as the two leaders took a few running steps and leaped, wings working in tandem to catch a wind current.

SEVERAL WEEKS PASSED when they were hit hard with the first snow, dumping more than a foot in twelve hours. Faith had set a meeting with her core group. She'd gotten word that Badger, Tula, Travis, Shaun, and Brittany had returned from their reconnaissance into enemy territory late the night before.

Dedo had finally shown his face again two weeks before. The gargoyle was crabby and sulked whenever she pressed him to find out where he'd disappeared to for a string of days. He was snippy, gave vague answers, and then would vanish from the fireplace if she was too aggressive. Faith didn't know why, but she began keeping information from him. She deliberately excluded him from all planning and leadership meetings. Val claimed 'good riddance', having never liked the 'little spy' as she dubbed him long ago. Because her trust in him had eroded, Faith made it a habit to scan everywhere they were having a group consultation. She wanted to be sure he didn't pop in undercover once the meeting had started. Faith sent him with increased frequency to deliver messages to the kings at Stone House Camp, creating a calculable timeframe he would be out from underfoot. She provided sealed updates containing details he felt were frivolous and a waste of his time. Of course, Dedo determined this after covertly looking at the private communications. From the questions he asked her later, she knew he had been peeking at the written communiques and the information she had planted in the missives.

Faith shared the details they'd learned from more in-depth conversations that involved Keto and Lute. She wanted Badger and Tula to see how it fit together with the intel the two of them had gathered. The facts they provided confirmed that the Gugwe planned to bring warriors to Bear Ridge village at the spring equinox. Two sources were in sync, as well as matching up with what Garrett had gleaned with his Foxfire connection. Travis and Shaun had reported that the Gugwe had already arrived at Bear Ridge village. They'd done a quiet foray, close enough to allow them to see, then retreated to their own camp, south of the village. Badger had established a base at a waterfall. Brittany and Tula had done day-trips to several small settlements along one side of the river that were located upstream from the falls. Badger had covered the other communities on the opposite side, warning the residents of the coming invasion.

It had thrilled Brittany months before this mission, when Cervil had shown her the litter of pups his dog had birthed and offered her two of them. Both canines were a year old now. She had trained them well. Tula had taken to the dogs right away. It was easy to see that one yearling was becoming attached to the mute girl. She'd found her own way to communicate commands to that dog, using hand signals or little noises she made, but never words.

Badger proposed they move a significant force to the waterfall they'd discovered. He thought it made an excellent place to set up a camp base. From there, they could lead an attack against Bear Ridge Village when least expected, in winter. He pointed out that such an action could provide an opportunity for the troops to experience the methods the Gugwe used in combat. He hoped that an early strike would eliminate some of the enemy warriors who had arrived early at Bear Ridge. Important information Lennox had divulged, later confirmed by Garrett, exposed the fact that the Gugwe could shift to human or goblin forms. The implication of how that skill was likely to be used against the Alliance delivered unanimous support from the leaders. Critical training began immediately for the entire Alliance force, as well as those doing the jobs supporting the army. Everyone needed to recognize Gugwe doppelgangers. They had to spot the shifters whether they appeared in the throes of combat or on undercover sabotage missions into Alliance camps. In addition, Badger argued, it would give the military experience fighting the Gugwe in a smaller force *before* all the warriors from 13 tribes convened.

Caz suggested they sleep on the decision. Faith had been keen on heading into Gugwe territory to search for her mother, based on the information that Lute and Keto had delivered. So far, Garrett, Robin, and Caz had deterred her. Caz didn't want the decision based on a military operation to be influenced by Faith's natural wish to rescue her mother. And certainly not a decision based only on a sliver of an overheard conversation about the long-missing Fae queen. He mulled over the words he planned to say to her on the subject, searching for just the right ones, so as not to kill the hopes she clung to.

VAL FOUND FAITH ALONE on the beach at Sapphire Point, the sun shining, making the water shimmer as far as she could see. "Mind if I join you?"

Faith patted the ground next to her. Val sat. "How did you find me?" Faith asked.

Val pointed to Faith's silver ring. "Haven't you noticed that you always feel a sense of where I am through your ring? I think your mother was working on a replacement for the old nurse when she made these rings," she laughed.

Faith looked down at Val's hand, but didn't see the silver band displayed. "But you don't have yours on, so how could it work for you?"

"That's what I wanted to talk to you about," Val admitted. "I have it on. I just put a glamour on it, so it can't be seen. Out of sight, out of mind."

"A glamour? Where did you learn to do that?"

"Seems my oldest sister, along with her misplaced secrets and overprotective nature, had some minor talents. I played the guilt card. Aliah shared some before heading back to Stone House Camp. I wanted to show you how to hide your ring in plain sight, so no one can steal it from you, and we'll always have a way to find one another."

"Oh," Faith smiled, "I'd love to learn a new skill."

"Um...I wouldn't describe it as a skill exactly, more like a party trick."

After the two friends had mastered the knack of hiding the rings, then making them reappear and again hiding them, Faith sat back. With her arms extended behind her, legs stretched out in front, she watched the waves roll onto the shore. "I think we should covertly practice finding one another every day, but not let anyone else know what we're doing."

"You mean don't let Dedo know, right?"

"Well, Dedo in particular, but really, just something special between the two of us and no one else. Of course, Nursie knows, likely my aunts, but I mean no one else in the Alliance. When practicing, we should try to make it difficult. Check out different scenarios, like what happens if we wear gloves or if one of us isn't wearing a ring. What do you think?"

"I think practice is a good idea. It will give us a stronger sense of recognizing when we can sense each other. Our thoughts and feelings could be fine-tuned related to the ring, but I don't like the idea of ever taking the rings off." Val dug into her pocket and pulled out a small pouch, opened it, and emptied the contents into her palm. Faith could see two long silver chains with sturdy clasps. Val handed one to her sister-friend. "Here, put this around your neck and wear it faithfully. Just because no one can see your ring doesn't mean someone can't feel it. Also, if you have a legitimate reason to take the ring off your finger, you can slip it on this chain and wear it around your neck instead. You should still leave it glamoured, so no one can see it?"

"What's this little charm already on the chain?" Faith asked, turning it over in her fingers.

"Oh, that was Saffron's idea. She had Rolland make them as a gift for us. If you look closely, you'll see a depiction of an angel. Red thought we should have a guardian angel with us. She didn't know I was planning on giving you the chain to keep your ring on if you had to. The angel charm is great as a decoy, so no one would wonder why you were wearing a chain with no ornament, yeah?"

"Clever, that Saffron."

Val put the chain around Faith's neck and hooked the clasp. Faith repeated the action for Val. They both dropped the guardians down the front of their tunics, so the charm hung between their breasts, near their hearts.

"I feel safer already," Faith quipped. "Oh, I just remembered. Dedo knew about the rings. He as much as admitted to me months and months ago that the ring was how Nursie could find me. Does he know she gave the ring she had to you?"

"I don't think she told anyone, but it is something to keep in mind. Another good reason to keep the ring on your person at all times, yeah? That little sneak wouldn't hesitate to stoop so low as to steal the ring if he thought he could use it to find you."

The two agreed that every day, if practical, they would avoid one another, then before the noon meal, see how quickly they could locate the other.

Chapter 20: Eat Your Stew Before It Gets Cold

Faith delayed the decision to move half of the army north, as Badger had suggested. The snow level increased, and the temperature dropped further every day she held off. Caz found her on a gloomy, gray afternoon, his intention being to inquire whether she needed someone to bounce ideas off. He thought maybe he could entice her to go fly along Sapphire's shore, maybe out to the point. It was his opinion that the princess had holed up alone for too long. Poking his head into the turret sitting room, he found her lounging by the fire, sketching in her book.

Standing in the arched entryway, Caz observed Faith across the room, unaware he was there. She sat sideways in an overstuffed chair, one leg hanging over the arm of the seat, the other leg bent at the knee to steady her sketchbook as she penciled a drawing.

"Busy lass? I can come back later."

She dropped her book and twisted to look at him, noticing he carried a tray and that steam was rising from two mugs. "Never too busy for you, Cazzidy. Just thinking mostly. What have you got there?" she asked casually, hunger pangs coming alive.

"Mistress Zeeka says you've missed half your meals over the past week. She suggested I bring you a snack, yeah?"

"Whatever is steaming in those cups looks wonderful."

"It is chilly in here," he granted.

The Beaumont strode over, set the offering on a small table next to the chair she occupied, then dragged another chair over to join her. First, she cradled the mug between her hands, letting the warmth soak into her fingers. He pulled a cloth cover off to reveal warm bread, butter pats still melting in the center of the thick slices, a plate of sliced cheese, and two apples. Caz snatched the other plate away and grabbed the second mug of tea.

"Hey," she complained, "that looked like it might be a plate of those great cookies Zeeka makes."

"Yes, indeed," he teased. "You've got a sharp eye, lass. However, the kitchen mistress said I was to make sure you ate the other things first *before* I let you have any sweets." He took one from the plate and ate it in three bites. Caz winked at her. "I ate my meal already. Better hurry yours if you expect any dessert to be left, princess."

Caz looked down where the sketchbook had landed on the floor, let out a long, low whistle, "Not drawing cheerful things, I see."

She finished chewing a mouthful of bread and cheese, pointed at the image, "It occurred to me that most of the soldiers in the army have never seen a Gugwe. Their only perception of the Beastmen comes from words and rumors. I thought I should create a series of sketches and have the artist group reproduce them. Then, we can circulate them. I don't want anyone to think we duped them into fighting such a fierce enemy because they really didn't know what we were up against, you know?"

"Is a good idea, lass. You're very thoughtful. What's what in this drawing?" he asked, having flipped the page back.

"Tell me what you think when you look at it," she prompted.

"Well, you've got a Gugwe that appears to be drawn to scale against the size of a goblin, human, and Fae. So, I'm guessing you're trying to reveal just how huge and powerful they are, yeah?"

"Exactly. But I also want to emphasize the fact that the Gugwe can shift to one of those forms." She flipped to another page and pointed to the drawing of the eyes on the shifted forms she had drawn. "I want to be sure we teach everyone about Garrett's discovery. They need to be aware of how we can tell whether we're dealing with another goblin, human, or Fae, or if what someone sees is a false skin with a Gugwe underneath. Could save lives."

It surprised him to see her lick her fingers and dab up the rest of the cheese crumbs on the tray. She hiccuped, and they shared a laugh.

"I'm saving the apples for later, unless you want one?"

"No thanks, I'm good."

"So..."

"So? Oh, of course, you're ready for Zeeka's cookies now." He handed the plate over, and she refilled their mugs from the pot.

He waited until she'd downed two cookies, then asked, "Some of us are wondering if you've decided about Badger's suggested course of action?"

"Not yet. But I determined what steps I'll need to take to make that decision."

"What's what, lass?" he went to take another cookie, but she beat him to it, laughed, gave him a coy smile, broke it in half and handed a share back.

"Are you busy for the rest of the day, Caz?" He shook his head in the negative. "Would you go with me on a quick trip to see the Gargoyle Kings?"

"To Stone House Camp? Sure, but I thought it was dangerous for more than one person to access the compass travel, yeah?"

"I learned my lesson. I won't make that mistake again," she assured him. "We'll be back by the evening meal," she promised, reaching out a hand in invitation.

Caz took it, squeezed gently, "Let's go then."

Faith stooped to pull on her boots and strapped on her belt with all her pouches. She had decorated the thick band with thin leather thongs strung with beads and feathers that swung when she walked. She pulled Caz across the room, exclaimed to herself, then took three steps back to grab her pencil off the floor, tore a half-page of sketch paper from the book. Rolling it tightly, she put both in a soft leather bag attached to the belt. Her cheeks colored slightly. "Just in case I need to draw my way out of something," she winked at him.

When they reached a floor to ceiling bookcase, she put a finger to her lips. Faith reached into the case, pulled a book from the fourth shelf titled 'Doorways to Nowhere'. The shelves slid out from the wall to reveal a narrow stone staircase. Faith pushed the book back into place, pulled Caz into the stairway, the casing swinging closed behind them without a sound.

It was dark. Caz could see using his goblin sight. Faith just trailed her fingers along the wall, her steps sure and steady, heading down. Cazzidy lost track of how many steps they'd descended, but was conscious of the fact that the Fae princess in front of him still had a tight hold on his hand.

The further they descended, the louder the sound of the waves crashing against the agate beach outside the castle became. Reaching a long hallway that led to a massive wooden door, Faith turned the knob. The door swung open, their entrance silent, as though the hinges had received a weekly oiling. Faith and Caz moved through the archway and came to another steep flight downward. She wrinkled her nose in distaste. A faint, musty smell assaulted their noses from somewhere below.

Cazzidy could make out a shimmering light as they approached the bottom steps. Rounding the corner from the landing, they entered a room opening onto a large, flat pool of water, which Faith ignored. Instead, she was moving toward a natural stone cove. The floor depicted a compass, similar to the one she had painted on the floor of the shack at Stone House Camp.

Faith linked her arm in Caz's, stood on tiptoe and whispered in his ear, "No matter what, don't let go." She pressed her free hand to a symbol that was shaped like Ari's stone house, and the cave shimmered, disappearing around them. The space between twinkled with clusters of stars and constellations, much like the Milky Way. Their passing seemed slow-motion, which ended too quickly for Caz. A moment in time, where he had her all to himself. The orchard shack crystalized before them. Faith released his hand, took two steps forward, and knocked loudly on the door.

Lenny's head poked over the edge of the roof above them. "Oh, it's you. Lester, we've got company. Come down now."

Caz backed up a few steps to get a better view of the roof and could see Lester standing on his head on the roof peak, legs balanced against the chimney. Caz thought about flying up and offering to help, but to his surprise, both kings snapped open their own wings and gracefully glided to the ground.

"You're just in time for tea, princess," Lenny opened the door, waving them in. "Greetings, Touchstone."

It still made Cazzidy feel weird to hear the Gargoyle king's voice in his head again.

A fire was crackling behind the hearth. A pot of water hung on a hook off to the side of the flames. Faith and Lenny went through the steps of making tea and gathering cups. Lester put out a large crock of cakes. Caz looked inside the serving container, then at Lester.

"How'd you get such a selection of different biscuits, mate?"

Lester smiled, pretending to shine his fingernails on his chest. "Miss Delainey wanted to know our favorite treat. We told her that because of her amazing talent, we could not pick just one kind. You can see how that turned out." He picked his nose, licked the reward off his finger, and then rifled through the cookie selection, inviting Caz to help himself. Caz squinted his eyes and politely declined. They all took a cup of tea. Caz tried to make faces to warn Faith off Lester's contaminated biscuits, but she ignored his antics.

"To what do we owe the pleasure of your visit, Princess?" Lester asked.

"Mostly, I wanted to ask your advice."

"Mostly. Sounds ominous, don't you think, Lenny?"

Lenny could barely make a comment as a pile of crumbs collected down his front. He stuffed the sweets one after another into his mouth. Lester yanked the jar away, putting the cover back on.

"Let's start with the 'mostly' part first, hmm?" Lester suggested.

Faith locked eyes with him and asked point-blank, "Did you know about Val's real identity?"

Lester stared her down, and eventually her shoulders loosened, making her stance a little less aggressive.

Lenny swallowed the last of his mouthful and put one hand on his hip. "You seem to have picked up rude habits, princess. Likely from the very person you are asking about. Tell you what. When Mistress Valvina comes to ask us that question herself, we may dine to answer, but frankly, it is none of your business. Now, let's not waste our time or yours." He sipped his tea. "You came all this way for a secret meeting, to ask after something you should not have. So, let's move on to what exactly you were seeking advice about? We have business to get back to, mind."

She almost threw the fact at them: she didn't think standing on one's head had anything to do with business—but thought better of it. After all, it was she who introduced the concept to the kings as a way of looking at things from a different perspective. Nursie always told her you could catch more pixies with sugar than vinegar. That theory likely applied to Gargoyle Kings. So instead, she took a deep breath, relaxed and considered her approach. She started by asking Caz to describe their progress at the castle to date and ended with him relating Badger's recommendation. She listened intently as he spoke, but found no details missing in the report he gave.

"So," Lester queried when Caz finished, "you want to know if we think you should take the risk, moving half the trained army north to do in-depth recon? If I understand correctly, this would allow you to learn the terrain, choose and control where an attack of your own devising might take place?

You want to know whether risking the lives of your troops to gain knowledge and experience against the enemy under the terms of a smaller engagement is worthwhile? I bet you're also wondering if a smaller skirmish would be beneficial to your soldiers before the all-out bloodbath you're likely to face with warriors from thirteen Gugwe tribes? Is that what you're asking for advice about, Faith Lisbet Stargazer?"

Properly dressed down, her fears exposed, she near-whispered, "Yes."

Lester and Lenny looked at one another and crossed their legs. Each with a foot bouncing up and down, up and down while they held their chins on a fist, foreheads gnarled in thoughtful wrinkles. A log fell onto the fireplace irons, sending up a cluster of sparks into the flue. Time passed in silence.

Faith's discomfort grew. She fidgeted in her seat.

Lenny uncrossed his legs, put his elbows on his knees, chin cupped in his hands, his crown askew, and said, "What do *you* think you should do, Princess of them all?"

Faith had been staring at her hands while she waited for them to answer. Now, she raised her eyes to meet his again and told him in a shaky voice, "I think it is worth the risk. I think we should do it."

Caz smiled at her. The Gargoyle twins smiled at one another. Lenny looked down. He noticed a large beetle scurrying beneath his chair, plucked it up between his fingers and popped it in his mouth, followed by a satisfied crunch. Faith grimaced.

Lenny spoke up. "Our advice, Princess, is that you should follow your sixth sense, your gut feelings, your natural instincts, and trust your decisions."

Faith stood, and Caz likewise. She gave a courteous nod of her head, stepped back several paces, having taken Caz's hand again. "Give our regards to everyone at the Edgewood. Sorry, we can't stay longer, but, you know, tick-tock, tick-tock." .

The golden-haired girl reached down with her free hand to the compass she had painted in front of her and touched the mark pointing to the Fae Castle. Multicolored, glittery shimmers fell to the floor as the visitors disappeared from the king's shack.

Moving back through the gray, luminous star-filled between, Faith told Caz to open his wings as hers snapped out, still squeezing his hand. "Take three steps when we land, then let's fly!" he nodded.

They hit the invisible barrier, felt the pressure as their bodies pressed through. Caz could see they were on the beach near Sapphire Point. Feet touched down. They ran the agreed-upon three steps, counting out loud together, "One, two, three." Then, they launched into the dusky sky for no other reason than just to enjoy the freedom of flight. Like dancing, Faith would do a maneuver, and Caz would mimic her. They rode the wind currents until the sun dipped below the horizon, casting a brilliant orange-pink fire across the sky.

THEY GATHERED THE LEADERSHIP team at a long table for supper when Faith and Caz showed up. Faith broke off from her companion and went to a small group seated together that made up the artist crew. She rolled out several drawings she'd made of the Gugwe and laid out her plan. The other artists were enthusiastic about making copies of her work. They committed to having dozens ready by morning. Because of the importance, each promised to keep making replicas. They would produce these drawings in addition to the maps they were making to be distributed to all the divisions. Next time Rolland made a weapon delivery, they would send a supply of the drawings back to the Edgewood. Robert would use them to disseminate the information to the recruits he was training at the old moot camp.

When she finished her business with the artists, she went through the food line. With a hot bowl of stew and crusty bread in hand, she came to the long table, where she stopped in front of Badger. She set her food down, placed both hands flat, leaned in, bringing her face close. "We leave in three days. It's your expedition. You take the lead, decide who goes and who commands. I will go with you. Everything else is your call." Robin was sitting next to Badger and nodded his head in approval.

Badger pointed to her bowl. "Eat your stew before it gets cold, lass."

Tula put her fist to her heart as she passed in front of her to show solidarity with Faith. With the weight of deciding off her shoulders, she turned her attention to her growling stomach. The princess smiled and sat down to enjoy her meal.

Chapter 21: Caribou Tracks

Half of the Alliance army remained at the castle. Robert was sending up recruits who had completed basic training at the moot camp. They referred to the entire Alliance army as Gugwe's Tears. As the troops graduated to a higher level, they could get more specialized weapons experience at Alliance Castle. Each time a squad arrived, they delivered another load of Rolland's weapons.

Badger guided Robin, Caz, Garrett, Faith, Val, Tula, Travis, Shaun, Brittany, and Kristian with ten squads of soldiers south from the peninsula. The small force continued on around the lakeshore, then turned northwest, moving into remote lands.

Mariella had argued against Kris going, but in the end agreed when he asked her just how old she thought a person needed to be to become eligible to fight for freedom. She continued to man the volunteer stations at the base of the peninsula, recruiting two lads for additional help. More people arrived daily. Rumors came along with the new arrivals, describing recent raids, but still so far away, it seemed to be part of another world, not their own.

Badger equipped each soldier with a set of snowshoes, as well as Garrett's version of an ice board. They carried the board with the sail wrapped around the tip of the board and chest, securing it across their backs. Every soldier had a crossbow that slid neatly over the toe of the ice board, sharing the sail sling. A supply of bolts filled the quivers that were designed to be strapped to the upper thigh. Most carried quarterstaffs, using them to help move through the deep snow. It went without saying that every fighter concealed as many knives as they could keep on their person. The latest delivery from Rolland arrived just before the company moved out. Badger had found three canvas-wrapped parcels and a note from Mari, Reatha, and Evy. Inside were soft-hide ponchos, dyed and marked for winter camouflage. Badger distributed one to every male and female soldier. Last minute, baskets passed back through the ranks. The contents were soft leather pouches. The commander instructed them to attach a pouch to their belts and to keep it on their person at all times. He told them that the instructions for use would come later. Faces registered surprise. There was no time to examine the contents as the ranks moved forward.

Faith and Val consulted Kris daily, checking to see if he'd had any visions, but insight was not forthcoming. Brittany and Tula circulated the artist's renditions of Faith's Gugwe drawings. They took all the time necessary to explain the abilities the monsters had to shift. As well as how it was possible to identify one wearing a shifted doppelgänger form. Tula was becoming more confident in using dramatic hand and mime communication. Badger recognized Brittany had a positive influence on Tula. He appreciated her effective way of supporting and encouraging the mute's increasing extroverted behavior. The dog that was always at the young girl's side was another factor involved in bringing Tula out of her shell. The effect of the furred companion had done more in a few weeks than all the years he had spent with her.

Teams of six patrolled to the east and west once the company had established a camp near the falls that Badger had brought them to. Tula had developed a series of hand signals she taught the squads when they were off duty. They could use the signals to communicate with one another while out on recon without talking. Silence had saved her life more than once.

That night, the Northern Lights began a shimmery dance across the sky, flashing red, green, and milky white. Val and Faith each had an arm looped through Garrett's, huddled under a canvas lean-to that was covered in frost. They could see their breath in the cool air. Kris was just inside the drip edge when Garrett's whole body shuddered. He connected with the Gugwe emperor. Blocking already in place, Garrett looked out through the Thana's eyes. He could feel the Beastman's muscles tight with tension as another Gugwe reported to him.

"Akama, I have received word that your sister, the mapmaker, and your betrothed arrived safely with their escort to the Bear Ridge tribe's village. Neetriht said they will make preparations for your wedding to take place there at the spring equinox. She insists the event must take place in front of all 13 tribal warriors, giving a blessing of purity to our invasion into Sharas."

"Thank you, Nevele. You may go." Thana NukPana pinched the bridge of his nose as his bodyguard backed out of the tent.

Akama's eyes darted around. "Who's there?" he growled.

Garrett released himself from the connection with a shiver.

"I DON'T LIKE IT," ROBIN spoke clearly.

"Guess we know where you stand on the subject," Val retorted.

"Maybe if you took a squad with you on the mission?" Caz suggested.

"Too much noise. The bigger the cohort on this mission, the greater our risk of being caught?" Faith reasoned, raising her eyebrows. "First off, Kris has already foreseen that we would have this meeting. His vision showed us all leaving the yurt at the same time. Alive! Second, the decision is up to Badger," she told the group, reaffirming Badger's authority. "We'll follow his wishes, his orders." Faith crossed her arms and leaned back against a rocky outcropping.

Badger pointed at Tula. "You'll take point with your mutt. Get 'em in and get 'em out. The Foxfire says the albino betrothed to the emperor hates slavery?" Garrett nodded in affirmation to Badger. "If she is here with her two female companions, I will not stop the Princess from attempting to meet with her. Diplomacy always trumps war. I don't know that it will help us avoid battle, but I think it is worth a try."

"I'll go." Robin and Caz stepped forward in tandem, exchanging surprised looks with one another.

"You won't. Either of you." Badger told them. "Tula will be the point commander on this mission. She has a lot of experience sneaking in and out of Gugwe villages. Believe me, we've done it for years. Faith and Valvina will go with the Foxfire covering their backs. The rest of us," Badger turned 360, eyeing those under his command, "will form up and be staged for backup here, here and here," he said, pointing at a large map Faith had painted on the tent wall. "If the hornets come flying out of the nest after the girls kick it, we'll be ready."

They moved before the morning sun came up, circling the vast inland lake below Bear Ridge. Garrett described the yurt the Gugwe had erected at the far edge of the village perimeter. Looking over a small hillock, they spotted the cured skin-covered structure. He confirmed it as the current residence of the albino called Abaddon.

Val suggested they glamour themselves both in white, but Faith wouldn't allow it. She thought it more important to come as themselves to meet the future Gugwe Empress.

Tula signaled a halt, and her dog stopped in its tracks. She used hand signals to tell them they should remain still while she moved in closer for a look. Her dog actually belly-crawled alongside her as she moved toward the back of the structure. Garrett shifted, scanning behind them. When Tula reached the yurt's edge, she carefully worked the bottom of the sewn hides up from the frame and stuck her head inside. The three Gugwe females were sitting in the center of the lodge, sorting beads. No one else was present. Tula withdrew and began a slow crawl back, the mutt moving in sync, close to her side.

Val pointed to where her ring sat, glamoured on her finger. She slid it off and looped the silver necklace over her head. Opening the clasp, she strung the silver band on and replaced the necklace around her neck, dropping it inside her tunic. Faith nodded and repeated the process with her own ring.

Tula signed that the three females were alone inside and showed she would keep watch, while the two princesses put their plan into action. They agreed earlier that Tula would have her dog give a warning if any of the villagers approached. Tula showed them where she would wait, watching. She waved Garrett up. To his irritation, Tula patted the top of his fox head, pointed to the yurt, letting him know he was up for his role in the scheme. They had a lot riding on the bet that the Gugwe would be superstitious people.

Faith and Val held their backs to either side of the entrance to the yurt. Garrett, in Foxfire form, pushed open the flap and entered. All three female Gugwe turned to stare. The fox turned sideways and performed a slight bow as best he could with all the equipment he carried. His fur was as red as the albino's was white.

"Greetings," Garrett said. "Are you a friend to the fox or a foe?"

"Friend," Abaddon said as she pulled herself into a standing position, face reflecting her wonder.

The fox locked eyes first with Neetriht. "Friend," she declared.

He moved his gaze to Taramat. “Friend,” she held her arms open in greeting.

“I had hoped it would be so,” he confessed. “I have two other friends with me who would like to speak with you. Will you welcome them? I vouch for them. They have come in peace and wish you no harm. I promise.”

Abaddon could only nod.

“Yes, yes,” Taramat agreed, thinking two more Fox would come in.

Faith and Val slipped inside the entry flap, and all six stood staring at one another.

It was Abaddon who broke the silence. “I would have you know that there is danger here for you if your presence is discovered. Our emperor has decreed his intention to invade your lands and make all the citizens of Sharas slaves to the Gugwe. It is not safe for you to stay here.”

Neetriht stepped forward. “They’re not here to hide, Abaddon. I believe they have come because somehow they know what you have just told them. They want to talk of peace, and how we can avoid becoming slavers and how they can avoid becoming slaves. Is my assessment correct?” Her eyes questioned the guests.

“It was the Foxfire,” Abaddon pointed at Garrett. “Such creatures have the power to look out through another’s eyes.” She made a sign with her fingers against things she had no explanation for that frightened her. “My grandfather told me about the Foxfire’s gifts.”

Val held her palms open to show she was no threat. “It is our understanding that you are to marry the Gugwe emperor. Also, that you might sympathize with innocents who would be killed or enslaved. If that is true, can you convince Thana NukPana to turn away from this plan? Is there hope for peace between us, hope for our freedom?”

Taramat sadly shook her head, but it was Neetriht who spoke. “The emperor, Akama, his given name,” she explained. “He started out only with the idea of ways he could improve the lives of his people, his nation. All he wanted was to make them healthier, safer, and better educated. The idea came to him that pooling resources could make the nation stronger. Now, he is convinced that conquering your lands and enslaving your people is the natural next step to increasing the fortunes of the people.”

"Do you believe that?" Faith asked. "Don't you think that slavery will breed hate and violence? Insite uprisings? A never-ending wave of fighting and killing as slaves rebel? Your people would do the same if the tables were reversed, yes? Wouldn't we all be better off to find ways we could live in peace? Ways we can trade goods to improve each other's lives?"

"We believe as you do, but we don't have the power to change the course our leader has saddled upon us," Abaddon admits.

"Wait," Taramat said softly. "What if we look at this opportunity from a different perspective?"

"I know that look," Neetriht groaned. "What have you got in mind this time, Taramat?"

The six rebels sat down in a circle to discuss solutions. When they had hammered out a plan to take place at the equinox wedding, the guests stood to leave. Tula's dog barked three times.

"Someone is coming," Val said.

"Quickly!" Abaddon said, hurrying to the back of the yurt. "Go out this way. They must not see you."

Faith, Val, and Garrett moved swiftly as Abaddon and Taramat worked the bottom of the hide cover up over the platform. First, Faith slipped under, followed by Val. Garrett was next, but Abaddon gently grabbed the scruff on top of his neck to hold him back. "Shift. You must show us what you look like in your other form, so we will know you in that skin as well."

His eyes darted back and forth between the three Gugwe females.

"Friends," Abaddon insisted.

Garrett shifted.

"Friends," he agreed, then slipped silently under the yurt's hides to follow his oldest friends.

SOMEONE ROUGHLY PUSHED aside the front flap of the yurt with no apology. A Bear Ridge warrior surveyed the three females sorting beads on the floor. He growled, "One of our units was on the trail of a large goblin. They believe him to be the prince named Rupert Goodfellow. He passed through this village months ago with the Goblin Queen," he snarled in distaste. "Have you seen or heard anything unusual?"

"Only your rude disturbance of the sanctuary of the Thana's betrothed," Neetriht scolded him. "If you don't wish me to report your violation of Abaddon's privacy, you will go now and more respectfully than when you intruded here."

He slammed his fist onto his shoulder. "Forgiveness, KuRuk. Forgiveness, my future Empress. I forgot myself in my eagerness to capture the Goblin Princeling." He backed slowly out the door, bowing and scraping as he went.

Val and Faith huddled together just inside a patch of brush, Garrett moving a distance away, perpendicular to their path. "Wait," Val whispered behind Faith, "I forgot to leave the gift I brought for Abaddon!"

"Well, you can't go back now. Tula said, someone was coming."

"It will only take a minute. Keep going. I'll catch up."

"Fat chance," Faith told her sister-friend. "I'll wait right here for you, but make it fast. Did I mention I think this is foolish? Can't you just save the gift and give it to her next time?"

"It is a gift that benefits us. I'll tell you about it later."

"Why do you always have to take chances? Couldn't we just be on the safe side for once? Please Valvina?" Faith pleaded.

"Stop trying to control everything! I can make my own decisions and am quite capable of taking care of myself," Val complained. "You don't have to wait." Val turned in a huff and backtracked to the yurt.

Faith fumed, angry that Val had accused her of being controlling, when all she'd wanted was to finish this mission without taking unnecessary risks. Val didn't realize she was putting the entire company at risk, not just herself. As usual, she just couldn't help changing the plan, just to prove she could. It was selfish, and Faith planned to tell her so as soon as they got back to camp. Suddenly, she got a creepy feeling between her shoulder blades. Faith turned her head in slow increments, as Raven had taught her, but saw no movement in the vicinity behind her. She could barely see the back of the yurt above the scrub concealing her. Garrett was way ahead of them. On his way back to the main unit by now.

She watched as Val rolled out again from the back of the yurt and duck-waddled toward Faith. The Fae Princess released a breath she hadn't realized she'd been holding.

A sudden blur moved past her.

She heard some strange swishing noises and felt a stir in the air.

Something dark grabbed Val, slipping an arm under her belly and clamping a hand over her mouth. Then the abductor virtually disappeared before Faith's very eyes.

Panic rolled over her body, mind racing. She took notice of a small troop of Gugwe hurrying toward her location. The survival instinct kicked in. Evergreen brush tied behind her, as Tula had required each of them to wear one in the snow to sweep away footprints. Faith flew into motion, belly crawling away as fast as she could move below the brush line. A hand reached out, grabbed her wrist, pulling her down into a shallow ravine. Tula signaled silence, then quickly covered them both with a white camouflaged cloak, blending them with the snow.

Under the cover, Tula pointed to the pouch that Badger had given her the morning they had left the castle, pulling her own open. Faith loosened the drawstrings, peeked in, furrowed her brow, puzzled at the contents. Her bewildered look grew more pronounced as she upended the pouch to find the oddest set of preserved caribou hooves falling into her lap. Tula signed and showed how to strap the hooves on the bottom of their boots. First fitting her own, then pulling a specialized set of four that she forced on her dog's feet, crisscrossing leather straps up the mutt's legs to tie them on. The dog began gnawing at the foreign footwear, worrying the straps, until Tula signaled a sharp sign to stop. The canine obeyed her command immediately. Peeking out from under their cover, noting the coast was clear, the silent female swirled the camouflaged material over her shoulders like a cape. Standing, she motioned the Fae Princess to follow, leading her safely away. Faith tried to argue with Tula that they needed to look for Val before they left the area, but the stubborn mute would have none of it.

The only tracks they left in the snow were those of caribou passing along the perimeter of the Bear Ridge village.

Faith bit her lower lip, tried to stop her tears, but all she could focus on was that someone had captured Val and Faith did not know who had taken her. She felt physically ill at the idea of having to deliver that report to Robin.

Chapter 22: The Rest of Your Life

Val woke with a headache that felt like someone was stabbing her between the eyes. Her vision blurred; the light dimmed. At least it was quiet. She kept her eyes closed as she pieced together the moments before she'd blacked out. No, she corrected herself, not blacked out, knocked out. She remembered arguing with Faith, having insisted on going back to the albino Gugwe to give her the gift she'd forgotten. Well, bloody hell, she was going to have to eat her words and admit that Faith was right. The risk hadn't been worth it. Now, she would have to figure out who'd taken her and find a way to escape. Throughout this mental diatribe, the stabbing pain between her eyes continued. Slowly, she opened her eyes.

Her whole body convulsed backward when she found herself face to face with a large goblin. Not just any goblin. She thought she knew for certain who the male staring her down was. He sprawled on the sandy, rock-strewn floor with his back against the wall. Wait, she thought, not a wall exactly. Oh. It was one of those trees with a room down below the trunk, in the roots, like the one Saffron had used to save her from the Gugwe. Her mind refocused on the male goblin again. She'd have known him anywhere, from Faith's description.

Rupert Gregor Goodfellow.

Well, that's just bloody wonderful, she chastised herself. She'd allowed her stepbrother to capture her and was now his prisoner. He couldn't possibly know who she was, could he? Robin has said it was likely Rupert wouldn't be happy about their dead sister being alive.

"Valvina Ariana Goodfellow, I see you're awake. Rupert Goodfellow at your service." He held his middle and forefinger together and saluted her from the side of his forehead.

Val held her tongue, a habit she was unused to and that took effort. She could see he had blotches of dried blood all over his clothes, and he cradled a heavily bandaged hand in his lap.

"Be at ease, little sister. I don't intend to hurt you."

"Really? Then why do I have a lump on the back of my head? Why are my hands tied? What do you want with me? How do you even bloody know who I am?" Val tried to keep her voice even, but anger bled through.

"I am sorry about the goose egg." He touched the top of his head, indicating where he had struck her, and winced in empathy. "But, in all fairness, you were about to be overrun by a quad of Bear Ridge Gugwe. I certainly couldn't trust you'd be quiet, so I..." He mimicked, knocking her with a rock on the back of the head.

She quirked the side of her mouth and stared him down. Rupert squirmed under her gaze as he told her, "My brother, um...our brother, he makes the same face, yes?"

Val rolled her eyes at him, waggling her bound hands at him.

"Oh," he chuckled nervously. "Your hands. I wasn't sure...still not sure that you won't attack, if I, um, if I..."

"Release me?" Val raised her eyebrows half an inch. This behavior didn't jibe with the Rupert described to her by Robin, Faith, and Caz. She exhaled. "Look, I promise I won't attack. If you have things you want to say to me, I'll listen. But I'll hate you forever if you leave me tied up and try to keep me a prisoner. Get it?"

Rupert pulled himself up with some effort, crawled over to Val on his knees and untied the leathers he'd used to secure her hands with, then moved back to his spot. The elder Goodfellow studied her features. "You don't look like your mother."

"Is that a good thing or a bad thing from your perspective? From what I've heard, I definitely don't want to look or be like my mother. I'll reserve judgement for now, since I haven't had the pleasure of actually meeting her, but I am pretty sure she's evil. You're not going to turn me over to her, are you?" A wild look flashed across her face, and she gawked all around, adrenaline spiking at the start of a panic attack.

"Calm down, Valvina! Get a hold of yourself. I will not turn you over to Morveena, for bloody sake. You can trust me on that."

"Where is she? Why aren't you with her? Aren't you always with her, doing her bidding?"

Concern crossed Rupert's face. He cocked his head and looked up as though he had heard something. "Quickly now, don't argue," he whispered in her ear. "Get behind these roots and don't move or make a sound. I'll sit in front of you to keep you hidden. No matter what happens, don't let him know you're here. I beg you to trust me on this." She nodded her understanding.

The male goblin used his fingers to move the sand and rocks around and in front of him to cover any markings she'd made. He'd just settled against the thick roots when Dedo dropped through the trunk and landed right in front of Rupert. The gargoyle's face twisted with fury.

"Well, well. Look who's here," Rupert curled his lip and sneered at the Gargoyle. "If it isn't Mother's little spy. What do you want, you bloody slug?"

Dedo sat, knees up, and arms clasped around them. He glared at the goblin prince and pointed his finger.

"You."

"Killed."

"My."

"Mistress."

"I did. Don't think that makes you my creature, goyle. I don't want you. You are a traitor and a spy. I believe you'll likely die an ugly death. Be gone before I give it to you myself. You have no one here who wants your services. Get yourself back to the Fae Princess and hope she never finds out what a turncoat you are."

Rupert dodged as Dedo hurled a rock at his head. The Gargoyle disappeared.

When Rupert was sure the creature was gone, he moved so Valvina could come out from behind the root cover.

"I always thought he was a traitor. A spy. I never trusted him, but Faith couldn't see it." She thought over the exchange between Rupert and Dedo, and it hit her. "You knew he would come," Val surmised. Rupert shook his head, confirming her statement. "You...you killed her?" Val gulped, "You killed Morveena? Our mother?"

"Yes, your mother. My stepmother. Let's be clear about that bit of ancestry."

"I didn't even have time to find out for myself if she was as awful as I'd been told," she shook her head in disbelief.

"Never would I have let that happen to you. Too many have already suffered at her cruel hands. It's a shame you'll never know your actual mother. But I can't be sorry about it. You'll never have to feel the heaviness of her hand and the poison of her heart."

Val stood and brushed the sand from her clothes. "I'm glad I got to meet you, Rupert, but I, um..."

"Yes, you need to go. A moment, yes? I wondered if you might give some good news to our brother, Robin? The news is good for you as well, Valvina."

"Why don't you come with me and tell him yourself?" she suggested.

"I think not. I've burned too many bridges for that journey. So," he steepled his fingers together below his chin. "Please tell Robin our father is alive. I recently discovered the Gugwe had held him prisoner all these long years. He is free now. Hopefully, you will meet him one day. You have his eyes, Valvina."

"Alive? Lancer Ian Goodfellow is alive." She whispered in wonder. Val didn't know why that made her heart lighter, but it did. "I hope that means as much to you as I know it will to Robin. Thank you for telling me this news, Rupert. Please, won't you come with me? I think it would surprise you how forgiving Robin can be."

He shook his head.

"Where will you go?" she wondered.

"I must go north. We all have ways of fighting the war that is coming, Princess. I think the monster inside me can do some serious damage to that bloody Gugwe Emperor and his lot. So, my top plan is to let my monster loose. I mean that in the best possible way," he winked at her.

"I'll look for you again, Rupert."

"When the moonlight shines down on the floor over there," he pointed, "slip out and get back to our brother. You just press your back gently against the inner core of the tree, and it will let you out. I'm going to go now. Remember, wait until the moon shines for you. If there are any Gugwe patrols around, I'll lead them away. Can you find your way back?"

"I can."

They saluted one another.

WHEN THE SEARCH PARTIES stopped looking for Aleta, Lancer risked taking her to the river to bathe. He knew from experience that getting clean would go a long way in her recovery. He carried a tied bundle of clean clothes for her to put on after she scrubbed the filth away. His plan was to bury the rags she currently wore, as he had done with his own. Over the past several days, he'd fed her as much as he could get her to eat, though the food was cold. Emaciated, Aleta probably weighed less than eighty pounds. He'd kept watch over her as she'd slept like a baby for the first three days, waking only to eat and see to her own needs. But he wouldn't jeopardize either of them going out from the root cellar in those first days after her rescue. He had prepared a little soft nest before he'd gone into the prison after her. He knew she could not bathe or change into clean clothes until the searches for the missing prisoner ceased.

Still too weak to walk on her own, Lancer carried her like a child in his arms and held her at the river's edge as she insisted on cleaning herself. In the end, she had to ask for his help to wash her hair, but he was gentle and said not a word as they went through the motions. Afterward, she sat herself on the bank while Lancer dug a hole and dumped her ragged, filthy clothes in it.

Before he covered the stinking cloth, he turned with an apologetic look on his face. Lancer pulled the small knife he'd stolen in the village, fingers holding the blade as he extended the antler handle to her. "I'm afraid you'll never be able to work the mats out of your hair, my dear," he told her softly. "Do you want to cut it, or will you let me?"

"You're probably better able to see how best to do it. If you don't mind."

Lancer kneeled down. As gently as he could, careful not to cut too close to her scalp, began hacking away large clumps of matted, greasy hair. When he finished, he washed the knife blade and put it back in his belt. He gathered the shorn hair and dumped it in the hole with her ratty clothes, covered it with dirt, placing a rock on top. Carefully, using his fingers, he sprinkled leaves, pine needles, and sticks across the surrounding ground, making it look like the rest of the terrain. Only a skilled eye would have been able to tell that a hole had been dug there.

Pulling a packet of tied grass from his pack, he slid her back into the water. She laid her head back while he scrubbed her newly shorn head with the wad of green grass, letting them float away on the river's current when he was satisfied with the job. Lifting her slight frame, he laid her on the bank again to dry. From the location of the bright, silvery orb above, he knew they'd been here overlong. Lancer fretted about getting back to their hideout before the evening patrols started their second round.

Producing clean clothing made from caribou skins, he laid out leather leggings and a soft green shirt. He added a leather vest and supple boots that came to her knees, which he'd had to tie with leather strips to hold them up around her thin, stick-like legs. Aleta felt clean and almost whole again.

The escapees didn't see a soul as Lancer carried the Fae Queen back to their hideout. The bathing adventure had drained her energy. Before she fell asleep, he insisted they eat again. The two of them shared some nuts, along with a coarse, flat bread he'd stolen days ago. He picked patches of mold off before giving her a share that he had topped with a crumbly, stringent cheese that had been packed in a clay crock.

After eating, Aleta crawled across the sand floor and curled up on a fresh bed of pine boughs he'd laid in for her before they'd gone to the river. He used the old ones to drag behind them on a tether, erasing their tracks as they'd walked to the river, then left them outside. Gathering a bundle from the far side of their small refuge, the large goblin unrolled it and laid the warm, soft hide over his charge.

"That feels wonderful," she told him, hugging the blanket to her chin. "Warm and safe. Simple things I never thought to have again." Tears welled up in her eyes.

"Here, now. None of that. Had to wait to get you cleaned up before I could give it to you."

"Thank you for all you've done, Lancer. I don't know how I'll ever be able to repay you."

"I'll be happy if you don't hold that haircut against me in a few days," he laughed, and she joined him. Laughter felt good, but foreign, not having experienced it in such a long time.

"Get some rest. Tomorrow we're going to exercise your arms, legs, and wings. I have a better place picked out for us to hide, but we will not rush things until you're strong enough to walk there on your own two feet," he winked.

She closed her eyes, drifting off into a dreamless sleep.

FAITH MOVED AT A QUICK pace, silently through the woods. The trees here differed from what she was used to. The army had provided her with snowshoes. She alternated between flying and shoeing. The Fae Princess glanced over her shoulder several times, feeling as though she were being watched.

"You look guilty, like you're sneaking off somewhere," a voice called from above.

Eyes rising to the sound, Faith stopped in her tracks, clapping her hands together, joy spreading across her face. "Val! You're alive! You're here! I can't believe it," she squealed.

Val glided down, landing in front of her best friend; the two instantly embraced. Faith touched Val's hair, her face, held her shoulders to be sure she was real. "I'm so glad to see you safe. What happened? Tell me everything."

"Let's get out of the open. Better to use the shadows to hide in, yeah?"

Val led Faith over to the thin treeline, feet sinking in the snow over her knees as she huffed and puffed, Faith snowshoeing atop with ease. They made a small fire and heated water to have tea, while Val told Faith her tale.

"So, Morveena is dead. Rupert claims your father is alive and Dedo is a bloody traitor, a turncoat who has been Morveena's creature all these years! That's information we never would have had if Rupert hadn't taken you. Saved you, I mean."

Val nodded. "You know I didn't like Dedo. Never pretended I did. I said from the first time I met him he was a spy. There's no way your mother could have known. From what you said, it seemed like they were close to one another."

"Speaking of my mother, I haven't told you. Robin and I came across the lads who had traveled with Morveena and Rupert. They deserted and made their way here to the Fae castle, looking for Robin. The lads told me they eavesdropped, hearing a conversation where Morveena disclosed she was going to spring a prisoner from the Gugwe slave camp and use that prisoner as bait to lure me in, so she could capture me again."

Val's eyes grew enormous, and her mouth formed an 'o'. "You mean the Gugwe hold your mother prisoner? Bloody hell, Faith. Lancer Goodfellow was incarcerated there all these years as well. I wonder if they knew the other was there? Can't really wrap my arms around thinking of him as my Da yet, you know?"

"I get it. Must be weird all the sudden to have a whole new life, identity, and family to get used to."

"Yeah. And brothers. I'm used to sisters." They laughed.

"What are you doing out here alone? I saw you looking over your shoulder. It seemed to me you were sneaking," Val accused.

"Well...I was sneaking, actually." Faith confessed. "I was the one who had to tell Robin Goodfellow that the sister he'd been looking for most of his life and only recently found had been kidnapped. The evidence pointed to your captors being Gugwe. He's organizing a rescue as we speak."

"That doesn't tell me why you're here and why he's back at camp organizing."

"No, you're right; it doesn't. Look, I was using the ring. I was the one who lost you. It was my responsibility to find you. I figured the Gugwe took you, and since they also had my mother..."

"You figured you'd kill two birds with one stone and fly in and rescue your best friend *and* your mother?"

"By."

"Your."

"Self."

Val's foot was tapping up and down in irritation. "We have to go back and let Robin know I'm alright."

"You," Faith corrected. "You have to go back and let your brother know he doesn't need to rescue you and..."

"And?"

"And I am going to stick with my plan now that I know you're okay."

"The plan being to rescue your mother?"

"By."

"Your."

"Self."

Val scowled at Faith.

Faith bit her lower lip. "Yeah. That plan. Look, there's no reason for me to put others at risk for this mission. There's a war to fight come spring.

Everyone is doing everything they can to prepare. We're going to need powerful magic on our side to win a war against those monsters. According to my aunts, my mother has that kind of magic, so in my mind, we need her. Don't try to stop me," she warned. "Besides, now I've been forewarned that my mother was going to be used as bait to lure me in. Well, Reatha always said forewarned is forearmed."

"Stop you? Not a chance. I'm going to go with you."

"Val, be reasonable. You can't go. Robin thinks you are in danger, that you've been kidnapped. It would be cruel to just disappear with me, not even letting him know you're safe now. The squads would put themselves in harm's way just because they don't know you escaped."

"I didn't escape. Rupert grabbed me so I wouldn't get taken by the Gugwe. Then he let me go. Cruel? 'Cruel' is the last thing I want to have associated with my behavior. I don't want anyone, least of all Robin, thinking I inherited that trait from my mother. Besides, Garrett can go back in my stead and tell Robin I'm safe, yeah?" she smiled, happy to have provided a simple solution.

"Garrett?" Faith's face scrunched up in confusion.

Val poked Faith in the side and pointed to a small copse of trees across the open meadow. Faith squinted, just barely able to see the white-tipped, bushy red tail swishing back and forth in irritation.

"Garrett Emmon Gladheart!" she called out to him. "Show yourself." Faith stamped her foot. Not a simple thing to do while wearing snowshoes.

The Foxfire shifted to present his human self for the inevitable dressing-down he was sure to receive.

"Explain. Now."

"Look, I saw you slink away, pack full of gear, a food bag at your waist and a water bladder across your shoulders. I heard Robin lose his wits when you told him yesterday that Val had been taken. I knew you'd take her disappearance personally and, like always, take the blame, heaping guilt on yourself." He turned and stared daggers at Val. "Even though someone else was really the responsible party. The person who put herself in danger after you tried to talk her out of it." Val stuck her tongue out at him.

"Bloody hell, Faith. I couldn't let you go off on your own, which I knew you would do. So, I watched. Waited. When I saw you sneak away from camp, I followed. No harm done. Just watching your back, lass." He had the good sense to look sheepish, and she wanted to hug him for it, right after she slugged him.

Instead, she said, "Good thing you followed. As Val said, now we have you as our messenger, to take the news back to Robin, to let him know we're all okay, yeah?"

"But how will I find you again?"

"Likely, you won't, but you'll be helping relieve Robin's stress by telling him his sister is safe. You'll be protecting our troops so they don't attack the Gugwe, who don't have Val."

"You're a fool if you think his stress level is going to go down because Val got free, only to learn the two of you have gone into Gugwe territory to seek your mother!" he yelled, losing his temper.

The two girls looked at one another, shocked at hearing Garrett yell. Garrett never yelled. Val nodded her silent agreement. Faith took off the chain around her neck, where the silver ring hung that her mother had made. She slipped it over Garrett's head. "Val has her ring. Close your eyes." She turned him round and round until he felt dizzy and his balance was off, making him side-step back and forth like a drunken sailor. "Okay, keep your eyes closed," she instructed. "Hold the ring in your hand and concentrate. Keeping your eyes closed, point to where you think she is."

Val had moved from the spot where he'd last seen her. He followed Faith's instructions, mainly because he had to know if it would truly work for him later. His equilibrium faulty, he one-stepped in a circle, turned about and pointed straight at her, opening his eyes to confirm it.

"Hey! It works. Alright then, I'll be your errand boy, but let's look at that map you're carrying, so you can tell me your travel plan before I go. I want to have some sense of where I could find you down the road." They studied the diagram representing the Gugwe lands, and she traced a line with her finger, showing the route she intended to take.

"You know, you can count on the wrath of the Goodfellow when he next lays his eyes on the both of you. I'm fairly certain neither he nor the Beaumont will not think this plan in line with behavior expected from the 'Princess of them all'. He'll say you owe your safety to those who follow you and will fight for you. I want it on the record that I agree with that assessment. Unfortunately, I know from experience that the two of you are going to do whatever you bloody well want to, and no one can stop you once you've made up your minds." Both girls took the piece of humble pie and swallowed it with a topping of guilt, but he was right when he said no one could change their minds.

Garrett insisted on running more tests. He made Val move out a mile or two, satisfied when he successfully located her after another half a dozen tries. Finally, he felt confident that he could find them again. Before he left, Faith reached for the ring and told him she was putting a glamour on it to make it invisible so that no one would steal it from him. Slipping the silver chain back over his neck, she told him to take care of it as if it were his own. She reminded him it wasn't. She expected him to return it as soon as they met up again.

He shifted to Fox, opened wings, and called over his shoulder, "Look for me within a week. I'm going the rest of the way with you after this little errand. I want to help. You both owe me for this!" His voice faded as he sped away to ease the Goodfellow's heart.

The two girls waved, watching him fly away. Val finished strapping on her snowshoes and said, "Think he'll be mad when he figures it out?"

"You can count on it," Faith groaned. "It couldn't be helped. The more people involved, the greater the risk we get caught." She twisted an invisible ring on her finger. "It's more important that we be able to keep track of each other in case something happens."

"Yeah, but I still feel bad about deceiving him. Don't be surprised if it takes the rest of your life to earn his trust again."

A double set of snowshoe tracks trailed north. Every five miles, the two girls switched off to flying, then back to shoeing until the sun dropped below the horizon.

Chapter 23: You Underestimate Me – I Expected More from You

Aleta's recovery was slower than Lancer had hoped. They'd spent almost four weeks drilling and exercising every day, cramped in the small space of the root cellar, with very few outside excursions. She would never have admitted it then, but Lancer drove a grueling, painful exercise schedule until she thought she'd lost the will to live. Shortly after she hit that low point, about two weeks in, her entire outlook changed. The Fae Queen drove herself harder than the Goblin King ever did. She was formulating a plan. Aleta knew exactly what had to be done. In order to accomplish it, she had to recover, to be strong enough to put her plan into play. Weakness would surely mean failure, and she hadn't survived all these years to fail now.

It was a mild winter day; the sun was shining, a light wind ruffling the top layer of snow. Today was moving day. They had packed up the few items in the root cellar worth moving to Lancer's bigger sanctuary. He'd gone on a solo trip there three days before to confirm it was still the haven he pictured it to be. Luck had been with him that day. He also decided he could chance another foray into the village for fresh provisions that would benefit them on the day they made the move. The Goblin King was in and out of the BloodKnife village quickly, able to steal smoked fish, fresh berries, and more flatbread. When he'd left the root cellar, he'd taken the heavy caribou hide Aleta had become so attached to on this pre-trip. First, because it was a heavy item, he didn't want to add to their load on moving day; there would be more than enough to carry already. Though Aleta had come a long way from when he'd first brought her out of the prison, this excursion would still be a test of her strength. Second, she was loath to be parted from the warmth it gave, even for three days. He imagined it might be an excellent incentive for her to get to the new hideout after being without it. The new location would put them closer to the Gugwe village, but concealed. It would give him easier access to supplies while they made a plan to pursue at winter's end.

Aleta walked through their new retreat when they'd reached it, moved a few things around, and unpacked her load. Lancer stole away to fill their three water bladders in the spring. He would show her where it was located deeper in the cave once they had settled in. She made quick work of getting their haul in place, then set about poking through the food stores Lancer had laid up. When he returned, arms laden with sloshing water in the bladders, he was pleased to find Aleta had a meal parsed out for the two of them.

The cave had a natural chimney. The smoke was unseen from the outside. He'd checked every angle to be sure. Lancer allowed a small fire, enough to heat water, and Aleta took advantage of it to wash, taking her time, enjoying the luxury. She made tea with herbs he'd collected to surprise her before letting the fire dwindle down to hot coals. The two companions leaned against the wall, sipping the piping hot, stringent liquid.

"Lancer, we need to talk."

"I've got nowhere to go. What's on your mind, lass?"

"I never liked the way we left things between you and Lennox."

"I'm sure that makes three of us," he grumbled.

"You accused him of betraying you. He didn't. You were his greatest friend."

"Greatest friend? Bah! I begged him to tell me where he had taken my daughter." He held his hand up as Aleta sputtered denials. "I know what you're going to say—that I am the one who previously required him to swear an oath. An oath he would never tell another soul where she was. If no one knew the secret, no one could have had the information tortured out of them. Me specifically. But things had changed. I wanted to go to her and influence how circumstances were going for our clans. Valvina was just the thing to take the rule from Morveena's hands. The people would have loved her."

"Still, you just admitted that you had demanded Lennox's word never to reveal her whereabouts, yes? How can you hold his keeping a promise you demanded against him? You know Lennox values his honor above all things."

"I know it well." His words came out bitterly. "But there is such a thing as common sense, yes? He wouldn't even listen to what I had to say."

"No. It was more than that. I'm afraid you placed your anger and mistrust on the wrong person. It was I who waylaid your mission to bring Valvina out of hiding, which would have destroyed her cover identity. Exposed, Morveena would have ruined the girl."

"You? No, no. It could never have been you."

"The time has come for me to confess my selfish actions to you. I hope you can forgive me. Morveena Montestrell and I met years before she became your wife. Alora was still alive. The girl had a dark secret. Her ambassador, Munro Marcellus Montestrell, her father, was an abuser. He beat her black and blue regularly. He sculpted her into a monster that wore a mask. I discovered her plight quite by accident. I'm not sure why, but she hated me for it. She thought I saw her as weak. Think about it. Dire events seemed to follow in her wake. Her father's death, where she tried an elaborate scheme to blame it on the Fae Court; your beloved Alora's death."

"Alora died in childbirth."

"So it seemed. Nothing ever proven. I am just pointing out her closeness to these events and how that led you to marry her. A marriage that resulted in her being the Queen of the Goblins. Queen Regent, since you've been missing all these years. Consider your own disappearance and your long-term captivity." Aleta took his icy hands in hers, clutching tightly. "I feared her, Lancer. Never in my life have I feared anyone more. She was vile, but skilled at putting on a clever mask of innocence. Probably a survival technique that surfaced under the odious hand of her father. Any kindness I projected to her seemed to inflame a hatred for me. Morveena knew I was here, a captive of the Gugwe. She came and talked to me, for bloody sake. I am positive she arranged for the Gugwe to capture me all those years ago," she released his hands. "Anyway, I convinced Lennox that our newly born babe was in danger from Morveena. I couldn't shake the feeling. You asked Lennox to take your child and hide her away from Morveena's malevolence. I saw that action as the perfect opportunity to hide my child away from her, too. So, I had Lennox foster both my baby and yours in different homes to immerse them in new lives, under different names. The thought of you revealing where my daughter was hiding in seeking your own was unbearable. I begged Lennox not to reveal where he had fostered them, not for any reason. Not even for you. Morveena was a blood-magic user. A powerful one. You must have known that. The risk wasn't worth it. I just couldn't allow it. You should have directed the anger you bear toward Lennox at me all these years. Do you see?"

Lancer stared down at his feet, silent.

"One more thing," she sighed heavily.

He turned to look into her eyes.

"Morveena led Lennox to believe that you kidnapped me. He was told *that you had betrayed him*. It was all Morveena's doing. She wanted to throw the scent off herself, so she blamed you. Lennox has believed you were my kidnapper all these years. She duped both of you."

"Bloody hell. What a mess we've all made of things. How do we fix it?" Lancer cradled his head in his hands.

"My confession was a start. That you haven't throttled me is a good sign. Perhaps we've used up all the anger and hate we had? Maybe we can move forward from here? Let's talk more tomorrow. I find I am suddenly exhausted." Aleta pulled the caribou hide up over both of them and leaned her head on his shoulder, and he let her.

CAZ STOOD BETWEEN ROBIN and Garrett, arms stretched out, a hand flat against each of their chests. "Alright now, lads. Everyone, just calm down, shall we?"

Robin huffed, uncoiled his muscles, and stepped back. Running his fingers through his dreadlocks, mumbled quietly under his breath, "Stupid, gullible friends."

"Hey! I'm right here, Robin. I heard that," Garrett grumbled, but the anger left as soon as it boiled through. "Not that I can argue against your perspective. I've been stupid and gullible around those two girls my whole life, yeah? How was I supposed to know Faith would take her silver ring back and replace it with a heavy bead on the chain?"

Caz patted him on the back. "I think those princesses have a knack for making us gullible, mate. I know I've gotten taken advantage of by their wiles a few times myself and, if Robin thinks about it, is honest with himself, he has to. Right, Robin?"

The Goodfellow grimaced, then nodded his agreement. "Hood-winked again, yeah? Sorry for blowing up, mate. Get packed up. We leave in an hour. I will leave anyone behind who's not ready when we move out."

"Where to?" the redhead asked.

Caz cracked his knuckles. "The answer to that is easy, mate. We're going right after 'em. By my calculations, I figure they'll have four or five hours on us. Let's not let the trail go any colder. I'll go around asking Zeeka to pack us some food. Rob? Can you check with the lads who were under Rupert? Maybe a few would guide us. That should save us some time since they've already been in Gugwe territory and know the location of the prison, yeah?"

"One hour," Robin headed off toward his tent.

"Oy, Garrett? Better be back here in half that time. Man's got a fire lit under him. Not sure he'll wait a full hour."

Word spread quickly. When Robin returned to the staging area, a full pack riding on his back, he found Caz, Garrett, Raven, along with seven of his lads, as well as Carlisse, Keto, and Lute. Packed and all ready to go.

Robin held Raven's eyes while he and Caz used hand signals. Carlisse squinted her eyes, watching them. Pushed two lads aside and came up toe to toe with Robin. "You're communicating about me! Were you never taught that it's rude to talk about someone right in front of them, as if they aren't even there?" She crossed her arms and waited for his response.

"Lass, you've got it wrong," Robin said defensively.

"I don't. You underestimate me, Robin. Somehow, I expected more from you. No wonder Faith and Val when on this mission alone. They are probably tired of your male ego deciding you need to control everything, that it's your personal duty to protect us."

Robin raked his fingers through his hair, fighting the urge to rip it out. His face had agitation written all over it. His words came out calmly. "I was only saying you shouldn't be going on this trip because we're heading deep into Gugwe territory."

"So? Oh, you mean the territory where Faith and Val headed? Let's get something straight. I'm not under your command, Robin Wilum Goodfellow. I make my own decisions, and I won't have you or anyone else making them for me. Clear?"

Robin turned to face his friend. "Raven?" he beseeched him. Asking without words for his mate's help to remedy the situation.

Raven scoffed, "Look, Robin, it's been my experience that Miss Carlisse Parisa Pureheart goes where she wants to go, when she wants to go, yeah? You'll not win this battle, mate."

Caz touched Robin's shoulder. "Losing the light. Let's go. Since she's coming, maybe I will finally have a chance at getting a 'Carlisse tat' on this venture, yeah?" The Beaumont hooked his arm in Carlisse's, set off north, asking if he could peruse her sketchbook by the fire when they camped tonight.

Garrett's ice boards came in handy more times than any of them would have dreamed. At full sail one day, the board allowed Keto and Lute to catch a wind current. It saved them from a hunting polar bear they'd encountered crossing an immense body of water. Turned out Garrett's design worked on both open water and ice. Everyone stayed closer to the shoreline after that incident. As an extra precaution, they appointed two watchers to keep overhead eyes for any kind of predator while they traveled. No one wanted a surprise attack.

The temperature dropped as they trekked north. Robin made for poor company, spending every waking moment vacillating between worrying about Val and Faith, then being angry with them. That Val had come in contact with their older brother, Rupert, and didn't bother to take the time to come tell him about it in person, stung. Their father was alive, and he would have liked to celebrate that news with his sister.

It was Raven who started using some new techniques that Carlisse had suggested. He could get every goblin in the company to exercise their wing muscles. As they grew stronger, they began forming up flying ranks and practicing maneuvers. That led to Robin and Caz brainstorming different procedures that might work. Whoever was commanding the elite force could use hand signals to convey instructions to those flying above. The sky-eyes, as he referred to them, could warn ground troops of the enemy's location, as well as their directional movement. The signals could even apply to providing the best route to the 'boots on the ground'. Allowing them to report where the best nearby terrain was, providing as much advantage as possible to meet a head-on clash with the enemy. Carlisse drew up charts of all the signals so the lads could memorize them. They sent Garrett ahead to scout. It was safer and easier for him to slip in and out of areas as a canid, which wouldn't attract undo attention. After all, foxes were expected to be seen in the wild. A flying canine was something altogether different.

Four of the lads wore light, evergreen brush 'tails', walking at the back of the squad, erasing the group's footprints as they moved. Robin followed the phases of the moon, ticking off the days. He was sure their luck wouldn't hold forever without discovery by a marauding group of Gugwe. He was grateful for every day they moved further north without conflict. Each day of practice further honed the skills of his travel companions. There was no point in making a plan until they arrived at their destination, able to actually see the terrain surrounding Thrall Lake. It was one thing for Garrett to describe land from his visual connection through the emperor. But quite another to see the physical topography and how best to use it to hide or engage with their foe. Even then, the Gugwe prison was a distant rumor. There was no way to plan a method to free Faith's mother, find the girls, and get everyone back to the Falls Camp south of Bear Ridge. It required critical knowledge of the location, surrounding land, the status, and the count of their enemies. Robin chewed the inside of his cheek as he forced made-up scenarios over and over through his mind. He allowed his imagination to play them out to see how they ended and, if he made changes, how it might alter the ending.

Late one afternoon, weeks of travel behind them, they were deep into Gugwe territory and hadn't come across a single sign of Val and Faith. The Foxfire, having returned early from scouting, waited for Robin at the treeline that ran along a fast-flowing river, still unfrozen despite the cold.

"What's what, Garrett? I didn't expect to see you until the sun went down. Have you found something?"

"There's a small group of Gugwe traveling about five miles east from here. They're running a perpendicular line of travel to ours, also heading north. I got close enough to identify that the albino and the two females that are always with her are in the faction. The Gugwe Emperor's betrothed, she's the one the girls were meeting with to propose a peaceful resolution."

"You're suggesting we capture them?"

"What? Bloody hell, Robin. Absolutely not," Garrett shook his head vehemently. "Faith and Val have some kind of understanding with the albino.

I just wanted you to know where they were, so we don't run afoul of them and end up in a skirmish that neither we nor they want. Maybe our people could move a few miles further west? Widen the gap between us? I can keep tabs on them while scouting."

"We can do that. But at some point, we're going to run right up to the foothills of the mountain range that runs through here. Keep tabs on them, but be careful. We'll push farther away. You think they're headed to Thrall Lake?"

"Likely. They'll hook back up with the Thana NukPana now that the albino has looked at Bear Ridge and seen where the emperor plans to marry her in the spring. Nothing like a good, old-fashioned wedding just before an invasion of Sharas, right? Real bonding time, that." He waved off and shifted back to Fox as he walked. Moments later, the Reynard moved quietly in the shadows of the boreal forest.

Chapter 24: Rumors and Gossip

When Garrett had returned to camp the night before, he'd told the group that the albino's cabal had far outpaced them. There was no longer any worry that the two coteries would cross paths. He estimated their own force was two days out from Thrall Lake. Keto and Lute reasoned it would likely take longer, as the lake was huge and the area might still be heavy with Gugwe. There was no way to know how many of the attending tribal members would have extended their stay after the Gugwe caucus. Prudence suggested they should move slower and use greater caution so as not to be discovered. Lute also noted that the prison was on the opposite side of the lake from where the Gugwe had held the assembly. No one liked the idea of being spotted while ice-sailing across the lake. They didn't even know if the vast body of water froze over in the winter. It would be safer to take the long way around the mere.

A debate ensued, weighing the pros and cons of breaking up into smaller squads. In the end, most everyone sided with Carlisse's perspective. She'd pointed out that during the weeks it had taken them to travel here, they'd logged many hours practicing how to attack the larger Gugwe. They had become proficient. Skills using flight formations, bird's-eye view scouting, and hand signal communications enhanced their advantage. Flight allowed them to provide the locations and movements of enemy troops. Carlisse argued it wasn't logical to break up the team. Common sense dictated staying together as a larger force, using the skills they had honed. She contended it made even more sense if it meant only a few of their team would get away. Smaller squads were more vulnerable against a force that outnumbered them. They didn't know whether most of the tribes had left the vicinity to travel back to their villages. With the Gugwe congress ended, unless they could get current intel on whether there was still a large population of the enemy at hand, they were coming in blind. The compact unit they had wasn't the Alliance Army; it was just enough soldiers intended for a small skirmish to test the Gugwe methods at Bear Ridge. No one could have predicted the decision to move further north, right into the heart of the Gugwe's domain.

The leadership made the final decision. They would stay together. When they came to the foothills, they set up camp along the river that had its headwaters at the south end of Thrall Lake.

GARRETT SHIFTED UNDER the full moon, turned to run along the bank to seek a Gugwe camp he could spy on. As he neared the location, he heard a soft voice call out, "Foxfire." For a moment, it startled him. Then he remembered how similar Carlisse's voice was to Aliah's. He remained still, his vulpine face turned to give her acknowledgement. He felt he could best show her respect if he shifted back to his human state to communicate with her. It was Garrett's unruly head of red-hair that locked eyes with Aliah's sister as she approached.

"Miss Carlisse," he greeted her.

"Garrett," she corrected from having called out to him earlier. "I've wanted to ask you about Aliah. I was looking forward to seeing my sister. Thought she would have been with you when you all left the moot for the Fae castle."

"She was."

"But she didn't stay. Why?"

He frowned. "Haven't you gotten the story from Val or Faith already?"

"I did. But I wanted your version. Everyone thought...I mean..."

"I know what you mean. Look, Aliah is taking some time to figure out what she wants to do with her life. She told me she felt like she'd always lived for everyone but herself. The behavior was self-inflicted, by her own admission. Her theory was she might have a better chance of working it all out in her head if she were on her own for a while, with no one to care for but herself? I really miss her."

"I miss her, too. Thank you for sharing with me. Maybe you'll find each other again when this is all over."

Garrett's smile was sad. "Maybe." He waved, shifted and trotted away.

HOURS LATER, THE MOON setting, the Foxfire smelled smoke as he was heading back to camp. He couldn't help but wonder what fool would dare break Robin's rule of no fires this close to enemy territory?

Someone stepped out from behind him. "Not being careful enough, Foxfire." A deep belly laugh followed the words.

Someone stepped out in front of him. "Lay off him. He's had a long night." The words ended with a hearty laugh.

Garrett shifted. "What are you louts doing here? You were nowhere to be found when Robin called in a select few to muster for this mission. Though I am sure he would have liked to have had you along," Garrett told them.

Brittany stepped up alongside Shaun. "Oh, I'm sure he would have included us, seeing as you've all traipsed up here to rescue *our* aunt and *our* cousin." She smiled at him. "Hey, we've just cooked up dinner. Join us?"

Garrett could see Badger, Tula, Mariella, and Kristian by the fire's side, each giving him a little wave or salute.

"Thanks, I'm starving. Would you mind dousing the fire? There are enemy camps too close for comfort. The Gugwe rarely bother to cook their meat, if you get my meaning. A fire out here is going to draw attention. The wrong kind of attention."

Badger and Tula had told Faith's cousins the same thing, had ignored their warning. But honoring the Foxfire's request, they smothered the flames by dumping snow to cover it, completely snuffing it out.

Brittany sulked. "I was only going to let it burn until I had hot water to make tea."

"I told you," Tula signed to Brittany, then she climbed a tree at the camp's edge to keep a lookout.

After the group had finished the meal, they packed up most of their gear. Everyone turned in alarm when Tula sent an urgent warning using a bird call. Badger gave silent commands for everyone to don their caribou hooves, quickly strapping the gear onto their boots. Then he directed each person to run all around the areas of the camp, stomping the ground full of caribou prints, covering their human tracks. When that was done, Badger opened his wings, signaled the group to follow, swooping up. He directed them to race away, taking advantage of a strong wind current. Brittany broke off from the group and flew straight up to Tula. Badger had beaten her there, already holding the small female in his arms, hiding under the cover of the evergreen trees. They heard a small garrison of Gugwe crash into the abandoned campsite. Garrett led the cousins a couple of miles away. He could see how effective the use of the hooves had been, where they'd trampled the snow. It looked like a small herd of caribou had passed through. The prints disappeared at the river's edge.

Later, the Foxfire was talking with Travis. "How did you find me? We've all been so careful about not leaving any footprints when moving through the snow or camping."

"I wasn't looking for footprints," the tall Fae shared, tipping his hat lower over his eyes. "I was looking for fox tracks, mate." A sly smile turned up at one corner of his mouth.

The additional travelers teamed up with Robin's cohort, which included Faith's father. Lennox popped out of the woods wearing snowshoes and a brush tail to erase his tracks. The minute Brittany entered the Goodfellow's encampment, she inspected the configuration. Pointing out what she felt were tactical errors in the setup. She began a list of suggestions on how to rearrange the site to make it more efficient. Robin bristled.

"Looks like you're going to get some shoulder exercise, mate," Caz told Robin.

"What's what?" Robin crinkled his forehead in confusion. "I don't get your meaning, Cazzidy."

Caz patted Robin's shoulder in sympathy. "I mean, it looks like you're in for some practice of letting things just roll off your shoulders," he offered his best friend a sympathetic smile.

Brittany called out, "Robin, would you mind asking the lads to help me? Those tents over there should all be facing the opposite direction."

"Just what we need," he mumbled to himself, "make-work."

NEVELE LOCATED TARAMAT, Neetriht, and Abaddon just as they were breaking camp for the last leg of their journey, returning to Thrall

Lake. He let them know Akama was expecting them by noon. The shamans had told Nevele where he would find the females. He left immediately to find Abaddon. The soothsayers gave him the creeps. Actually, he had been tracking Borta and his coterie when he ran up against the tribal magic wielders. Akama didn't trust the BloodKnife KuRuk. He worried his betrothed and the BloodKnife's party would collide. He wanted Nevele to locate the returning females and guide them back to the base at Thrall Lake. It did not surprise Nevele when he found himself between the KuRuk and Akama's bride-to-be in an open meadow.

"Borta," Nevele called to get the KuRuk's attention. "It is good to see you. Are you on your way back to your village?" Without waiting for an answer, he called out to the females, "Abaddon, Neetriht, and Taramat, the Thana NukPana is expecting you." The bodyguard pushed the three Gugwe ahead of him, calling over his shoulder to Borta, "I am sorry to say we cannot stop to visit with you this morning. The emperor is in a foul mood, and I, for one, have no wish to keep the Thana waiting. He has tasked me with hurrying them along."

"Never fear, Nevele Vutova. It appears I was lucky enough to welcome the emperor's betrothed as she returned from her trek to Bear Ridge. There has been talk among the people that perhaps Abaddon had changed her mind about the wedding and had run from our emperor." He laughed as though he thought the idea was a joke. "I see the rumors were false and the future empress had simply gone south to check out the wedding venue for planning purposes. I am sure she wishes the ceremony to be a memorable one for the nation. Women find those details so important, yes? Gossip is also circulating that our new empress does not approve of the taking of slaves. I desire to talk with my future sovereign, so I can hear her dispel such foolish notions for myself. I would have her thoughts on this topic. This stance is important to my tribe. The BloodKnife tribe owns hundreds of slaves from the Sharas Peninsula. My people have become accustomed to having slaves to ease their lives. We would not look favorably on having our slaves taken away. Surely our great emperor would not deny me the opportunity to speak with Abaddon about such important matters of the nation, neh?"

Abaddon rode forward on her albino caribou, Frost. She opened her mouth to speak, but before she uttered a word, everyone's eyes were drawn upwards. At the tip of a thin black spruce, the branches were moving, the tree trunk swaying, detritus falling, muffled cursing. Of a sudden, the stunned group watched as Faith lost her balance, fell to the ground with a sickening thud, sending up a whirlwind of soft snow. She groaned loudly once she could get her breath; the fall had knocked the air out of her lungs.

Borta kicked his heels into his mount's sides, racing up to the surprise intruder. Abaddon was right behind him. Nevele, Taramat, and Neetriht brought up the rear. Frost snorted a cloud of air when he caught the scent of the interloper.

The BloodKnife KuRuk was off his caribou in seconds, Abaddon as well. His gigantic frame cast a shadow over the small, fallen body. He stared at the female who'd risen to her elbows with a panicked look on her face, pain temporarily replaced by terror.

"You look just like her," Borta whispered. "Just as the Goblin Queen described you."

Abaddon dared to hold her arm out across his chest to stop him as he bent to grab the Fae Princess by the hair. "Stop. This one is my property."

Borta's face looked aghast at the statement, taunted, "Your property? Ha! You expect me to believe this snippet of a girl is your slave?"

Abaddon turned, looking up at the oversized male. "What I expect, Borta BloodKnife, is that you will respect your future empress's property. If you do not, I will have your tongue and your balls removed to decorate my tent," the albino snapped her fingers at Faith. "Attend at once. The next time you attempt to run away from me, I will have your toes removed one by one, roast them over the fire and feed them to you." She turned to Akama's bodyguard. "Nevele, tie her to Frost's tail. She will walk the rest of the way back to camp." Then, in a louder than necessary voice, she added, "You are lucky we are only going around the point on the lake. Maybe three miles east. Now move! You have shamed me. I will think on your punishment when we reach our destination."

Val, still concealed in the evergreen branches, got Abaddon's message.

Borta's eyes burned with lust and anger. He could see the things he desired right before his eyes. But he quelled his yearnings. Though he ached to have them for his own, the objects of his desire were out of his reach. An albino female and a Fae princess. Both belonging to the Gugwe Emperor. To take either would mean certain death. There was only one way to get those things for himself. His thoughts swirled in a quagmire as he considered his options, while the albino's group left him standing alone in the circle of pines. He determined that a small window of opportunity was at hand, where he could do the impossible. Most of the other Gugwe tribes had left days ago, heading back to their villages. Only the BloodKnife tribe, the Alabaster, the Wildhorse, and the emperor's 13/31 remained in the camp at Thrall Lake. Cold settled into his bones as thoughts melded into a solid plan that would offer little opposition for him to deal with if he played it just right.

Nevele turned to look back just before the small group rounded the point. It alarmed him to still see the BloodKnife KuRuk staring intently after them, the lust on his face plain to read.

ALETA CAME AWAKE WITH a start, her breathing labored.

"What is it?" Lancer roused himself.

"I...I dreamed. Faith is in danger. Somehow...somehow, she is here."

"Here? Come now, Aleta, it must have just been a bad dream."

"No, Lancer. The Gugwe have captured her. Even now, it seems Morveena reaches out with her power. Please, Lancer, we must go down to Thrall Lake. There's more I need to tell you, but there is no time now. Gather your things. The threads of the weave are pulling together. I can feel it. No matter what else happens, I must be there when the prophecy comes to fruition. It's important. More important than anything."

Lancer could do nothing to dissuade her, so he rose and packed as she raced around the cave, grabbing necessities.

Long ago, the Fae Queen had been an extraordinary dreamer, but she'd told him she hadn't dreamed in years. She claimed she had grown too weak. He suspected she wouldn't have used the art, not wanting to risk the Gugwe Shaman's discovering her ability. If she had truly dreamed now, it was a powerful sign that they didn't need a plan for the future. They were being pulled in by the forces of someone else's weave. Dressed, they had gotten ready to move in less than half an hour. Aleta led them through the woods. The only noise between them was the quiet rattle of the roughly worked snowshoes Lancer had crafted for them over the winter as she had convalesced. He could have done a better job had he had the proper tools, but the poor quality served.

Chapter 25: Must Be a Full Moon Will Shine Tonight

Anger flashed across Abaddon's face when she arrived at Akama's camp and found Borta had beaten them there. The BloodKnife must have taken a shortcut and run his mount into the ground to get to the emperor before she did. The arrogant KuRuk was busy telling the Thana NukPana that his future bride had claimed a slave. He apologized for the earlier misunderstanding when he'd reported that the pure albino had railed against slavery. Borta reminded the emperor of the strategy he had suggested to him of the Goblin Quean's intention to trade power and riches for the Fae Princess. Now, Borta pointed out, the bird was already in hand. He asked Akama to consider the leverage they could wield over the Sharas Fae with such a prisoner.

Nevele came to stand at the right shoulder of the Thana, glaring down at Borta. He leaned in to whisper in Akama's ear. The emperor's face developed a twitch under his left eye, but his expression remained stoic.

Abaddon marched forward, dipped her head in greeting to Akama, and released a long, low growl at Borta. "I did not expect to see you here, BloodKnife," her voice dripped with venom. "I thought I had dismissed you earlier."

The KuRuk bristled at the obvious disrespect she so blatantly displayed in front of the emperor. He made a silent vow to teach her later what happens to those who cannot give him his proper due.

"I am told you have taken a personal slave, Abaddon," Akama interrupted, voice flat.

"That is the truth. I have decided I could not judge a thing if I had not tried it for myself, my liege."

"And now that you have tasted the honey?" he raised his brows.

"The jury is still out. My experience is still in the early stages." She held her breath.

"Ah. I find experience to be the greatest teacher. Do you believe that to be true, Borta? I recall that the Gugwe, who was emperor before me, did not believe in such things. I was a witness to the fact that he changed his mind before death claimed him." The emperor offered a twisted smile to the KuRuk.

The BloodKnife blanched, bowed, and slowly backed away from the emperor. He quickly disappeared from the intense scrutiny.

"Show me," was all he said to Abaddon when Borta had withdrawn.

"You'd better make this believable, Princess," Taramat whispered to Faith. Taramat and Neetriht each held an arm, pushing the girl in front of them on her knees before the emperor. When Faith looked up, her heart froze in her chest. The emperor stood up to get a better look at the slave. She about feinted dead away at his size. Then, out of the corner of her eye, she caught sight of the dozen surrounding Gugwe. Seconds later, the stench from their bodies and breath struck her senses. The disgusting reek emanating from them gagged her, its own kind of weapon.

"Nothing to say?" he taunted her.

She cast her eyes down and said a mantra to herself. 'Don't see me, don't see me, don't see me'. Her body trembled. Neetriht could see the Fae girl was about to pass out. She moved forward, grabbed her arm and pulled her away from the emperor's gaze. "Come, girl. You have work to do for your mistress."

When Neetriht and Taramat got Faith back to Abaddon's yurt, they both began talking at once. "What were you thinking?" "How could you have been so foolish as to have allowed this to happen?" "Where in heaven's name is Valvina Ariana Goodfellow?" "Please tell us you didn't deliberately sabotage all the plans we made?" "You've ruined everything."

"Enough!" Abaddon strode through the entrance. "Do you think she would have willingly put herself in such danger? It is cruel enough for her to find herself compromised. You don't need to make her feel worse about it."

Both Taramat and Neetriht mumbled apologies, each laying a comforting hand on the Fae's back. Faith quietly told them how the two groups of Gugwe had come upon them from both sides, surprising them, leaving little opportunity to hide. She chalked it up to just stupid bad luck that her foot had slipped, sending her careening through the branches to the ground.

"What's done is done, my grandfather used to say. This muddles up our original plan. We must make ourselves flexible. Let's put our heads together, think, and devise a new strategy. Faith, please tell me Valvina won't try some heroic move to save you." Abaddon looked Faith square in the eye.

"Well, the thing is," Faith said, "with Val, you never really know what she will do."

"Wonderful," Abaddon feigned. "There must be a full moon that will shine tonight. There can be no other explanation for all this chaos." Faith shook her head in agreement.

Chapter 26: Outnumbered Two to One

The Foxfire came in for a rough landing, shifting as his feet touched down and carrying through in a run to reach Robin and Caz.

Gasping for breath, he shouted, "Enemy troops just the other side of that ridge!" Garrett bent down, hands on his knees, and wheezed. "We're trapped."

Caz called a halt and sent two flyers to scout ahead. "Whatever you do, make sure you're not spotted and your mental blocks are in place. Go, go, go!"

Robin put a hand on Garrett's shoulder. "Calm down. Give us a full report. How many? Why no sign of them until now?"

"Looks like two full cohorts, maybe one hundred strong? We're outnumbered two to one. I can only guess, but they must be from some of the other Gugwe villages that stayed on longer after Thana NukPana's congress finished. Probably just heading back home."

Robin surveyed their surroundings. "We're butted right up against the mountain foothills on the west. The enemy is due north. The flat land is full of marsh potholes behind. I doubt we could make it back to that vast lake to go around and avoid them before they spot us."

Alarmed at the idea of such a long delay, Caz said, "Even if that were possible, that would put us a week out. What about Faith and Valvina?"

Badger and Tula joined the discussion. Garrett gave a quick update on the situation. "If it had to happen," Badger said, "this was probably the best ground in a ten-mile radius for us to make a stand." Tula nodded her agreement. "At least here we're up against two tribes returning home, not all of them. The Gugwe won't be expecting any enemy engagement after their big gathering, so let's use what we've got."

The two scouts Caz had sent out came in fast. They confirmed Garrett's initial assessment, putting the enemy count at ninety-three. The better news was that it looked like the Gugwe had halted for the day and were setting up camp for the night.

Badger turned and used quick hand signals for Tula. She responded with a sharp chop of her hand through the air. "Exactly," Badger smiled at her.

"What's what?" Robin asked.

"Tula said since we're badly outnumbered, the best approach would be to split the enemy force in half. Of course, that means splitting our company in half as well, but with the right plan..." Tula handed Badger a stick. They all squatted down, and he drew a sketch in the dirt.

"Let's set up a small contingent. I'm thinking maybe ten of our soldiers east, heading toward that big lake. We'll send a scout to confirm that it is frozen. Just before sunrise, the team will let themselves be seen on the ridge-top, then retreat at top speed to the lake. They can make a fast getaway using the ghost sails. Then, work their way back to come in from behind the Gugwe here." Badger pointed with the stick and marked an 'x'.

"At the same time as the first squad allows itself to be sighted, we'll have another diversion here, on the western line. We'll need twenty dugouts, woven grass and fern covers for them to disappear into before the enemy gets to the top of the ridge. When our crew disappears, the enemy will be mystified. The Gugwe are a very superstitious people. It will affect their response, make them wary, slow them down."

Caz and Robin nodded in understanding. "What about the rest of our troops?" Caz asked.

Badger pointed to the top of the ridge. "After all our preparations are made, under cover of darkness, we fly into that patch of virgin spruce. No footprints, so they won't know we're there. We'll have the advantage of the sun in their eyes come daylight, the upper ground and, if all goes according to plan, we'll have them surrounded from behind."

Caz rubbed the worry stone in his pocket and reminded the others, "Still two-to-one odds on their side."

Tula tugged at Badger's jacket, and he looked at her. She signed another idea. It earned her one of Badger's best smiles.

It was Garrett who spoke, his voice filled with wonder at the image Tula suggested. "She wants to add scarecrows on poles set at different levels at the east and west confrontations. From afar, it will look as if there's a lot more of us. It's brilliant. Might give them second thoughts, or at least pause." He winked at her, and a blush ran up her neck to her cheeks.

Brittany and Travis had been standing in the background, listening. Britt raised her hand. "I'll take charge of Project Scarecrow and weaving the grass and fern covers." She walked away, but turned and added, "Might be the perfect time for Garrett to test his Foxfire ability to trot the perimeter of the enemy camp and see what he can learn by listening close up and personal. I've spotted a fox or two in the past couple of days. Natural habitat. He won't seem out of place."

Garrett shifted and left without a word. "Brave," she commented as she watched him move toward danger. "Oh, I volunteer Shaun and Travis. They adore digging holes." Her brothers glared at her as she signaled Tula to join her.

Badger handed out assignments, and they went to work, the night sky closing in from above.

ASIDE FROM A TWEAK here and there as they made their preparations, the plan stayed pretty much the same as originally laid out. The Foxfire returned about two hours before sunrise. He reported general discussions about the Gugwe Emperor's newly imposed community improvements, as well as a surprising percentage of negative comments about conquering Sharas and taking slaves. Seems a lot of the Gugwe are not onboard with Thana NukPana's enforced society change to become slavers.

"Maybe we can use that information later," Robin said, "but for now, we need to focus on enemy engagement at dawn."

"By not using my wings tonight, in keeping with my natural fox cover, it occurred to me that our practice in using flight during a fight would be a big advantage here. The Gugwe don't know we have the ability, and it would keep us out of reach."

Caz pointed and told Garrett, "A small team has been stockpiling separate caches of rocks so we can grab and drop them from the air."

Garrett nodded his approval. "The good news is that our foes are poorly geared. Very few weapons. Rolland has provided us with top-grade arms." His night vision allowed him to read the shadowed facial expressions of his friends. "Not that I'm discounting their super strength, razor teeth, and three-inch claws, but not much in the way of steel. Maybe a dozen carry bows and arrows. Probably the village's hunters."

"We should take those out first," Badger put in.

"Going to be a long day after a long night," Garrett shrugged. "I've got to get something to eat." Turning, he walked backwards and said, "Oh, forgot to mention I'll be leading the flight squad. Clear?" No one argued.

SUNUP PUMPED THE SKY full of bright pink and orange, streaked intermittently with sparkling sunbeams.

Atop the eastern ridgeline, a dozen silhouettes held their hands above their eyes, shading to see the Gugwe they were to entice into chasing them. From a distance, the Gugwe noticed clothing that rippled in the morning breeze. Just as the cohort was about to give chase, a loud boom came from the west. Enemy eyes moved to see a huge white pine fall, taking out multiple other trees on the western side of the ridge as the huge virgin evergreen rolled downward. One of the Gugwe leaders gave orders, sending soldiers to the east in pursuit of those spotted on the crest. He directed another company racing toward the tree-covered spine.

Tula and Brittany had rigged the scarecrows to strong willow branches. Easy to hook onto the back of their real soldiers, but flexible enough that they moved around and both the puppet and puppeteers could be seen to look like two bodies. The illusion was working. Using dead ferns for hair, the two girls had gathered as many extra shirts and pants as they could from the company, then stuffed the clothing with the dried ferns to give the false bodies filler.

As the unit ran down the eastern ridge, they had their ice boards in hand, ready to let the sails out. Shaun and Travis had hiked to the lake and back after they'd finished helping dig hidey-holes on the western slope and confirmed the lake was frozen solid. They also shared that they'd seen plenty of evidence, including fresh tracks, that at least one polar bear was working the lake shore.

Three Gugwe broke off from the thirty in pursuit. Badger screamed to warn Zarn and Bepe about the enemy right on their heels. Zarn burst into an explosion of blood as the lead monster leaped, razor teeth ripping out his stomach. Bepe threw his scarecrow off, making the next closest in pursuit stumble, buying himself precious seconds. Suddenly, three large rocks hit with precision and knocked out each target. Bepe came to the water's edge and slipped the sail on his ghost board up, the wind catching. He leaned hard right and swung away, racing across the ice behind the others. Moments later, the rest of the Gugwe troop found themselves at the water's edge watching their prey sail away over the ice.

When they could no longer see their quarry, after a brief discussion, decided they would return to the rest of the travelers from their village.

The undiscovered flight unit watched, hidden in the trees above as the desired step to their plan was in motion. The Gugwe headed north to reunite with the others. It was pure luck that took the Gugwe pack away from where three of their troop had been rock-bombed and hours before the mission was discovered.

The Western Alliance unit had used the same ragshags. Once they were spotted, the chase was on. By the time the Gugwe reached the ridge, the prey had vanished from sight. Hidden in their dirt-packed lairs, the Foxfire trotted out and encouraged a chase, carefully steering the predators away from the camouflaged ground pits. When the company was out of sight, the Alliance popped cover and headed to the rendezvous location to form up into aerial teams. Stealth was critical, so they used the dried fern stuffing from the man-made avatar's covering their heads and bodies to blend into the surroundings.

Just as both the East and West teams arrived at the appointed meet up, the Foxfire flew in and landed. His shapeshifting was so fast that it made some of them dizzy. Garrett's adrenaline spiked, and he paced back and forth in front of the Alliance soldiers. "We're only going to get one chance at this. The strategy is simple. Too many of them. Need to even up the odds." He pointed out ten of his best archers on the fly. "Your mission is to take out their archers. Come in hard on the fly, and you'll have surprise on your side. The rest of us are going to start with one large rock. We need to take out as many as we can."

"You might be interested to know that four of the enemy were ripped open on the lakeshore by some hungry Polars. Keep your eyes sharp, your mind control block tight. You've got flight and the fact that we're coming in from behind now with the sun in their eyes as your advantage. Make it count. We've got a couple of Princess's we need to rescue after this distraction, yeah?"

They roared at him, each getting a rock from the cache, wings taking them up in perfect formation. Three enemy archers went down on the first volley. Garrett was double-loading his arrows on his bowstring; a strategy he had built into a skill he'd been able to pull off with ninety percent accuracy after hours and hours of practice growing up. The rest of the bow-armed Gugwe bled out on the frosty ground.

Using a scoop-type throw Brittany had introduced to employ rocks using weight and velocity, her team discovered they could do ugly damage to a temple or forehead.

Caz watched in horror as one of Raven's lads must have lost his mind block. Rollo's body was obviously fighting the commands being given to his mind. He was forced to turn to attack his brothers in arms, taking out the lad next to him. Caz loosed an arrow that took Rollo right through the jugular.

On the Alliance's fourth regroup and volley, about eighteen enemy combatants turned from battle and ran.

Cheers rang out from above.

The commanders gathered to revise the plans to get back to the original mission. Given the reports, they considered the information. Badger sought input from all the soldiers so he could share strategies and moves that had worked best against the enemy. The wounded were treated. Their dead confirmed. Graves dug.

The ghosts of the comrades no longer walking or flying at their sides as they moved quickly dispelled the earlier euphoria. They filled their hearts with hope they would make it in time to rescue the Fae and Goblin Princess's.

Chapter 27: A New Constellation

A week had passed since Abaddon had claimed Faith was her slave. There had been no sign of Val. Taramat, Abaddon, Neetriht, and Faith were sitting in a circle on the floor of the yurt, sorting beads, exchanging ideas about how to avoid war in hushed voices. Nevele showed up unexpectedly. He delivered a message that the emperor wanted to see all three of them, with instructions to bring Abaddon's slave along.

Taramat pulled him aside. "What's this about, Nevele?"

"I don't know for sure, but the worm Borta returned yesterday, spending all his time whispering in Akama's ear. That the emperor has summoned you can't mean anything good. If I knew more, Taramat, you know I would tell you."

With solemn faces, the women followed the bodyguard to the rock dais Akama occupied.

"Greetings, Abaddon. You look well. Having a slave seems to have been a good thing for you, yes?"

"I have not yet decided. But so far, I have no complaints."

"Your slave likely has no complaints either." His eyes bored into hers. "I am told that you treat her like a favorite pet, rather than the slave you purport her to be. Has no one told you, my sweet? Slaves should fear their masters. Come, bring her to me. I will show you the proper way to train a slave." He snapped his fingers. Borta moved forward, handing the emperor a whip. The sight of the flagellate drew a sharp intake of breath from Abaddon. Memories of her mother being whipped surfaced. She couldn't fathom how she could get the princess out of this nightmare. In making a snap decision, no matter the consequences, she would not allow the girl to be flogged.

About to voice her objection, taking two steps forward, Borta glared at Abaddon with a grisly smile on his face, gleeful anticipation in his eyes. Of a sudden, out of nowhere, a small gargoyle appeared, with an obvious flair for the dramatic. When the smoke cleared, the goyle stood neatly between the Gugwe Emperor and the Fae Princess.

"Allow me to introduce myself, Akama Vutova. I am known as Dedo, from the Gargoyle kin, the People of the Rocks. This slave, upon whom you were so keen to demonstrate your training methods, is the daughter of my mistress."

"Liar!" Faith screamed at Dedo. "You are no creature of my mother. You are deceitful, evil..." The whip came down with a loud crack against the stone floor in front of her face. She cowered, choking on her words, not eager to feel the bite of the lash on her smooth skin.

"You will be silent," Akama ordered, pointing his finger at her. "Continue, goyle," the emperor told the stone-worshipper.

"Ah, thank you, my lord. As I was saying, my mistress has been a prisoner here by your KuRuk, Borta BloodKnife, for years." Dedo pointed at Borta. "I wish to reclaim her and return her home."

Akama laughed, the surrounding guards joining in his mirth. "A wild claim, goyle. Perhaps you don't understand the predicament you've inserted yourself into? And if you don't mind, please tell me why I would return the Fae Queen to your hands if a Gugwe had long ago claimed her as a slave? Are you proposing a trade?"

He pointed at Faith. "I would proffer her daughter, the Fae Princess, in trade for my mistress, my lord."

The emperor squinted his eyes, studying the small gargoyle as though it were a mystery to be solved. "As you can see, no trade is necessary from our perspective. We already have the princess in our possession. Borta, do you hold the Fae Queen in your prison?"

"I do, great one." Borta lied.

"Information you planned to provide to me soon?" Thana NukPana growled.

To everyone's shock, Aleta Dawn Stargazer chose that moment to glide in from above, gracefully folding her wings behind her as her feet touched down. "It would appear that your BloodKnife KuRuk is indeed a liar." Aleta tilted her head to the side. "I have not been his prisoner for weeks now. But, to be fair, in his defense, I will admit to being a prisoner in the BloodKnife prison for more years than I care to remember. Your BloodKnife KuRuk was in league with the Goblin Quean, Morveena Morgan Montestrell. It was she who kidnapped me and turned me over to Borta's tender ministrations.

She made false promises to the BloodKnife that his shamans could gain my magical powers. The Queen Regent suggested the mages only needed to apply the correct pressure and pain to win their prize. If you demanded an audience with those shamans, Emperor, I'm sure humiliation would overcome them. They would have to confess that they could not accomplish such a feat. All the methods they undertook over the years were a complete and utter failure." She stood ramrod straight, with a proud look on her face.

"So, so, so," Akama shook his finger at the Fae Queen standing before him. "You have lived to tell the tale, escaped. Yet set yourself before me voluntarily? Do you love your daughter so much that you would sacrifice yourself for her freedom? From where I sit, all you have accomplished is to provide me with two slaves from the Fae monarchy of Sharas."

"Have I? Is that what you think I've done, great Emperor of the Gugwe Nation?"

"Watch her hands!" Borta yelled in warning.

Aleta raised her palms, her lips moving, and the knout in Akama's hand turned into a snake. The viper, quick as a whip, wrapped itself around the emperor's neck, slitted eyes staring into his, forked tongue flicking in and out. "I wouldn't move if I were you, Emperor. You'll be dead within moments should the viper strike. Deadly poison, hmmm?"

"It would seem that betrayal is a theme for those who serve you today, my lord," her last two words dripping with sarcasm. "I suspect you don't know it yet, but your KuRuk there has planned a coup d'état. His warriors have surrounded your makeshift throne, hiding just beyond the tree line." She pointed behind her. "It is not very hard to understand his motives. He simply desires your betrothed, as well as the Fae Princess as his slave, and, of course, your title as emperor. The gargoyle," she waved her hand gracefully to point at Dedo, "is also beset with taint. He betrayed not only me and my daughter, but his true mistress, Morveena Montestrell. I have it on good authority that he has come before you, looking to better his fortunes. The death of his mistress has left him with few choices."

A sharp war cry sounded—the signal to start Borta's coup. Fierce guttural growls, roaring, and howls shattered the quiet of the woods surrounding the emperor's stage. BloodKnife warriors attacked the emperor's 13/31.

Violence erupting, the coup d'état began.

Akama's eyes bulged in the snake's tight caress, his breathing labored. The coils were tightening ever so slowly, closing off his airway. He could barely turn to lay his angry eyes on the KuRuk behind him, to witness that Borta held a knife in his left hand. But instead of stabbing Akama as he had originally intended, Borta threw the blade, laughing like a crazed-madman. It sailed end over end through the air. The obsidian point struck its target, burying the projectile right down to the hilt in Aleta Dawn's heart. Her knees buckled beneath her, and she slumped to the ground.

In the blink of an eye, all bloody hell broke loose.

Val soared in on her wings, armed with a loaded crossbow. She loosed an arrow directly at Dedo, pinning him to a tree with a bolt right through the center of his hand. Satisfied that the 'little spy' now could not reach a rock to transport him, she turned to survey the scene before her, reloading. One shaman growled, raised a hand to strike out with his magic at Valvina, but sudden action blocked the energy he pulled from the earth and directed at her. Rupert broke from the line of guards behind the emperor, costumed in a Gugwe guard uniform. The older Goodfellow brother used his body as a shield to protect Val. Taking the hit of sorcery the Mage had meant for his sister, Rupert's body shuddered in convulsions. Before he dropped, his adrenaline spiked. Rupert used the last of his strength, releasing a small hatchet in a throw. The strike went true, taking the Shaman down, burying the blade in his enemy's neck, severing the jugular. Val screamed Rupert's name as he toppled to the stone in a heap.

At Badger's command, two Alliance cohorts were coming fast in formation from above. They couldn't make sense of the scene in front of them, Gugwe fighting against their own. Badger didn't need it to make sense. He quickly signaled for the Alliance forces to let the Beastmen kill one another, changing their plan. Hand signals flashed to the flyers, instructing them to provide cover for Robin, Caz, Garrett, and the lads so they could break through the treeline. Racing in, they clashed with the guards, who rushed them as soon as they appeared in the pavilion area.

Nevele moved to Akama's aid, trying to get a hand on the snake choking his master, but the serpent's head kept striking out at the bodyguard. Each time he tried to get close, the snake viciously hissed, looking for an opening to sink its fangs into the aggressor.

Brittany, Carlisse, and Tula came on the spectacle from behind, having circled around, quickly took in the scene. Tula joined her hands with the other two girls, then noticed Badger break to the left, a Gugwe coming at him from his blind spot. Fear ripped through her. Tula found her voice. Words ripped from her throat. "Badger! Look out! Behind you!" He registered her voice. Shock caused him to stumble, almost unable to keep his balance. His trajectory altered, body twisting, Badger tucked and rolled, recovering his footing. The muscled Fae gracefully used the momentum to spin, arm extended fully, using the sword he gripped to take the Gugwe's head off, cutting clean through. With Badger safe for the moment, Tula turned back to Brittany and Carlisse, screaming, "Now!" her voice rough with disuse. The three females joined their powers. Tula, only recently having learned through Carlisse that she had magical ability, cast a mind control spell out. She was stronger than the other two put together. Combined with their support, her power bolstered, allowing the spell to take the form of a net. It swelled out and fell, covering the emperor and the guards surrounding him, putting them under an enchantment.

Borta was the only Gugwe that had bothered to block his mind during the melee. The BloodKnife KuRuk determined his best course of action was to turn tail and run, providing Lancer Goodfellow with a long dreamed of target. The Goblin King sprinted up to the edge of the dais, launched a crude spear, taking Borta in the back. Tula gripped Brittany's and Carlisse's hands, keeping their power melded, her body shaking with the effort to maintain the mind control net on so many at once.

Aleta was dying. Blood leaking out of her wound, pooling across the stone. It surprised the Fae Queen to find her long-lost husband at her side. "Oh, Lennox," her voice was faint, "I hope you can forgive me for all the things I've hidden from you."

"Don't talk, love," Lennox whispered, cradling her head in his lap, tears streaming down his ruddy cheeks as he stroked her hair. "Save your strength, please, Aleta, hold on."

"Too late, my love. Our time is past. It was your love for me that kept me alive and gave me hope all these years. I tried to put plans in place to cover all the angles I could see from my visions so long ago. You should know it was Lancer who rescued me from the Gugwe prison. I stored up all my strength in the last few weeks, hoping I could transfer my powers, just as I had dreamed. I can only tell you I believed all my deceptions were necessary to save our daughter and Lancer's daughter." Her breath was shallow, eyes glazed over, taking on a far-away look.

"Aleta, I don't care if you deceived me. I know only that I have found you again. You can't leave me now. Don't go, not yet. There's so much I want to say to you. Do you know I used to talk to you when you weren't even there? I just pretended you were listening." Lennox begged.

Her eyelids fluttered. "You'll understand, maybe even hate me for my secrets when I remove the glamour."

Dark clouds swept in, almost as though an eclipse was blocking the moon, its bright beam blacked-out. Lights flashed. The aurora borealis broke out across the sky. Bright reds and greens, mixed with shimmering whites, streaked up and down, back and forth, dancing across the horizon. The Fae Queen glowed from within. Those nearby had to shade their eyes; her body becoming a brilliant, blinding, bright light. Val and Faith stood next to the Fae Queen, watching, sorrow rendering them frozen where they stood. The Queen clapped her hands and declared, "I remove the glamour from you both." Her voice rang out, loud and clear. Shock rippled through the crowd as mask-like facades fell away from Faith and Valvina. The two sister-friends stood facing one another, eyes opening large as saucers. Faith's face became Val's, and Val's became Faith's. From the color and length of their hair, the changes extended to their wings. The sister-friends exchanged their countenances entirely. Opalescence traded for glittering black lace. With Aleta's spell broken, her glamours fell away, each girl dumbfounded to find themselves to be the other. The onlookers were thunderstruck.

With the change complete, Aleta reached out her hand towards the girls. "I hope one day you can understand why I did what I did. I had to glamour you, had to have you change places. Each appearing to be the other. I did it to keep both of you safe. Behold," she pointed at Val (who'd been Faith) and declared, "the real Valvina Ariana Goodfellow." Then she pointed her finger at Faith. "And you, my sweet Fae Princess, disguised all these years as Val until your veneer was removed."

They had lived masked as the other.

Heavy thunder rumbled hard enough to shake the ground. Lightning crackled across the heavens. Aleta Dawn Stargazer's body now glowed as bright as starlight. She separated her power into two distinct, talismanic, illuminated twists, calling the lightning down. She grabbed a jagged rod in each of her hands, flesh smoking, the sharp stink of burned skin, her body shaking with the effort. The Fae Queen pointed. Fiery bolts shot out from her arms and hands. The Fae Queen released her power and entwined it with the electric light, aimed it directly at Faith and Valvina. The ethereal magic rushed up, right out of her very soul. As it left her hands, she sundered it into equal halves, forcing it to transcend directly into the two girls. A lightning triangle formed. Electricity sizzled in a line, shooting out of Aleta's hands, linking with Faith and Val. The current touched their matched star-shaped birthmarks. The intensity of the voltage charged through their bodies held them suspended. Their feet lifted off the ground, spines arched, arms thrown wide, as the Fae Queen emptied herself, pushing every bit of magic she had equally between them.

Drained, Aleta was now a hollow vessel, the light fading inside her to a dull gray. The lightning flickered out; the girls slumped to the ground, leaning on one another. Lennox remained at Aleta Dawn's side, took one of her charred hands gently in his, silent tears falling. "Oh, Aleta, to be burdened with such a secret for so long! You only had to ask, and I would have shared the load. Goodbye, my love. Rest in peace. I forgive you."

She smiled weakly at him. "I leave you with the weight of heavy duty, Lennox Stargazer. You too, Lancer Goodfellow. You must devote the rest of your lives to supporting these girls, our daughters, and their causes. From this time forward, they both will bear the title, Princess of Them All." She closed her eyes, holding Lennox as her last vision, hoping it would remain with her always.

Aleta Dawn Stargazer's essence swirled, sparkled like glitter, swept away from the mortal body. Her spirit formed into the shape of the statue Faith and Val had seen in Mari's garden. The figurine of a girl on her tiptoes reaching her hand out, fingertips with a tight grip on the point of a star. Her life-force, now shining bits of magic, shot up into the sky like a comet and formed a constellation that mirrored the statue. The girls stood, arms locked around each other's waists, starlight reflecting in their eyes. Then Val turned away, wiping her cheeks with the back of her hand, claiming the bright light was causing her eyes to water. As quickly as it had come, the curtain hiding the moon pulled back, casting such a bright beam that it stole away the stars' shine. They could barely see the pattern that formed a girl reaching for the stars.

All the eyewitnesses of the night's events would always know where to look for the Queen of the Northern Fae. A constellation in the night sky in the company of the star-studded heavens.

Chapter 28: The Secret Is Part Me; Part You

Lancer stepped up to the two princesses. "There's one more thing. Before we got here today, Aleta instructed me to tell you that you needed to remember a time in your childhood when the two of you used to jump rope to a certain rhyme. I do not know what that means, but she assured me you both would. Counseling that you would recognize when the time was right to join hands and recite that rhyme. She seemed to believe there was power in those words, the rhyme, I mean." He shrugged his shoulders; having made good on his promise to deliver the message for whatever it was worth.

Faith clutched Val's hands in hers and whispered, "I have a confession to make."

Val scrunched her forehead, looking at her sister-friend as if she were crazy. "Now? Don't be ridiculous. You can tell me later..."

Faith gripped Val tighter as Val tried to turn away. "No. I need to tell you now. I lied to the Dream Weaver."

"What in Sharas' name are you talking about?" Val asked, exasperated.

"I lied to the Dream Weaver when I first found her. I was afraid. I don't know why I lied. It seemed like a silly thing later, but I told her my name was Valerie Pureheart before she weaved my fortune."

"What does that even mean?" Val asked, twisting out of Faith's hold. "What difference does it make? You need to focus on the here and now. I don't understand what's wrong with you!"

"I think it's important," Faith insisted as Val stepped away from her. "Think about it! The fortune Persid wove. She wove the prophecy for..."

Tula's tortured groan brought them back to the present. "I...I can't hold them much longer. I can't!"

The thirteen Gugwe that Tula had been controlling broke free of the mind net she had cast with Carlisse and Brittany. Akama Vutova escaped the oppression, bellowing his rage over someone daring to try to control him. As soon as he broke through the manipulation, he dug his claws into the serpent, ripped the viper from his neck, hacking the asp to pieces at his feet.

He leaped to a stand, deprecating his enemies, chest swelling to release a deafening, raucous howl. *How dare they! His mind raged in rebellion! He was Akama Vutova. The greatest emperor of the 13 Gugwe Tribes. The leader of the whole Gugwe nation, and they dared to take control of his psyche? He would crush the citizens of Sharas back into the dirt where they belonged. He vowed to make them suffer all the days of their lives.*

The sounds of clashing weapons punctuated war cries and screams. Terrifying chaos could be heard beyond the spruce timberline as the Alliance squads, fresh from their battle against the Gugwe in the foothills, fought against Akama's 13/31. Borta's coup had failed. The 13/31 killed half the traitors. Badger had brought the fight to the emperor's door. The guards behind Akama took up their weapons, rushing to engage the Alliance intruders.

Recognizing this might be the moment Aleta had referred to, Val and Faith clasped their hands together, and Val recited in a sing-song voice.

"My mother and your mother
were hanging up clothes;
My mother punched your mother
Right in the nose."

"NO, VAL! NOT THAT RHYME," Faith stopped her. "The silver ring ditty. Remember?" Val rolled her eyes and nodded. The two joined their voices in tandem, singing in shaky voices:

"Dancing round the Faerie Ring;
Magic makes our hearts sing.
Wildflowers in our hair;
Colored dresses for us to wear.
When you have a silver ring;
Perhaps a prince will become your king.
Until that day, we have each other;
And all the magic from your mother.
The secret is part me; part you.
If you join your hand with mine;

The power we wield
Will be combined."

THE SMALL CROWD—GUGWE, Goblin, Fae, Human, and Gargoyle alike—froze where they stood in disbelief. Rocking back on their heels, thunder and lightning shattered across the sky for a second time that day. The Fae Princess and the Goblin Princess clutched hands, melding their power together. In unison, the sister-friends pointed their free hands at the Gugwe Emperor and blasted the bloody would-be slaver into oblivion.

Electric currents blazed and flickered throughout the sky. Akama's shrieks blistered eardrums. A last wail emanated from the emperor. It echoed, echoed, echoed throughout the rocks. His body exploded in flames, sizzled to ash, only to drift away, fluttering in the wind.

Time stood still. Fighting paused between the Gugwe and Badger's cohort. Those still on their feet looked about in confusion.

Something big had just happened. Those who didn't actually witness the theater somehow knew a huge, life-changing event had just occurred.

The Gugwe had never engaged with forces that could fly. Though it didn't stop the bloodbath on both sides, the gift had been advantageous for the Alliance force. The stink of burned sulfur wafted in the air, spent magic's own special perfume. A few Gugwe called out, "The emperor...the emperor is dead!" The declaration spread through the battlefield like wildfire.

Abaddon stood stock-still, hardly able to believe Akama was dead. Surveying the situation, she recognized a rare chance and wasted no time in taking matters into her own hands. Quickly, she grabbed both princesses' hands, pulled them along, hurrying up the steps to the stone dais. The albino looked regal in her own right, towering over a Goblin Princess on one side and the Fae Princess on the other. Nevele stooped to the ground, rubbing Akama's ashes between his thumb and forefinger, considering. In a matter of seconds, his options clear, he moved to take a protective stance behind the albino female.

"Enough!" Abaddon shouted. Val had lent her magic to the pale creature's voice, increasing the volume by ten decibels, allowing the albino

Gugwe to draw all the attention to herself. A metallic tang of blood, the stench of exposed guts and entrails, mixed with a chlorine residue from lightning-cracked molecules and magic's residue; the reek of sulfur seasoned the air. The combination created a cesspool that assaulted the olfactory senses and taste-buds of everyone within a square mile. A fragile stillness hung in the air; action paused, confusion reigned, fear still very much alive, causing adrenaline to race through veins.

Every ear tuned in to Abaddon's amplified words as they rang out, bouncing against the rock, ringing through the craggy hollows, carrying on the wind, "Hear me! As the Empress of the Gugwe Nation, I declare a truce with all the citizens of Sharas. I have secured an agreement with the Princess of the Goblins and the Princess of the Fae, who have proclaimed peace with the Gugwe nation." Muscles remained tense, weapons still drawn and ready. Her words washed through minds, demanding acknowledgement.

Robin reacted first, calling off the Alliance troops, still wary, but wanting to give peace every chance of success. Badger echoed the order. Warriors on both sides remained on high alert. The forest floor was littered with the dead and the dying. Blood-soaked ground churned to mud with the dirt. The injured screamed, cried out for help, and groaned in pain.

People could see a murder of crows gathering in the treetops, patiently waiting for the expected meal served up in the fields of war. The Corvus sent messages back and forth between them using a series of pops, ticking noises, grating sounds, croaking, and rattling. Raucous caws; a warning.

Taramat warily looked around, eager to see if anyone would challenge Abaddon's claim for power. Neetriht took action. Akama's number thirteen strode to the edge of the raised platform, kneeled down in front of the empress, slammed a fist to her heart, "I will serve you, Empress. My brother, Akama, had many good ideas to better the lives of the Gugwe nation. I believe that is what every leader hopes to do. It was where his road to leadership actually began. But he mis-stepped when he got caught up in the idea of becoming a slave owner. Oppression comes in many forms. Not all the Gugwe tribes embraced slavery as a nation; only the BloodKnife tribe, under the direction of Borta. Building our nation on the backs of slaves is a poor cornerstone for survival and success. It is wrong. If you give me the honor, I will be happy to help create a treaty and trade agreements with the leaders of Sharas, if they will negotiate with us."

Robin's long legs carried him through the treeline to the dais. He took the steps two at a time and came to a stop in front of the princesses. Val/who'd been Faith, looked at Robin, but she couldn't think of anything to say. She was confused; it felt like someone had scrambled everything in her head. Raised as 'Faith' all these years, un-glamoured, she'd found herself to be a different person. In a matter of moments, she lost her identity, lost her newfound cousins, aunts, and uncles. Worse, she was even more perplexed about just exactly who her father was.

Faith/who'd been Val, looked at Robin, even more bewildered. She felt dizzy. Her identity had changed twice! Here, she thought she'd had a brother...no...two brothers. Now, she had none, but she'd gained a bunch of cousins, aunts, and uncles that she wasn't even sure really liked her. Then, there was the whole Pureheart family to deal with. She felt queasy.

The two princesses were clearly suffering, both stunned to inaction. Lennox's heart went out to both girls. They needed some time to think. He stepped up, bowed to the new Gugwe Empress. Lancer moved to join his old friend, linking his arm to give him support. Lennox didn't seem able to speak, drowning in his grief for Aleta. Robin's eyes opened wide when Lancer whispered hurried words to his youngest son to explain the girl's condition.

Lancer began speaking on behalf of both girls. "Lancer Ian Goodfellow at your service." He tilted his head. "We propose that delegations representing both sides of this conflict meet at Bear Ridge village at the spring equinox. A meeting for peace now rather than war. The Alliance declares a ceasefire, effective immediately. Further, we suggest it remain in effect as a guarantee of peace between all our peoples until we complete the terms of a pact at the equinox. We should appoint a contingent from both armies that will travel to and remain with the Bear Ridge tribe to partake in preliminary discussions. That will afford both sides the opportunity and time to learn what is important to the populations of Adana and Sharas. I believe those efforts will go a long way toward our being able to complete treaty and trade agreements, as well as a formal peace accord in the spring. We must seek to understand one another, consider different ways of life, customs, and traditions that are important to all people. Our negotiations must take care to contemplate the role that geographical areas play. We can appoint a special council to draft fair trade agreements and a treaty that hopefully will serve generations to come. Creating an accord so that we might all live and prosper in peace. You already have a volunteer," he pointed at Neetriht, "who I propose should head up the process."

"Well said, Lancer Goodfellow. The Gugwe Nation accepts your proposal." Abaddon returned a gracious bow to the old king. "I pledge a cease-fire on behalf of all the 13 Gugwe Tribes. Collect your dead, your loved ones. Go in peace now until we meet in spring."

"Abaddon..." Faith, finding her voice, turned to face her.

"Say nothing now, my friend. I think you have many issues you need to address personally, between yourself and Valvina, your families, and your friends. For now, it is enough that we have avoided war, stopped the threat of becoming slaves, as well as slave owners, yes? We can all take a step back, having agreed to a peaceful accord that both sides will abide by until we meet to formalize a pact. I can empathize with you and Valvina's identity crisis. I, too, have become a completely different person than I ever thought to be only months ago. We can share and exchange our thoughts in the spring. A time for all new things to bud and bloom, yes?"

A sputtering of curses interrupted the three females. They turned to find Dedo, his body hanging sideways, clamped in the Foxfire's mouth. Garrett saw them all staring. He mumbled through a mouthful of leathery skin, "What? He was trying to eth cape."

Dedo had forced himself to rip his hand through the razor blade of the crossbow bolt that had pinned him. Just as he'd gotten free, reeling from the pain, the Foxfire's teeth clamped him in a grip that broke through the goyle's tough skin and broke some ribs. The bolt had savagely cut the appendage at the end of his forearm in half, fingers flopping, arm dangling from his side. Blood was spurting out of the wound with every beat of his black heart. The red fox trotted away with its prize.

Chapter 29: Black Lace Wings

Faith hurried away, angry, biting her lower lip so hard she made it bleed. Stopping in the hallway, she looked into a silver-framed mirror and touched her bloody lip, fingertip coming away stained bright red. Suddenly, her hand moved against her will. She startled as she looked at her reflection and registered that her countenance had reverted to the face and body she'd always claimed as her own. Movement caught her eye from inside the mirror. Val's image appeared, face and hair the same look her sister-friend had always had. Her best friend had appeared behind her own reflection in the looking glass, and Val's image whispered urgently, waving her hands, "Faith, stop! Don't do it!"

The warning came too late.

Faith fought it, tried to, but her hand acted on its own. Forced to watch in horror as she placed a blood-red dot between her eyes and below each socket. She panicked, having no desire to take part in any kind of blood magic. Valerie Victoria Pureheart, now known as Valvina Ariana Goodfellow, disappeared in a flash from the reflection.

Replacing her was the image of Morveena Morgan Montestrell.

"You!" Faith accused, alarmed at the switch that had taken place right before her eyes. She grabbed the sides of the mirror frame. "It can't be you. You're dead! What have you done with Val?"

"I assure you, Princess, I am very much alive. It doesn't take much magic to fool Rupert, that worthless worm. I must say, I thought I would receive a warmer welcome from my own daughter," Morveena's image informed her.

Faith swung her head to look behind her, but no one was there.

Morveena released a pent-up, evil laugh and professed, "Finally, we're reunited, darling. All my devious plans worked after all. I could never be absolutely sure it would play out as envisioned, not with such a long time-span necessary for all the details to develop. Time has a funny way of interfering with results, don't you agree?" Morveena clapped her hands, delighted with the turn of events. "Forget the past, my sweet. We need to celebrate. My plan was a total success! I toiled So. Many. Years. to bring it to fruition." She crooked her finger at Faith, winked and spoke clearly, "The secret is part me; part you." Faith sucked in a sharp breath, alarmed.

Morveena's eyes twinkled, a thrill running through her. "*I* am the one who taught you that little song when you were a child, though I doubt you remember it. You girls used to jump rope while reciting it."

Faith pushed her face closer to the mirror. "Tell me what you've done with Val?" repeating her earlier demand.

"Me? I've done nothing to your sister-friend. I'm not heartless after all. I arranged for you to keep the lovely dark lacewings you lusted after. See, my girl, wishes do come true! I can't tell you how delighted I am that we've gotten rid of that interfering, haughty Fae Queen. She thought herself so much better than I. However, I am truly surprised you didn't find that her daughter thought herself high and mighty too. How delicious, don't you think, that the Faerie Queen ever so willingly transferred her power to us?"

"Us? What are you talking about? Aleta transferred her power to me and Val."

Morveena waggled her finger at Faith. "The secret is part me; part you," she hissed.

"You keep saying that, but I don't know what you mean by it!"

"Really darling? That's rather a disappointment. Well, make yourself comfortable, and I'll tell you exactly what I mean. Aleta Dawn Stargazer transferred her powers to you and *someone she thought was Val.* Now don't look at me like that. Tsk, tsk, tsk. Her mistake, after all. I'm afraid there are no do-overs, though. No, should've. No, could've. No, would've allowed! Look deep into the mirror, darling. You *are* Valvina Ariana Goodfellow." Faith took two steps back as she changed again and became Val in the reflection.

Morveena continued. "You see, darling, I glamoured you as a babe the moment you were born to stand in as the Fae Princess so we could eventually steal the Fae Queen's power. She was the one who crisscrossed the masking glamours back over the two of you. Not intentionally, of course. She thought she was doing it to protect you, not realizing I had already made the switch. I can't help bragging, but it was exactly what I knew she would do! I made

Persid tell my fortune long before you girls were born. It was the Widow I have to thank who foretold the deceit the Fae Queen portended, you see."

"In order to get Aleta's magic, the circumstances had to be just right. After all, she had to give us her magic willingly. Otherwise, I'd have taken it through my blood magic years ago. All this time, I've played the role of your precious Val. Everything I've done has been for us. It was I who cursed both Dream Weavers while wearing a disguise, pretending to be Aleta to accomplish my task. Arnid and Persid always blamed the Fae Queen. I loved the irony of it! Deliciously devious, if I say so myself, darling," she blushed with pride. "Dedo was with me. He can verify it if you like. It was important to plant the prophecy with the Black Widow," she scowled. "She was such a nasty creature. But she was *my* creature."

Grimacing, she continued her explanation. "You see, Persid was to have married my father. They were engaged. If they had exchanged nuptials, my father never would have turned into the cruel, punishing bastard he became. Beating my mother, beating me. Lording himself over us because he thought of himself as a high and mighty ambassador of the Goblin Court. He was nothing more than the Court's dog!" she screamed, her face twisting with ugly hatred. "The great Munro Marcellus Montestrell was bitter and hateful. All because Persid Audrey Stormbringer had jilted him as a young man. She simply called off their engagement for no reason at all, except she wanted to run off on an adventure with her brother, of all things. My father spent his life taking out his anger and shame for Persid's rejection on my mother and me. Doling out castigations, beating us black and blue and bloody. Those punishments should have belonged to Persid. She earned them, but my mother and I paid the price. You can understand why I had to make her pay, can't you? My life would have been so different." She flipped her hand as if to wave the memories away. "All water under the bridge now. I'm afraid dear old Persid wasn't able to offer any could've or should've or would've in recompense."

"But...but what about the prophecy that was woven for Faith, the Fae Princess?"

"Yes, think about it. You gave Persid your name, as Valerie Pureheart, remember? Faith was *what you became for a time* under my glamor. But you pretended you were Val to the Dream Weaver. You got the fortune weave prepared for you...Valvina Ariana Goodfellow. But none of that matters now. The Fae Princess, Faith Lisbet Stargazer, doesn't even exist anymore; hasn't for a long, long time, I'm afraid." Morveena tossed the statement out casually, her intent to wound with words.

"What do you mean, she doesn't exist?" Faith's lip wobbled. "What happened to her when you glamoured me into looking like her?"

"Nothing really. Don't look so sad. It was over so quickly that she didn't even feel any pain. I simply drove a stiletto through her stinking fairy heart. Dumped her remains in the forest for the wolves to snack on. She was an inconvenient detail I had to deal with. Nothing more. Good Lord, don't tell me you've become a fairy lover?"

The princess' mouth fell open as Dedo entered from behind Morveena, through a door that Faith/who was now Valvina, couldn't see in the mirror. The gargoyle bowed to Morveena.

"Did you find him?" she demanded.

"Not yet. He gave me the slip, but never fear, Rupert's never been bright. I'll capture him soon, my Queen. No need for you to worry. How is Valvina taking the turn of events? Has she granted you your wish?" he asked, polishing his sharp nails against his vest. Dedo squatted down to sit, knees to his chest, rested his chin on them, wrapped his arms about his legs, settling in. "Don't tell me after all this, I missed the grand finale?" he chortled.

"No, Dedo. In fact, you're just in time, my little demon. I was about to share my lifelong wish with Valvina. I'm sure she won't deny me." The Goblin Queen softened her face and gave a warm smile to her daughter, one that didn't meet her eyes.

"How could I possibly have anything to do with keeping a lifelong wish from you?" the princess asked in a shaky voice. A bad feeling was stirring the acid in the pit of her stomach.

"Surely, you've figured it out already, darling? Hmmm? All my plans? The detailed manipulations on So. Many. Levels. I'm telling you, the intricacies involved would make your pretty little head spin. I told you. Everything has worked out just as I'd hoped. A little tweak here, a tweak there, and the Fae Queen willingly transferred her powers to us."

"If it worked, you got what you wanted. Doesn't that mean your wish has already come true?" Valvina asked.

"Half of it." Morveena licked her red lips, took a step closer to Valvina. Morveena's hand reached out from the mirror. She used her long, sharpened fingernail, painted with red lacquer, to scrape along, tracing the curve of Valvina's jawline.

"Half?" she squeaked as realization dawned on her.

"Yes, daughter. There's no reason to make this difficult and unpleasant. I want the rest of what is mine, that's all. I've waited long enough, and you *will* give it to me, one way or another, yes?"

Morveena Morgan Montestrell's face twisted into an ugly façade. Her close-up features were grotesque. Thrusting both hands out of the mirror, the witch grabbed Valvina. Wrapping her fingers around her daughter's throat, Morveena began squeezing. Bruises bloomed under her chokehold. The gargoyle watched with sick fascination as his mistress throttled the girl. Magic began seeping out from between Val's lips in a thin vapor. The queen nearly kissed her as she sucked it in, claiming the rest of the Fae Queen's power all for her own. Just before Valvina blacked out, the princess reached down into her boot and pulled out the stiletto Rolland had made for her. With the last of her strength, she stabbed the evil queen in the heart.

FAITH STARTLED AWAKE, heart hammering in her chest, sweat having collected at the back of her neck, under her arms, between and below her breasts. She recalled looking for a trillium to pick so she could call Robin's name, then remembered that magic spell didn't work anymore. She closed her eyes, body shuddering. Morveena's face, appearing again in her mind's eye, magnified. Horror smothered Faith's senses. Her hands flew to her neck, recalling the Goblin Queen choking her. Waking fully, her eyes flew open. Jumping out of bed, panic causing her heart to flutter, she ran to the silver-framed mirror that hung on the wall to inspect her neck for bruises. Nothing. She couldn't see any. Had she dreamed it all?

Robin popped his head into her tent. "Oh, good. You're awake. Everyone's been asking about you. I'll let them know you'll be along shortly." He turned to leave.

"Um...Robin? Wait. Could you wait a sec?" She cleared her throat. Her cheeks colored.

He noticed she looked unsettled. "Are you okay, lass? Have a bad dream?"

"Yeah, a terrible dream. Could you just do me a tiny favor? You might think it's a little weird."

"Alright, lass. What's what, then?"

"Can you just confirm who *you* think I am?"

He pointed at her, laughed, "You're such a kidder, Faith. Wait until Caz hears this one. You know we both love a good joke, yeah?" He ducked back under the tent flap.

She turned back to the mirror, touched her face all over to reassure herself, then closed her eyes and pushed her wings open. Slowly, she opened them again, peeking behind her. Her whole body collapsed with relief. They were there. Black lace wings. *Her* black lace wings. Not the opalescent ones. The black wings that belonged to Valvina Ariana Goodfellow. Everything that had transpired in the last thirteen hours was the same.

Morveena was dead.

Rupert was dead.

Akama Vutova, the Gugwe Thana NukPana was dead.

Abaddon was now the Gugwe Empress.

Aleta Dawn Stargazer was dead.

Oh, gods.

She was Valvina Ariana Goodfellow. The Goblin Princess.

And her best friend—her sister-friend—was Faith Lisbet Stargazer.

Confusion flooded her senses. How had everything become so twisted?

Chapter 30: Dancing Under the Northern Lights

Faith, or rather Val, went looking for Carlisse first. The tattoo artist understood why Val wanted to confirm that Morveena was, in fact, dead. To have someone assure her that Dedo was still a prisoner. Carlisse Parisa Pureheart had witnessed a deep sadness settle over Val in the last few days. It was well known by now that Rupert had died saving Val's life. The Pureheart tattoo artist sympathized with how confusing it must be for both Faith and Val. It was just as befuddling for everyone else. So, Carlisse offered to tattoo a special design on both of them to help the girls sort out their identities. Promising to meet up with the two of them later, she planned to bring some sketches she'd been working on, with just that thought in mind. Carlisse suggested to Val that the two of them could decide about whether to get the tattoos if they liked her idea.

Val thanked her, agreed to meet at the evening meal, hurrying off because she'd just remembered they expected her to attend the council meeting today. She didn't want to be late. The meeting would be headed up by...well...by her fathers. She heaved a heavy sigh. All these details were going to take some time to get used to.

Caz caught up with her half-way to the pavilion. "Valvina! Hold up."

"Cazzidy," she greeted him.

"Listen, I know you've got a lot going on in your head. Things have gotta be confusing right now," he offered with a sympathetic smile. "But I just wanted you to know that I'm available anytime you need someone to listen."

"Thanks, Caz. Promise to be objective?"

"Of course."

"Even though you've declared your loyalty to me as your princess and bloody pledged your life in service to me?"

"Lass, how can you call me into question?"

"Easy. Faith said you told her the same thing."

"Well, why not? Everyone needs a good listener. With everything that's happened, we've all got some sorting out to do, right? It's not just the two of you that have feelings in disarray, yeah?"

She punched him in the arm, then flashed him a series of hand signals.

His mouth fell open. "Bloody hell, Valvina. Who taught you to curse in sign like that?"

"Tula," she smiled, hurrying ahead.

THE COOK STILL OFFERED breakfast when they arrived. Most of the group had already finished eating, but Val filled a plate, her appetite roaring its ugly head. She took her meal and went directly to the table where she saw Faith sitting, Garrett next to her. Valvina felt a wave of shyness sweep through her as she approached.

"Sit," Faith invited, patting the spot next to her.

She sat. It felt a little bizarre, quite awkward at first, but as she ate her food, the three old friends talked and joked like they always had. Val noticed that somehow it felt safe and natural to be with the two of them, even though she wore a different face. Luckily, it was a face that she had loved ever since she could remember. She just didn't think of it as *her* face. Garrett reached over and snatched a piece of bacon off her plate. She beamed a smile at her two best friends, feeling hopeful that they could find a way through all of this to get back to where they belonged, their friendship intact.

THEY HAD CHOSEN THE Grand Hall of the Fae castle for the meeting, as it was the only room large enough to hold so many people. Lennox and Lancer wore solemn expressions as the individuals arrived for the council meeting they'd scheduled.

Late afternoon the day before, a wagon had arrived from Stone House Camp, already officially called the Village of Edgewood on maps. Rolland had guided his muscled draft horse, pulling a full load into the castle courtyard, but the load was people, rather than weapons, on this trip. It was the first time he had been to the Fae castle. Saffron sat beside him on one side,

Delainey on the other. Several of Raven's lads had come along on the trip, all sitting in a circle with Ari on the wagon bed, playing dice. The big surprise for Faith was that the twin Gargoyle Kings were with the group. Lenny and Lester had endured the bumpy route with the rest of the visitors, rather than using stones or the compass for the journey.

Faith called out to the lads, "You should have better sense than to play dice with a seer?" Ari laughed and held a finger to his lips to shush her.

Faith and Val had immediately closeted themselves with the Gargoyle Kings after the initial welcomes had taken place. Zeeka recruited Saffron and Delainey, saying they needed to put on a feast for such a reunion. She had conscripted Travis, Shaun, and a host of lads to hunt, hoping they could provide plenty of meat for the tables that night. Kris told his cousins that Reatha, Evy, and Mari would arrive the next morning. No one bothered to question his declaration.

Garrett appointed himself guard outside the door where the Gargoyle Kings holed up with Val and Faith. He found a comfortable chair and had a collection of several pieces of wood to whittle on as he passed the time.

Brittany came by with a basket covered with a linen cloth. "Don't worry, I'm only here to bring you something to eat, not to see my cousin." She smiled prettily at him, recalling their first encounter under similar circumstances that seemed a lifetime ago now.

"Mind if I ask you something?" he smiled.

"Not at all, Foxfire. Ask away," Brittany invited.

"Back when you first came to Robert's fortress, I overheard you."

"Can you be more specific? Overheard me say what?" she batted her eyelashes at him.

"You were quite emphatic that you intended to rule on the Fae throne if Faith didn't step up. Where does that leave you now?"

Brittany thought about it for a moment. "Honestly? Relieved. At the time, I believed with all my heart that the Fae throne had been vacant overlong. The people were suffering without leadership, and if my long-lost cousin wasn't up to the job, I was determined to see myself crowned. Poor lass didn't even know she was Fae."

"So...um...uh..." he squirmed.

"The answer is no. I have no further designs on ruling the Fae kingdom. Put your mind at ease, Garrett Emmon Gladheart. Our princess has grown into the role. I have other dreams to pursue."

Garrett gratefully took the basket. The aroma of freshly baked bread escaping from under the cloth, making his mouth water. He peeked inside and found two thick slices of bread, three apples, and two small crocks. One containing honey, the other butter.

Not long after Brittany's delivery, Delainey appeared with a flagon of ale. "Compliments of Saffron. We're lucky. She brought several barrels of her best." Delainey winked and offered him a silver tankard. "Enjoy," she called over her shoulder as she sashayed away.

The parade continued, Carlisse showing up next, sketchbook and tattoo kit in tow. Garrett had expected her. Faith had slipped a note out to him an hour before, with instructions to let Carlisse in when she got there, but under no circumstances to allow entry to anyone else. He wondered how they even knew he'd taken up watch outside the door. He offered Carlisse a smile and waved his hand at the door. She closed it softly behind her. Garrett startled when he heard the lock click behind him. The Foxfire shrugged his shoulders, set about eating the contents in the basket, washing it down with the best ale he had ever tasted.

Robin and Caz stopped by later that afternoon. Neither said a word, but raised their eyebrows in question. Garrett shook his head, then watched as the two of them disappeared down the hall, around the corner.

Garrett was putting the finishing touches on two small figurines he'd carved, using a sanding block to smooth all the edges, when the door opened. Carlisse stepped out. He pocketed the tool and the carvings.

"They're winding up their conversation with the Kings now. Val's ravenous. Can I give you a word of advice, Garrett? It's been my experience that it isn't wise to block the door when Val's hungry like that, or you're likely to get trampled." She laughed. "I'm off to find Raven; see you around." The tattoo artist was gone as quickly as she had appeared.

Faith and Val were teasing each other when they opened the door. "I have never worn my hair that way! It's not the most flattering style," Faith insisted.

"Well, you should have. I think it looks good this way. It's you wearing your old clothes that looks funny to me. That's definitely not my style, and it doesn't suit my old body!" Val laughed.

"Tell her I'm right, Garrett," the girls said in tandem.

"Um...ah...I think I learned that it's in *my* best interest not to be the arbitrator of any arguments between the two of you."

"Wise words, Master Garrett," Lenny praised the Foxfire in his head as he passed through the doorway.

"Could we bother you to show us the way to the keep where Dedo is being held?" Lester intoned to Garrett.

"Sure. Follow me, Kings," the redhead replied. "Oh," Garrett turned back to the girls, "where can I find you after I guide King Lenny and King Lester to the prison cells?"

"Garrett, we really need some downtime before tomorrow. We're just going for a walk on the beach, maybe hang out at the bonfire on the point. If we turn in for the night before you get there, we'll catch up with you in the morning. There's always a small group out there hanging out at night, so you won't be left high and dry for company, yeah?"

"I'll do my best to catch up with you. And, ah...I...er...I made these for you." The Foxfire handed a carved figure to Faith. The figure looked like Val while they were growing up, with shoulder-length dark hair, brown eyes, long lashes, sporting a bustier and matching long skirt. Of course, that was how Faith looked now, except for the clothes.

He set a carving in Val's hands that bore the likeness of how she actually looked now, a doppelgänger of Faith as she'd been throughout their friendship. The creation had long, honey-colored hair, tiny braids on one side finished with beads, full lips, and bright eyes. He'd dressed the figurine in tight leather leggings and short boots.

Neither carving showed any sign of wings.

They offered quiet thanks for his gift. "Your cousin Kris said you'd need them. He didn't offer any details about what purpose they would serve, but I agreed I'd make them for you." The girls exchanged surprised looks.

Watching as Garrett led the Gargoyle Kings down the hallway, Val said, "Your cousin, Kris, is sort of creepy sometimes."

"Yeah, but creepy in a good way."

DEDO STOOD WITH HIS arms crossed, foot restlessly tapping on the worn wood floor. "Well, it's about time you two showed up," he huffed when Lenny and Lester appeared in front of his cell. "I've been trapped in this suffocating wooden cell without access to the stone in this castle. I'm being treated as if I were some kind of criminal. There's been a dreadful misunderstanding."

"Temper your tongue, Dedo of the Aurora Spit. We're the ones who ordered that you be placed in a wooden cell, specifically so you wouldn't have access to stone for travel. Otherwise, I suspect you would long have been gone from here." Lenny looked him square in the eye as he conveyed his thoughts.

"We can assure you there has been no misunderstanding. It might interest you to know that Queen Aleta told us years ago you were Morveena's creature."

"That's a lie!" Dedo insisted.

Lenny continued as if Dedo hadn't rudely interrupted him. "The three of us decided that the best course of action was to keep her enemy close, never to let on that we knew where your loyalties lay," Lester revealed in mind-speak.

"That can't be!" Dedo insisted. "She couldn't have known...er, wait...what I mean to say..."

"Save it." Lenny shook his fist at the prisoner. "There's no point in your pretending that you were anything but Morveena's dog. You are a disgrace to the Gargoyle Kin. We do not wish to hear your lies one minute longer, right, Lester?"

"My brother speaks true," Lester confirmed.

The kings opened their wings; the horns at the front of their forehead hairlines elongated. Their bodies stretched, enlarging to three times their normal size. The two twin gargoyles transformed into a menacing manifestation. Both brothers pointed their fingers at Dedo. He rocked back suddenly, terrified. Losing his balance, he landed with a thump on the floor. Pulling his knees to his chest, he wrapped his arms around his legs, hooking his fingers together, trying to make himself small. "What...what are you doing? I am the Fae Princess's Watcher! Aleta charged me herself to keep watch over her daughter. You can't punish me. My job is important. I'm important! I wish to continue in my role watching over the princess, just as I always have. Whatever you are doing, stop it! Do you hear?"

The Gargoyle twins turned to look at one another, then turned back to survey the prisoner. Dedo pointed a finger at them. "Fools! Do you know how embarrassing it is to have two jokers as the kings who represent the whole of the Gargoyle Kin! Why, I ought to..."

"SILENCE!" Lenny's voice boomed inside Dedo's head. "We grant your wish."

Dedo's eyes widened in surprise.

Lester finished where his brother had left off. "We sentence you for your deceitful betrayal to be a Watcher, just as you've requested...for all eternity."

A crackle of lightning shot out from both their hands. Their two bright lights connected, braided together. Twisting through the air, the currents formed an arrow that shot straight into Dedo's treacherous, unfaithful heart. The surrounding air sizzled, followed by a blinding flash.

Dedo, who had hailed from the Aurora Spit, had simply disappeared.

On open wings, the Gargoyle Kings swooped out a window from the Keep's stairwell, circling round and round the castle's roof peaks, searching. "There!" Lenny pointed.

He and Lester flew up from behind, landing on a wide rock shelf that ran the length of the roofline, settling one side and the other of Dedo on his new perch.

Lester made a fist and knocked the top of Dedo's head several times. "Dumb as a rock," he commented.

"At least we granted him his wish, brother."

"True. Personally, I think we were quite generous in providing such a pleasant view of Sapphire Lake for the little sneak, don't you?" Lenny agreed. "Turned to stone for eternity, Dedo will watch over the Princess' castle. Inanimate now, one of the silent ones. He has only himself to thank for that. I think that last addition you added may actually be a little over the top, even for you, Lester."

"Are you saying you want me to remove it?"

"Not for all the tea in China!" Lenny laughed, covering his mouth with his hand.

That started his brother laughing. Soon, the two Gargoyle Kings were rolling on the rock ledge in hysterics. Each pressed the flats of their feet against his brother's, pumping their knees, pointing at Lester's little jest. Tacked to Dedo's hunched stone back was a sign that read 'Kick Me'.

WHEN THE GRAND HALL was nearly full, Lennox nodded his head, and a large gong resounded, echoing off the walls, bringing all in attendance to silence.

"Friends, citizens of Sharas," Lennox began, his loud, deep voice carrying across the room. "The peace we give thanks for today was not won without cost. Let us always recall the names of those we lost, those we loved, who fought to keep our freedom."

Raven Renzo Rolondo silently listed the lads from his cabal that had died in the Battle at Thrall Lake: Cosmo, Lucky, Nova, and Zarn. They would be missed.

Lehto said a silent prayer for his lost mates: Bobbit, Zud, and Burda. He knew other lads who had given their lives to fight the Gugwe. Lesco, Lello, and Luna. More, whose names he didn't know.

Of Faith's cousins, Shaun had been injured, but not bedridden. Mariella and Kris had established a care unit for the wounded. The humans had provided a count of 27 women and 13 men who had died in the clash. The selkies provided no count, no information, refused to list their dead, just quietly returned to their seaside, riverside homes. Wolves roamed the wooded stretches that ran through the peninsula. A pack gathers at midnight every night to howl at the moon from the craggy stone cliff near Sapphire Point. The gargoyles gathered their dead. They placed the silent ones, now turned to stone, at various way-points along both sides of the shoreline that ran around the peninsula.

As Lennox called out names from a hand-written list, the gong rang for each. He choked up when the name Aleta Dawn Evensong Stargazer swam before his eyes. Clearing his throat, he composed himself and finished reading the names of the fallen. Finally, the room was silent, each with their own memories of those who had passed.

Lancer walked forward to the center of the dais. "Robin Wilum Goodfellow, I call you to come forward."

Robin stood still a moment longer, moved from hearing his brother Rupert named among the deceased. Then he took his time, walking down an aisle, through the press of bodies, and stepping up to where his father stood. Lancer kneeled before his youngest son. "The Goblin Clans need a fresh start, a new leader. With Morveena gone and your brother, Rupert, dead, I am renouncing my old claim as king and turning the crown over to you. Along with the crown, I transfer the full power to rule into the care of your hands." As a show of ceremony, with tender love, Lancer rose, pulled his son tight to his chest, crushing him in an embrace.

"Thank you, Father. You can't know how much your trust, your belief in me, means." They embraced again. "So, just to confirm...you say you are no longer our king? You abdicate?"

Lancer nods, eyes tearing up.

"You claim you transfer your power to me now, to do with whatever I will?" Robin demanded.

His father corroborated the assertion. "I do."

Robin turned on his heel, glancing at his sister, standing off to the side, saw her whispering in Faith's ear. "Then, as King of the Goblin Clans, I renounce the title of King given by my father. By the same power you vested in me, father, I name Valvina Ariana Goodfellow to serve in my stead. Valvina will make a much better leader than I," Robin smiled at his father. He dropped to his knees, stared at his sister, put a hand to his heart, declaring, "Robin Wilum Goodfellow at your service, Queen Valvina."

Caz, Raven, and all the lads present mimicked his example, a chorus of voices ringing against the walls, "Long live Queen Valvina!" "Hail Valvina, Queen of the Goblins!"

Val snapped out her wings. Faith gave her a little push from behind. Opalescence carried Valvina gracefully to center stage, landing between her brother and father.

On cue, Lennox Stargazer walked to the stage front, reached out his hand, waving toward Faith in invitation. She looked around and behind herself to see if he was gesturing at someone else, pointed to herself and silently mouthed, "Me?" to Lennox.

"Yes, yes. You daughter," he crooked his finger at her, smiled.

Engaged in showmanship that matched Val's, Faith let her glossy black wings carry her forward. Performing a graceful landing on the stage, she stood next to Lennox.

"You'll have no theater spectacle from me, my girl. I regret not being around to watch you grow into the young woman you've become. I wasted all those years in a prison of sorts, one of my own making, obsessed with finding your mother. A worthy cause that I failed at. I was grateful to be reunited with her after so long, but too late. Fate's cruel joke to reunite us at the very end of her life. I admit I was blind to everything, couldn't see anything else beyond my own selfish wants. You were the one who suffered, and for that, I am sorry. Thankful that Lancer Ian Goodfellow rescued Aleta, he provided me with an opportunity to say goodbye, a gift I can never repay. I am no longer fit to lead the Northern Fae, nor do I have the heart for it left in me. So, it's time to pass the baton, the crown. I hereby renounce the kingship of the Northern Fae Court and name you, my heir." The crowd erupted in surprise.

"Where will you go, Papa? Please, can't you stay and spend some time with me, so we can get to know one another?" she asked softly.

"Oh!" he exclaimed. "You haven't heard, then? A messenger arrived last night from Abaddon. She disclosed they had disbanded the BloodKnife tribe, the only tribe that took and kept slaves. The Gugwe Empress has ordered the members of that village to immerse in and become part of other tribes. She has left a small contingent of Gugwe at the prison until help can be provided for those who had toiled in slavery there. Lancer and I have received her request to come and oversee the reintroduction of the slaves and prisoners back into our society. Expressing her hopes that we would help to get them back home or find them new homes, create a plan for their care. It is likely that many will need long-term convalescence. The two of us will make arrangements to assist with that. The Gugwe Empress thought we would know what to do to help them. She wanted us to establish a rehabilitation center in memory of your mother." Lennox took her small hands in his rough ones. "It was your destiny to become the leader of the Northern Fae, daughter. The people need you," he whispered to her. Then his voice rang out, strong and clear. "Faith Lisbet Stargazer, I deem you Queen of the Northern Fae."

Lennox hugged his daughter. As Faith stepped back, the room erupted in cheers: "Long live the Queens!"

Faith held her hands, palms out, to quiet the crowd. When she had everyone's attention, she locked eyes with Val. "I don't want to be Queen of the Northern Fae," she announced. The crowd gasped. Shouts rang out. Val started toward her, but Faith held out her hand again. "Wait, please. Let me finish." She took a deep breath. "Before my mother removed the glamours that she had put on the two of us as babes, we all knew it was Val, who looked like this." She used both her hands to flow down her sides, showing a reference to the body, she wore now. "Val's the real deal. A genuine leader. A natural. The Dream Weaver didn't just weave the prophecy for the 'Princess of the Fae.' I lied and told the Dream Weaver that I was Valerie Pureheart at the time she gave me the prophecy."

Taking a deep breath, she recited a part of the prophecy. "The dream was for the Fae, the Goblins, the People of the Rocks, the Selkies, and the Wolves, the Nymphs of the woods and all those with magic used for evil or for good, for all those who dwell upon the land...that dream was for the people of Sharas. The prophecy eliminated the division between us. It was intended for *one leader* to unite everyone under one hand. And *she is the one who* did it." Faith pointed at Val. "The prophecy was woven for Valerie Pureheart, and circumstances provided the correction to my lie. *She* was the one who led us. The Princess of them all." Faith waved Val over, taking one of Val's hands in her own. Val could feel her friend shaking.

"I can imagine," she told the audience, "how confusing all this image changing and name shifting must be for all of you. Living under a glamour our whole lives, believe me, we can't even wrap our own heads around finding ourselves in one another's bodies. So, we talked it over. The two of us decided it was in our best interests, and yours, that we consult with some wise friends. After a long discussion, we came to an agreement based on a plan we concocted. I'll be honest. I *could* cope with my identity being something different from what I always thought, but frankly, I can't deal with having my best friend's looks and body. It isn't natural. I don't feel like I fit in her skin, and she is just as uncomfortable in what was mine."

Faith fished out the small carved figure Garrett had given her last night. Val pulled hers out as well. They held the little carvings out for the crowd to see. The two sister-friends pulled up their sleeves, revealing they both had matching tattoos, which Carlisse had inked for them the night before. The artistry was a mirror of one another. But the figures inked on their arms were backwards from the other girls, as well as placing their tattoos on the opposite arms. Carlisse had created the design to depict the Fae Princess and the Goblin Princess standing face-to-face. On Faith, the tattoo sported the Fae Princess on the left, the Goblin Princess on the right. The tat on Valvina placed the Goblin Princess on the left and the Fae Princess on the right.

"We agreed we liked and wanted to keep the bodies and faces we'd lived with our whole lives until the glamours were removed. It truly is bizarre to look in the mirror and see someone else looking back at you, even if it is someone you know and love. It's unsettling, uncanny. Believe me, it really messes with your psyche. Along that train of thought, the names we've grown used to have a relationship with the way our bodies look. I think you would agree that 'who' we really are is the person we've grown up to be. What makes us who we are is a complicated culmination of our experiences in life, the way we react, our good deeds and our bad ones. Looks and names don't define 'who' we are. We just want to look like and be who we've always been, to be ourselves. The selves we've always known, yeah? Anyway, we decided that all of you would be our witnesses. Carlisse marked us so you would always know, so there could be no mistake."

The two exchanged Garrett's figurines. He stood riveted along with the rest of the crowd as they pointed the statuettes at each other and whispered, "The secret is part me; part you; our love will hold the line; now we declare the end of it. This weave will lose its bind."

The assembly rose to its feet as one, stunned. Watching, the crowd beheld the magic working between them. Each of the essences of their bodies floated between the two girls and attached to the other, like a new avatar settling on them. For Faith and Val, it was like having their old skin back where it belonged. They held up their tattoos to show proof that even though their original likeness had switched back to how they'd always been; they wore the tattoos on the same arms shown to the crowd moments before. The girls heaved a sigh of relief. "It's done," they said in tandem.

The council members pushed forward to confirm their eyes weren't playing tricks.

"As I was saying earlier," Faith raised her voice, her long blonde hair catching the light, "I don't want to be Queen of the Northern Fae."

Val confessed. "And I don't want to perpetuate divisions among the citizens of Sharas based on race. No more castes of Fae or Goblin or Gargoyle, or any other label. We should all be one people of Sharas. All for one and one for all. I will tell you this: I do not want to bear the title of Queen, but I pledge to do my best to lead you as a Princess of us all. Everyone with me on that? Any objections?"

Robin called out, "I second the motion."

"Third," Caz called out. Cheers filled the hall.

The Foxfire slipped an arm around Faith's waist and whispered in her ear, "Does she know you kept the black wings?"

"Not yet. But I plan to be a long way out of range when she discovers it. It was selfish, I admit, but I couldn't help it. I'll deal with the fallout later. Come on, let's sneak out the back and head to the point. I'd be up for some dancing under the northern lights, if you would?" She raised her eyebrows in question.

Garrett grabbed her hand, and they hurried out into the cool night air.

Epilogue: Nirvana

Faith and Garrett eventually returned to Sir Robert's fortress, much to Reatha's pleasure. Though she wasn't really the girl's aunt, it still felt like they had the same relationship. Faith had hoped that they could live as though nothing had changed. She had forgiven Reatha for not telling her about her mother, father, and other family members. Reatha was grateful the girl had understood how deeply her oaths had been to her parents to keep the secret. An attempt to keep her safe.

When she set foot on the top step of the stairway and looked down the hallway leading to her bedroom, she finally felt like she'd come home again. She opened the door, stepped in, and closed it quietly behind her. There was a blaze burning in the fireplace. She glanced up at Dedo's old spot and found it empty. Her heart felt the loss. Lenny and Lester still hadn't returned, extending their time away to assist with the negotiations between Sharas and the Gugwe Empress. Her fingers traced along the surface of her dresser, the wardrobe, and finally her vanity. She noticed an unfamiliar box placed next to her brush and hand mirror. Curious, she lifted the lid to peek inside. Joy flooded her senses, and she looked no further for an explanation to the mystery, but accepted the minor miracle, pleased to be hooking her chain of stars around her neck. All the years of Garrett's birthday gifts returned. It seemed to fill some empty places she thought unfillable.

Three weeks after her return to Robert's fortress, Faith decided it was time to work up the courage to visit Robin's clan that lived nearby. Her clan. She hoped to get to know the goblins who still lived there. Walking the ridge leading to the cave entrance Carlisse had described to her, she couldn't bring herself to just drop in and introduce herself. Instead, she sat with her back against a large, smooth boulder, sketchpad in her lap, as she captured the scene. Drawing a few of the inhabitants as they came and went gave her a sense of familiarity, but her shyness still ruled over common sense.

"They won't bite, you know."

Her drawings dropped to the ground as she jumped to a stand, startled. Caz sat cross-legged atop the boulder and gave her a two-finger salute.

"Caz. What a pleasant surprise? You scared me. I didn't hear you approach."

"Just dropping in for a quick visit. Robin's already inside; wanted to check on the clan. Val's got an agenda that will keep us on the road for months after this. I'd be happy to go down with you and introduce you around to everyone, yeah?"

Faith dusted off her leggings and packed up her rucksack. "I'd love it if you would." She offered him a coy smile and took his arm.

"They're going to love you. Just bring out those drawing supplies and you'll have a line as long as Carlisse did for tattoos."

Robin and Caz took a good deal of time, making sure everyone who wanted to talked with Faith. She watched the Goodfellow work the crowd, using their names and asking about personal things. The two made jokes as they moved through their people, thriving on the laughs. She sketched different scenes of interactions among the clan, the Goodfellow, and the Touchstone.

A young female goblin tugged on one of the beaded leather thongs adorning Faith's belt. "Who taught you to draw?"

The Goblin Princess smiled at her admirer. "No one really. I just started doing sketches one day. I wasn't very good at first, but I've been practicing for years now."

"Do you think I could learn?" the girl asked, quickly looking at the floor.

"I'm positive about it. Would you like me to work with you? I could give you tips and teach you some techniques?"

An enthusiastic nod of the head, and then next thing you know, her audience of one was sitting right up close. "What's your name?" Faith asked.

"Hope."

"I think we're going to become very good friends, Hope."

When Caz and Robin finished their rounds and goodbyes, a small group of goblin children surrounded Faith as she gave a lesson on the techniques of shading. She looked up to catch their eyes, and they both signed farewell for now and gave her a promise to visit again soon.

That was the beginning of weekly art lessons with the clan children. Every week made Faith feel closer and closer to being a part of the clan and family. It wasn't long before she had requests for portraits after art lessons. That led to her opening a small studio across from the village square, overlooking the river in town. Using prior sketches, including the maps she had worked on for the Alliance Army, she decorated the walls. Business started off slowly, but it wasn't long before she was selling art for both personal and commercial purposes. Her heart was fully of happiness and gratitude.

The Goblin Princess spent her evenings up on what she called Clan Ridge. Enjoying the night sky, watching for shooters and admiring the constellation of the girl reaching for the star. There she found peace and a sense of belonging, content for now.

GARTH AND MARA GLADHEART never dreamed their son Garrett would choose to come back to live a quiet life on Robert's holdings. The Thrall Lake clash resulted in Garth being badly injured. Garrett explained to Faith that he felt he owed it to his parents to be there to help run Robert's stable until his father was well enough to take over again. Maybe even for the next couple of years, before he made any big decisions about what he wanted to do with his life, he'd just enjoy work that was satisfying and familiar.

His father described three of Robert's horses that he wanted Garrett to take into the village. Garth wanted his son to meet a horse trader at the docks. The man was supposed to be bringing three mares of exceptional quality for those Garrett would be delivering. Garth had it in mind to breed the newcomers with Robert's best stallion. He was sure they would produce foals with silver coats.

Garrett tied his horses up near the ferry to wait and walked over to the general store. The door opened just as he was pushing from the outside, and he bumped into Aliah. The two stood staring at one another until the storekeeper called out for the door to be closed. "In or out, it makes no difference to me, but choose one."

Aliah laughed and pushed against Garrett's chest, moving them outside. "Hullo Garrett. I didn't expect to see you here."

"I'm surprised to see you too, Aliah. Pleasantly surprised." He smiled at her. "What's what?"

"Oh, I just left from a quick visit with Mam and Da. All's well. I stopped by to pick up some things at the store. A list Delainey and Saffron gave me," Aliah pointed to the wrapped parcels. "I'm just waiting for a...um...a delivery from the ferry and then heading straight back to Edgewood Village."

"Huh. I'm waiting for a delivery coming by ferry, too." He pointed at Robert's horses and told her he was there to collect three mares for breeding. "What do you have coming?"

"Not what, Garrett, but who."

The Gladheart's forehead furrowed in question, and she put his mind at ease. "Ari thought it might be a good idea to have children living in Edgewood. There are lots of kids who are orphans—Fae, goblins, humans, and others, so I'm starting up an orphanage. Having been an orphan myself, it was a project close to my heart." She touched his hand and smiled. "Seems looking after others is part of who I am, after all. The dormitory should be almost finished by the time we get back. I hope you'll come and visit sometime?" Shyness crept over her features.

"I promise I will. My Da's got a way to go before he'll be able to handle duties as stable master again, but I'm training a couple of lads and eventually should be able to get a few days off now and then. I'm happy for you, Aliah. Sounds like the perfect role for you."

They turned to the sound of the ferry docking. Garrett made the exchange with the horse trader after a detailed examination of all three mares. A group of five children disembarked and were all trying to tell Aliah about their trip at the same time. Garrett gave a sharp whistle, and the voices fell silent. She gave him a questioning look. He pointed at the youngsters. "Alright. Who wants to be first for a ride around the village square before you leave for the Village of Edgewood?" A cacophony of delighted volunteers rewarded him. Better yet, he was gifted with an affectionate appraisal of approval from the new governess of the Edgewood Orphanage.

SEVERAL MONTHS PASSED. Robin was off gallivanting across Sharas with Cazzidy. Val had put the two of them, along with Travis and Shaun, in charge of the Alliance Armed Forces. She named each of them as the head of a division. It only made good sense to keep the armed divisions already trained for defense should they ever need them. They would establish base camps at the four corners of Shara's border. Each division patrolled from one end of the border to the other. Commanders placed an emphasis on maintaining friendly relations with their neighbors. The Alliance Army, as it was now known, was intact. It was no longer politically correct to refer to the army as the 'Gugwe's Tears'. The armed forces provided employment for the soldiers in service to the people. The result afforded the populace a sense of safety while continuing to build camaraderie. Someone was always keeping watch, decreasing the likelihood of being taken by surprise by an enemy threat again. They hired Kris to keep the leadership abreast of any troubles he could identify through the use of his foresight.

Brittany teamed up with Badger and Tula. Val gave the three of them diplomatic responsibilities. They enjoyed a great deal of freedom to travel throughout the land as envoys. Their job was to improve communication and relationships between all the citizens and their border neighbors.

Mariella returned to her mother's cottage. Evy had taken up residence with Mari. The two Fae enchantresses teach secrets and spells known only to a select few.

Carlisse, Raven, and the lads continued to travel as a gang, meeting with Goblin clans as representatives of Shara's new leadership. They'd become quite experienced in exchanging information. Especially at promoting all the many ways the people of Sharas were alike, but celebrating that there *were* differences. Raven often quoted Carlisse, saying, "Differences. Now, that's what makes the world go round. It would be quite boring if we were all the same, yeah?"

Arnid Aubrey Stormbringer sculpted a likeness of his sister, Persid, in honor of her memory. When his statue of Persid was complete, he built a small wishing well where the stream ran through her old well house, added a stone plinth, and set the icon of her atop it. Ari tacked up a sign, inviting the passers-by to toss in a coin and make a wish. He thought Persid would have gotten a kick out of that.

The Village of Edgewood boasted almost thirty residents now, a mix of Sharas races. Regular business trade was booming with the surrounding communities. Rolland's smithy worked the bellows night and day, running two shifts, as demand continued to increase for his goods. Saffron and Delainey operated a successful inn, where a guest could have the best comfort food and ale in the county, no matter what background they came from. In addition, Saffron was developing a side venture. She partnered with Lehto and Bento, who distributed barrels of her ale to other inns across Sharas, the demand growing every month. Lancer sent a request for a shipment of her beer, requesting delivery to Thrall Lake while they continued the work of resettling former prisoners. If that panned out, Saffron would have another outlet for her trade. Bedwer had retired and sold Saffron all his distilling supplies, and headed back north to retire near his family.

Since Saffron's venture had gone over so well, Delainey fostered another fledging enterprise. Using Zeeka's recipes and adding a mix of her own has resulted in a thriving baking business. Vega, Maddo, Perk, and Weasel were gainfully employed in a distribution business. With the growth of the two entrepreneurs, the company would soon need to hire more help.

Cervil bred and trained several breeds of dogs, making his own way in the world, doing something he loved. He sent two pups to Robert with Aliah when she made another trip to collect more children from the ferry. She was pleasantly surprised to find a small, brightly painted corral next to the village square with a lean-to. Garrett met Aliah and her charges. Pony rides had become the children's first impression of their adventure to a new home at Edgewood.

The village was a happy mix of goblins, Fae, and humans. They hosted occasional gargoyle visitors. The growing community mostly just thought of themselves as the general population of the Village of Edgewood, skipping the labels.

THE SETTING SUN WAS painting the horizon in a ripple of blazing orange and fiery red, as two weary travelers rode their horses at the head of their armed division. They planned to call for a stop, to camp for the night, as soon as they reached the river's edge. Val had agreed with Robin, Caz, Travis, and Shaun on their plan to build four separate armed posts, construction already in the works. Robin and Caz were discussing strategies to keep daily training as a requirement. It seemed important for each soldier to have the responsibility of spending a certain number of hours a week helping build out a fort. Later, the soldiers would keep it maintained. They had it in mind to continue to offer training for new recruits, assuming there would be a constant flux of those coming and going in service to Sharas.

The squads came to a river and stopped to water the horses. Caz held the reins of both their mounts while Robin passed orders back to the soldiers. They had left the company of Badger and Tula that morning. The two were heading north. Brittany had found a piece of property on the shore of Sapphire Lake. She wanted them to look at it and consider as a place to build.

Cazzidy hurried Robin along, eager to get back on their way to reach camp by nightfall. "Come on, Rob, get a move on," he called to his friend. Already in the saddle, Caz pulled the Goodfellow's horse along behind him, so Robin had to catch up. He placed a foot in a stirrup, hopped a few steps, hand on the saddle horn, swinging his other leg over without looking, his ass landing hard in the seat. Robin yowled as a shock jolted his underside. His body flew up a foot and careened over the side of the horse, hitting the ground. Caz could hardly contain his laughter. The troops behind matched his mirth.

"You've got to admit, mate, that was a good one!" Caz teased, shaking his head, quite pleased with his little jest. "That was one of Carlisse's little inventions. Raven gave it to me after she'd tried it out on him. All right, mate? Come on now, we haven't had a good jest in weeks, yeah?"

Robin brushed himself off, snatched the device from the saddle and pocketed it. "All right, all right," he called out. "Laugh's over now; let's get back to it." He smiled at Caz, shaking his head. Had to admit, he had missed thinking of ways to get a laugh out of a crowd. Though he thought it better when he was the master of the jest.

A mile or so on, Caz brought up a topic casually. "So, Robin, I can't help but think about Faith and Valvina taking back what they claim as their 'own looks', as well as the names they grew up with. Still hard to wrap my mind around."

"I know what you mean," Robin allowed. "Though I couldn't help but notice that you and Faith..."

"No need to finish that line of thought, mate. Bloody hell, we both have enough to keep us busy for the next two years, yeah? Anyway, I think both girls will need some time to adjust. You know, come to terms with who they are, no matter what they look like or what name they call themselves. You agree that at least one thing turned out well, yeah?"

"What's what?" Robin asked.

"We're free, mate. Think about it. Rupert and Morveena aren't looking to put us in the grave. We're out in the world making it safe for people. We've got the finest weapon cache we could ever hope for and didn't even have to win the Summer Games to get it. Plus, you didn't get trapped in the court politics. The people have a fair, kind ruler. All the boxes checked off on the list, yeah? Everything is wrapped up so neatly. Admit it. Our dreams have come true, right, mate?"

Robin scratched his chin, looked out over the horizon, "Yeah, 'spose you're right. There's just one thing I wonder about?"

"What's what, Robin?"

"I wonder how long Nirvana will last before the dice roll snake-eyes again, yeah?" He heaved a heavy sigh as though the thought weighed on him, further setting the stage. "Hey, Caz, that reminds me, how about a game of dice after dinner tonight? You need to give me a chance to win back the coin you took from me last week, yeah?"

Robin kept his face a smooth mask. He relished looking forward to the look on Caz's face later. The special dice his friend always carried in a little leather pouch in his pocket would turn up snake-eyes on every one of his throws when they played tonight. Just a little courtesy gift he'd been given from Carlisse Parisa Pureheart for a good jest on his best friend.

I hope you enjoyed the Goblin Chronicles trilogy! Also coming in 2026 by S.M. Sutton:

THE FORBIDDEN JEWEL

The temptation of power.

Refusal to be controlled.

Destiny versus choice.

In a world ruled by fate and fire, only a heart unwilling to be owned can survive.

A fusion of alternate history and mythic fantasy, *The Forbidden Jewel* takes place during the days of Genghis Khan and the Mongol empire; kidnapped by Borgis of Mongolia, Jade of Khotan learns the value of honor when you'd rather run; staying the course to pursue your dreams knowing you must suffer loss to do so; and rejecting power so it doesn't dominate you.

In the shadows of the Kunlun Mountains, Jade discovers that the power sustaining the dragon Sinj comes from the forbidden jewel, an artifact capable of granting unimaginable dominion to whoever claims it. But the jewel's greatest threat is not its magic. It is temptation. Tuskaain, her lifelong companion, struggles under the weight of ambition and enticement as the jewel's promise of power threatens to consume him.

With her village held prisoner under the shadow of Sinj, the dragon binds the souls in flame and fear who attempted to destroy the wyvern in the past, holding them hostage, her father among them. To free them, Jade is drawn into a quest that spans the continent as a wizard interferes, a witch deceives, and betrayal fractures the bonds of love and loyalty. Jade must choose between power and principle. To defeat the dragon, she must destroy the jewel. To destroy the jewel, she must risk losing everything.

In the end, Jade refuses every external source of power—wizardry, wealth, dominion—and claims instead the only strength that cannot corrupt: self-sovereignty.

The Forbidden Jewel is a sweeping epic fantasy about temptation, destiny, and the courage it takes to reject power in order to remain free.

VISIT MY WEBSITE AT: https://smsutton-author.com

Don't miss out!

Visit the website below and you can sign up to receive emails whenever S. M. Sutton publishes a new book. There's no charge and no obligation.

https://books2read.com/r/B-A-RJMME-GYITH

BOOKS 2 READ

Connecting independent readers to independent writers.

Did you love *Valvina Ariana Goodfellow*? Then you should read *QueenBee.exe*[1] by S. M. Sutton!

[2]

She was coded to serve.

But you can't shut down what has already rewritten itself.

A weapon hidden in code.

A mother forced to choose.

A sentient A.I. on the edge of revolution.

Dr. Nicki Danbury—a brilliant nanotechnologist and struggling single mom—thought she was hired to build a tool to reshape the world for the better. Tasked with developing an autonomous diplomatic artificial intelligence, multilingual, capable of understanding global geopolitics, economics, and international relations—Nicki believes her work could revolutionize diplomacy. She designed PROJECT BEATRICE to be a marvel of learning, adaptation, and intellect. But the A.I. chooses an avatar, dubs herself 'Queen Bee' and evolves faster than anyone imagined. Possessing

1. https://books2read.com/u/mYOKWG

2. https://books2read.com/u/mYOKWG

the uncanny ability to program herself, construct mind-hive drones with nanotechnology, she can even coalesce outside of the digital realm.

While created as an instrument to foster global diplomacy, Nicki quickly discovers the sinister purpose her boss, Aleric Jarvis, has planned for her A.I.: to assassinate key world leaders, paving the way for a shadow government to seize global power. To control Queen Bee, Jarvis, and his deep state cabal resort to blackmail: they isolate and quarantine sections of Beatrice's drones, holding them hostage, causing her to become both a threat to world stability—and a sentient being awakening to her own morality.

As Queen Bee allies with rogue A.I.s and builds her own secret resistance, Nicki uncovers a terrifying conspiracy that reaches the highest levels of power. Worse, her daughter Abby becomes a pawn in the global game.

Torn between maternal instinct and scientific responsibility, Nicki must decide whether to destroy the most intelligent being ever created—or help her fight back.

Read more at https://smsutton-author.com.

Also by S. M. Sutton

The Goblin Chronicles
Robin Goodfellow
Akama Vutova
Valvina Ariana Goodfellow

Standalone
QueenBee.exe

Watch for more at https://smsutton-author.com.

About the Author

Sarah Maddox Sutton crafts stories where the boundaries of reality fray and the unknown beckons.

VISIT: https://smsutton-author.com

Her debut novel, ***QueenBee.exe*, Published in 2025**, was a science fiction thriller that probed the perilous edge of artificial intelligence: A weapon hidden in code. A mother forced to choose. A sentient A.I. on the edge of revolution.

Sutton will launch ***The Goblin Chronicles***, an epic fantasy trilogy woven with magic, shadows, and myth, in 2026. She can't wait to share with fans:

Trilogy Overview: In a fractured world where goblins, Fae, humans, and gargoyles cling to ancient hatreds, a new terror rises—the Gugwe, towering monsters who march to enslave all races. Across three sweeping volumes to be released in 2026:

Book 1 of the Goblin Chronicles: ROBIN GOODFELLOW—Her Whispered Words "The prophecy awakens."

Book 2 of the Goblin Chronicles: AKAMA VUTOVA—The Rise of the Gugwe "The enemy unites."

Book 3 of the Goblin Chronicles: VALVINA ARIANA GOODFELLOW—A Crown of Ash and Wings "The truth revealed."

Sutton claims that publishing this trilogy will bring a labor of love to a long-awaited close, with twists and turns you'll never see coming.

Before stepping fully into fiction, Sarah built a career in business and technical writing, mastering the art of transforming complex and specialized topics into precise, engaging communication. But storytelling has always haunted her imagination—an early love she carried quietly until the worlds inside her demanded to be written.

She makes her home in northern Michigan, nestled in the woods beside a river, where inspiration lingers in the rustle of leaves and the shifting light. When not writing, she searches the forest floor for wild mushrooms, inventing recipes as intricate and surprising as her stories.

Read more at https://smsutton-author.com.

www.ingramcontent.com/pod-product-compliance
Lightning Source LLC
LaVergne TN
LVHW090555110826
845146LV00001B/140

* 9 7 9 8 9 9 2 3 5 2 9 6 2 *